PRAISE FOR JAMES GRIPPANDO AND *MOST DANGEROUS PLACE*

"**G**rippando gets underway with a bang and never lets up, springing a series of carefully calibrated surprises in and out of the courtroom guaranteed to catch even the canniest readers unaware."
—*Kirkus Reviews*

"**G**rippando weaves a complicated but compelling plot. Much of it unwinds in the courtroom . . . Readers will find themselves liking this lawyer."
—*St. Louis Post-Dispatch*

"**P**ardon the pun, but Grippando grips from the first page."
—Harlan Coben, *New York Times* bestselling author

"**G**rippando is a very intense and ingenious storyteller."
—Nelson DeMille

"**T**he thriller writer to watch."
—*Wall Street Journal*

"**G**rippando is able to make his characters jump off the pages."
—*USA Today*

"**G**ripping . . . Grippando keeps the tension high."
—*Publishers Weekly*

"**G**rippando has been at the top of the legal-thriller ladder for some time."
—*U.S. News & World Report*

"**J**ames Grippando is a dependable author who delivers a few hours of thrills every time. . . . You can always count on [him] to offer some time away from the humdrum."
—*Kingston Observer* (MA)

"**G**rippando is one of the very few lawyers who can write a great book."
—*Contra-Costa Times* (CA)

"**I**f you go with Grippando, you'll get a plot you won't soon forget."
—*San Jose Mercury News*

By James Grippando

*Most Dangerous Place**
*Gone Again**†
Cash Landing†
Cane and Abe
*Black Horizon**†
*Blood Money**†
Need You Now†
*Afraid of the Dark**†
Money to Burn†
Intent to Kill
*Born to Run**†
*Last Call**†
Lying with Strangers
*When Darkness Falls**†
*Got the Look**†
*Hear No Evil**
*Last to Die**
*Beyond Suspicion**
A King's Ransom
Under Cover of Darkness†
Found Money
The Abduction
The Informant
*The Pardon**

Novellas and Short Stories

The Penny Jumper
*Death, Cheated**
Green Eyed Lady†
*Operation Northwoods**

And for Young Adults

Leapholes

* A Jack Swyteck Novel
† Also featuring FBI agent Andie Henning

JAMES GRIPPANDO

MOST DANGEROUS PLACE

A JACK SWYTECK NOVEL

HARPER
An Imprint of HarperCollins*Publishers*

This novel is a work of fiction. Any reference to real people, events, establishments, organizations, or locales are intended only to give the fiction a sense of reality and authenticity, and are used fictitiously. All other names, characters, and places and all dialogue and incidents portrayed in this book are the product of the author's imagination.

First Harper premium printing: October 2017
First Harper hardcover printing: February 2017

Print Edition ISBN: 978-0-06-244058-7
Digital Edition ISBN: 978–0-06-244057-0

Cover design by Gregg Kulick
Cover photograph © Tiffany Bjellméus / Getty Images

17 18 19 20 21 QGM 10 9 8 7 6 5 4 3 2 1

To Tiffany, with love.
Always.

MOST DANGEROUS PLACE

Spring

1

Baby doll definitely has your hair," said Keith.

Isabelle Bornelli shared a weary smile with her husband. They were twenty-two hours into a flight from Hong Kong to Miami. First class on a Boeing 777 is a 1–2–1 configuration. Isa and Keith were separated by an aisle. To Isa's left was their five-year-old daughter, Melany, sound asleep with her head in Isa's lap, her face buried beneath chestnut waves of silk.

"It's a strong gene," said Isa.

Isa was a stunning brunette who didn't look back fondly on her childhood pageants, but getting tapped at age six by a top beauty academy in Caracas fed her mother's vicarious pursuit of the coveted "Miss" titles. In a country whose unmatched number of Miss Universe winners was a source of national pride, pageantry wasn't just the poor girl's ticket out of the barrio: it was a shot at a better life for the entire family. But not for the Bornellis. Isa's father abhorred pageants, espousing the revolutionist's view—as proclaimed by then president Hugo Chavez—that plastic surgery was "monstrous." Ultimately it was Felipe Bornelli's faithful service to the Chavez regime that lifted the family out of a crumbling apartment in the hardscrabble hills west of Caracas. Isa was eleven when her father landed a diplomatic post with the Consul General of the Bolivarian Republic of Venezuela in Miami. Isa got a top-flight education at Miami's most prestigious international middle school. Even better, she managed to avoid butt implants at age twelve, the surgical shortening of her intestines at sixteen, a mesh sewn to her tongue that would turn eating into torture, and other extreme measures that the "Miss Factories" encouraged girls to take in pursuit of someone else's definition of "perfection."

Isa brushed away a curl that had fallen across Melany's face, and a hint of sadness creased a mother's smile. That beautiful hair also hid the hi-tech gadgetry that enabled Melany to hear.

"Time to wake up, sweetie," said Isa.

Melany had barely moved since their brief and only stop in San Francisco, which left Isa with no one to talk to. Keith was head of wealth management in Hong Kong for the International Bank of Switzerland, and he'd spent the entire flight on his laptop, except to eat or nap. Isa hadn't slept at all; this was no family vacation.

Melany wasn't born hearing-impaired. When IBS offered Keith the post in Hong Kong, Melany was like most other twenty-two-month-old girls in Zurich—which meant that she had not yet completed her full sequence of vaccinations against haemophilus influenzae type B. "Hib," however, wasn't included in Hong Kong's childhood immunization program. Two months before her third birthday, Melany developed bacterial meningitis, caused by Hib. Doctors gave her a 90 percent chance of survival, which sounded good in theory, until Isa thought of the last ten people she'd said hello to and imagined one of them dead. Weeks later, when Melany started to improve, doctors warned of a 20 percent chance of long-term consequences, anything from brain damage to kidney disease, from hearing loss to limb amputation. By her fourth birthday, it was confirmed that Melany had landed at the unfortunate end of the spectrum: the infection had destroyed the tiny hairlike cells in her cochleae and left her profoundly deaf in both ears, unable to hear even sounds in excess of 95 decibels—a lawn mower, a drill, or even a jackhammer.

Hearing aids were ineffective. Their only hope was a bilateral cochlear implant in the inner ear—a tiny mechanical device that essentially did the work of those ravaged hair cells that stimulated the auditory nerve. Melany's surgery was a success—for a time. Six months into Melany's auditory rehabilitation, something went wrong in the right ear. The doctor in Hong Kong assured them he could repair it, but Isa wasn't taking any chances. A second failure would lead to further ossification of the cochlea and leave Melany permanently deaf in one ear, no longer an implant candidate. In March,

Isa flew her daughter to Miami for evaluation by the surgeon who had pioneered cochlear implants at Jackson Memorial Hospital. He undid surgery number one and sent Melany home to heal. In April, after the risk of infection had passed, they were back for surgery number two.

"We'll be landing shortly," said the flight attendant. "I'll need you to buckle your daughter's seat belt."

Isa adjusted Melany's audio processor. She didn't normally sleep with the device, but it wasn't a big deal if she did. The only external parts were the microphone and speech processor, which fastened behind the ear like a hearing aid, and a transmitter that was worn on the head just behind the ear.

"Wake up, honey."

Melany's eyes blinked open, and Isa breathed out her anxiety. Ever since things had gone awry with the right ear's implant, there was a palpable sense of relief when Isa got confirmation that the left was still functional—that Melany's brain could perceive the sound of her mother's voice, even if she wasn't actually "hearing" in the traditional sense.

Melany sat up, still half-asleep as she put her arms around Isa's neck and nuzzled against her shoulder. Isa glanced again in her husband's direction. He was typing on his smartphone.

"What are you doing?" asked Isa.

"Letting Jack know we're on time."

Jack Swyteck was Keith's friend from high school. He was picking them up at the airport.

"You can't text from an airplane," said Isa.

"Actually, I can. I have one bar."

"I mean it's not allowed."

The floor vibrated beneath her feet, followed by the hydraulic whine of the landing gear. The flight attendant returned. "Seat belts, please. And, sir: no texting."

"Sorry," said Keith.

Isa lifted Melany and maneuvered her into her seat. "For God's sake, Keith. You're going to get us arrested."

Keith tucked his phone away, then reached across the aisle to hold Isa's hand. "Honey, you're really stressed. It's going to be okay. I promise."

"What's going to be okay?" asked Melany.

She'd missed the first part of her parents' conversation—the part that had landed mostly on her right ear, the ear that needed fixing.

Keith captured a gentle kiss from his lips in his fist and passed it across the aisle to Isa, who then planted it on Melany's forehead. It made her smile.

"Everything, sweetie," said Keith. "Absolutely *everything* is going to be A-okay."

Jack Swyteck maneuvered the three-wheel jogging stroller through a crowded International Terminal at MIA. His wife hurried to keep up, and two-year-old Riley was squealing with delight as the pram zigzagged around passengers like a test car around cones.

"Hey, Jeff Gordon, can you slow down, please?" said Andie.

"We're late," he said.

They were always late. It was an immutable

axiom of parenthood that the amount of stuff a daddy Sherpa schlepped from the house on any given car trip was inversely related to the size and weight of the offspring. It was equally well established that no matter how well planned the journey, it was impossible to reach the ultimate destination without having to return to the car and fetch a stuffed animal, a blankie, a sippy cup, or some other thing that, quite naturally, was the very item that Riley couldn't live without at that particular moment.

A TSA officer stopped them at the security post at the end of the international terminal. They could go no farther, having reached the airport version of a velvet rope: nylon barricade tape connected by stanchions. Jack staked out a spot that offered a clear view of the exit doors from U.S. Customs, and there they waited.

"Think you'll recognize him?" asked Andie.

Jack hadn't seen Keith Ingraham in more than a decade, and it would be the first time each had met the other's wife and daughter.

"Yeah, but only because I checked out his photo on the IBS website."

"Does he look that different?"

"Looks exactly the same, except for the shaved head."

"That's quite a difference."

"Not really. His hairline was already receding our senior year of high school. I guess he finally threw in the towel. Looks good on him. Like a younger Bruce Willis."

Riley made an unusual noise from the stroller. She was mimicking the elderly couple beside her, who were speaking Chinese. Andie apologized in Mandarin—she'd learned a few basics on one of her undercover assignments—then continued.

"Why did you guys lose touch?"

"A typical story, I suppose. Keith stayed in Miami and studied business at UM. I went away for undergrad and law. By the time I came back to Miami, he was working on Wall Street for Sherman & McKenzie."

"So while you were living on a shoestring budget and defending death-row inmates at the Freedom Institute, your ol' buddy Keith was making money hand over fist at S and M."

"'SherMac' for short. Never 'S and M.'"

"Funny, but when I was spending seventy hours a week on mortgage fraud investigations at the height of the Great Recession, most of us at the Bureau referred to them and their inflated balance sheets as 'S and M': smoke and mirrors."

That was one of the many interesting things about being a criminal-defense lawyer married to an FBI agent: it was one surprising revelation after another, the number of friends who had perhaps come close to getting burned by Andie Henning and the long arm of the law but who, unlike Icarus, lived to fly another day. "Keith is with IBS now," said Jack.

"Ah, S-S and M. Swiss smoke and mirrors."

"Such a cynic," he said with a smile.

A steady flow of travel-weary passengers continued through customs. Eager friends and family waited alongside Jack and then greeted loved ones with hugs, smiles, and tears of joy as they proceeded to the other side of the tape. Jack kept an eye on the exit. Finally, even from the other end of the long corridor, the recognition was instantaneous.

"There they are," he told Andie.

Keith returned Jack's wave as he and his family approached. Keith was pushing a fully loaded luggage cart. His wife and daughter walked hand in hand beside him.

"Wow," said Andie. "If that's what his wife looks like after flying halfway around the globe, your ol' buddy sure married himself one beautiful woman."

Andie wasn't the jealous type, though it still puzzled Jack the way women checked out other women. Not that he wasn't thinking the same thing.

The big moment was a typical male reunion: mutual backslapping and hugs that weren't quite hugs, followed by Jack's insistence that he help with the carry-ons—a tug-of-war that ended, predictably, with Keith piling the smaller bags atop an already overloaded luggage cart and asserting, "I got it." The adults were halfway through the introductions when Riley climbed out of her stroller to say hello. She clearly wanted to be Melany's instant best friend. Melany was more reserved or, perhaps, just worn out.

Jack put Riley back in the pram, and they were

ready to roll when a pair of officers approached. Jack recognized the uniforms of the Miami-Dade Police Department. The taller one spoke.

"Isabelle Bornelli?" he asked.

Their caravan stopped before it really got started. Smiles faded, and a sudden uneasiness fell over the group.

"Yes," she answered.

"You're under arrest."

The second MDPD officer stepped toward Isa and quickly cuffed her hands behind her back. She did not resist.

"Whoa," said Keith. "What is going on here?"

The arresting officer gave Isa the familiar Miranda warning, but Keith kept talking. "This is crazy. Look, if this is about the text message I sent from the airplane, I—"

"Keith, stop talking," Jack said firmly, kicking into his defense-lawyer mode.

"No, I need to know what this is about."

"Keith, listen to what I'm telling you," said Jack.

Keith pressed on. "What is my wife being arrested for?"

The officer was stone-faced. "Murder."

"What!"

"She's under arrest for the murder of Gabriel Sosa," said the officer.

The next few words stumbled from Keith's mouth. "What—how? I—we don't know anyone named—"

"Keith, I'm very serious," said Jack. "Stop talking. Isa, do not answer any questions or speak to the police about this. Say only that you want to speak to your attorney. Do you understand?"

The expression on her face was one of terror, but she nodded.

"Mommy, where are you going?" asked Melany in a voice filled with concern.

"Give her thirty seconds with her daughter," Jack told the police, and they did. Isa got down on one knee and tried to explain things to Melany. A crowd of onlookers had gathered, forming a rough semicircle on the public side of the TSA security tape. Jack moved a half step closer to the officer, speaking loud enough to be heard but not overheard, making sure that the police understood the situation.

"I'm an attorney," said Jack.

"Are you *her* attorney?" the officer asked.

"He is now," said Keith.

"I'd like to see the arrest warrant."

The officer handed Jack a copy. It was just one page and, as was usual, did little more than reference the applicable provisions in the penal code and recite the judge's finding that, based on the affidavit of an MDPD detective, probable cause existed to believe that Isa Bornelli had committed the specified crime. The details would be in the detective's supporting affidavit, which Jack would have to get from the court or the state attorney.

"Let's go, ma'am," said the officer.

Isa instinctively tried to hug her daughter, but the handcuffs wouldn't allow it. She was fighting back tears as she kissed Melany on the cheek, and her knees wobbled as she rose.

Jack handed Keith a business card and told him to tuck it into Isa's front pocket, which he did. "That has my cell number on it," Jack told her. "We'll follow you to—"

Jack stopped himself, not wanting to say "detention center" in front of the children. "To where you're going," he said. "But call me if you need to talk before we get there."

Isa said nothing; she looked numb. Keith started toward her for one last embrace, but Melany started to cry, so he went to her instead, lifting her into his arms.

"It's okay, baby. Mommy is just going to have a friendly visit with the nice policemen," he said in a voice that wouldn't have fooled Riley, much less a five-year-old.

The police took Isa away, but not toward the main terminal exit. They retreated to the other side of the security tape, and a TSA agent escorted them through the secure area, making it impossible for her lawyer or even her husband to follow.

"We love you!" Keith called to her, speaking for Melany, too.

Isa glanced over her shoulder as the police led her farther and farther from her family. Jack took a good look at her expression, and then he grabbed a quick glimpse of Keith before his gaze returned to Isa. Her focus was on Keith, but Jack stole a moment of eye contact before she looked away.

Jack didn't share his thoughts with Keith, but from his vantage point, there was no mistaking what Isa was telling her husband without words:

She knew Gabriel Sosa. Isa knew exactly what this was about.

2

Jack and Keith hurried to his car in the Flamingo parking garage. Andie queued for a taxi and took the girls to the house on Key Biscayne.

Jack was on his hands-free phone as he steered toward the airport exit. It was after business hours, so he dialed Abe Beckham at home. Abe was a senior trial counsel at the Office of the State Attorney for Miami-Dade County, one of several go-to prosecutors in first-degree murder trials. He wasn't exactly a friend, but Jack had tried two capital cases against him, and there was mutual respect.

"Sorry, not my case," said Abe. "This one belongs to Sylvia Hunt."

"I don't know Sylvia."

"I'll let her know you reached out."

"I need to speak to her ASAP. Tonight, actually."

"I'll see what I can do."

Jack thanked him and hung up. There was more than one route to the detention center, but the evening rush hour was over, so Jack hopped onto the Dolphin Expressway.

"You think the prosecutor will call you?" asked Keith.

Jack kept his eyes on the road. "If we don't hear from her in five minutes, I'll call her."

Keith breathed a heavy sigh. "Well, this certainly wasn't the way I had planned for you to meet my wife."

Jack could have been a friend and simply offered reassurance, but he was in a lawyer frame of mind. "How well do you know her, Keith?"

"We've been married six years. What kind of a question is that?"

"I didn't ask how long. I asked how *well*. What's a normal workweek for you? Seventy, eighty hours?"

"We have quality time."

Quality: code for *not enough*. "You travel a lot, I'm sure."

"Once a week to Zurich. Every other week to Singapore or Tokyo, depending on where we have the Asia private-wealth meeting. Then there's the incidental travel—business development, high-net-worth-client events, that sort of thing."

"So on average, you're home—what, three nights a week?"

"Sometimes four. If you're suggesting that I didn't really know the woman I married and it turns out she's a murderer, then you're talking crazy."

"I'm just asking the questions I need to ask. Does Isa have a criminal record?"

"No."

"Are you sure?"

"I've never run a criminal background check, if that's your question."

"What do you know about her family?"

"Her mother died before I met Isa. Her father lives in Caracas—last I heard, anyway. I've never met him. He and Isa have no relationship. Isa didn't even want to invite him to our wedding."

"Why not?"

"Politics. He was a Chavez crony when Isa was growing up. I won't put words in her mouth and say it was rebellion, but could the daughter of a card-carrying member of the United Socialist Party have married a bigger capitalist than a private-wealth manager for a Swiss bank?"

There was a time when Jack, a young criminal-defense lawyer who defended death-row inmates, stopped speaking to Harry Swyteck, the "law and order" governor who signed more death warrants than any governor in Florida history. Jack used to tell people it was about politics, too; it was never *just* about politics.

"I suppose I can relate," said Jack.

"This whole thing has to be a mistake," said Keith. "Isa hasn't set foot in Miami in years. She left the U after her freshman year and finished her degree at the University of Zurich. She was working on her doctorate in psychology when I met her."

"Isa has a Ph.D.?" he asked, sounding more surprised than he intended.

"Not yet. That's been on hold since Melany was born. Actually, pretty much everything has been on hold since the ear trouble started. It's Isa's full-time mission."

Jack steered over to the right lane of the expressway and took the Twelfth Street exit. His cell rang as they waited at the red light at the end of the ramp. It was Sylvia Hunt. She wasn't willing to say much to him on the telephone, but she did agree to e-mail Jack a copy of the affidavit in support of the arrest warrant, which was what Jack really wanted. One question, however, Jack wanted answered right away:

"When was Gabriel Sosa murdered?"

"Twelve years ago this month," said Hunt. "April seventeenth, to be exact."

"So this was a cold case?"

"Yes."

"I presume there is some new evidence that links Isa Bornelli to the crime, allegedly?"

"Yes. It's in the probable-cause affidavit."

"You can't just tell me what it is?"

"I'm preparing for a suppression hearing in another case. I'm not focused on Ms. Bornelli right now and I don't want to be accused of mischaracterizing anything. Read the affidavit, and then I'll be happy to schedule a time to sit down with you and discuss it."

Some prosecutors played cautiously, especially with criminal-defense lawyers they had never dealt with before.

"You're e-mailing it now?" asked Jack.

"As soon as we hang up."

"Okay. One other quick question. I noticed that the arrest warrant alleges first-degree murder with special circumstances. What are the special circumstances?"

"Kidnapping and torture."

The traffic light turned green. So did Keith's pallor.

"You mean kidnapping for ransom?" asked Jack.

"I really have to get back to my other case. Read the affidavit, please."

Jack thanked the prosecutor, hung up, and merged into traffic toward the Justice Building. Keith was looking truly nauseous.

"You okay?" asked Jack.

"Kidnap and torture? Seriously? This is a fucking nightmare."

Jack didn't want to make matters worse, but he needed answers. "Where was Isa twelve years ago this month?"

Keith took another deep breath. "She was a student."

"Where?"

Jack glanced in Keith's direction, but he was staring through the windshield, as if hypnotized by the string of red taillights ahead of them. "Here. At the University of Miami."

They rode in silence, neither man having to say that the quickest way out of trouble—the ironclad alibi that Isa hadn't visited the U.S. since college—had already evaporated.

3

The criminal courthouse was dark, but the lights were burning across the street—Lucky Thirteenth Street, as it was known—at the pretrial detention center. Jack parked in the jury lot, which was empty for the night. It was after eight o'clock when he and Keith entered through the visitors' entrance on the ground floor.

The multistory detention center north of downtown Miami housed 170 inmates who were awaiting trial on charges that ran the legal gamut from traffic offenses to capital murder. Men and women were held on separate floors, but the same visitation rules applied. Family visits were strictly noncontact, and visitation outside of normal hours was allowed only by court order.

"Are you saying I can't see my wife?" Keith asked.

They were in the lobby, standing on the visitor side of the glass window for guest registration. The corrections officer answered from inside the booth, speaking into a gooseneck microphone. "Visitation for female inmates is Thursdays and

Saturdays, five thirty p.m. to nine fifteen p.m.," she said.

Keith blinked, and Jack could almost see the fog of jet lag surrounding him. "Today is Tuesday," said Jack.

"I'm here all the way from Hong Kong," said Keith. "There must be exceptions."

"Only for attorneys and bail bondsmen," said the officer.

"How fast can I become a bail bondsman?" he asked, but Jack knew he wasn't serious—at least not entirely.

Jack leaned closer to the glass and followed up with the corrections officer about an attorney visit. A check of the computer confirmed that Isa had already gone through the booking process and that Jack Swyteck was registered as her legal counsel. Isa was in a temporary holding cell awaiting bed assignment. Jack and Keith took a seat in the waiting room. After about fifteen minutes, a guard escorted Jack to the attorney-client conference room, where Isa was waiting for him.

Jack entered. The guard closed the door and locked it from the outside, leaving Jack alone with his newest client.

Isa was seated at a small table, still dressed in the clothes she'd worn on the flight from Hong Kong. She rose to greet Jack as he approached.

"Thank you for coming."

"I'm glad I can help."

She settled back into her chair, and Jack sat opposite her at the table. They were surrounded by windowless walls of yellow-painted cinder block.

Bright fluorescent lighting lent their meeting room all the warmth of a workshop.

"How are you holding up?" asked Jack.

She shrugged. "Just kind of going through the motions, I guess. It's all pretty surreal."

"I understand."

She folded her arms, as if cold, but it was probably the total experience that was making her uncomfortable—not to mention the fact that Jack was her husband's old buddy. Keith had pointed out that these were less than ideal circumstances for a reunion, and it had to feel even more awkward for Isa. Jack decided to address it up front.

"Look, I don't want you to feel locked into hiring me as your attorney. This happens to be my line of work, which is convenient in the short term. But choosing a lawyer is a very personal decision."

"Thank you for saying that."

"I'm willing to help as long as you want me to help. But once we sort out these preliminary matters, I can come up with a short list of topflight criminal-defense lawyers for you to interview, and you can make your own decision."

"Keith has told me all about you and the work you did at the Freedom Institute. You sound pretty topflight to me."

The Freedom Institute, where Jack had started his career right out of law school, was Jack's first introduction to capital cases. "We can talk more about that later. For now, let's tackle the problem at hand. I have a few questions. But first, is there anything you want to ask me?"

"How is Melany?"

"She's fine. Andie took her back to our house with our daughter."

"Tell Keith that it's okay if Melany wants to wear her audio processer to sleep. Being in a strange house might make her feel too disconnected if she can't hear out of both ears."

"I'll be sure to tell him. He's here, in the waiting room." Jack explained the restrictions on family visitation.

"Thursdays and Saturdays? I won't actually still be here on Thursday, will I?"

Jack hesitated a bit too long.

"I need to see my family," said Isa, "and I can't bring my daughter *here.* How soon can you get me out?"

"Let me explain how the process works. Arraignment is your first court appearance. That won't happen until tomorrow. You'll be lumped in with all the other felony arrests, starting at nine thirty."

"So I have to spend the night here?"

"Yes."

Isa breathed in and out, as if coming to terms with it. "Okay. I'll deal with that. Then I get out?"

"I'll try to get the prosecutor to agree to that."

"Do you think he will?"

"She, not he," said Jack. "So far I've had one phone call with her. She promised to e-mail me a copy of the affidavit of the MDPD homicide detective, which lays out the evidence against you. I had to leave my cell phone at visitor registration, but as of twenty minutes ago I still didn't have her e-mail. If it's not in my inbox when I pick up my cell, I'll go over her head."

"That doesn't sound like a great start. What if the prosecutor won't agree to let me out? Will the judge release me?"

She'd hit on the first bit of bad news, and Jack tried to be gentle. "In a first-degree murder case, the legal presumption is no bail."

It was as if Jack had punched her in the chest. She looked away, then back. "I can't stay *here*. Melany has her surgery on Friday."

"We may be able to use that to our advantage."

"It's not a question of *using* it. She's five years old. She can't go without her mommy."

"Sorry. What I meant to say is that we have a situation where there are extenuating circumstances that favor your release."

"Yes," she said, "lots of extenuating circumstances. Starting with the fact that I didn't do it. I didn't kill Gabriel Sosa."

"I don't always get the answer to that question from my clients. It certainly doesn't impact my decision to take the case. All I want is the truth."

"That is the truth. I didn't kill him."

Jack didn't respond right away. He gave her a moment to live with her assertion of "the truth," assessing her demeanor. It wasn't exactly a lie-detector test, but he did note that she didn't feel the need to fill the silence with nervous jabber.

"All right. If you want to go down that road, we need to go all the way down it. Do you know who did kill him?"

"No."

"Let's back up even further, all the way to the beginning. Call it lawyer's intuition, but when the police escorted you away at the airport, I got the impression that the name Gabriel Sosa was one you'd heard before."

"Uh-huh."

"So tell me: Who is Gabriel Sosa? Or who *was* he?"

She drew a deep breath. "A boy I knew in college."

"How well did you know him?"

"Not as well as I thought I did."

"What does that mean?"

She hesitated, and Jack was certain that she was going to tell him something that she had never told her husband.

"He raped me," she said.

Jack had reached a point in his career where he truly thought he'd heard it all. And then there was this.

"I'm sorry, Isa. But you're going to have to tell me all about that."

4

I'd like to make a phone call, please," Isa told the guard.

The meeting with Jack had lasted until 9:30 p.m. He'd warned her about the overcrowded conditions at the detention center, which explained why she was still waiting for a bed. He'd also told her that a charge of first-degree murder meant a cell in Protective Custody Level One, the high-security section. She would get one hour a day to take a shower and sit in the dayroom. She could access books from a library cart to take back to her cell, but Level One inmates had no television or computer privileges. Most important, she could make collect calls from the jail phone.

A corrections officer escorted Isa from the holding cell to the jail telephone, and Isa took her place at the back of the line. At least a half dozen inmates were ahead of her, depending on how many were also holding a spot for a friend or cellmate. All Isa could do was wait. A little more time to choose her words was probably a good thing. She needed and wanted to speak to Melany—if she was awake at this hour—but she still wasn't sure how to explain. Isa tried to script something out in her head, but it was hard to focus. From the moment the police had taken her away at the airport, she'd felt untethered from reality. No watch. No cell phone. No talking allowed. She especially didn't like the way the correctional officer was looking at her. It wasn't the first time a man had undressed her with his eyes, but in this situation, where she was literally his prisoner, it was especially creepy.

"I'm not going anywhere," she told him. "You don't have to wait here with me."

The guard seemed to take her point. He made a quick assessment of her wait time and said, "I'll be back in an hour."

Sixty-five minutes passed. The guard had yet to return, and Isa was still waiting in line. The day was weighing on her. She should have been lying on a king-size bed at a luxury hotel sleeping off jet lag. Instead, she'd been forced to endure endless periods of unexplained waiting, interspersed with bursts of pointless activity that seemed driven by nothing more than the correction officers' personal whim. Up and down several flights of stairs. In and out of different holding pens. She'd been shackled, unshackled, and shackled again. The body search had been especially memorable.

"Hey, you gonna use the phone or not?" the inmate behind her asked.

Isa opened her eyes. She'd nearly fallen asleep standing up. Finally, it was her turn. She went to the phone, and her hand shook as she dialed Jack's home number.

Please, someone answer.

On the fourth ring, she heard Jack say hello. He was about to bring Keith to the phone, but Isa stopped him.

"Did you tell him?" At the conclusion of their meeting, she'd asked Jack to tell Keith everything.

"I did."

"So he knows that I was—"

"Isa, stop," said Jack. "Remember what I said about jail phones."

Jack had given her compelling examples of men and women who had, figuratively speaking, hanged themselves on prison lines. The sign on the wall—ALL CALLS ARE MONITORED BY LAW ENFORCEMENT—reinforced his words. She was under strict orders not to discuss Gabriel Sosa, the sexual assault, or anything else about her case.

"I understand," said Isa. "Does Keith know the rules?"

"Yes, we've covered it. He's eager to talk to you. Let me get him."

It took just a few seconds for Keith to come on the line, but it seemed to take much longer for him to say something.

"I don't even know where to begin, honey."

"I can only imagine," she said.

"I just don't understand why you never told me about any of this."

He was talking about the rape, of course. "Keith, you know we can't talk about this right now. Don't make this call harder than it already is."

"I'm sorry. That wasn't what I was trying to do."

"It's okay," she said, and then she came around

to what really mattered. "I'm worried about Melany."

"Don't be. She's doing pretty well. She was busy playing with Jack and Andie's little girl, until she went to bed."

"Melany's asleep?"

"No. I meant Riley is out. Melany slept so hard on the plane she'll be up 'til at least midnight. Let me get her for you."

Isa's grip around the phone tightened. The wait seemed much longer than it was. She hoped she was strong enough to get through this.

"Hi, Mommy."

That little voice—it almost killed her. "Hi, baby. Did you make a new friend today?"

"Yeah. When can I see you?"

A second near-mortal wound. "Pretty soon. Is Riley nice?"

"Yes, she's real nice. Are you coming over here tonight?"

"No, honey. Not tonight."

"Why not?"

"I can't tonight."

"Why not?"

Isa struggled, silently chiding herself for having no prepared answer. "Tonight will be your night with Daddy."

Melany didn't reply. There was muffled sobbing on the line. Isa closed her eyes and then opened them, trying to absorb the blow. "Don't cry, big girl. Please don't cry."

She could hear Keith in the background telling Melany that everything was going to be all right.

"Good night, Mommy. I love you."

It was enough to make Isa cry, but she didn't. "I love you too."

Keith was back on the line. "Are you okay?"

"Not at all," said Isa.

He gave her a moment. "So, I wouldn't read too much into that. Melany is really doing well. I think she's just tired."

She knew that Keith was only trying to ease the pain, but it wasn't working. "Will you be at my arraignment tomorrow?" she asked.

"Of course."

"Jack said I'll be in prison clothes. Don't bring Melany."

"No, I get that."

"And be mindful of what's on the TV when she's in the room. Jack said this case could get media attention. I don't want Melany to see any of that."

"Actually, I didn't know if I should say anything, but there was a segment on tonight's news."

Of course there was. *Former UM Coed Arrested for Murder of Her Rapist.* A headline that catchy could go viral. "I can't believe this is happening to me."

"Don't worry about things you can't control. That's Jack's job."

A lump came to her throat. She hoped her reading of his words was correct, but he seemed to be telling her, "*I believe in you; I know you're innocent.*"

The woman in line behind her grunted something to the effect that Isa's time was up. Isa wasn't aware of any time restriction, but the woman was built like a UFC champion, and she didn't want her first night in prison to end with the snot getting beat out of her.

"Keith, I have to go now," she said into the phone.

"Okay. Hey, we'll get through this."

"I know we will."

"I love you."

"I love you, too."

They said good-bye. Isa hung up, and the next inmate in line practically knocked her to the floor in her rush to the phone. Isa stepped aside and waited for the corrections officer. It was well past his promise to return "in an hour." Isa could only hope that they were still having trouble finding a bunk for her.

Maybe they'll let me go home.

It was short-lived optimism. The guard's return immediately burst her bubble.

"Got a bed for you, sweetie," he said.

I'm not your "sweetie." She thought it but didn't say it.

Isa followed the guard down the long corridor. She focused straight ahead, her gaze like a laser, making no eye contact with anyone inside the cells she passed on the left or right. At the end of the cell block, the door buzzed open. They continued into the east wing.

"Lucky for you," said the guard. "No cells in level-one custody, so you'll be here with the hookers and druggies tonight."

Isa didn't answer. She wasn't feeling lucky.

It was "lights out" by the time they reached her

assigned cell. Isa entered quietly, careful not to disturb the inmate on the top bunk as she climbed onto the mattress below. It squeaked as she settled in. The cell door closed, and then reality hit her.

I'm in jail. I am actually in jail.

She felt imprisoned in every sense of the word; telling her lawyer how she was the victim of date rape in college hadn't proved to be liberating at all. It merely stirred up a past that she had managed to compartmentalize and suppress for years.

She was thinking again of the television coverage Keith had mentioned. She didn't have to ask how bad it was. And she had no doubt it would get worse—that the story would be embellished as news worked its way from Miami to Hong Kong and then back across the globe to her old neighborhood in Caracas. Her entire life, Isa had fought adversity. A mother who had pushed her into the beauty academies. A father who had condemned her for it.

And now, her college nightmare would have a name the world over: Gabriel Sosa.

She tried to close her eyes, but the scary voice of the woman in the top bunk startled her.

"So, what'd you do to land yourself in here?"

"Nothing," said Isa, her voice a mere peep.

The woman chuckled. "Just like the rest of us." She hung her head over the edge of the mattress and peered down at Isa, her long dreadlocks dangling in the shadows. "Come on, princess. You can tell me."

"Really, I didn't do anything."

The woman's smile drained away. "You think I'm a snitch, don't you?"

"What? No, I—"

"You think that if you tell me what you did, I'll run to the state attorney and cut a sweet deal to save my own ass."

"I didn't say that." *But now that you mention it.*

"Fucking bitch. You go around callin' people a snitch, you better sleep with one eye open."

Isa caught her breath, praying to God that the woman didn't jump down from the top bunk to continue this discussion face-to-face—or, worse, fist-to-face. The mattress above her didn't move, which triggered the closest thing to a sense of relief that Isa had felt since her arrival. Sleep, however, was out of the question. She lay awake in the prison silence, listening, trying to grow accustomed to what she could label as "normal" prison noises. Survival meant being able to quickly identify any sound, any movement, anything at all that wasn't normal.

Sleep with one eye open.

Her entire adult life, Isa had kept secrets, but never had she been up against a criminal justice system intent upon turning her inside out for the world to see. It bordered on terrifying, and she couldn't stem the emotions that were welling up inside and begging to escape. She'd flown across the world to be with her daughter when Melany needed her most. Now, Isa might never be with her again.

Isa struggled to hold it in, but a tear fell in the

darkness. And then another. The words she'd shared with Melany echoed in her mind.

Don't cry, big girl. Please, don't cry.

"You cryin' down there, princess?"

Her cellmate's voice made her shiver. "No."

The dreadlocks were suddenly hanging down in the darkness again, and Isa could see the glint in her cellmate's eyes. "Yeah, you is."

"I'm *not*," she said, but her voice cracked.

"Aw, poor princess. It's Tayshawn who got you so scared you could piss your pants, ain't it?"

"Who's Tayshawn?"

"The guard who brought you in here. Everybody know he like Latina pussy."

Isa went cold. Her instincts had been dead on. *I'm not your sweetie.*

"You gonna be just fine, princess. You got me as a cellmate."

"What does that mean?"

"It means I ain't gonna look the other way when Tayshawn come in here for some bullshit inspection and shoves his big dick down your throat. That won't happen," she said, and then she disappeared into her bunk, finishing her promise in the darkness:

"Tonight."

5

Jack was in downtown Miami by five a.m., in time for his first interview with local television. He had four of them lined up, and all would air before Isa's arraignment. By 5:30 he was wired up and on the set.

"Good morning, Miami!" the primped and perfect blond host said into the camera.

Jack wouldn't typically work the media so soon, but in this case it was justified. Sylvia Hunt had never sent the promised e-mail. Jack had tried to go over her head, but the state attorney didn't return his calls. It was clear to Jack that the prosecution had no intention of sharing the sworn affidavit in which the MDPD homicide detective laid out the evidence to support "probable cause" for Isa's arrest.

"With me this morning is Miami criminal-defense attorney Jack Swyteck."

Technically, the state attorney wasn't legally required to share the MDPD affidavit; the defense could get a copy from the courthouse file—but not until 9:00 a.m., when the clerk's office opened. Jack therefore needed to send a message to the entire office of the state attorney: if they weren't willing to extend the courtesy of sharing the affidavit before Isa's arraignment, it was a huge mistake to issue a press release before Jack could get inside the courthouse and secure his own copy.

"Mr. Swyteck, you've handled dozens of murder trials before. Tell us a little bit about the state attorney's somewhat unorthodox case against your latest client."

"Honestly, the prosecution has been unusually tight-lipped, so I know virtually nothing about the case except what the state attorney deigned to put in a press release that was issued last night just before the late edition of the news."

"Well, we know from that press release that your client is a thirty-one-year-old woman. At the age of nineteen she enrolled at the University of Miami, and in the spring of her freshman year she was the victim of sexual assault. Now, all these years later, she is arrested and charged with first degree murder, allegedly for having killed the man who raped her. Do I have those allegations right?"

"Yes, that's essentially the prosecution's case. And thank you for not mentioning my client by name—even though her name appears in the state attorney's press release."

"Let's talk about that. I understand you're pretty upset about it."

"I'm appalled, frankly."

"Why?"

"The clear implication of the state attorney's press release is that my client's motive for the murder of Gabriel Sosa was the fact that he sexually assaulted her. Like most states in this nation, Florida has a shield law that prohibits law enforcement from releasing the name of a rape victim to the media. The idea is to avoid making her a victim twice: once when she is assaulted, and a second time when her identity goes viral. The Miami state attorney has ignored the law, apparently taking the position that a rape victim accused of murdering her attacker is entitled to no such protection."

"But wait a second. Should those shield laws apply in this situation?"

"In my opinion, yes. Look, my client is innocent of that murder charge until proven guilty. The only thing we know for certain is that she was sexually assaulted. I might not fault a news organization for deciding in good faith that the shield laws don't apply here. But I don't think the state attorney's office should be leading the way by revealing her name in a press release within hours of her arrest."

"I would tend to agree. As an editorial note, I must concede to our viewers that this station did reveal the identity of Mr. Swyteck's client in last night's eleven p.m. newscast. We did so based on the information in the press release from the Miami state attorney's office. I don't know what our official position will be going forward. But as a matter of principle, I can tell you that this *Good Morning Miami* host definitely will not repeat her name.

"Thank you very much for joining us this morning and sharing this fascinating case and this important issue, Mr. Swyteck."

"You're very welcome."

"Coming up: a live interview from Mercy Hospital with British tourist Ginger Radley, who somehow survived a twenty-story fall after breaking her bungee cord. It's Ginger snap, Miami style! Next on *Good Morning Miami.*"

Jack unclipped his microphone and stepped down from the news set, so glad he didn't do this every day for a living.

Sylvia Hunt was standing in her bedroom, staring at the flat-screen television on the wall—and fuming. Jack Swyteck on *Good Morning Miami* was not something she had anticipated.

Sylvia was not one to be outmaneuvered by any criminal-defense lawyer. She'd paid her dues as a "pit assistant," a C-level prosecutor of adult felonies, working sixty-hour weeks under supervising attorneys, earning the astronomical sum of forty thousand dollars a year. An unmatched combination of courtroom skills and tireless preparation opened doors for her, and she could have moved up to any unit. She chose sexual assault, where she took more cases to trial and earned more convictions than anyone else in the state of Florida. She was the youngest prosecutor in the Miami office to hold the title "Senior Trial Counsel," which put her among the elite—the seasoned few who prosecuted the most controversial and complicated capital cases. It was an honor and a distinction she'd earned.

She sure as hell didn't deserve this stain on her record.

Sylvia grabbed her cell phone from the nightstand. It was fully charged; so was she. It didn't matter if it wasn't yet six a.m. She dialed her boss at home and got her out of bed.

"Swyteck is doing the morning circuit."

Carmen Benitez was midway through her fourth elected term as state attorney. No one questioned her commitment to the job. She worked late into the evening, weekends, and holidays. Phone calls at one or two a.m. were no problem. But she had never been known as an early riser.

"Record it on your DVR," said Benitez. "I'm going back to sleep."

"No, wait. We are getting pulverized for revealing the name of a rape victim in last night's press release on Isabelle Bornelli."

The state attorney hesitated, and Sylvia could sense her confusion over the line. "Wait—we didn't do that."

"Yes, *we* did. I called the station to confirm. They sent me a copy of the release. Isabelle Bornelli's name is in it."

Benitez groaned over the line. "Oh, boy."

"Yeah. 'Oh boy' is right. That's not the version of the press release I reviewed and approved last night. I said do not use her name—not until the press made its own decision and the horse was out of the barn."

"Obviously somebody in media relations fucked up."

It wasn't the first time. "That's not a very satisfactory explanation. Don't underestimate this, Carmen. We are going to have huge backlash from victims' rights groups. I guarantee it."

"We'll have to talk damage control. When's the arraignment?"

"Nine thirty."

"That doesn't give us much time."

"I can meet you in the office in thirty minutes," said Sylvia.

"Ohhhh," she said. It was some combination of a yawn and a groan.

"I'll take that as a yes. See you in thirty."

Sylvia hung up, grabbed the remote, and changed channels. There he was again, Isa's hotshot lawyer on another network: "I think it's a sad situation when the state attorney's office is leading the way against the spirit, if not the letter, of rape shield laws."

Sylvia switched off the set and grabbed her purse. Her anger was still smoldering, but as she started toward the door, she glimpsed a framed photograph of her parents that she kept on her dresser. They were partners in every sense of the word, married for over thirty years and even had their own law firm—Hunt & Hunt—while Sylvia was growing up in Pensacola. They'd been gone long enough for the pain to ease, and Sylvia mustered a little smile as she recalled something her daddy used to say whenever opposing counsel crossed the line.

"You stepped on the wrong dog this time, Mr. Swyteck," she said on her way out.

6

Courtroom 1–5 at the Richard E. Gersten Justice Building was packed.

Felony arraignments started every weekday at nine a.m. Wednesday's docket included Isabelle Bornelli and everyone else in Miami-Dade County who'd been arrested in the previous twenty-four hours on a felony charge. The routine played out in a spacious old room with high ceilings and a long mahogany rail that separated the public seating from the business end of the justice system. A junior assistant state attorney was seated at the government's table in front of the empty jury box, working his way through the stack of files, one at a time, as each case was called. Jack watched from the first row of public seating, waiting his turn as the parade of accused armed robbers, drunk drivers, and others proclaimed their innocence and then were either released on bail or remanded to custody. Keith was to his left on the long bench seat.

"More spectators than I thought would be here," said Keith. He spoke quietly so as not to disturb the seventh arraignment of the morning, which was under way on the other side of the rail.

Both Jack and the state attorney's office had underestimated the public outcry in response to Isa's arrest. Interested observers filled several rows of public seating behind them. The media section was at capacity. Last night's press release from the state attorney had sparked some local interest, but not until Jack's morning interviews did the media firmly latch on to the case. The Internet was already abuzz with tweets, blogs, and other electronic chatter about the beautiful former Miami coed who was "hiding out" in Hong Kong and finally got arrested for murdering the young man who had raped her in college.

"When do I see Isa?" asked Keith.

Hopefully not too soon. A lawyer from the Freedom Institute was in line at the clerk's office to get a copy of the affidavit that Sylvia Hunt had neglected to send him, and Jack wanted it for the arraignment. "Isa's number eleven on the schedule. The deputy will bring her in when it's her turn."

"Next case," said Judge Gonzalez. He was moving quickly. They were at number nine.

Judge Gonzalez was the oldest judge on the criminal circuit. Some said he no longer had the stamina for lengthy trials, but he still seemed to enjoy the frenetic pace of arraignments. It had been several months since Jack's last appearance before him, and it had been a defense lawyer's dream, starting at 9:07 a.m. and ending at 9:08 a.m. The state attorney dropped the assault charge against an elderly woman who reminded

Jack of his own *abuela*. She was a Cuban expat who had fled the Castro regime on a *balsa* in the first wave of refugees, and she just couldn't help herself when a clueless college student walked into her cigar shop in Little Havana sporting a T-shirt that bore the iconic image of Che Guevara, the supreme prosecutor during the Cuban revolution. If the state attorney hadn't dismissed the charge, Judge Gonzalez would have. He might have pointed out that his family of five had also left Cuba on a raft, that only four of them had made it to the Florida coast, and that this was Miami, not the People's Republic of Berkeley.

Jack wondered if Judge Gonzalez had seen any of the early-morning media coverage, some of which had mentioned that Isa's father had served under Hugo Chavez, Fidel Castro's protégé. It was a complication Isa didn't need—especially before Judge Gonzalez.

"Case number seventeen oh-three oh-one," announced the bailiff. "State of Florida versus Isabelle Bornelli."

"Rape victims matter!" a woman shouted from the back row.

Judge Gonzalez smacked his gavel. "There will be order in this courtroom."

Silence. It was an isolated outburst, clearly not yet a coordinated movement. Jack hadn't noticed any demonstrators on his way into the courthouse, but he sensed that something was brewing. Injecting the rights of sexual assault victims into this case could well backfire, but Jack wouldn't have been doing his job as a defense lawyer if he weren't already thinking about how it might help his client.

The side door opened, and a deputy brought Isa into the courtroom.

"Oh, my God," Keith said softly, like a reflex. It was the first time he'd seen his wife in prison garb and shackles. Jack rose, pushed through the swinging gate at the rail, and met his client at the defense table. Isa made brief eye contact with Keith, then looked squarely at Jack.

"Jack, you *have* to get me out of jail," she whispered.

There was desperation in her voice, and Jack would have liked to get to the bottom of it, but arraignments move quickly, and this was not the time.

"Good morning, Ms. Hunt," Judge Gonzalez said with a smile. "I don't have the pleasure of seeing you at arraignment very often anymore."

The junior prosecutor who had handled the first ten arraignments stepped aside. Sylvia Hunt assumed the lead post at the prosecutor's table. They were bringing in the big gun for *State v. Bornelli*.

"I don't do many arraignments these days," she said.

"Well, it's always a pleasure to have you. And you as well, Mr. Sweet. Sorry, Swat—"

"Jack Swyteck for the defendant Isabelle Bornelli, Your Honor." There wasn't a gray-haired judge in Florida who didn't know how to pronounce the name of the former governor, and Jack interpreted Judge Gonzalez's brain fart as a sign of either Alzheimer's or animosity, neither of which boded well for his client.

"Good morning to both of you. Ms. Hunt, may I have the date and time of Ms. Bornelli's arrest?"

"Yesterday at approximately seven twenty p.m."

"Ms. Bornelli, the purpose of the proceeding is to advise you of certain rights that you have, to inform you of the charges made against you under Florida law, and to determine under what conditions, if any, you might be released before trial. Do you understand?"

"Yes, Your Honor," said Isa.

"You have the right to remain silent," the judge said, and for the second time in as many days, Isa listened to the full recital of her Miranda rights. She looked no less numb the second time, Jack observed.

"We'll waive the reading of the charges," said Jack.

"That's fine. Ms. Bornelli, how do you plead?"

"Not guilty, Your Honor."

"So noted." The judge's gaze shifted to the other side of the courtroom. "Ms. Hunt, what is the state's position on bail?"

"Judge, thanks to Mr. Swyteck's whirlwind tour on the morning show circuit today, we are well aware of his view that the rules should be different in this case because Ms. Bornelli is the alleged victim of a sexual assault. As the court knows, I have successfully prosecuted scores of sexual offenders, and I'm very sensitive to the rights of victims in our judicial system. But this is not a case in which Ms. Bornelli is the accuser. She is the *accused*—charged with first-degree murder. Under the law, the presumption in a first-degree murder case is that bail will be denied in the absence of clear evidence that the defendant is not a flight risk. We urge the court to follow the law."

"What evidence do you have that the defendant *is* a flight risk?" the judge asked.

Hunt had done a nice job defusing the rape shield issue. Jack expected her to take the judge's question and run with it, moving from defense to offense.

"Ms. Bornelli is a citizen of Venezuela. She moved here at the age of eleven, when her father served as a diplomat in the consul general's office under the Chavez government."

Judge Gonzalez sat up with interest. "Is that so?"

Jack bristled. It wasn't really a question. The judge might as well have said, *"That's all I need to hear."*

The prosecutor continued. "She was a nineteen-year-old college student in Miami when she claims she was sexually assaulted by Mr. Sosa. His body was recovered six weeks later near the Florida Everglades. Detectives from MDPD were two months into a homicide investigation when Ms. Bornelli left Miami and moved to Switzerland. The murder investigation went cold. Two years ago, right about the time MDPD reopened the investigation, Ms. Bornelli moved to China."

A Communist country, Jack noted. Hunt knew how to play her cards in front of this judge, but that blow was below the belt.

"Hong Kong," said Jack, rising.

"Yes, Hong Kong," said Hunt. "But since coming under control of the Communist Chinese government, Hong Kong has made extradition to the United States extremely difficult. Every move that the defendant has made since Mr. Sosa's death has been a calculated and clear attempt to evade prosecution, confirming her risk of flight. Bail should be denied."

The judge shook his head, but not in disagreement. He was passing judgment. "Well, I have to say—"

"Judge, may I respond?" asked Jack, futile as it might be.

"Quickly."

"My client left Miami because she was sexually assaulted and wanted to leave this place behind and start someplace new. She lived in Switzerland for eight years because she was pursuing a doctoral degree from the University of Zurich and married a man who worked for IBS. They moved to Hong Kong because her husband—Mr. Keith Ingraham, who is sitting in the front row—was promoted to head up the IBS office in Hong Kong."

"Is Mr. Ingraham Swiss?"

"No," said Jack.

"He's a U.S. citizen," said the prosecutor. "Which raises another interesting point. Since moving to Hong Kong, Mr. Ingraham has traveled to the United States fourteen different times. The defendant traveled with him on just two of those trips, both of which were related to medical treatment for her daughter. We are still trying to gather evidence from the Communist government in China," she said, hammering the communism point, "but we believe those two trips to Miami were the *only* times Ms. Bornelli has left Hong Kong since moving there."

The judge seemed ready to rule, taking his gavel in hand. "So what you're saying, Ms. Hunt, is that ever since MDPD reopened this homicide investigation, the defendant has been living on an island on the other side of the world, holed up in China, from which she probably couldn't be extradited."

"Precisely. I would also point out that she currently has a flight booked in her name to Hong Kong, which is scheduled to leave on Saturday."

"Is that so?" Another judgment, not a queston.

"Your Honor, this is getting ridiculous," said Jack. "My client flew to Miami because her daughter is profoundly deaf in one ear. On Friday she is scheduled to have corrective surgery performed at Jackson Hospital by one of the leading cochlear-implant experts in the world."

"But what Mr. Swyteck fails to inform the court, Your Honor, is that the defendant's husband and daughter are not scheduled to fly back for another twelve days. Ms. Bornelli's daughter can't fly immediately after ear surgery, but this stay-at-home mom, who has no pressing need to get back to Hong Kong, is scheduled to fly out the day after her daughter's surgery. The only logical inference is that the defendant is determined to get out of Miami and back to China as fast as she can. She is a flight risk. Bail should be denied."

Jack glanced at his client. Isa had neglected to tell him about the curious flight schedule.

"Judge, what I'd like to do—"

"I've heard enough, Mr. Swyteck."

"Judge, if I may. I'd like to request a full evidentiary hearing to flesh out these issues, after which the court can make a final determination on bail."

"That's fine. Cynthia, when do I have a free hour?"

The judge's assistant thumbed through the calendar. "Two weeks from tomorrow, at eleven a.m."

"Book it," the judge said. "Until then, I'm remanding the prisoner to custody."

Isa grabbed Jack by the arm. "I have to be at Melany's surgery," she said firmly, but soft enough so that only Jack could hear.

Jack did what he could. "Judge, I would propose that arrangements be made for my client to be released on a temporary basis so that she can be with her daughter on Friday for the surgery. Perhaps an eight-hour window."

"Let's see a show of hands from the taxpayers in the audience who want to pay for a police escort to and from the hospital. No one. Denied."

"She could be released with a SCRAM bracelet."

"This court doesn't do ankle bracelets in a first-degree murder case. The prisoner is remanded to the detention center. No bail," he said with a crack of the gavel.

The bailiff called the next case. Another lawyer and her client hurried forward and took Jack and Isa's place at the defense table.

Jack and Isa walked to the rail. Keith was standing on the other side, and he did his best to embrace his wife over the bannister. The deputy approached and took Isa by the arm.

"Jack, I can't spend another night in that place," Isa whispered—but with urgency. The desperation in her eyes that Jack had seen earlier had turned to terror. "You can't let that happen!"

"I'll come by this afternoon. We have a lot to discuss."

"Jack, about the plane ticket—"

"Mr. Swyteck," the judge intoned from the bench, "can you please take your client conference back to the detention center?"

Jack apologized to the court. The guard took Isa and escorted her across the courtroom toward the prisoners' exit. She glanced over her shoulder, mouthing the words *I love you* to her husband, and then disappeared behind the heavy door.

The next arraignment was under way, so Jack and Keith continued in silence down the center aisle toward the double doors in the back of the courtroom. The prosecutor followed, and as they reached the doors she handed Jack a file. "Here's the probable-cause affidavit I promised," she said in a church voice. "Sorry I couldn't get it to you last night. I got serious pushback from MDPD about sharing it without redactions. It turned into such a bureaucratic hassle. I just couldn't get it sorted out in time."

"That's a crock of shit," said Keith.

They were well out of Judge Gonzalez's earshot, but Jack still shot his friend a glance to shut him up. The prosecutor pushed the glass door open and stepped into the lobby.

"I don't trust her," said Keith.

Jack gazed through the glass and watched her walk straight to a flock of reporters outside the courtroom. She was handing out copies of the affidavit that she'd kept from Jack until the arraignment was over.

"I wish I could disagree," said Jack.

7

Jack started grilling Keith as soon as they were outside the courthouse and well away from anyone who might be eavesdropping. It wasn't literally true that courthouse walls had ears, but in a world where anyone on social media had the power of a journalist, the old adage was truer than ever.

"What's the story with Isa's plane ticket?" asked Jack. They were heading down the granite steps, side by side.

"I honestly don't know what the prosecutor is talking about. I've seen our tickets. We're all on the same flight home. If anyone was going to change flights and go home early, it was me."

"Is it possible that Isa bought two return tickets, just in case?"

They stopped at the curb across the street from the parking lot. "In case what?" asked Keith.

"In case she needed to get out of Miami sooner than planned," said Jack.

Keith considered it. "Now you sound like the prosecutor."

"Sometimes that's my job," said Jack.

Jack's office was just a few blocks from the courthouse. Keith drove. Jack plugged in the GPS coordinates so he wouldn't have to navigate from the passenger seat while combing through the MDPD probable-cause affidavit. He was reading it for a second time—aloud, for Keith's benefit—as they pulled into the driveway at the old house near the Miami River.

"This is your office?" asked Keith as the car came to a stop.

The ninety-year-old house, built by south Florida pioneer Julia Tuttle, was home to the Freedom Institute. The coral-rock façade needed cleaning, the front porch needed painting, and more than a few clay tiles were missing from the roof; it had changed little on the outside since Jack joined the Freedom Institute as a young lawyer fresh out of law school. Four years of defending the guilty had proved to be enough for Jack, so he'd struck out as a sole practitioner. A decade later, when his mentor passed away and the Institute was on the brink of financial collapse, Jack came up with a plan to save it.

"The Institute owns the building. I lease space here," said Jack.

Keith opened the screen door. The hinge made a loud pop, as if shaking off a century of rust. "Why?" asked Keith.

It was a question Jack had heard from his wife, too. Technically, Jack didn't head the Freedom Institute. Neil's daughter did. But Jack was there for guidance on a daily basis, and his inflated rent payments helped subsidize operations. As his accountant had pointed out, "The time you give them is time you can't bill a paying client, and your rent is higher than it should be."

"It's a great location," said Jack.

Another pop, as if the screen door might come unhinged, and then it stuck in the open position. "I have a great location, too, but it comes with a view of Hong Kong Harbor."

They went inside, and Keith's double take made Jack smile. The outside needed work, but the interior renovation was a source of pride. The original floors of Dade County pine had been sanded and refinished. The high ceilings and crown moldings were restored. The upstairs bedrooms, once uninhabitable, were now fully usable, so the foyer no longer doubled as a box-filled file room. The bad fluorescent lighting, circa 1970, had been replaced in a total electrical update. The living room was now an impressive reception area decorated with Oriental rugs, authentic antiques, and silk draperies.

"This is expensive stuff," said Keith, admiring the Jacobean secretary in the foyer.

"We picked it up on the cheap from a group of investment bankers so greedy that even I couldn't keep them out of prison."

"*Touché*," said Keith.

Jack's assistant was seated at the reception desk, and Jack introduced his friend to Bonnie "the Roadrunner," so named because she knew only one speed—full throttle—when zipping around the office. The rest of the crew was in court.

Jack led Keith to his office—formerly the dining room—to talk business. Jack sat behind his desk and Keith was in the striped armchair facing him.

"What's your take on the affidavit?" asked Keith.

Jack didn't want to discuss *his* take with Keith. "Now is probably a good time to clarify some things. My client is Isa."

"Of course."

"My point is that I'm interested in hearing your reaction to the affidavit. But 'my take' is something I'll share with Isa."

"I'm sure she'd want us to talk about this."

"That's not how the attorney-client relationship works."

He didn't look happy. "Okay, if those are the rules."

Jack had read the affidavit aloud in the car, but now he handed it to Keith and let him read it for himself, which he did quickly.

"My reaction is that there isn't much here," said Keith.

"Legally, it doesn't take much to establish probable cause to make an arrest."

"That's something I'm confused about. Where's the grand jury in all this?"

"A grand jury indictment isn't required unless the state attorney is seeking the death penalty. For tactical reasons the state attorney might take other cases to the grand jury. In this case, my guess is that they didn't find out Isa was traveling to Miami until the last minute. They didn't have time to present evidence to a grand jury, so they went the quicker route. They drafted what's called a 'criminal information,' which is a bare-bones recitation of the charges, and then ginned up an affidavit that laid out just enough to get a judge to issue an arrest warrant."

"It seems like they should have to do more to arrest someone for first-degree murder. Essentially, all this affidavit says is that Isa went to a bar with her boyfriend and two of his friends on a Friday night in April. She pointed out Gabriel Sosa and told her boyfriend that Sosa raped her in her dorm room sometime in March."

"Well, it says more than that," Jack said as he retrieved the affidavit. "It's says that 'in accordance with the plan that was orchestrated and choreographed by Isabelle Bornelli, coconspirators identified herein as John Doe 1 and John Doe 2 did forcibly abduct Gabriel Sosa, murder him, and dispose of his body."

"I thought you only wanted to hear what I thought."

"I can say enough to ask you intelligent questions. Did you have any idea that she was sexually assaulted?"

"No."

Jack paused, taking a mental step back from the details. "Is Isa the type of person who believes in forgiveness?"

"You mean in a spiritual sense?"

"In any sense," said Jack.

"Isa has a big heart. Yes, I would say she is a forgiving person."

"But she cut her father out of her life, right?"

"Well . . . she told me it was politics."

Jack jotted down a note to follow up with Isa, then continued through his mental list of open questions.

"Is it true that, aside from the two recent medical trips with Melany, Isa hasn't left Hong Kong in almost two years?"

Keith reflected for a moment. "You know, I hadn't thought about that until the prosecutor mentioned it. I've been so busy with work, and Isa has been so busy with Melany's speech and hearing rehab, that I guess I never noticed we hadn't taken a vacation."

"And for the eight years that you were together in Zurich, you never once came to the States?"

"I did. Isa never did."

"You never said, 'Hey, honey, why don't you come with me on this trip? We'll do a Broadway show in New York. We'll catch some sun on South Beach.' That sort of thing?"

"I might have. But it wasn't like she had nothing to do. She was a doctoral candidate before we had Melany."

"Have Isa and Melany ever met your parents?"

"Yeah. I've flown them over several times to visit us."

"Where were they living when you and Isa lived in Zurich?"

"They were still here in Miami. They moved to North Carolina about a year ago, when Dad retired."

"So even before Melany got sick, and when it

was the dead of a freezing-cold winter in Switzerland, you couldn't get Isa to fly to Miami? She was that busy with her doctoral program?"

"It wasn't just that. I think it goes back to politics again."

"What do you mean?"

"I told you before. Her father was a diplomat for Chavez in the Miami office of the consul general. He did that for years."

"What does that have to do with Isa visiting Miami?"

"Her father didn't just leave Miami. The whole office closed because of terrorist threats."

"Terrorists? You mean like al-Qaeda?"

"No. Cuban exiles. Here," he said, checking his smartphone. "Let me see if I can find the website Isa showed me."

"What website?"

"The consul general's. I believe their office is still closed. Here it is," he said, handing Jack his phone.

Jack read it aloud: "'The government of the Bolivarian Republic of Venezuela has verified with extreme concern the increase in threats against Venezuelan consular personnel in Miami, Florida. Accordingly, the Miami office shall remain closed until criminal and terrorist individuals and organizations that the U.S. government harbors in the state of Florida no longer pose a danger to the personal safety of our personnel.'"

"I presume they're talking about the Cuban exile community," said Keith.

"As if Judge Gonzalez is a terrorist."

"He wasn't very nice to my wife today," said Keith.

Keith wasn't the first friend to forget that Jack was half Cuban. His mother died shortly after his birth, and he was raised by his Anglo father and stepmother—"a half-Cuban boy trapped in a gringo's body," his *abuela* called him. She'd been trying to teach him all things Cuban after finally escaping from Castro's Cuba and coming to Miami when Jack was in his thirties. So far, she gave him an A for effort, about a C-plus for execution.

"So you're saying that the reason Isa didn't come to Miami is the so-called terrorist threat?"

"That's what she told me. Honestly, it did seem like overreaction to me. Knowing what I know now, it obviously wasn't politics at all. She didn't want to come back for the same reason she left: she didn't want to relive the memory of being sexually assaulted."

Jack had made that point at the arraignment. "That would make sense."

"Agreed," said Keith. "Now here's something that makes *no* sense to me: the prosecutor's whole argument that Isa was hiding out in Hong Kong. If that was the case, why would she pick Miami of all places for Melany's surgery?"

"The first surgery was botched."

"Yes. So go to Australia. Go to western Europe. Go to Boston, if you have to go to the U.S."

"I see your point," said Jack. "But I've watched my own wife change before my eyes since Riley was born. Your daughter was facing permanent deafness in the right ear if the second surgery wasn't successful. If you're a mother bear, you don't take your child to see Dr. Nobody in Australia. If you can afford it—and you can—you take her to the doctor who invented cochlear implants."

"I suppose that's true," said Keith. "Anyway, speaking of things I can afford . . . The outside of this place still looks like the Clampett residence before Jed was shootin' at some food."

"What are you doing?" asked Jack. Keith had his checkbook out.

"I asked around. In a case like this, I'm told a retainer of a hundred thousand dollars is fair."

"You're giving me a check?"

"Well, some of your clients may deal in briefcases filled with cash, but—"

"That's not what I meant. I'm not going to take a hundred thousand dollars from you."

"Please. We're old friends, but I'm a firm believer that you get what you pay for. I'm not looking for a freebie."

"We'll work something out."

"No, let's work it out now. These last two days have been the worst days of my life. Don't give me something else to worry about. I want this case to be your top priority. Take the check, and let's be done with it. Please."

Keith pushed the check halfway across the desk, within Jack's reach. These weren't the old days of Jack Swyteck, P.A., when getting paid was something to worry about later. Jack had a wife and daughter. He took it. "You *did* break my door."

Keith returned the smile, and Bonnie entered the room. "Sorry to interrupt. There's a man here to see you, Jack. He says it's imperative that he see you."

"Who is it?"

"His name is Felipe Bornelli."

Jack and Keith exchanged glances. "That's Isa's father," said Keith.

"Did you know he was in town?" asked Jack.

"Nope," said Keith.

"What should I tell him?" asked Bonnie.

"Tell him I'll be with him in a minute," said Jack.

Bonnie left, and Jack picked up his phone.

"Who are you calling?" asked Keith.

"Your wife, if I can reach her," said Jack. "I need to know what the hell is going on."

8

Sylvia Hunt had a short walk from the criminal courthouse to her office.

The official name for the main facility of the Office of the State Attorney for Miami-Dade County was the Graham Building, but Sylvia called it the Boomerang. The building had two wings, and the structure's footprint was angled like a boomerang, but the appellation had more to do with the fact that it seemed she could never leave without coming right back.

This time, however, it felt as though an actual boomerang had flown in, high and hard, caught her unawares, and smacked her right in the face.

"Rape victims matter! Rape victims matter!"

The chant followed Sylvia all the way across the street and up the sidewalk. It was led by the woman who had been gaveled down in Judge Gonzalez's courtroom at the start of the arraignment. About a dozen more demonstrators had gathered outside the Graham Building, mostly young women. Their signs and posters spoke not to Isa but to the broader issue of victims' rights, though Sylvia didn't see any reference to RAINN—Rape Abuse and Incest National Network—or other leading organizations that she'd supported over the years. It was a small but vocal group, and Sylvia knew that the evening newscasts would make it look much larger and louder than it actually was. A reporter and her cameraman from the local *Action News* approached as Sylvia passed the demonstrators.

"Ms. Hunt, do you have any mixed feelings about prosecuting a rape victim?"

The camera was rolling, and Sylvia kept walking. The reporter matched her stride for stride and thrust a microphone in Sylvia's face.

"Do you think it's fair to charge a rape victim with first-degree murder?"

A breeze kicked up as they neared the building, and Sylvia had to hold her hair out of her face. The band of demonstrators followed behind the reporter, and their chant continued: "*Rape victims matter!*"

"I can't comment on the evidence at this time," said Sylvia, picking up speed.

"I'm not asking about the evidence. I'm asking if you think it's fair to lock up a victim of sexual assault before trial the same way you would lock up a serial killer."

Sylvia stopped at the revolving door at the main entrance and dug deep for a newsworthy but unassailable sound bite. "Ms. Bornelli is a proven flight risk. Judge Gonzalez followed the law by holding her without bail until she stands trial for the murder of Gabriel Sosa."

"But many people would argue—"

"That's all I can say at this time," Sylvia said, and then she ducked into the building.

The *Action News* reporter and cameraman stayed outside with the demonstrators. Sylvia hurried across the lobby and got into an open elevator. She rode alone to the top floor and didn't say a word to anyone on the walk to her office. She closed the door, sat behind her desk, and took a deep breath.

Do you have mixed feelings about prosecuting a rape victim?

Of course she did. The decision to charge Isa with murder in the first degree had tormented her; a lesser charge might have been enough. Sylvia had opposed bail without enthusiasm, but agreeing to pretrial release here would create a precedent that another defense lawyer would use against her in a future murder case. Arresting Isa before her daughter's surgery was a decision that Sylvia had initially opposed, but the MDPD Felony Apprehension Squad convinced her that the risk of flight was too great.

There was a knock on her office door, and Carmen Benitez didn't wait for an invitation before entering. She had a file tucked under her arm, which she rested in her lap as she took a seat.

"How are you doing, Sylvia?"

"I'm fine."

"That's the answer I would have expected." She smiled a little, like a proud parent, and then turned serious. "I heard about the 'rape victims matter' outburst at arraignment."

"Not a big deal. It was just once."

"Security sent me an e-mail about the *Action News* ambush and the demonstrators downstairs."

"Yeah. There was that, too."

"Look. I know that in the long list of cases I've steered your way, this is not your favorite. You're going to get heat for prosecuting a victim of sexual assault."

"I knew that when I took the case. I told you I would do it. That's the end of the matter."

Benitez paused, and Sylvia felt the weight of concern in her gaze. "I'm not sure that is the end of it. Something's bothering you. I know you can handle the media, no matter how sensational. Is it the demonstrators? Did they get to you?"

Sylvia shook her head. "No."

"Then what?"

She breathed in and out. This was starting to feel like true confessions. "I did something I never do. I lied."

"Hopefully not to the court."

"No. Jack Swyteck called me last night and asked for a copy of the probable-cause affidavit. I told him I would send it. I didn't."

"So what? He can get his own copy from the court file."

"I made a promise, and this morning I made up a b.s. excuse why I broke that promise."

"It sounds to me like you're making a big deal out of nothing."

She looked away, then back. "It's part of a deeper problem. The evidence laid out in that affidavit was bare bones."

"That's not unusual."

"I get that. But it's not the right thing to do in a case like this. That's what put me in the position of lying to Swyteck's face."

"I don't follow you."

"The evidence laid out in that affidavit is so skimpy that any defense lawyer could make this case sound like a prosecutorial witch hunt against a victim of sexual assault. If I had sent that affidavit to Swyteck last night, he would have turned this morning's arraignment into a public embarrassment for us. That's why I didn't send it to him."

"That will change," said Benitez. "We'll have to put some cards on the table at the preliminary hearing."

"I don't want to wait that long," said Sylvia. "I don't want to be spending all my energy between now and the hearing trying to convince the public that this case has merit."

"Then don't talk to the media."

"That's not an option. Swyteck already has a leg up in that department. If we stand mute, it will only get worse."

"What do you propose?"

"I want to go to the grand jury, get an indictment, and be in a position to state publicly that this case wasn't just cooked up by a misguided prosecutor."

Benitez considered it. "Well, it's certainly not unheard-of to take a case to the grand jury even after the state has filed charges."

"And I think it makes sense in this case," said Sylvia.

The state attorney seemed to agree, but perhaps for different reasons. "It might also work to our tactical advantage. I don't like the idea of Swyteck cross-examining our witnesses at a preliminary hearing. We don't have to worry about that if we go to the grand jury."

It was a valid point. Florida law required a preliminary hearing only if there was no grand jury indictment. "So you approve?" asked Sylvia.

"I do. We need to change the perception that there is no public support for this prosecution."

"Thank you," said Sylvia.

Benitez took the bulging file from her lap and laid it on Sylvia's desk as she rose. "I don't want you to read these now. Just keep the file. Go to it when the trial gets tough, and you're second-guessing your decision to prosecute this case."

"What's in there?"

"Letters," said the state attorney, "from Gabriel Sosa's mother."

Sylvia peered inside. "That's quite a stack."

"Nine years ago an MDPD investigator told her the case had gone cold. Every month since then, without fail, Fatima Sosa has written me a letter begging me to seek justice for her son."

"Did you ever answer her?"

"I did. I let her know how pleased I was that the best prosecutor for the job was on it."

Sylvia didn't respond, but she appreciated the words.

"Keep up the good work," said Benitez, and she closed the door on her way out.

Sylvia took the file. It was tempting to read at least one, but she took the state attorney's advice. She put the letters in her desk and closed the drawer, saving it for that low point on the long road ahead.

9

Jack was at his desk, phone in hand, trying to arrange for Isa to call him back.

Contacting an inmate at the detention center could be like phoning the pope, even for a lawyer who needed to reach his client. It wouldn't have mattered if Jack were calling to say "Your husband is tied to the railroad tracks, a speeding locomotive is approaching, and he's in serious distress." The dance was always the same. This instance was no exception, having started with the usual first step.

"You say her name is Jezebel?"

"No—*Isabelle*. Isabelle Bornelli."

"Sorry, we got no inmate by that name."

"Yes, I can assure you—"

"Hold, please."

Jack had been on hold for nearly five minutes.

The door opened and Bonnie the Roadrunner poked her head into the office. "Mr. Bornelli asked me to tell you that he came here purely as a courtesy to you and that he's going to leave if you can't see him right now."

"Wow," said Keith. "Isa wasn't kidding. He *is* a pompous ass."

"This is pointless," said Jack as he hung up the phone. "Bonnie, does he know Keith is in here with me?"

"I didn't tell him who you were with."

It felt like a strange question, but Jack put it to Keith anyway: "Do you want to meet your father-in-law?"

"I'm not sure I do, but it seems pretty stupid for me to sneak out the back door."

Jack agreed. "Bonnie, bring him in."

She disappeared in her usual flurry and returned in a flash with Mr. Bornelli. Jack and Keith rose for the introductions.

"An unexpected pleasure," he said, as he shook the hand of his son-in-law for the first time.

Felipe Bornelli spoke with ease in English, despite the heavy Spanish accent. He was not much taller than his daughter, and not nearly handsome enough to account for Isa's elegance; Jack could only surmise that Isa's mother must have really been something. His hair was a distinguished shade of silver, and he wore it combed straight back, like the Gordon Gekko character in the *Wall Street* movies. He had that same intensity about him, too—spoke a little too fast, shook hands a bit too firmly, and didn't wait for others to finish talking before speaking.

"Keith was just leav—"

"Stay, please," said Bornelli.

"I don't want to intrude on—"

"It's no intrusion at all. In fact, I would prefer that you hear what I have to say to Mr. Swyteck."

They moved to the sitting area of Jack's office, each taking a chair around the coffee table in front of a fireplace that hadn't seen a burning log since LBJ was president. *One more thing to fix.*

"Does your daughter know you're here?" asked Jack.

Felipe crossed his legs, giving Jack an eyeful of noticeably yellowed toenails. The golf shirt and pressed slacks were perfectly appropriate, but too many men in Miami interpreted business casual to mean open-toe sandals.

"You mean *here* in your office, or that I came *here* to Miami?" asked Felipe.

"Both."

"No to both," said Bornelli.

"When is the last time you spoke?"

"Nine and a half years ago. At her mother's funeral."

"That was before Isa and Keith met?" asked Jack, trying to keep the timeline straight.

"Yes," said Keith. "But we did send you an invitation to our wedding."

"Did you personally put my invitation in the mail?" asked Bornelli.

"Not me personally. Isa took care of that."

"I never received an invitation."

It was possible that he was lying, but from the look on Keith's face, Jack surmised that it was equally possible that Isa had lied about mailing it. Jack shifted gears, but only slightly. "Is it too personal to ask why you and your daughter stopped speaking to one another?"

"She hasn't told you?" asked Bornelli.

"It would be helpful to hear your side of the story."

"Well, aside from being too personal, your question is way outside the point of my visit."

"That's fine," said Jack. "Then what brings you here?"

"I mean no disrespect to you, sir. But I must be direct: I do not approve of the lawyer my daughter has chosen to represent her."

Keith chuckled nervously, but Jack knew immediately that the man was deadly serious. "I'm sorry to hear that," said Jack, and he left it at that.

"I feel as though I should tell you why," said Bornelli.

"I feel as though it doesn't matter," said Jack.

Bornelli continued nonetheless. "You probably know that I served in the Venezuelan Office of the General Consul here."

"I heard," said Jack.

"And for most of my term of service, the governor of Florida was, of course, Harry Swyteck."

"He was elected twice, so there definitely would have been some overlap."

"There was more than overlap," said Bornelli. "Antagonism would be a better word. Perhaps even hostility."

Governor Swyteck wasn't of Cuban descent, but Jack's mother had come to Miami as a teenager under "Operation Pedro Pan," a humanitarian program under which thousands of Cuban parents—Jack's *abuela* included—put their children on some of the last Miami-bound flights to leave Havana. Abuela's plan was to meet up with her daughter later. She never did, and it took another thirty years for her to get out of Cuba and meet her grandson. Miami's Cuban-exile community had seen no better friend in the governor's mansion than Harry Swyteck.

"Seriously?" asked Jack. "You came here because my father was staunchly anti-Castro and anti-Chavez?"

"You minimize this," he said, and there was a hint of anger in his tone. "But, yes, I am serious. I will not have my daughter represented by a lawyer whose last name is Swyteck."

Jack moved forward in his chair. "Let me explain something, Mr. Bornelli. We're not taking a vote on this. The selection of a lawyer is not up to you. It's Isa's decision."

"And mine," said Keith.

"No," Jack said firmly. "Just Isa's."

Jack didn't like rebuking Keith in front of Isa's father, and Keith clearly didn't like it either, but it needed to be said.

"I am only looking out for my daughter's best interest," said Bornelli.

Jack doubted it, but he chose to avoid further confrontation. "Your good intentions are irrelevant. Isa chose me. That's the end of it."

"I disagree," said Bornelli, his voice taking on an even sharper edge. "It is my right to choose the lawyer who will put an end to the disgrace that my daughter has brought to the family name."

"What disgrace?" asked Jack. "Your daughter is innocent until proven guilty."

"I'm not talking about the murder of Gabriel Sosa."

The words hit Jack like a mule kick. Keith appeared on the verge of eruption.

"Wait a minute," said Jack, barely able to comprehend. "Are you suggesting that Isa disgraced your family because she was raped?"

Bornelli's expression tightened. "Who says she was raped?"

"Isa does," said Keith.

"Exactly," said Bornelli.

"Fuck off," said Keith, and Jack had to reach across like a boxing referee to keep him in his chair.

"All right, all right," said Jack, trying to keep things calm. "At the risk of dignifying this discussion with a follow-up question, I'll bite. Mr. Bornelli, do you have evidence that Isa *wasn't* raped?"

Felipe paused, as if searching for the perfect response. "Whatever evidence I have, I will gladly share—with Isa's new attorney. Now, I think I've made myself clear. I must be going," he said, rising. "Gentlemen, it has been a pleasure. Thank you both for your time."

There were no handshakes. Jack and Keith watched as he showed himself to the door and left the room.

"I should punch him in the fucking mouth," said Keith.

"Let him go," said Jack.

"He comes in here and tries to fire you. Then he calls my wife a liar to my face. What does he think—he owns Isa?"

"That's not the right question," said Jack.

Keith looked confused, and Jack clarified.

"The question is, does *Isa* think he owns Isa?"

10

At four p.m. Jack paid a second visit to Isa at the detention center.

It was a quick walk from the state attorney's office, where he'd spent a good chunk of the afternoon trying to work out a plea agreement—not for Isa, but for the owner of a neighborhood *farmacia* that had been driven out of business by the opening of "El Walmart" across the street. The landlord refused to let Jack's client off the hook for five remaining years of rent, and now he stood accused of torching the building to get out of the lease. Jack had fought for no jail time, but there was only so much you could do for an amateur arsonist who'd got so close to the accelerant that he'd singed away his own eyebrows.

Jack and Isa sat alone at the table in the same windowless conference room where they'd first met. She wore her hair in a ponytail. Her fingernails, once beautifully manicured, had been clipped short for safety reasons, but the nail on her left index finger was much shorter than detention center policy required. She'd been chewing on it, Jack noted.

"I'm guessing that you never got the message to call me," said Jack.

"No. I would have called if I did."

"I wanted to talk to you because your father showed up unexpectedly at my office."

She looked genuinely surprised. Jack gave her a quick summary of their conversation, and as the story progressed, it was hard to tell if she was more hurt or angry.

"He never did believe me." Her gaze drifted away, and she shook her head slowly, as if still amazed. "My own father never believed I was raped."

Jack gave her a minute to collect herself; it was still an obvious source of pain. "You mean from the very beginning?"

"Yes."

"Tell me about that."

Her voice softened. "After it happened, I didn't know what to do."

Jack could have asked her to back up—he needed to know more about "it"—but the fact that even after all these years she still referred to the rape as "it" told him how difficult this was for her. For present purposes, he would let her skip over the "it" and start with the "after."

"Where were you?"

"My dorm room. Alone. Gabriel left me there on the floor. I must have lain there for, I don't know, an hour. Maybe more. I felt so worthless—

like a thing. I didn't want to exist. I wrapped myself in a blanket and couldn't stop crying."

"Where was your roommate?"

"She'd gone home for the weekend. We weren't really friends anyway. She's not someone I would have confided in."

"Did you think about calling the police?"

"And tell them what? I went on a date, we came back to my dorm room, and if you asked Gabriel, we 'had sex,'" she said, making air quotes. "What were the police going to do, other than make me feel worse about myself?"

"So what did you do?"

"I called home. I wanted to talk to my mom."

"How did that go?"

"Unfortunately, my father answered the phone."

"Did you tell him what happened?"

"I wish I hadn't."

"What do you mean?"

"I didn't want to talk to *him* about this. I wanted my mother. But he could hear the hysteria in my voice, and he wouldn't hand over the phone until I told him what was the matter. What was '*wrong with me*,' to use his words."

"So you told him?"

"I tried. I got to the part where I invited Gabriel up to my room, and that was all my father needed to hear. He absolutely blasted me. '*What? You invited a man to sit on your bed when your roommate was out of town! What did you* think *was going to happen?*'"

That reaction didn't surprise Jack, and not just

because he'd met Isa's father. The same questions were often asked of women with black eyes and broken ribs.

"I'm sorry you had to go through that," said Jack. "I'm also sorry to tell you that your father's views have not changed."

"I'm not surprised. My father will never admit he's wrong. He never apologizes."

"Did you get to tell your mother about the attack?"

"Yes. Not that night, but later."

"Did she believe you?"

"Yes, of course."

"Did she have no influence on your father's views?"

"Not in this case. It's a very screwed-up situation. My father blamed me *and* my mother for what happened."

"I don't understand."

She paused, as if trying to figure out where to begin. "Growing up in the Bornelli house, I didn't hear my parents argue over very many things."

"They had a happy marriage?"

"Not really. My mother just always gave in to whatever my father said. Except when it came to pageants."

"Beauty pageants?"

She nodded. "I was six years old when my mother put me in my first contest. I won, which was the worst thing that could have happened. From that point on, my mother was like millions of other mothers you could find in Venezuela. She had a picture of Hugo Chavez hanging in the kitchen, yet she would spend half the family budget sending her daughter to a beauty academy, and she'd drive hundreds of miles to the next pageant. It was like, 'Yes, I'm a revolutionary . . . but please, please let my daughter grow up to be Miss Venezuela.'"

"How did you feel about that?"

"I hated it. But not nearly as much as my father did. I can remember being nine or ten years old. It was a five-hour drive to the pageant, so we got up at four a.m. My mother had me practice my walk in high heels in the kitchen before we left. Yes, ten-year-old girls walked in heels. Anyway, I guess all that click-click-click on the floor woke my father up. He came out of the bedroom, took one look at me, and screamed at my mother. '*You're turning her into a whore! She looks like a prostitute!*' And it wasn't just the shoes. It's the way you're taught to carry yourself, to express yourself. It's a game of seduction. We are hypersexualized at a very young age. My father was totally against it."

"That must have ended when your father took the post at the consulate."

"No way. I was eleven when we moved to Miami. That's the age when things kick into high gear. The Venezuelan community is huge here. My mother found an academy on South Beach, next to one of the modeling agencies. Beautiful girls from Venezuela, Brazil, Argentina, all getting a good education in the States while keeping up their beauty training."

"How long did that last?"

"'Til I was fourteen. *Ocean* magazine did a story about South American beauty academies in south Florida. I was one of the featured girls. It was a huge embarrassment for my father. I think Chavez was even going to call him home."

"So he put his foot down?"

"No. His fist. He punched my mother in the face so hard that he knocked her out cold."

Jack felt as though he, too, had just been punched. "I'm so sorry."

"Yeah. It was pretty monstrous."

Jack chose his next question carefully. "Did your mother report it to the police?"

"Of course not," said Isa, and then Jack could almost see the wheels turning in her head. "Are you implying that's the reason *I* didn't call the police?"

Her response served to remind Jack that he was practicing pop psychology on a student of psychology. "I don't know. What do you think?"

"I think we've about covered this," said Isa, and her gaze intensified. "What I really want to talk about is how to get me out of here."

"You heard what the judge said. We have a hearing in two weeks."

"That's too late."

"I have my assistant working on it. I can't promise anything, but Bonnie has been with me for almost twenty years, and if there is any way to cajole a judge's secretary into giving us an earlier date on the judge's calendar, Bonnie will find it."

"I really cannot stay in this place," she said.

"Keep in mind that we have work to do before you go back in front of the judge. It will be our job to show you're not a flight risk. One thing we need to explain is why you bought a plane ticket to fly home with your family in two weeks, and why you also have a ticket to fly home without Melany the day after her surgery. I'm sure you can see how that looks like a contingency escape plan."

"Of course that's what it looks like. That's what it was."

Jack did a double take. "You booked the early flight as an escape plan?"

"Yes."

"An escape from what?"

"Oh, I don't know," she said, scoffing. "What's the right answer? My demons? The threats from Cuban-American exiles that shut down the Venezuelan consulate? My father?"

"This isn't the time to be flip."

"I'm sorry, but I've had it with this. I came to Miami to be with my daughter on the day of her surgery. Instead, where am I? Locked in this room, dressed in this lovely prison jumpsuit, trying to tell my lawyer how to explain an airplane ticket at a stupid hearing that's two weeks away. I need to be with my daughter on Friday, and I need my lawyer to get me out of here in time for me to be there."

"I hear your frustration. But bail in a first-degree murder case is the exception, not the rule."

"Are you saying it's impossible?"

"No. But it's not going to happen before Friday. Can you postpone the surgery for a couple of weeks?"

"In theory, yes. But every day we put this off, the chances of a full recovery for Melany diminish. So as much as I want to be there, that's not an option. Keith will have to take her."

"I think that's the right decision."

"Yeah. But it still sucks."

"Unfortunately, that's not the only hard choice you have to make. In fact, this one might even be harder."

"What?"

"Are you going to tell me why you booked a contingency plan to fly back to Hong Kong the day after the surgery? What did you think you might have to escape from? What were you afraid of?" Jack leaned forward to put a finer point on his question. "Before you got on that plane in Hong Kong with your family, what did you know, Isa, about the investigation into the murder of Gabriel Sosa?"

Their eyes locked, but there was only silence.

Jack packed up and rose.

"Where are you going?" asked Isa.

"I'm going to let you sleep on it. Think very carefully. And understand that when we talk again tomorrow, it will be very bad for our relationship if you try to bullshit me."

She didn't answer.

Jack knocked on the door. It opened, and the correctional officers entered.

"I'm sorry you can't be there for Melany," said Jack. "I truly am."

Jack left the conference room, his footfalls echoing in the corridor as he headed for the visitors' exit.

11

It wasn't even five a.m. when Keith left their hotel room at the Four Seasons, took the elevator down to the motor port, and waited. A stretch limousine pulled up and four young women climbed out, stepping carefully onto the stone pavers in their five-inch heels and tight skirts. They were laughing about something, a silly laugh that said they were still feeling the effects of a night on South Beach and too many Red Bulls and vodka.

"Cool earbud," said the blonde as she passed Melany. One of the other ladies shushed her and said, "That's not an *earbud*," but it only triggered another round of giggles all the way into the lobby.

The limo pulled away, and Jack's wife drove up.

"There she is!" said Melany, meaning Riley.

The news that Mommy wouldn't be at her surgery had left Melany almost inconsolable. It had been Andie's idea for Riley to go with her to the hospital, which helped stop the tears. Keith hoped it would last at least through the pre-op.

Keith strapped Melany into the extra car seat in back and got in the passenger seat up front. Brickell Avenue ran through the heart of Miami's financial district, but the predawn traffic was light, making the hospital just a ten-minute ride from their hotel.

"Did you find an apartment?" asked Andie.

Jack had warned Keith that this ordeal wouldn't likely end soon. Keith addressed it with his supervisor and an executive decision was made to let Keith work from the Miami office of IBS for the next four weeks. They would then reevaluate.

"We move in this afternoon. Fully furnished. Don't even have to change buildings. Just pack our bags and get in the elevator." The Four Seasons was mixed use, both hotel and condo. "We'll be on the sixty-first floor, which Melany thinks is pretty cool."

On the green arrow, Andie made a left and steered onto the Expressway. "Must be a great view."

"Yeah," Keith said without heart. "If you go out on the west balcony you can see all the way to the pretrial detention center."

They were first on Dr. Balkany's surgery schedule for the day, and they reached the surgery center sooner than expected. The receptionist steered them to the waiting room. Keith and Andie found seats in the corner, while Melany tried to teach Riley the Hong Kong version of hip-hop.

Andie smiled. "Melany's such a great kid."

"She always loved music. It will never sound the way it sounds to you and me, or even the way it used to sound to her before the meningitis. But that doesn't seem to make a difference. She still loves to dance."

"That's a wonderful thing."

"It is. Isa gets a lot of the credit. The implant surgery is a miracle, but mainstreaming a child with a cochlear implant is work. Isa really stepped up."

"I'm sure you deserve some credit, too."

He smiled a little, but it was a sad smile. "Not really. I love Melany with all my heart. People say I'm a good father. But all this makes me realize that, for the most part, my job is to be 'Fun Daddy'—playing games, reading to her at night, taking her to the ice-skating rink where she pretends to be a princess from *Frozen*. It was Isa who got up in the middle of the night when Melany was scared. Isa who comforted her or took her to the doctor when she was sick. Isa who knew what to say and how to calm her when her anxiety was up."

Andie's gaze drifted toward Riley. "It's work being a mommy. I can vouch for that."

"Oh, you get no argument from me. Isa was working on her doctorate when we got married. Looking back on it, I kind of took for granted Isa's decision to put her studies on hold and be a stay-at-home mother."

"It's good that you recognize that."

"I didn't always. I never criticized her to her

face, but in my mind I sometimes questioned that choice—for focusing exclusively on motherhood and not being one of those supermoms who somehow manages to do it all. Husband, kids, career, triathlons in her spare time. You know what I'm talking about."

Andie fell silent, and Keith realized that he was talking to a supermom. "Sorry, I wasn't making any judgments or comparisons."

"It's okay."

"It's just that your mind goes in strange directions in circumstances like these. This wasn't something I had time to prepare for. It was like a light switch. Boom: Melany's mom is . . . not gone, but suddenly out of the picture. I mean, I tell Isa all the time how beautiful she is. But I can't really remember telling her what a great mom she is. What an amazing job she's doing with Melany. I'm rambling. I'm probably not making any sense."

"You're making total sense," said Andie.

"Am I?"

"Yes," said Andie, and he could hear it in her voice that she meant it. "More than you realize."

Sylvia Hunt and a junior prosecutor entered the grand jury room at 8:03 a.m. Inside were twenty-three grand jurors who had sworn an oath to keep secret all matters that occurred before them, and to consider all evidence presented against Isabelle Bornelli.

The proceeding had begun Thursday afternoon.

Sylvia had read the charges aloud, explained the law, and given the grand jurors a broad overview of the evidence that she intended to present. They adjourned for the evening. On Friday morning, the prosecution was ready to call its first witness.

"Let's get started," said Sylvia.

The junior prosecutor opened the door, and a pair of Florida state troopers escorted the witness into the room.

Everything presented to the grand jury is eventually disclosed to the defense, and Sylvia had no intention of tipping her prosecutorial hand. She and the state attorney were in complete agreement that the proper strategy was to present just enough evidence to the grand jury to secure an indictment—to dispel any notion that the case against Isabelle Bornelli wasn't strong enough to take to trial. Depending on how things went this morning, one witness might suffice.

"State your name for the record, please," said Sylvia.

"David Kaval."

Kaval seemed relaxed, slouching in the hardwood chair, his tattoos swelling as he folded his forearms across his chest. He needed a shave and a haircut, but he had handsome features, and Sylvia detected potential "jury appeal" beneath the rough exterior. The rugged and unpolished look was good enough for this proceeding. For the actual trial, Sylvia would groom him, dress him up, and have him looking like the humble and responsible architect that women in romantic comedies brought home to Mom and Dad before dumping him for "the One."

Losing the ankle shackles and orange jumpsuit wouldn't hurt, either.

"Mr. Kaval, where do you currently reside?"

"Raiford, Florida."

"Where in Raiford?"

"Florida State Penitentiary."

"Are you currently serving a prison sentence?"

"Yep."

"For what crime?"

"Armed robbery."

Sylvia checked the jurors. She had their attention. "What was your sentence?"

"Ten years in the state penitentiary."

"How much longer do you have to serve?"

"About two years."

"Are you currently facing any other charges?"

"Yes. Conspiracy. But it has nothing to do with the robbery."

The prosecutor nodded, confirming it. "The conspiracy charge relates to what we're here to talk about today, correct?"

"Yes."

"Have you reached any agreement with the state of Florida regarding that charge?"

"Yes."

"Could you please describe that arrangement to the grand jury?"

He turned in his chair and faced the jurors. "I will plead guilty and receive a sentence of ten years. But I get credit for time served."

"So at the end of the day you would have two felony convictions, and you would spend a grand total of ten years in state prison. Then you're free. Is that right?"

"Right, that's what I just said."

"And under this arrangement, what are you required to do in exchange?"

"I have to testify against Isabelle Bornelli."

"You have to provide *truthful* testimony in the case against Ms. Bornelli, correct?"

"Yes. Truthful testimony."

"Thank you, sir." The prosecutor stepped closer, signaling to the grand jury that the next part mattered. "Mr. Kaval, do you know the accused, Isabelle Bornelli?"

"Yes, I do."

"How do you know her?"

He smiled a little. "I was her boyfriend when she was in college."

Sylvia glanced again at the grand jurors. Some were taking notes—a good sign. "Now, Mr. Kaval, I want to take you back to Ms. Bornelli's freshman year of college. To a certain night. A certain Friday night."

Keith checked the clock on the waiting room wall: 10:07 a.m. A whole two minutes had passed since his last time check.

Andie had stayed until the start of surgery, and then she had to drop Riley off at preschool and head to work. Time passed more slowly with no one to talk to. The procedure was supposed to take three hours, and they were only a few minutes over the estimate. Keith wasn't worried—no more worried than he should have been, at least. But a "Melany update" from the nurse would have been nice.

He rose and was walking toward the reception window when the pneumatic door opened. Dr. Balkany emerged from the surgical suite. And he was smiling.

"Everything went great," he said.

Keith could have hugged him. He did, in fact, but he wanted details. "When you say it went great, you mean—"

"We'll know for certain when the incision heals and she's fitted with the external components. But I fully expect her right ear to be every bit as functional as her left."

That took Keith's breath away. They were due for some good news, and this couldn't have been any better. "Thank you so much, doctor. When can I see her?"

"She's in recovery now. We used general anesthesia, but she'll come around soon. The nurse will take you back."

Keith thanked him again, and a few minutes later the nurse arrived. She led him through a maze of color-coded hallways. A green line embedded in the tile floor led to the recovery room. Melany was in bay number 3, behind a plastic privacy curtain that hung from the ceiling. Another nurse was checking the dressing behind Melany's ear when Keith entered. The surgeon had shaved a two-inch patch of her scalp for the incision, but Melany had plenty of hair to cover it.

With a push of a button the nurse raised the

mattress so that Melany was almost in a sitting position, but her eyes were not really open.

"How you feeling, big girl?"

Melany didn't respond.

"She's still kind of out of it," said the nurse.

She also wasn't wearing her external audio processor on the left ear, so she wouldn't have heard him even if she were fully conscious. The new audio processor wouldn't be programmed and operational until they returned to Hong Kong—if they returned to Hong Kong.

Keith stood at the bedrail and took his daughter's hand. Slowly, she was coming around. The nurse retrieved Melany's existing processor from her bag of personal items and attached it behind her left ear. It only took a minute, but that was enough time for the fog of anesthesia to lift and for her to recognize her father.

"Welcome back," said Keith.

Melany smiled. He leaned over the rail to give her a hug. She wrapped her arms around his neck and squeezed the breath out of him.

"Mommy," she said, still hugging him.

Apparently the fog had not yet lifted completely. "No, honey. It's Daddy."

"Mommy, Mommy! She's right behind you!"

Keith turned around, his mouth agape.

Isa was standing at the foot of the bed, dressed in the clothes that she'd worn on the flight from Hong Kong.

"Wha-a-t?" he said, but the words seemed to be on a several-second delay. Isa went to him, and they hugged until they laughed. Then it was Melany's turn.

"You're back!" said Melany as Isa wrapped her arms around her.

"Yes, honey. Mommy's back."

12

Jack spent the morning at the civil courthouse in downtown Miami, miles away from his usual criminal haunts. He was trying to convince a very skeptical judge that eleven years wasn't too long for his client to wait before suing the college professor who'd flunked her for refusing to do what he'd required a half dozen other women to do in exchange for a passing grade. Jack powered-on his cell phone as he left the courthouse, and he was preparing to tell his client that she could appeal the judge's dismissal of her case when Keith's text message popped onto the screen.

Isa is out on bail. Call me!

Jack had to read it twice, and even then he didn't fully comprehend. He continued down two tiers of granite steps, hurrying to put distance between his phone and the ninety-year-old courthouse with its impressive limestone façade and Doric columns—and its notoriously bad cellular reception. Some said the historic old building was falling apart, but from the standpoint of handheld technology, it was a veritable fortress. Jack had been on zero bars all morning.

He found a seat at the bus shelter on the corner and dialed Keith's cell. He got no answer, which was frustrating. He'd left three messages for Isa at the detention center on Thursday and had heard nothing in response. Jack's last communication with his client was on Wednesday, when he'd told her that there was no chance she would be out in time for Melany's surgery.

His cell rang. Keith's phone number appeared on the screen, but it was Isa on the line.

"Surprise!" she said, her voice filled with excitement.

"You took the word right out of my mouth. Where are you?"

"In a taxi, heading back from the hospital. Keith and Melany are with me."

Melany. Jack had many questions, but one seemed more important. "How did the surgery go?"

"Absolutely perfect. By the time I got to the hospital the surgery was already over, but I was there when she woke up. It was the most wonderful moment in my life. I'm so grateful to Manny."

"Manny? Who's Manny?"

"Manuel Espinosa. He said he knows you."

Espinosa was a high-profile and successful attorney, but not one Jack held in high regard. "Slick" would have been a polite way to describe him. "I know Espinosa. But what does he have to do with this?"

"I was really down after you and I spoke on

Wednesday. My cellmate—who frankly scared me to death when I first met her—turned out to be an amazing help. She recommended I call Espinosa. So I did."

The bus stopped at the curb, and the driver opened the doors. Jack didn't move.

"You called another lawyer?" asked Jack, a cloud of diesel fumes covering him as the bus pulled away.

"Yes. I hope you're not mad."

"I'm not mad. I just need to understand. Am I off the case?"

"No! Not at all. Manny's expertise is bail."

Jack knew that wasn't true. "Is that what he told you?"

"Yes. He guaranteed that he would get me out on bail."

"Isa, no lawyer can guarantee that in a first-degree murder case."

"Well, he did. And he got me out."

"This still makes no sense to me. I never got a call from the judge's secretary about a hearing. I never heard from the prosecutor, or from Espinosa. I said a minute ago that I'm not mad, but actually I am mad. I don't work this way. I can't work this way."

"I'm sorry. This may sound selfish, but your feelings weren't the first thing on my mind in all of this. I just—"

She stopped, and Jack could hear the emotion in her voice.

"I just wanted to be with my daughter."

"I understand," said Jack. "This is not about

me. We can file a simple substitution of counsel and Manny will be your new lawyer. No big deal."

"What are you talking about? I want both of you."

"You want us to be cocounsel?"

"Yes. Keith will pay both of you. You'll be a great team."

"I don't know about that."

"Please, Jack. Let's all meet at Manny's office. He can explain how he got me out on bail, and we can all make a plan going forward."

Jack was definitely interested in the former—how Manny pulled this off. "All right," said Jack. "I'll set something up with Espinosa."

"Great. And thank you, Jack. I would never have reached out to Espinosa if you hadn't been so honest with me about not being able to get it done."

It didn't exactly feel like a compliment, but he supposed she meant well. "Any time," said Jack.

The call ended, and before Jack could even pull up a phone number, Espinosa's secretary called to confirm a one o'clock meeting at the Espinosa Firm, LLP. Jack was just a few blocks away—he didn't even have to move his car—so he agreed.

Jack rose from the bench and started down the sidewalk along Flagler Street. Reception continued to improve and more messages populated his inbox as he walked toward Espinosa's office.

A voice mail at 9:52 a.m. from Sylvia Hunt caught his attention.

He pressed the phone to his ear, straining to hear over the excited chatter of about fifty Brazilian tourists who were headed back to the green-and-yellow motor coaches after cleaning out the electronics shops.

"Jack, I've been trying to reach you all morning," said the prosecutor, "but your secretary said you're in court. The state attorney and I met with Manuel Espinosa, and he showed us the letter signed by Isabelle Bornelli indicating that he is in fact her attorney. In any event, I wanted to let you know that we have investigated Mr. Espinosa's allegations, and we have agreed to release Ms. Bornelli on bail in the amount of one hundred thousand dollars. Call me if you have any questions."

Mr. Espinosa's allegations?

Jack would have liked to return the call immediately, but he would lose all credibility if she knew just how deep in the dark he was.

Never have friends for clients.

Jack walked a little faster down Flagler, not wanting to be even a minute late for the meeting with Espinosa.

13

The meeting started just after one o'clock. Jack, Isa, and Manny were at a round table in Manny's spacious office. Jack took the seating arrangement as a conciliatory gesture—an olive branch of sorts. Espinosa could have put Isa and Jack in the armchairs facing his desk, and he could have run the show from a position of power. The round table left neither lawyer visibly in control.

"The first thing I want you to understand, Jack, is that this is not a coup. I did not come on board to replace you. We are building a legal team."

"I'm open to that," said Jack.

"I'm so relieved to hear you say that," said Isa. That "relief" was all over her face. A shower and change of clothes were part of the transformation, but it was deeper. "Being there" for Melany had turned Isa into a new person.

"But we have to act like a team," said Jack.

"Agreed," said Manny.

"Some differences are a matter of style. Other things are fundamental."

"That's what makes the world go 'round," said Manny.

"That's not exactly the point I was making," said Jack. "Let me start with a concrete example. I never guarantee results to my clients. When I spoke to Isa on the phone, she told me you guaranteed that she would be released on bail."

Espinosa smiled. "She may have *heard* it as a guarantee. But I never said it that way."

"No, that was your exact word," said Isa. "'I *guarantee*.'"

He was still smiling, but it was a bit awkward. "Well, if I used that word, it must have been after you told me what happened to you in your cell."

Jack looked at Isa. "What happened?"

She lowered her gaze.

Manny answered. "A male correctional officer was planning to sexually assault her."

Jack took a moment. "I couldn't be more sorry to hear that happened to you, Isa. And forgive me for probing, but I need to be clear on the facts. The plan was never executed, I'm hoping."

"No," said Isa.

"How did you find out about it?"

She took a breath, and the radiance Jack had seen just moments earlier seemed to fade.

"At first it was just a feeling I had about this particular guard. I tried to not let it get to me. I told myself that I was being paranoid—that the resurrection of Gabriel Sosa had me seeing a rapist in any man who had control over me. But it turned out I wasn't imagining things."

Jack waited for her to continue, but she was silent.

"Her cellmate blew the whistle," said Manny.

"She told me that the guard had a plan," said Isa.

"Can I ask what the plan was?"

Isa held her head in her hands, elbows on the table. "Do we really have to talk about this?"

"Sorry."

Manny answered for her. "In a nutshell, the security cameras inside each jail cell don't record every minute of the day. They're motion activated. The guard used threats and coercion to get Isa's cellmate to agree to stand motionless in front of the camera's sensor—effectively freeze it—while he assaulted Isa."

"Would that work?" asked Jack.

"Thankfully, we'll never find out. The cellmate told Isa and gave her my name. We met this morning, I took it to the state attorney, and we had a deal in twenty minutes."

"That's fast."

"My sense is that the state attorney knows she reached too far in charging Isa with first-degree murder, and that whole team is feeling the prosecutorial equivalent of buyer's remorse. All I had to do was spell out the headline they narrowly avoided: 'Rape Victim Jailed and Raped Again after State Attorney Opposes Bail.' They caved immediately."

"That helps to make sense of the message I got this morning from Sylvia Hunt. She made a vague reference to allegations."

"Oh, she called you?"

"Yes. Interestingly, neither of you did."

"That was my decision," Isa said softly.

"This isn't about hurt feelings, but I'm going to need an explanation," said Jack.

"The bottom line is that I didn't want Keith to know about this. It would have just made him worry about something he couldn't fix. It's the same reason I didn't tell him about Gabriel Sosa. I didn't want our marriage to become one long therapy session where every time we made love, my husband asked me, '*Oh, are you okay with this, honey? Was that too traumatic for you?*' There was no reason for him to know. This was for me to deal with."

Jack wondered if the old adage about lawyers—"The lawyer who represents himself has a fool for a client"—applied to psychologists. "I understand what you're saying, and that's your decision. But I'm not Keith."

"But I felt that if I told you, you might tell Keith."

"No. What you tell me does not go to Keith."

"I know," she said.

"Do you? Because if you don't believe it, then I can't represent you."

She paused, then answered. "I'm sorry. You're right. It won't happen again."

Jack had no idea if he could believe her. But he had a good place to start—a test question.

"On Wednesday we talked about the flight you booked to Hong Kong on the day after Melany's surgery. You said the prosecutor was right: it was a contingency escape plan. I need you to tell me what you thought you might have to escape from."

"Okay, then, I'll tell you: my college boyfriend. David Kaval."

"What made you think you might have to escape from him?"

"Because he's a crazy man," said Isa. "I know that doesn't sound like a term that someone who holds a degree in psychology would use, but trust me when I say this: David Kaval is crazy."

"Is he still in Miami?"

"I have no idea where he is."

"Why did you think you might have to escape from him?"

"Because—" she started to say, then stopped, struggling with the question. "Let me put it this way. When I left the University of Miami to finish college in Switzerland, it was as much to get away from him as it was to get away from the memory of Gabriel Sosa. He's not just crazy. He's scary crazy."

Jack had a long mental list of follow-up questions, but Isa's phone rang. She answered, and a smile came to her face. "It's Melany," she told her lawyers. Jack listened to one side of the conversation.

"Hi, honey. Are you being a good girl and resting? . . . You're bored. . . . Oh, yeah, Daddy's real busy, sweetie. But I'm just finishing up now. I'll be home real soon. . . . Fifteen minutes. I promise, okay? . . . I love you, too."

She hung up. "Guys, David Kaval is a very long story, and right now I need to be with Melany. Can we continue this later?"

"Sure," said Manny.

Jack was eager to learn more about Kaval, but it wasn't urgent enough to keep Isa from her daughter. And it couldn't hurt for him to do his own checking on Kaval before having a more in-depth conversation with Isa.

"No problem," said Jack.

Isa thanked them and left the room. Manny rose and shook Jack's hand. "Looking forward to working with you, Jack. This should be very interesting."

"Yeah," said Jack. "It will definitely be interesting."

14

Friday was date night. The marquee event was the Adele concert at the arena; but first, an early dinner. Jack ordered the churrasco with chimichurri, and Andie had the Peruvian ceviche with avocado. A bottle of Malbec was on the table between them.

They were at one of their favorite sidewalk cafés at the quieter end of the street, where the residential stretch of Miami Avenue transitioned into restaurant row. Farther south, sprawling royal poinciana trees and a few Old Spanish houses harkened back to an era before high-rises, when Mary Brickell pioneered the area in true Miami style, platting out beautiful wide boulevards and then selling off parcels of her extensive landholdings to entice the insanely rich to build waterfront estates. A few of the early mansions remained, owned by the likes of Sly Stallone and Madonna, when Jack had opened his first law office, but even those weren't on Brickell Avenue proper. What made the Brickell area worth a drive for locals was the upscale district of bars and restaurants, which were also popular with the wealthy South American crowd that fueled the surrounding condo market.

Jack's cell vibrated on the table. He checked the number and put it away.

"Who was that?" It was a question Andie wouldn't have asked before Riley was born. Something about motherhood had activated the "need to know" gene, as if every call that interrupted a date meant that an inquisitive two-year-old had stuck her spoon in the toaster and was being rushed to the emergency room.

"Another reporter," said Jack. "They've been calling all day since Isa was released."

"Do you need to return it?"

"No."

"Are you sure?"

"I couldn't even if I wanted to. Manny negotiated Isa's release. Part of his deal with the state attorney was that we wouldn't talk to the media until an internal investigation into the corrections officer's misconduct is complete."

"And you're bound by that agreement?"

"Yes. Manny and I are cocounsel." Jack left it at that. As a rule they didn't talk much about Jack's cases, but there were always the gray areas around the fringe where basic communication between husband and wife trumped confidentiality between criminal-defense lawyer and FBI agent.

"How's that working out?" asked Andie. "You and Manny, I mean."

"We'll see."

"You know he does ninety percent drug cases, right?"

"How did you know that?"

"One of our narcotics agents texted me: '*Hey, Henning, your husband has stooped to a new low.*'"

From the standpoint of most of Andie's colleagues, it was better that Jack defended death-row inmates than drug dealers. "Does that bother you?" asked Jack.

"No. Does it bother you?"

He was quiet.

"It *does* bother you, doesn't it," she said.

"It's not the drug clientele."

"Then what?"

Jack hesitated. Her question was a little deeper than the "gray area around the fringe."

"I don't know if we should talk about that."

"Jack, I'm your wife. There's obviously something on your mind, and it's turning you into a not very fun date. Talk to me."

It was on his mind, and the conversation he and Keith had in his office with Felipe Bornelli wasn't privileged. He put down his fork and told her.

Andie poured more wine, listened, and held her comment until Jack finished. "So Isa's father wants you off the case?"

"That's what he told me," said Jack.

"Do you think *he* went out and found Manny Espinosa to replace you?"

Andie had a way of knowing exactly what he was thinking. "That's not the way Manny, Keith, or Isa tell me it came about. In fact, from what I'm told about Isa's relationship with her father, never in a million years would she hire a lawyer he recommended."

"How did she get Manny's name?"

"From her cellmate."

"The same cellmate who said that a correctional officer was planning to rape Isa?"

Jack did a double take. "How did you know about that? That hasn't been made public."

"The Civil Rights Division of the Justice Department is getting involved. Our office has been called in to investigate. I'm not breaching any confidentiality by telling you. It'll be in the newspapers tomorrow."

Jack drank from his wineglass—much more than just a sip. He couldn't count the number of times he'd been afraid to talk about one of his cases and possibly "spill the beans" to Andie, only to find out that she knew more than he did.

"It makes sense that the feds would get involved," said Jack. "But to your first point—who hired Manny—there's something fishy about the sequence of events here. On Wednesday the judge denied bail. Two hours later Felipe Bornelli showed up in Miami to tell me that he doesn't approve of the lawyer his daughter hired. Less than forty-eight hours later, Manuel Espinosa has her out of jail, and Isa is eating out of the palm of his hand."

"Nobody thinks you're a lousy lawyer, Jack. Put your ego aside: Why would Isa's father hire Espinosa?"

"I don't know. I'm not buying his story that he doesn't want Governor Swyteck's son representing his daughter. But I got the clear vibe that for some reason he wants to control the case."

"What are you going to do about that?"

Jack thought. "I could talk to Isa again."

She shook her head. "Before that."

"I could go straight to Felipe."

A grimace. "Or?"

Jack thought for a moment. "I could talk to Isa's cellmate."

"Bingo. And at the risk of crossing a line I shouldn't cross, you might want to do that before the feds interrogate her."

They were in that gray area again, but Jack was glad they'd gone there. "I feel better. Thank you."

"You're welcome," she said, and Jack felt her foot sliding around his ankle. "I'll think of some way for you to pay me back."

He smiled hopefully. "Where do you put the odds of Riley staying in her own bed tonight?"

Lately it seemed that whenever Mommy and Daddy went out, Riley had a bad dream. Their last two date nights had ended in slumber parties: Jack, Andie, Riley, and Dora the Explorer.

"Fifty-fifty."

"Do you think she might leave us alone if we swore on a stack of Bibles that she has nothing to worry about—she's going to be an only child?"

Andie laughed. "Our little girl is smart, Jack. But not that smart."

Friday was their first night in the new condo at the Four Seasons residences, and Keith was loading the refrigerator. Home delivery was the way to grocery shop in the Brickell area. Most stores would even unpack and put things away for you, but Keith liked everything "just so"—dairy on the top shelf, bottled water and soft drinks on the bottom, expiration dates facing out. He couldn't help doing it himself. But he still tipped well.

"Wow, *gracias*," the deliveryman said.

A few dry goods remained on the kitchen counter, but the perishables were taken care of. Melany was sound asleep in her new bedroom, which was adjacent to the master suite. Isa had said she was exhausted and wanted to lie down, but Keith spotted her out on the terrace, which was accessible from the master at one end and the breakfast nook at the other. She was wearing a bathrobe, her hair pulled back in a clip. He joined her at the rail.

"Couldn't sleep?" he asked.

"No," she said quietly.

It didn't surprise him. He wondered what nightmares had followed her home from the detention center.

They had a north-facing view, which was spectacular. The financial heart of Miami was at their feet, and they could almost reach out and touch the city lights along Biscayne Bay.

"A little like Hong Kong," said Keith.

"Yeah. That's what Melany told me." Her voice was flat, and even though the vista was sprawling, she seemed intensely focused, as if she had picked out something of interest.

"You okay?" he asked.

Her gaze remained fixed. "See that building down there? The west side of Brickell Avenue, next to the Marriott?" she said, pointing.

"The glass one on the corner?"

"Uh-huh. When I was a girl living in Miami,

that was the Office of the Consul General of the Bolivarian Republic of Venezuela. Where my father used to work."

"Did you ever go there?"

"Nope. Not once."

They'd never had a real conversation about her father, and Keith wasn't sure if this was the right time. But he was still bothered by the way Felipe had shown up at Jack's office and made it clear that he wanted Jack off the case. "He's an unusual man," said Keith.

"Tell me about it. It's funny how you get images in your head about people. In my mind's eye, I will always see my father wearing one of those red T-shirts that everyone in the Chavez government used to wear. A red T-shirt and a windbreaker in the colors of the Venezuelan flag."

"That's not what he was wearing when Jack and I talked to him."

"Have you heard from him since then?"

"No," said Keith. "Have you?"

"I would tell you if I had."

"Would you?"

She looked at him. "Yes, Keith. Why would you even ask that?"

He was taken aback by the question, given what secrets had been revealed in the previous two days. But he wasn't looking for an argument. "I just want to make sure he's not here to stir up trouble."

"I'm not going to worry about that. Manny and Jack can handle it."

He noticed that she'd mentioned Manny's name

first. "Okay. But I don't want you to be too taken with Manny."

"What do you mean?"

He chose his words carefully. "Your father didn't just say that he wanted Jack off the case. He said that he planned to share information that will bring into question your claim that Gabriel Sosa assaulted you."

Isa closed her eyes slowly, then opened them, absorbing the blow. "He is—" She paused, searching for the right word. "He's just unbelievable."

Silence came over them. Keith thought of his own daughter—how he would react if a nineteen-year-old Melany called to tell him she'd been assaulted. "I can't get over your father's reaction. How could he just reject out of hand any possibility that you were raped?"

Isa hesitated, as if reluctant to talk about it. "You don't know my father. I can't say that I have a perfect recollection of the phone conversation, after what had just happened to me. I was already numb, and when he started blasting me for inviting a boy up to my room on the first date, I just went—I don't know, catatonic."

Keith felt his anger rising inside, but he didn't know if he should show it. He didn't know how to deal with any of his feelings or sudden developments that had changed their lives from the moment they'd landed in Miami.

"It was a huge mistake not to report it," said Isa.

"You can't beat yourself up about that."

"I hung up the phone with my father and I didn't know what to do. I don't know how much time passed, but then another wave of panic set in. What if I got pregnant? I went to the campus clinic to see a doctor. The nurse at the desk must have sensed how traumatized I was. She asked if I wanted to report anything to the authorities. All I could hear was my father's booming voice in my head. Not even my own father believed I was raped. So I told her no. I had nothing to report. When I got in to see the doctor I told her I had sex without protection. I got the morning-after pill. And that was the end of it."

"You did the best you could," said Keith.

Tears came to her eyes. "I wasn't thinking at that time. I felt ashamed. I felt guilty. I didn't want to come forward because I didn't want anyone to know."

Keith held her in the darkness. "It's okay," he told her. "It's totally okay now."

"I'm going to try to lie down again," she said. "I need to sleep."

"I'll join you."

Keith opened the door and they went inside. Isa went straight to the bed. Keith made a stop in the bathroom, and by the time he emerged, Isa was already asleep. He quietly climbed under the covers and rested his head on the pillow. The air conditioner kicked on, then off. He didn't check the time, but the A/C cycled on and off two more times, and he was still unable to sleep. He, too, felt ashamed. And guilty. He thought of the things that he and Isa had done in the bedroom, the things he'd said to her in moments of passion, and he wondered if they had made her cringe inside.

Sex had never been anything but a strong point in their relationship. Or so he'd thought. Was he that insensitive? Had she tried to tell him and he wasn't listening?

He watched her sleep for a moment and laid a hand on her shoulder—and she started, sitting bolt upright at his mere touch. She was breathless.

"You scared me," she said.

Keith comforted her, and she settled back into the bed. But it was as if she slept with one eye open.

Keith worried about what was to come. They hadn't even reached the hard part yet. He wondered how he and Isa would cope, how Melany would fare, when a trial would force his wife to relive in a public courtroom the most traumatic experience a woman could face.

He wanted to stroke her hair and kiss her gently on the temple, but he didn't. He didn't dare disturb the rest she'd finally found.

15

Jack woke early Saturday morning. Andie was asleep on the other edge of the mattress. Between them, stretched sideways like the horizontal line in the letter "H," lay Riley. He slid out of bed quietly, trying not to wake her, but she was already up.

"Daddy, let's play Swiper."

Swiper was the mischievous orange fox on *Dora the Explorer*, Riley's favorite TV show. He swiped everything. Precious stones. Blueberries from Blueberry Hill. Jack and Andie's sex life.

I could strangle that fox.

"How about we cook breakfast for Mommy?" Jack whispered.

It struck her as an excellent idea, and they tiptoed out of the bedroom like Swiper making off with the loot.

The view from the kitchen was one of the things Jack loved about his house, and an air of nostalgia colored his appreciation of the morning sunlight twinkling on the bay beyond their tiny backyard. They were down to their final months on Key Biscayne, and Jack was missing it already. For eight years he'd been a "key rat," dating back to life before Andie, thanks to a sweetheart lease on one of the original "Mackle houses." Hundreds of the two-bedroom concrete shoe boxes were built for World War II veterans who were willing to brave what was, at the time, little more than a mosquito-infested swamp. Jack's was the last remaining Mackle on the waterfront. With the landlord unwilling to renew the lease, Jack's only hope of saving the old house from the bulldozer was a winning lottery ticket worth at least $7 million.

"Make pancakes. Okay, Daddy?"

"Perfect," said Jack, his gaze sweeping the kitchen. He had no idea where the griddle was stored, but he was slightly proud of himself for at least knowing that he needed one.

The *tick-tick-tick* of a dog's nails on the tile floor echoed in the hallway, and a sleepy golden retriever entered the kitchen. "Hey, Max," said Jack as he opened the French door to the backyard. "Need to use the bathroom, buddy?"

"Max already made potty," said Riley. She was pointing at the puddle in the family room. Max was well trained, and his one accident a year was always the fault of the knucklehead named Jack who forgot to let him out the night before.

Jack grabbed a roll of paper towels and was cleaning up Lake Okeechobee when his cell rang from the kitchen counter, where he'd left it to charge overnight. It was a new ringtone: "Hello," by Adele. She'd sung it as the encore to last night's concert, and on the way home Andie had programmed it into Jack's cell.

"Oh, Mommy's favorite song!" shouted Riley, and then she sang alone, plugging in her own lyrics:

"Hello from the other kitty . . ."

The thought of Riley and her mother tooling around town in the SUV singing their Adele–Hello Kitty parody made Jack smile. But the voice on the line was Manny's, which took the smile away.

"Good morning, Jack. Sorry to call on a Saturday, but I just got off the phone with Sylvia Hunt."

"What's up?"

"You went after her pretty hard for not sharing a copy of the probable-cause affidavit, so she said this time she wanted to give us a heads-up."

"What do you mean 'this time'? She didn't change her mind about bail, did she?"

"No. The grand jury returned a true bill last night, and she's unsealing the indictment at nine a.m."

"Why an indictment on top of the existing information? Are there additional charges?"

"She wouldn't tell me why. Strategic reasons, I presume."

Jack could see strategic value where the prosecution of a victim of sexual assault had proven controversial, and the state attorney wanted a grand jury's stamp of approval. But he'd done too many capital cases to overlook the Fifth Amendment of the U.S. Constitution, which required a grand jury indictment in only one type of case—where the state was seeking the death penalty.

"Let's hope it's just strategy," said Jack.

16

The team met at the Freedom Institute at 9:30 a.m. Jack, Manny, and Isa gathered around the Formica-top table in the so-called conference room. Keith waited in Jack's office, apart from the lawyers' conversation with their client.

The interior renovation of the Freedom Institute was transformational, but not without nostalgia. One room hadn't changed a bit, and by unanimous vote of the team it never would—the sixties-vintage kitchen was a time capsule in honor of Jack's mentor. It was not only where lawyers and staff had eaten their bagged lunches since the Institute's founding, but it also served as the main (and only) conference room. Hanging on the wall over the coffee maker was the same framed photograph of Bobby Kennedy that had once hung in Neil's dorm room at Harvard.

"I think Keith is mad that we keep excluding him," said Isa.

"He understands he's not the client," said Jack. "It's important that you do, too."

"Aren't things that a husband and wife say to

each other protected by some kind of privilege?" asked Isa.

"To some extent," said Jack. "But there's no good reason for Keith to be here. If he ever has to answer questions under oath, the less he knows the better. Every time he says 'I refuse to answer because the things my wife told me are privileged,' it sounds like you're hiding something."

"Could Keith be a witness at trial?" she asked.

"Impossible to know for sure," said Jack. "Right now, let's focus on what we do know. The indictment lays out two charges against you. Count one: felony murder in connection with a kidnapping. Count two: conspiracy to commit murder. The conspiracy count means that you formulated a plan with others to murder Gabriel Sosa. The agreement is the crime."

"I didn't agree to anything," she said.

"The felony murder count means that you participated in the kidnap and abduction of Gabriel Sosa. During that kidnapping, someone—but not you—killed Gabriel."

"I'm confused. Am I charged with kidnapping or murder?"

"First-degree murder," said Jack.

"That doesn't seem fair."

"It's a well-established principle. People have been executed for driving the getaway car when it was their partner in crime who actually shot and killed the bank teller. It makes no difference who committed the murder. If you participate in a crime like kidnapping or robbery, and somebody ends up killed, you are guilty of felony murder. That's the way the rule works."

"You said 'executed.' Am I facing a death penalty?"

"No," said Jack. "I was slightly concerned about that when I heard the case was going to a grand jury. It's possible that the prosecutor asked for it, but the grand jury didn't bite. Under the current indictment, even if you are convicted on all charges, there is no possibility of the death penalty."

"I'll take that as a bit of good news," said Isa. "But how bad could the sentence be?"

"Worst-case scenario?" asked Jack.

"Yes. Worst case."

"Life without parole."

She shrank a little in her chair. It wasn't the death penalty, but it was daunting enough.

"We'll never get to that point," said Manny.

"How can you be sure?" asked Isa.

"This is not a case the prosecution wants to take to trial. As long as you're willing to consider a plea to a lesser charge, life without parole should never enter your mind."

"I'm not going to plead guilty to something I didn't do. Even if it is, as you say, a 'lesser charge.'"

Jack and Manny exchanged glances, as if each were wondering how many thousands of times the other had heard similar assertions from clients.

"Let's take a look at the indictment," said Jack.

"Before we get into this," Manny interjected, "I

just want to say that, as your lawyers, we are well aware that there are always two sides to every story. An indictment is just one side—the government's."

"Okay."

"I should also add that the indictment does not include all of the evidence that the prosecution presented to the grand jury. That will come later, when we get the actual transcripts of the proceeding."

"When is that?" asked Isa.

"Soon," said Manny. "We'll work out a schedule with the prosecutor. But I didn't mean to interrupt. Go ahead, Jack."

"Thanks. The first couple of paragraphs track the previous allegations. You went to a bar with your boyfriend and his friend. You pointed out Gabriel Sosa and said that he had sexually assaulted you earlier that spring in your dorm room."

"And as I said before, all of that is true."

"Who was your boyfriend's friend?"

"I can't remember his name. I'm not sure I ever knew. Never saw him before or since."

"The indictment doesn't name him either," said Jack. "But my guess is that when we do get the transcripts, we will find out that the chief witness is your boyfriend, David Kaval."

"I told you I don't know where he is."

"My investigator nailed that down last night," said Jack. "He's in Florida State Prison serving time for armed robbery."

"Which makes it even more likely that he is testifying against you," said Manny. "He probably cut a deal."

"Almost certainly," said Jack. "Regardless of who the informant is, the indictment says that when Sosa left the bar and went to his car, you, along with your boyfriend and his friend, followed Sosa in a white van. True?"

"That's true."

Jack hesitated. He'd expected her to say the opposite. "Why did you follow him?"

"David said we were going to scare him."

"Scare him how?"

"I don't know. David didn't say."

"Whose van was it?"

"It belonged to David's friend. I didn't even want to go."

"But you did."

"Yes."

The old refrigerator behind Jack grumbled. Isa's response hung in the air until the mechanical groaning ceased, and Jack continued. "The indictment then says: 'About a mile into the drive, the van intentionally rear-ended Sosa's car. When Sosa got out of his car to check the damage, Isa's boyfriend and his buddy jumped out and confronted Sosa.' True?"

She didn't answer.

Jack tried again. "Is that true, Isa?"

"Yes."

Another unexpected admission. "How did Kaval and his friend confront him?"

"We pulled off to the shoulder of the road, the way anyone would after being in a fender bender. Sosa was standing between the back of his car and the front bumper of the van. David and his buddy blocked him in, David on the driver's side and his bigger friend on the other side. So Gabriel was trapped and couldn't go anywhere."

"Where were you?"

"In the front seat of the van."

"Did you hear what was said?"

"No."

"Did you see anyone touch Sosa?"

"David shoved him."

"Hard?"

"No. It was like middle-school stuff. They were trying to scare him. I got out of the van and told David to stop it. But he ignored me. He shoved Gabriel again."

"Harder?"

"Mmm-hmm. He knocked him to the ground and then started yelling at him. 'Get up! Get up, you pussy!'"

"What did you do?"

"I screamed at David. I told him to stop it and leave Gabriel alone. But he just yelled back at me. 'Get outta here, Isa! Go! Get lost!'"

"What did you do?"

She drew a breath, then started to shake. "I ran."

"Where?"

"To my dorm room. We were less than a mile away from campus. I started running, and I didn't stop until I got there. And I locked the door."

"Did you call the police?"

She averted her eyes, staring down at the table. "No."

"Why not?"

She took a moment, then looked at Jack. "Do you have any idea what David would have done to me if I had called the police?"

"Given the fact that he's now in prison for a violent crime, I suppose I can imagine," said Jack.

"Your imagination is not that dark," said Isa. "At least I hope not."

Jack would need to hear more about her boyfriend, but first he wanted to get through the chronology. "When did you hear again from David and his buddy?"

"I never heard anything from his friend. The next morning, David called me."

"How did that go?"

"I said, 'I hope you didn't hurt him.' And David said he didn't. They just scared him. 'Scared the shit out of him,' were his exact words. And then he said, 'You can sleep easy now. You don't have to worry about him coming around and bothering you anymore.'"

"What did you take that to mean?"

"That Gabriel was so scared he wouldn't dare enter the same zip code I lived in."

"It didn't occur to you that he wouldn't be coming around because he was dead?"

"No."

The old refrigerator whined once more. Jack gave the electric motor a moment to stop shrieking, and when silence was restored, he gave Isa a few more seconds to consider her answer. She added nothing.

"Anything else you want to tell us?" asked Jack.

"No. That was it."

Jack reviewed his notes, making sure he'd asked all the necessary follow-ups. Then he checked the indictment again. "The indictment tells a different story. It says that your boyfriend and his buddy threw Gabriel into the back of the van and drove to an automotive shop. And it says you were there."

"That's not true. I ran back to my dorm."

"It says that Sosa was systematically tortured over a period of hours at the automotive shop. On Saturday morning, his brutalized body was found dumped on the side of Krome Avenue in south Miami-Dade County."

"I don't know anything about torture or finding a body. The last I saw they were standing between the van and Gabriel's car, bullying him."

"Why did you run?" asked Jack.

She didn't answer right away, but from her body language, Jack guessed that she'd asked herself the same question many times before. "I don't know. I was scared. I was angry. I couldn't stand the sight of Gabriel Sosa again. I just suddenly knew that I couldn't possibly stay there another second. So I ran."

"Before Kaval and his friend took Sosa to the automotive shop?"

"Yes. This is the first I've heard of any automotive shop."

"The last line of the indictment alleges that the entire scheme was planned, orchestrated, and choreographed by Isabelle Bornelli."

"That doesn't even sound like something David would say."

"These are not his exact words. This is a summary written by the prosecutor."

"Whoever said it, that's just not true."

Jack leaned into the table a bit, not to intimidate, but to let her know that something was troubling him. "Let me ask you this, Isa. What did you think was going to happen when you pointed out Gabriel Sosa to your boyfriend in the bar?"

"I don't know."

"You have to do better than that," said Jack.

She collected herself and then answered. "I thought he would tell Gabriel that he wasn't going to get away with what he'd done to me. Tell him that he'd better not have any ideas about coming back a second time."

"*Tell* him?" asked Jack. "Let's be real, Isa. You knew he would do more than have a conversation with Gabriel."

"I thought he would do what any boyfriend would do when he found the man who raped his girlfriend. But this whole idea that I came up with a plan to *kill* Gabriel is crazy."

Manny rose and leaned against the counter. "Especially if he didn't rape you."

"Excuse me?" said Isa.

"There was no reason for you to point him out to your boyfriend, to kidnap him, to scare him—and definitely not to kill him—if, as you told the doctor at the campus clinic, all you and Gabriel did was engage in unprotected sex."

"But that's not what happened," she said.

"That's not the issue," said Manny. "Can the state attorney *prove* that anything more than that happened?"

"I don't understand," said Isa.

"Technically, the prosecutor doesn't have to prove motive. But in a case like this, if the government can't prove motive, a jury will never convict you."

"But they shouldn't convict me for any reason. I didn't do anything."

"Just listen to what I'm saying. There's no way the government can prove you were sexually assaulted. You didn't report it. Your attacker is dead. There was no medical examination of your body to confirm sexual assault. If Jack and I are right, the case is built on the testimony of your ex-boyfriend, who is a convicted felon serving time for armed robbery. We'll shred him on the witness stand as a scumbag who cut himself a nice deal in exchange for his testimony against you."

"But what am I supposed to do?" asked Isa. "You want me to lie about what happened and say I wasn't raped?"

"No," said Manny, speaking in a flat, calm voice. "I want you to shut up."

She bristled at his words.

"I want *all* of us to shut up," said Manny. "We need to stop telling the prosecutor, the media, or anyone else that you were raped. I don't want to put anything out there that could be used against us at trial to prove that Gabriel Sosa sexually assaulted you. Because as it stands now, I don't see any way for the prosecutor to prove rape. No rape means no motive. No motive means no conviction."

"I don't like that approach," said Isa. "I don't like it one bit."

Manny shrugged. "Then maybe you'll like spending the rest of your life in prison."

She glanced at Jack, reaching out for help.

"Manny, tone it down," said Jack.

"I say it like it is," said Manny.

"No, you say it as you want it to be."

"What do you think, Jack?" asked Isa.

Jack still had his doubts about Manny, but he had listened with an open mind. "This is the toughest issue a criminal defendant can face: Should I speak up and explain my innocence or should I stand silent and say the government can't prove my guilt beyond a reasonable doubt?"

"But do you agree with Manny?"

He looked only at Isa as he spoke, sensing that she needed the reassurance. "To some extent. If you say publicly that you were raped, under the rules of evidence your statement can be used against you at trial. It's an admission. So I agree that you should make no public statement."

"Good," said Manny. "Then we're all on board."

"Not so fast," said Jack, shifting his gaze toward his cocounsel. "I don't agree that we should *all* shut up. The prosecution deserves every bit of the public backlash it's getting for bringing murder charges against Isa. If the *lawyers* tell the media that Isa was raped, the prosecutor can't use that against our client at trial."

"Now you're splitting hairs," said Manny.

"No," said Jack. "It's an important point. Yes, Isa should be silent. But her lawyers will continue to work the media and keep the pressure on the state attorney's office for building a first-degree murder case where the charges, if any, should have been far less serious."

"Are you saying that I won't testify at trial?" asked Isa.

"That's a call that we'll make way down the road," said Jack. "Right now, the goal is to keep you from making some public statement before trial that will make it easier for the prosecutor to prove her case."

Isa breathed in and out. "I guess I can live with that."

Manny shook his head. "Well, what Jack says is very nice in theory, but the fact of the matter is that *none* of us can say anything about the sexual assault."

"Why?" asked Isa.

"That's the agreement I made with Sylvia Hunt. She agreed that the state attorney would not oppose bail as long as we agreed to have 'no comment' until the investigation into the misconduct of the correctional officer is completed."

"'No comment' on the investigation doesn't mean that you and Jack can't talk about what Gabriel Sosa did," she said, and then she looked at Jack. "Does it?"

"I agreed to a blanket gag order," said Manny. "The defense cannot talk to the media. Period."

Things suddenly came clear to Jack. Manny had a strategy firmly in mind—Sosa didn't rape Isa—and he'd single-handedly committed the defense team to it.

"That doesn't seem like the best result," said Isa.

"It's the best *possible* result," said Manny. "You're out of jail."

Isa closed her eyes and massaged between them. "This is giving me a major headache."

"We've covered enough for one morning," said Jack.

"When should we meet again?" she asked.

"Soon," said Jack, and then his gaze drifted toward Manny. "But first, the lawyers need to have a talk. A good, honest talk. Just the two of us."

"Okay, call me when you need me," said Isa. "Thank you both," she added, and then left the room.

"I gotta take off, too," said Manny. "If I hurry, I can still make my tee time at La Gorce."

"I was serious about having a lawyers-only conversation," said Jack.

The refrigerator was acting up again. Manny kicked the side of it, and it went silent. "Cute little setup you have here, Swyteck. Let's do that talk at my office."

Jack rose. He didn't want to have it out with Manny with Keith and Isa in the other room, but it was getting hard to hold his tongue. "Is this the way you want to play it, Manny?"

"I have no idea what you're talking about."

"If we're going to be a team, you need to stop acting like you're the captain of the ship."

"I am the captain. It wasn't you who got Isa out on bail."

"That's exactly what I'm talking about, Manny. I haven't said a single negative word about you to Isa. But everything you say and do is calculated to convince her that this is a one-lawyer operation. You decide what we say to the media. You decide the trial strategy. You're the legal magician who got his client out of jail with the wave of his wand."

"I assure you, Jack, it wasn't magic."

"I have no doubt. But, boy, wasn't it one hell of a funny coincidence the way this case just fell in your lap? Especially within hours of Isa's father coming into my office—my 'cute little setup'—and telling me that he didn't want me to be her attorney and that he would share his evidence that she wasn't raped only with her new lawyer."

"Jack," he said with a reproving shake of his head. "Are you accusing me of dirty pool?"

"How many Venezuelan clients do you have, Manny?"

"I've had many Venezuelan clients. It's the nature of my business. Caracas is the new Medellín."

"Let me put it another way: How many Venezuelan clients named Bornelli do you represent?"

He smiled a little, then turned serious. "The same as you, Jack. Same as you."

Jack met his stare.

"My foursome's waiting at the country club," he said, the first to blink.

Jack's gaze stayed on him like a laser until his cocounsel showed himself out and closed the door behind him.

17

Jack drove to Coconut Grove at noon. It was related to Isa's case, but it wasn't exactly a working lunch. He was paying a visit to Theo Knight.

Theo was Jack's best friend, bartender, therapist, confidant, and sometime investigator. He was also a former client, a onetime gangbanger who easily could have ended up dead on the streets of Overtown Village or Liberty City. Instead, he landed on death row for a murder he didn't commit. Jack literally saved his life. With his civil settlement from the state Theo went on to open his own tavern—Sparky's he'd called it, a play on words and double-barreled flip of the bird to "Old Sparky," the nickname for the electric chair he'd avoided. Sparky's success led to a second bar in Coconut Grove—Cy's Place.

Cy's Place was better known for its late-night jazz than its lunch menu, so Jack had his choice of barstools. He took one in front of the television, which was permanently tuned to ESPN. Theo came over, reached over the bar top, and gave Jack one of those multistep handshakes that Jack could never keep up with, even if Theo did sometimes call him a brother.

"Whassup, dude?"

"Same old," said Jack.

"You hungry? How 'bout a Riley Special?"

Theo had anointed himself Uncle Theo, and the Riley Special was a hot dog, no bun, cut into a hundred tiny pieces.

"No, there's a reason we call it the *Riley* Special."

"You could have brought my little niece, you know."

"Next time."

Andie wasn't crazy about bringing a two-year-old to a bar and feeding her hot dogs. But what happened at Cy's Place stayed at Cy's Place—until their last visit, when Riley had gone home singing her own version of "*Ninety-nine bottles of beer on the wall.*"

"Is your wife still pissed at me for teaching Riley to count backward?"

"First of all, she wasn't mad. Secondly, I don't think ninety-tenty, eleventy-twelvety qualifies as counting, let alone counting backward."

"It was her first attempt, okay?"

The couple seated at the other end of the bar flagged Theo's attention. He broke away to check on them.

Jack knew he wasn't kidding about bringing Riley around more. Four years lost for someone else's crime had left Theo in a perpetual mode of "anything worth doing is worth overdoing." Theo wasn't just an uncle; he was going to be the Willie Mays of uncles. Cy's Place wasn't just a jazz club; it was the reincarnation of Miami's Overtown in its heyday. No one had to remind Jack what a special place this was. Creaky wood floors, redbrick walls, and high ceilings were the perfect bones for the club that Theo's great-uncle had always dreamed of owning. Art nouveau chandeliers cast just the right mood lighting. At night, crowded café tables fronted a small stage for live music. More important, on these very barstools, at the grand opening, sparks had begun to fly for Jack and FBI agent Andie Henning. They'd talked and laughed till two a.m., listening to Uncle Cy give them a taste of Miami's old Overtown Village through his saxophone. A few months later, on the second anniversary of Jack's thirty-ninth birthday, Jack put a ring on her finger. Good times.

Why does all that seem like a million years ago?

"Be back in one second," said Theo, as he breezed past Jack on his way to the kitchen. "I got some info."

Jack knew Theo wouldn't let him down. Andie had given Jack good advice: if he wanted to know the real story behind bail, Jack needed to talk to Isa's cellmate before she was swallowed up by the Justice Department's investigation into the guard's misconduct. The chances that she would talk to Jack seemed remote. It was the perfect job for Theo.

The café doors swung open. Theo emerged from the kitchen, delivered a couple of sandwiches to the other end of the bar, and went back to Jack.

"Were you able to set up a meeting?"

"Yep. And you don't have to worry about me doing anything illegal to make it happen, either. No bribery, no threats."

"How'd you do it?"

"One of my old waitresses is locked up over there. Drug charge. I asked if she knows Foneesha Johnson. She did, and she put in a good word for me. Foneesha and me met this morning."

"How did it go?"

"Pretty good. I'm gonna take her to a Heat game in about six months, if she's acquitted. In about twenty-five years if she ain't."

"I meant—you know what I meant."

"Yeah, I know. But I'm not totally messin' with you. See, I think the chances are real good that she'll be acquitted. You know why?"

"I'm guessing that it's not because she's innocent."

"You exactly right. She's got herself a top-flight lawyer."

"Yeah, I know. Her lawyer is Manuel Espinosa."

"But did you know *this*? Manny is doing it for free."

"Manny is defending her for free?"

"Is there a fucking parrot in here?"

"Sorry," said Jack. "I'm just trying to wrap my head around this. Manny's a drug lawyer. He wouldn't represent his own mother for free."

"No shit. But it has to be true, dude. No way can Foneesha Johnson afford Manuel Espinosa."

He had a point there. "Okay. So how did Isa's cellmate pull off a freebie?"

"According to Foneesha, he reached out to her. He offered to be her lawyer free of charge if she met with him face-to-face. She said deal."

"There has to be more to it than that."

"There is. But this is where she got a little fuzzy on me. See, to get the free lawyer, she had to do something in exchange."

"Something like what?"

"A favor. I don't mean a sexual favor."

"I *know* you don't mean *sexual*. Theo, just spit it out."

Theo leaned closer, as if sharing the world's biggest secret. "She had to help Isa get out on bail."

"How?"

"She wouldn't tell me. Well, she wouldn't tell me yesterday. She said she'll tell me at the Heat game. Can you swing tickets? I'll take anything. Even the sorry-ass Knicks."

"Theo, forget the Heat, okay? This is major what you're telling me."

"Well, if it's major I'll take Golden State."

"Fine. You can have any game you want. Just shut up for sixty seconds and let me sort this out." Jack closed his eyes, then opened them, thinking aloud. "Here's what Manny told me. Follow the timeline here. A guard went to Isa's cellmate. He tried to coerce her into being part of his plan to sexually assault Isa."

"Foneesha didn't tell me anything about that."

"That's fine. Stay with me. The cellmate went to Isa and told her about the guard's plan."

"And then Isa called you?"

"No," said Jack, shaking his head. "She called Manny. Because Manny was Foneesha's lawyer."

They looked at each other for a moment, trying to make sense of it.

"That doesn't really add up," said Theo. "Foneesha told me that she got Manny for free after she promised to help get Isa out of jail."

"Right," said Jack. "And Manny says the opposite—that he offered to help Isa get out of jail because he was already Foneesha's lawyer."

"What do you think really happened?" asked Theo.

"No idea."

"What do you think could have happened? Worst case."

Jack processed it for a few more moments. "Manny found out who Isa's cellmate was. Manny met with Foneesha, and he offered to represent her for free if she would tell Isa that the guard was planning to rape her."

"So you don't think the guard was actually planning to rape Isa?"

"You asked me for the worst-case scenario."

"You think Manny put the words in Foneesha's mouth?"

"I'm just saying it's *possible.*"

"Whoa. A lawyer can get disbarred for making shit like that up."

"Yes, he can," said Jack. "If someone can prove it."

"But I'm missing something. Why would Manny even want to help Isa get out on bail? He wasn't her lawyer. You were."

"True. But this would be one way to become her lawyer."

"Come on, man. I Googled this guy. Espinosa isn't hurtin' for clients who got coin."

Jack thought back to the conversation in his office with Isa's father—Felipe Bornelli's pull-no-punches disapproval of the lawyer Isa had hired.

"Maybe this isn't about Manny getting a new client," said Jack. "Maybe it's not even about Isa getting a new lawyer. It could be about control."

"Control over what?"

"Over Isa," said Jack, "and her case."

"Serious shit," said Theo, as he wiped down the bar. "'Course, all this depends."

"On what?"

"Whether anybody can believe anything Foneesha says."

"You trusted her enough to invite her to a Heat game."

Theo laughed.

"What's so funny?"

"I wouldn't invite her to sit in the seat next to me if I was wearin' an ebola suit. Those tickets are for me and my girl—Riley."

"So you don't have any follow-up plans with Foneesha?"

"Nah. I was lucky to get one visit with her. I got what I could. But don't take her word as gospel."

"All right." Jack rapped his knuckles on the bar top and climbed down from the stool. "Thank you, pal. I will take this for what it's worth."

18

At about two p.m. Sylvia entered the Village of Merrick Park, an outdoor shopping mall of upscale shops in Coral Gables. She valeted her car and followed the line of towering royal palms to the center of the open-air courtyard. A young woman was seated on the bench facing the fountain. Sylvia hadn't seen her in almost five years, but as she approached from behind, she immediately recognized the posture, the hair, and the contour of her shoulders.

"Hello, sweetie," said Sylvia.

The woman turned and caught her breath, startled. Sylvia smiled sadly. *Still jumpy.*

Sylvia hadn't visited this spot in almost five years—not since her last meeting with "Jane Doe." Valerie Hinds was twenty-four years old now. Sylvia had met her when she was just a seventeen-year-old junior at Coral Gables High School. The mall was off limits to students during school hours, which made it the perfect meeting spot, because Valerie didn't want any of her classmates to see her meeting with a prosecutor. She didn't want anyone to know that she'd been sexually assaulted.

It was Sylvia who'd prosecuted the three men who had raped her at knifepoint.

Valerie rose and gave her a hug. "So good to see you."

They took a seat on the bench, shaded by palm fronds and surrounded by the shops of Tiffany, Gucci, and the like. They caught up briefly. Valerie was engaged. She showed Sylvia the ring.

"Congratulations!" said Sylvia as she gave her a hug.

Valerie thanked her and smiled. Then she turned serious. "I haven't told him."

"About?"

"Us. What happened to me."

"I see," said Sylvia. She wasn't shocked. The thought of testifying at trial had been so traumatizing to Valerie that she'd begged Sylvia to cut a deal—even to drop the charges, if necessary—so she wouldn't have to face her attackers in court. Sylvia spent countless hours supporting her, consoling her, telling her that it would be all right. But in the end they cut a deal. Valerie just couldn't do it.

"When we talked about taking the case to trial, you mentioned the rape-shield laws that would prevent my name from being reported in the media."

"That's true. You still have that protection."

"But now I see that you're involved in this case against Isabelle Bornelli. It made me wonder if the state attorney's office is changing its position. Is the identity of rape victims no longer protected?"

"Isabelle Bornelli is a totally different situation," said Sylvia.

"I just wanted to make sure."

"Rest assured. You have nothing to worry about."

"Because I *really* don't want this to be out there," she said, the old agony resurfacing. "It's not something I want to talk about with my husband or anyone else. It's over. I want it behind me. Do you get what I'm saying?"

"I do," said Sylvia. *Better than anyone.*

Valerie took a breath. "Can I ask you a question?"

"Sure."

"Why are you prosecuting Isabelle Bornelli?"

"I'm a prosecutor," said Sylvia. "A grand jury indicted her. She has to be prosecuted as charged."

"I understand. But I'm asking something a little different: Why does it have to be *you*?"

Sylvia looked off toward the fountain, then back at Jane Doe. "This may sound strange, but the fact that you ask that question makes me feel even stronger about this: It *should* be me."

"You're right," said Valerie. "That does sound strange."

Silence hung between them. Then Valerie rose. "Okay. It was good seeing you, Ms. Hunt."

Ms. Hunt. That's what Valerie had called her when she was a teenager. "I think it's finally okay for you to call me Sylvia."

"I'll stick with Ms. Hunt," she said. "Thanks again for meeting with me."

Sylvia watched her turn and walk away. *Ms.*

Hunt. It was a crushing blow, and it made Sylvia wonder how many other Jane Does felt the same way. Betrayed.

Sylvia rose. It was a Saturday, and for once she didn't have work to do. She could have window-shopped at the mall or called a friend to meet her for lunch. Instead, she went back to the valet stand and retrieved her car. She was headed back to the office.

This seemed like the time to take Carmen Benitez's advice. She was suddenly feeling the need to go back to her desk, open that file Carmen had given her, and read one or two of those letters from Gabriel Sosa's mother.

19

Jack was ridding himself of a five o'clock shadow, the left side of his face still covered in shaving cream, when Andie stepped into the bathroom.

"Our babysitter is asleep," she said as her face appeared in his mirror.

Jack pulled the razor away from his chin and spoke to her reflection. "Already?"

Andie laid her smartphone beside the sink in front of him, showing him the proof: a photo of Jack's grandmother in their recliner with her eyes closed and mouth agape. Riley was sitting on the floor in front of her, putting on lipstick. Max lay right beside her, probably wondering what Dusty Rose no. 23 tasted like.

"That's a good color for her," said Jack.

"Not funny," said Andie. "I love Abuela, and I know she loves Riley. It's great that she's independent and still lives alone in her town house, but she's too old to be alone with a two-year-old. I don't care how much she says otherwise. You have to put your foot down."

Abuela had missed the full grandmother experience with Jack, having found a way out of Cuba only after he was a grown man. It would break her heart to hear that she was "too old" to be left alone with her great-granddaughter, but Jack knew that Andie was right. "I'll tell her," said Jack. "Can you call in reinforcements for tonight?"

"I'll try."

Jack finished shaving and entered the bedroom to select a shirt. One thing he wouldn't miss about the old Mackle house was the bedroom closet, which was only big enough to hold Andie's things. Jack kept his clothes on a freestanding rack along the wall. He was deciding between a dress shirt and short sleeves when the television on the wall caught his attention. Isa's photograph flashed on the screen. The local news had an update on the Bornelli case. Beneath her photo was a red banner with bold white letters:

"REVENGE KILLING," SAYS MIAMI PROSECUTOR.

Jack grabbed the remote and turned up the volume. The *Action News* anchorman finished his introductory remarks, and the segment switched to prerecorded video. Sylvia Hunt was standing at the podium in the press room inside the Graham Building, reading a prepared announcement of the grand jury indictment:

"It's important to understand what this case is and is not," said the prosecutor. "This is not an ambiguous case where a jury will be asked to decide if Ms. Bornelli acted in self-defense in the confusion of the attack. It's not a case in which the victim of sexual assault, acting out of fear and desperation, retaliated against her attacker because he continued to stalk and torment her. This was a carefully planned, cold-blooded act of vengeance that took place weeks after the sexual assault. The victim in this case, Mr. Sosa, suffered multiple stab wounds. These include the loss of three fingers on his left hand—defensive wounds that an unarmed victim would receive when fighting off a vicious attack. This was, in plain English, a revenge killing."

The anchorman reappeared on-screen and closed out the segment. Isa's photo disappeared, and the coverage shifted to a house fire in Miami Shores, but those two words were already burned into Jack's mind: *revenge killing.*

The prosecutor and the media-relations team had finally come up with a viable handle. A good one. One that required a response from the defense team.

Whether Manny liked it or not.

Keith and Isa went for a run along Brickell Avenue. A five-year-old was at the upper limit for a baby jogger, but Melany was small for her age and needed to get out of the apartment as much as anyone.

The Financial District is quiet on Saturdays, and the evening rush to nearby Restaurant Row had not yet begun. Eating outdoors was the big draw, and with spring already starting to feel like summer, the sidewalk cafés would remain empty until after sunset. It was almost too hot to run. At the half-mile mark, Keith was breathing heavily enough for Isa to be concerned. The professional life of a banker was sedentary, save for running through airports, and Keith was no longer the man who used to take her cross-country skiing in Zermatt or hiking in the shadow of the Matterhorn. She relieved him of jogger-pushing responsibilities as they reached the westerly bend on Brickell Avenue, where mixed-use high-rises yielded to strictly residential condominiums. At one mile, Keith's shirt was soaked with sweat. He needed a break.

"Let's make it to the church," said Isa, and they pushed on.

Nestled in the midst of towering giants of steel and glass on the waterfront side of Brickell Avenue is St. Jude Melkite Catholic Church, one of the area's few remaining historical buildings. The only Miami church built of Indiana Bedford stone—the same stone that adorns the exteriors of the Empire State Building and the Pentagon—St. Jude's managed to withstand several powerful hurricanes and, even more impressive, a string of building booms that had sent countless other architectural gems the way of the wrecking ball.

They stopped outside the church, beneath the shade of palm trees.

"Are you okay, Daddy?" Melany asked with concern.

"Uh-huh," he said, huffing. "I'm"—two more breaths—"fine."

"I have to go potty," said Melany.

"Good," said Keith. "Let's get—a cab—back to—"

"Seriously, Keith?"

"Sorry," he said, still breathless. "I'm hurtin'."

"I really have to go," said Melany, grimacing.

Isa jogged up the granite steps and checked the double entry doors to the church. They opened. "Come on. There has to be a bathroom in here."

Keith pushed the jogger up the handicap ramp and followed Isa into the vestibule. The bathroom was behind the stairwell, and it was barely big enough for one person. Isa got Melany situated and waited outside the door. Keith stepped into the chapel, admiring the Romanesque arches surrounding a beautifully tinted ceiling as blue as the south Florida sky. Painted icons graced the altar and surrounding walls, and arched windows of stained glass commemorated various saints. Rows of old wooden pews stretched before him.

A sense of peace came over him. More peace than he'd felt since setting foot in Miami. He needed a touch of God's grace, after a day that had started with his wife's indictment. He didn't like being excluded from Isa's meetings with her lawyers. He wanted to trust his wife's assurances that she was telling him everything that was discussed. But how would he know?

"Beautiful church," said Isa as she came alongside him.

"Very pretty."

They were standing behind the last row of pews; the vestibule and bathroom were just a few steps away. Isa's gaze swept the ceiling.

"When I die, this is the kind of place where I would want the funeral service."

Keith shot her an uneasy glance. "Why would you even say that?"

"We're all going to die, Keith."

"But why are you even thinking about dying?"

"It's probably the way you nearly croaked on a one-mile run," she said, smiling. Then she turned serious. "And everything else that's happened in the last few days."

"Oh, honey," he said as he put his arm around her.

She was suddenly trembling, as if trouble wasn't far below the surface. "Sorry. It's all so crazy. I can't stop thinking about it."

"It's going to be okay," he said.

"No, it's not. Nothing is ever going to be the same."

"Don't say that."

"It's true."

Keith held her close, speaking more softly. "Did Jack and Manny tell you something this morning? Something you forgot to tell me about?"

"No."

"Are you sure?"

"It's not anything that anybody said. I'm just so scared."

"Of course you are. I'm scared, too."

"Not like I am," she said, her voice quaking. "I

just feel like he's back. After all these years he's back in my life."

Keith laid his hands squarely on her shoulders and looked her in the eye. "Listen to me, okay? That's not anything you have to worry about. Gabriel Sosa will never be back to hurt you."

"I know," she said. "I didn't mean him."

Keith was confused. Then he thought of the meeting in Jack's office. "Do you mean your father?"

"No, no. I mean David Kaval."

"He's in prison."

"What if he gets out? Jack and Manny both think that he cut some kind of deal with the prosecution."

Keith wanted to reassure her, but he couldn't hide his own surprise. "After all that has happened, that's what you're most afraid of? David Kaval?"

She lowered her gaze, as if unable to explain.

"Mommy, I'm finished!"

The bathroom door swung open. Isa started away, but Keith squeezed her hand, stopping her. "I want to talk more about this."

The expression on her face was one of pain and desperation, as if she were begging him to let it go and forget she'd ever raised it.

"We have to talk about this. Okay?"

"Mommy!"

"I'm coming," said Isa as she broke away.

Keith let her go, watching as she hurried into the vestibule, wondering what the scary truth was about David Kaval—and not at all certain that he would ever hear it from Isa.

It was 6:45 p.m. Jack and Andie were still at the house. Abuela had moved from the recliner to the guest bedroom, pouting. Almost ninety minutes had passed, and the backup babysitter was still "on her way."

"Where's she coming from, Bulgaria?" asked Jack.

They were standing in the kitchen. Andie shifted Riley from her left arm to her right. "Let's give her fifteen more minutes. Then I'll pop the popcorn. You pick the movie."

"*Frozen!*" said Riley.

"Sounds like a plan."

Jack went to the family room, took a seat on the couch, and scrolled through the movie offerings. *Frozen* for the fifteenth time was not going to happen, even if it meant Jack's total surrender to an On-Demand double feature of *Sex and the City* and *The Devil Wears Prada*. Out of the corner of his eye, he spotted Abuela walking quietly toward the front door. It was understood that she slept over whenever she visited. She was toting her overnight bag.

"Abuela, where are you going?"

She stopped and turned. "I go where wanted."

Oh, boy. Jack pushed himself up from the couch, stopped her in the foyer, and took the bag from her. "Abuela, please. Nobody said you're not wanted."

"*A donde te quieren mucho no vengas a menudo.*"

The Spanish would have been beyond Jack's ability but for the fact that it was one of Abuela's oft-used expressions, the Cuban equivalent of "A constant guest is never welcome."

"Abuela, you don't have to work to earn the right to visit. We want your company, not your services. Let the babysitter do the hard part. Just enjoy Riley."

Her expression tightened. "*Y quién es la bebé-seeder?*" she asked in Spanglish.

"Her name is Catalina."

"Catalina? Hmm. *Como la jinetera.*"

Like the prostitute? Jack sighed, surmising that there must be a Catalina of ill repute in one of Abuela's telenovelas. "No, she's not a prostitute. She's the oldest daughter of Andie's friend at the FBI."

Jack's cell rang. MICHAEL POSTEN flashed on the screen—the crime reporter for the *Miami Tribune*.

"Abuela, I have to take this call. Will you please stay?"

"No."

"Just until I finish this call?"

"No."

"Por favor?"

She smiled warmly. "Ah, *español. Muy bien.* I stay, *mi vida.*"

Mi vida—literally "my life"—which summed up the way she felt about her grandson.

Abuela wheeled her bag back to the guestroom. Jack answered the call, but he'd already missed Posten. Almost immediately his cell chimed, and a text message from Posten quickly followed:

I need a comment in two hours or the headline and first sentence will run as filed in Sunday's paper. See below.

Jack scrolled down and read:

ACCUSED "REVENGE KILLER" TO POLICE:
"I WENT ALONG WITH IT"

The *Miami Tribune* has obtained a twelve-year-old police report, including statements from alleged sexual assault victim Isabelle Bornelli, which reveals powerful new details about Bornelli's connection to the brutal murder of her alleged attacker, Gabriel Sosa.

The message ended there. Jack read it again, more slowly, trying to understand. *Police report? What police report?*

Jack redialed Posten, but it went to voice mail. At the tone, he left a message: "Michael, thanks for the heads-up. I will definitely have a comment for you, but I'll need the full two hours. Call me if you can give me more information or if the deadline changes."

To be sure, Jack also typed the same message and sent it by text. Then he walked back to the family room and dialed his client's cell.

"Did you pick a movie?" Andie asked as she entered the room.

Jack had the phone to his ear, listening to Isa's cell ring, willing her to answer. "Yeah," he said to Andie. "How about *Dial M for Murder*?"

20

Reaching across a bay as dark and calm as the cloudy night, alight with a stream of glowing headlamps, the interconnected bridges of the Rickenbacker Causeway, like a strand of floating pearls, tethered Key Biscayne to the mainland. Brickell Avenue was roughly halfway between Jack's house on the key and Manny's place on Miami Beach, so they met at Isa's apartment at the Four Seasons. The legal team gathered on the terrace around a glass-top patio table. Keith retreated to Melany's room to read to her.

"Went along with it," Isa said with a bite in her tone. "I can't believe any newspaper would print such a thing."

For the first time, Jack heard real anger from his client. Perhaps it was the shoddy journalism, or it could have been the cumulative effect of five days from hell. Either way, the shell-shocked and numb Isa was not at this table.

"I'm glad to see more fight in you," said Jack. "But let's break this down. You're angry because you never said those words—'I went along with it'—to the police. Is that right?"

Isa hesitated.

Jack tried again. "You told us that you never talked to the police, right?"

"Well, what I told you was that I didn't report the sexual assault. And that's true. I didn't. But—"

"But what?"

"I know this is going to sound like a lie, but I'm telling the truth. About a month after I was raped, a detective from Miami-Dade Police came to see me."

"About the sexual assault?"

"No. It had nothing to do with that. I told you before that Gabriel and I went on a date. My number was in his cell phone records. The police were talking to everyone he called in the month or so before he died. It was routine."

"So this was a homicide detective who came to see you?"

"Yes. I guess so."

"Do you remember his name?"

"No. Until you brought this up, I didn't even remember talking to the police. This was so long ago. In my mind, I've blocked out the attack and Gabriel Sosa. These are suppressed memories. I'm not playing psychiatrist on you, but there is such a thing. It's part of the post-traumatic stress disorder, and it's real."

"I don't doubt that," said Jack, though he was starting to question far more things than he would have liked. "But let's stay focused. Did you or did you not tell the police that you 'went along' with the attack on Gabriel Sosa?"

"No! That headline is beyond misleading."

"'Misleading' is what you call it? So you actually did say those words?"

"Yes. But it had nothing to do with any attack on Gabriel. I was talking about Gabriel's attack *on me*."

A warm breeze rustled Jack's notepad on the table, and with the wind, Isa's emotions shifted. The anger was giving way to the pain and anxiety she'd displayed in their earlier meetings.

"Can you tell me more about that?" asked Jack.

She nodded, but she didn't jump right into it. Jack gave her the time she needed, his gaze drifting off toward the blanket of city lights that stretched for miles up the coast.

"Gabriel walked me home from the Rathskeller," she said. "Neither one of us was tired. He was fun to talk to. He knew my old neighborhood in Venezuela, so we had things in common. I invited him up to my room."

"What time was this?"

"About eleven, I'd say. So we got to my room. We talked a little more."

"Sorry to interrupt," said Manny. "Did you close the door or leave it open?"

"I closed it," she said in a firm voice. "Does that make this my fault?"

"No, not at all. I'm just getting all the facts. Continue, please."

"I showed him some of the old beauty-pageant

photos of me when I was little, just for laughs. Then he sat on the bed and said something like, 'So, we're going to have sex, right?' I laughed, thinking he was joking. He wasn't. I said he should leave. He said I was being a tease. I told him he needed to go. But he didn't move."

"Again, sorry," said Manny. "Did you open the door?"

The question clearly annoyed her. "No. I didn't open it," she said.

"Then what happened?" asked Jack.

Isa paused and then continued. "I—he asked me to lie down on the bed. And I did. But this was not to have sex. We just talked. He tried to kiss me, and I got up and asked him to go again."

"My apologies," said Manny. "But I have to ask another question: Did you get up and open the door?"

Her eyes narrowed, and Jack sensed that Manny's "no rape" theory of the case wasn't exactly growing on her. "No. The door stayed closed."

"Okay, got it," said Manny.

"What happened next?" asked Jack.

She swallowed hard. It seemed to be getting more difficult for her. "He started pulling off my clothes," she said, looking away from her lawyers. "I wound up on the floor."

Jack gave her another moment. "Where was Gabriel?"

"He was on top of me. We were struggling and I seriously don't know how I ended up there, but after he got my pants off, I stopped trying to fight. I figured it would be better for me if I pretended that I was going along with it. I kind of just blanked out. That's what I told the police—that 'I just went along with it.' I was nineteen years old and barely a hundred pounds. Gabriel was probably one eighty, and mostly muscle. I was scared, I couldn't believe what was happening, and that seemed like the safest thing for me to do."

Another minute passed. Isa wiped a tear away. "I'm sorry," she said.

"No need to apologize," said Jack. "Did you tell the homicide detective everything you just told us?"

Isa thought about it. "Probably. Most of it, anyway. I definitely told him that I went along with it—or something like that."

Jack looked at Manny and said, "We have to clear this up with the *Tribune*."

Manny shook his head. "The state attorney reversed her position on bail on one condition—that we not talk to the media."

"That's ridiculous. The *Tribune* wouldn't know about the detective's report unless MDPD or someone at the state attorney's office told them about it. Whoever leaked it clearly distorted the facts. We have a right to explain what Isa meant when she said 'I went along with it.'"

"Let's not jump into the cesspool of a media trial," said Manny.

"We don't have a choice," said Jack. "Posten said if we don't comment, he'll run the story as written."

"Call Sylvia Hunt," said Manny. "Tell her to kill the story."

"Why would she do that?" asked Isa.

"Because the story is inaccurate," said Manny. "I trust Sylvia to do the right thing before I trust some scumbag reporter to give us a fair shake. If we call Posten and try to straighten this out, the *Tribune* won't kill the story. The headline will be even worse. '*Lawyer confirms: Revenge killer told police she "just went along with it."*' The state attorney's office already has a PR mess on its hands with this case. Throw this one right in their lap and tell them to fix it."

Jack had his points of disagreement with his cocounsel, but he had to give credit when due. Manny was making excellent sense.

"I agree," said Jack.

Isa did a double take. "What?"

"I agree with Manny. Sylvia is the one to clean this up."

Manny smiled. "Are you patronizing me, Rick? Or is this the beginning of a beautiful friendship?"

"Who's Rick?" asked Isa.

The *Casablanca* reference was lost on her, but if Manny was an old movie buff, that might be one more thing that the lawyers could see eye to eye on.

"Let's not get carried away," said Jack, as he reached for his cell. "I'll call Sylvia."

21

Isa went to Melany's room to say good night. It was just the two of them in the apartment.

She'd overheard Jack's end of the conversation with Sylvia Hunt, and it had been short and to the point. The prosecutor had made no promises, but she'd at least confirmed that the planned story was inaccurate and that she would do her best to make it right. All they could do was wait. Isa had encouraged Keith to go down to the hotel bar and have a beer with Jack, partly because it would be good for him, but mostly because she didn't want to be hounded for a full recap of the meeting with her lawyers.

"How are you doing, muffin?"

Melany looked up from her favorite board book and smiled. She was on her back, propped up by two pillows. "I'm okay."

Isa sat on the edge of the mattress, took the book—*Olivia Saves the Circus*—and laid it on the nightstand. Melany had read it so many times, and it was probably no coincidence that she was drawn to the story of a circus that needed saving because all of the performers were out with an ear infection.

"Let Mommy have a look at that boo-boo."

Melany turned her head so her mother could check the pressure dressing on the incision site. She was limited to sponge baths for five days, so apart from obvious problems like bleeding or drainage at the ear, it was important to make sure that Melany didn't somehow get it wet. "You're good," said Isa.

Melany straightened her head just enough to lift her functioning ear from the pillow. "Mommy?"

"Yes, honey?"

"When will we know if the operation worked this time?"

"Twelve more days. You'll get a processor, just like the one in your other ear."

"What if it doesn't work?"

Isa had put her faith in the Miami doctors and tried only to look at it from the flip side: if it *did* work, a bilateral implant was Melany's ticket to hearing speech in noisy places, and it would even enable her to determine the direction a sound was coming from. "The doctor isn't worried about that. We shouldn't worry, either."

Melany looked away, then back. "Did you worry when you were little?"

"Sure."

"What did you worry about?"

"Silly things."

"What kind of silly things?"

Really silly things—things that her mother had

put in her head. *Am I skinny enough? Are my eyebrows too thick? Is my nose too "native"?* Things so trivial that Isa sometimes wondered if God had given her precious daughter this burden to make a point. "Worrying is normal, but it doesn't get you anywhere, honey."

"Did you worry about being deaf?"

"No. I never did. And neither should you." She leaned closer and kissed her on the forehead. "It's time to go to sleep. Do you want to take your processor off tonight?"

"No. Can I sleep with it? Tomorrow night I'll take it off."

It had taken a while to wean Melany of that habit after the first surgery. Returning to a world of profound deafness was a scary notion, and it still wasn't something that she embraced outside her familiar bedroom in Hong Kong.

"Sure. You can wear it. Are you having any pain?"

"A little."

"Let me get you something."

Isa rose from the bed and went to the kitchen. The acetaminophen was on the top shelf in the cabinet. She poured out the cherry-flavored dosage into the plastic cup, taking care to get it exactly to the line, but her phone rang, startling her, and she spilled.

"Damn it."

She cleaned up the mess with a paper towel and answered her cell with the other hand. "Hello?"

There was a pause on the line, followed by the

voice of an operator. "I have a collect call for Ms. Isabelle Bornelli from Y-three-seven-nine-eight-zero. Will you accept the call?"

Isa froze.

"Ma'am, will you take the call?"

Isa didn't answer. She couldn't speak. Her hand shook as she lowered the phone and pushed the button to end the call. She knew who it was; she recognized that inmate number. But it had been years since he'd tried to call her from prison.

Why? Why are you doing this to me?

22

Jack and Keith took the elevator down to the seventh floor, and Manny accepted the invitation to join them at Edge Steak & Bar. The restaurant was packed, "reservations only," but they found three open stools at the quieter end of the four-sided bar in the center of the cavernous room. Jack and Keith ordered a craft brew, Hop for Teacher, just because they liked the name and had never tried it. Manny went for a specialty cocktail of cigar-infused bourbon and told the bartender to send an "Original Cin"—cinnamon-infused vodka and a splash of cherry liqueur—with his compliments to the leggy Latina at the end of the bar. It was Keith's suggestion that they "talk shop" for a minute, and neither the lawyer to his left nor the one to his right objected.

"I'm not an attorney," he said, the usual preface from a layperson who was about to play one. "But with the exception of Melany's surgery, I have thought of pretty much nothing but Isa's case since we hit the airport."

The waiter set a basket of homemade potato

chips in front of them. They smelled irresistible and tasted even better. "Can we get another basket of these?" Manny asked the bartender. "Sorry, Keith. Go on."

"To me, the biggest problem I see is that Isa didn't report the assault to the authorities when it happened."

"That's not a problem," said Manny. "That's our advantage."

"Manny, we know your view," said Jack. "Let's hear what Keith has to say. Why do you think failure to report is the biggest problem?"

"Because the jury might see it as evidence that Isa intended to take matters into her own hands—that from the very beginning she had 'revenge killing' in mind."

Manny reached for another chip. "That's exactly why we have to make it as difficult as possible for the prosecutor to prove that she was actually raped."

"Let's put that aside for a minute," said Jack. "Keith, you know that Manny and I can't talk to you as if you were the client—because you're not. The fact that we're three guys sitting at a bar doesn't change that. But I'm guessing that you have something you want to say to us about this."

"I do," said Keith. "I want to make sure that Isa has told you everything she's told me about this."

"Do you have something specific in mind?" asked Jack.

"In a nutshell: that she called home and spoke to her father right after she was attacked; that her father blamed her for the rape by inviting a man to her dorm room on the first date; and that she was made to feel as though it would bring shame on her family if she reported the rape."

"We've heard all of that," said Manny.

"Good," said Keith. "Because you're kind of an expert in this field, aren't you, Manny?"

"What field?"

"The abuse defense," said Keith. "I did some research on some of your early cases."

Manny hadn't started out as a drug lawyer. His most famous case as a young public defender involved one of the first successful uses of the "battered spouse" defense in Florida, in which he earned an acquittal for a woman who killed her husband after suffering years of his abuse.

"That was many years ago," said Manny. "But even so, I don't see how that applies here. Isa and Gabriel Sosa had one date. There's no history of abuse."

"No history of abuse by Sosa," said Keith.

"Are you suggesting that Isa was abused by her father?" asked Jack.

Keith shifted one way and then the other, as though not entirely comfortable with Jack's articulation of what he was thinking. "I don't know. The only time I met the man is when he came to Jack's office and said Isa wasn't raped. All I can tell you is that Isa has absolutely no love for her father. I believe her when she says he berated her when she called home and told him about the assault. And then we have this latest statement in the detective's report. Isa's words: 'I just went along with it.'"

"How does that tie in with her father?" asked Manny.

Jack saw where Keith was headed, and picked up the line of thought. "It makes you wonder if her father's reaction on the telephone was the sign of long, dark history," said Jack. "To frame the issue: Was Isa's reaction to the sexual assault—'I thought it was best just to go along with it'—the mark of someone who was abused as a child?"

Manny shook his head. "You two are making this case so much more complicated than it needs to be."

"My only point is this," said Keith. "The impact of that phone call to her father was huge. It's more than enough to explain why she didn't report the rape."

"There are a million reasons why a woman wouldn't report a rape. She doesn't want to face her attacker in court. She doesn't want anyone to know. In our case, it happens to be extremely helpful to leave the jury wondering: did she not report the rape because it wasn't rape? Trust me on this. There's a time to play the abuse excuse, and a time not to. This is not that case."

"I wasn't suggesting we *play* anything," said Keith. "I just want to get the facts out."

"The facts are only those that the state attorney can prove," said Manny. "Right now, the fact is that Isa had no motive to revenge-kill. The prosecution can't prove she was raped."

"But she told an MDPD homicide detective that she was assaulted."

"That was two months after the fact, and we

haven't even seen that alleged report yet," said Manny. "If it does exist, we might still find a way around it."

"Why would we want to do that?"

"Because it's crazy for us to prove rape for the prosecution and hand them a motive. It's even crazier to shoot ourselves in the other foot by arguing that she was emotionally or physically abused by her father. The prosecutor will run with that information and tell the jury that she acted on years and years of pent-up anger when she orchestrated the murder of Gabriel Sosa."

"That's a risk," said Jack, throwing Manny a bone. "But we should be discussing those risks with our client, not Keith."

"Well, hold on a second," said Keith. "It's time to just stop beating around the bush. Manny, have you been in contact with Felipe Bornelli?"

"Huh?"

"Just answer the question," said Keith.

"No. I've never talked to him."

Keith took a long drink from his draft, and then set down the mug a little harder than necessary. "So you're telling me it's a fluke that Felipe told Jack that Isa wasn't raped and that he didn't approve of her choice of attorney, and then two days later, you're on the case pushing the theory that Isa wasn't raped. You're saying that's all just a coincidence?"

Manny shrugged, dismissing it. "There are coincidences, and there are coincidences."

"What the hell does that mean?" asked Keith.

"A lightning strike twice in the exact same spot

is a coincidence. A hiker attacked by a polar bear and grizzly bear on the same day—that's one hell of a coincidence. But two men looking at the same set of circumstances and coming to the same conclusion on how Isa can keep herself out of jail? I don't call that a coincidence. That's two people who thought things through independently and reached the right conclusion."

"Whoa," said Keith. "Are you suggesting that Felipe told Jack and me that there was no rape because he's trying to *help* his daughter?"

"I don't know what Felipe is doing or for what reason. I've never met the man. I'm on this case because Foneesha Johnson gave her cellmate my number, and Isa called me. I like Isa. I want to help her. I want to stay on this team. Jack and I don't agree on everything, but the final decision belongs to the client. Not to me. Not to Jack. And not to her husband. It's good for a client to have options. That's in your wife's best interest."

Manny climbed down from the bar, opened his wallet, put down a fifty-dollar bill. "I think that's enough shop talk for tonight. If Isa wants me off the case, that's her decision. But just so we're on the same page, I hope you read my engagement letter. I keep the hundred-thousand-dollar retainer you paid me. Good night, gentlemen."

Jack and Keith watched as Manny walked to the far end of the bar and checked on the woman sipping her complimentary Original Cin.

Keith reached for a chip. "He's a piece of work, isn't he?"

"I've tried cases with all kinds," said Jack, "and

it takes all kinds. There's no cookie cutter for a successful lawyer."

"I'm not going to keep him around just because I wrote him a check. That hundred grand is a sunk cost. If you think he should go, he goes."

Jack drained what was left of his draft. "So far I'd say he's been an asset. I can work with him, if that's Isa's decision."

"I get it that this is Isa's decision. But as her lawyer, and as my friend, you can't let tonight be the final word on how Manny and Isa's old man came to be of like mind on the sexual assault."

"Don't worry about that. Another talk with Felipe should clear things up."

"Good luck finding him. He still hasn't reached out to Isa. Since that meeting in your office, it's as if the guy has dropped off the planet."

"Have you been looking for him?"

"No, but he didn't exactly leave us with the impression that we'd heard the last from him. Then nothing."

Jack retrieved his cell and pulled up Theo's number. "If he's still in Miami, I know someone who can track him down."

23

Sylvia was sitting in front of the vanity mirror and applying her makeup when Swyteck called.

After two months of duds from an online dating service, she was less than an hour away from an actual second date. The trial against Isa Bornelli was turning into her most high-profile case in years, however, so she took the call. But she made it clear that a call at home on the weekend was not going to be standard operating procedure.

"This had better be important, Swyteck."

It was. Sylvia thanked him, promised nothing, and called the state attorney immediately.

"This had better be important, Sylvia."

It caught her off guard—the way the state attorney's greeting had echoed her own warning to Swyteck. Sylvia took a minute to update Benitez about the *Tribune*'s proposed article. The two prosecutors agreed that it was a mixed question of law and public relations, so Sylvia conferenced in the director of media relations, Alex Cruz.

"If the story is inaccurate, you need to correct it," said Cruz. "We're already losing the social-media battle in this case."

"Define losing," said the state attorney.

"Bloggers are really starting to chime in," said Cruz. "Uniformly, they are sympathetic to Bornelli. I've been sending you the links by e-mail."

The state attorney barely had time to read e-mails, let alone the links inside them. "Give me the gist, Alex."

"Naturally you have outliers—the extremists who not only applaud Bornelli for killing her attacker but hope that she castrated him, too. But there are also some serious discussions. The most credible one, with tons of hits and comments, simply asks, 'What responsibility does a rape victim bear for the murder of her rapist?' The general view seems to be 'some responsibility,' but almost every commenter agrees that first-degree murder with a sentence of life in prison without parole is a case of the prosecutor overcharging."

"That's because they don't know the facts," said Sylvia.

"Exactly," said the state attorney. "Which is exactly why we can't let the *Tribune* run a Sunday story that gets the facts dead wrong."

They agreed that Sylvia should make the phone call to Michael Posten. He'd covered many of her trials over the years, and she knew how to handle him. She hoped.

She dialed his cell, then startled herself with her own reflection. The left side of her face was ready for date night; the right looked like the bad "before" photo on a morning-show segment of extreme makeovers.

Posten was pleasant, and she got straight to the point.

"I had a phone conversation with Jack Swyteck," said Sylvia. "He tells me that you have a copy of a report prepared by the MDPD homicide detective who interviewed Isa Bornelli."

"So what if I do?"

"I shouldn't have to tell you that a homicide investigation is considered 'active' through trial until conviction. That report is not public information."

"Oh, so now you're threatening to put rape victims *and* journalists in jail? Making all kind of friends, aren't you, Sylvia?"

"This is not a threat. Right now I'm just trying to figure out how you got it so wrong if you actually have a copy of the record."

"All right, I'll be honest. I bluffed Swyteck. I don't exactly have the report. I've been told what's in it."

"By whom?"

"You know I can't tell you my source."

"Inside or outside the department?"

"Can't say."

"Fine," said Sylvia. "Swyteck sent me your headline. Whoever told you that Bornelli admitted to police that she 'just went along' with the murder of Gabriel Sosa is dead wrong."

"Can I see the MDPD record and draw my own conclusion?" asked Posten.

"It will be released to the defense on Monday along with the other evidence presented to the grand jury. The judge will decide what will be made public. If you intend to print your story before then, I want to be quoted on the record as follows: 'The alleged admission is a complete distortion of the MDPD investigation record and of the evidence that the state attorney presented to the grand jury.'"

"Ooo-kay," he said. "I'm not a *complete* idiot. But if you're taking that position, you have to give me something else. You just killed six paragraphs."

"I'm sure you'll think of something."

"Yeah, I have one thread I'm toying with."

"Tell me."

He chuckled. "Not so fast. Let's go about this a little differently. What evidence do you have that Isa Bornelli was actually raped?"

Sylvia paused, deciding how much she should give him. "She told it to an MDPD homicide detective. It's in the report you almost mischaracterized."

"The interview that happened more than a month after the alleged assault."

"Approximately. Yes."

"That's all you have?"

"I have no further comment on that."

"Well, maybe you'd like to comment on this: I've been told that Ms. Bornelli more than went along with the rape. That she wasn't raped."

The prosecutor froze. Still, she could sense the enjoyment on the other end of the line as her mind raced with the implications that story would have on her case. *No rape. No motive.*

"You still there?" asked Posten.

"Yes. Do you have a source on that?"

"Do I have a source?" he said, his chuckle dissolving into a serious tone. "I have *the* source."

24

"The grand jury materials are here from the state attorney," Jack's assistant told him. "I put them on your desk."

It was Monday morning. Bonnie was always the first one into the office, and she never looked like she had just rolled out of bed. Sometimes Jack wondered if roadrunners actually slept.

"Thanks, Bonnie. Call Manny and let him know."

"Already did. He has a morning hearing and will be here at eleven."

"Good. Call Isa and tell her to come then, too."

"Already did that, too."

Of course you did.

Jack went into his office. Following an indictment, court rules required the prosecution to share all evidence presented to a grand jury, and the evidence against Isa Bornelli was laid out across his desk. Bonnie had been with him so long that she knew how to organize things before he even reviewed them. On the far left was the indictment, followed by the transcript, and so on, all in neat and labeled piles. Jack switched on the lamp, settled into his desk chair, and started with the transcript, making notes on his pad as he worked through it.

"Knock, knock."

Jack looked up from his desk. It was Hannah Goldsmith, the head of the Freedom Institute—Neil's daughter and successor.

Hannah was a foot shorter than Jack, but what she lacked in stature she made up for in energy. Her mother had asked Jack to step in after Neil's death. "Hannah's too young," she'd pleaded, overlooking the fact that her daughter had already passed the age at which Neil had founded the Institute.

"Need any help with anything today, Jack? I'm kind of slow right now."

Jack smiled and shook his head. "Here's a concept: go to the beach."

She stepped into his office and pulled up a chair, sitting the way she always did—on the front edge and leaning forward slightly, like a schoolkid who knew the answer to every question and was primed to thrust her hand into the air.

"Eve, Brian, and I have been talking. The Institute would have gone under if Jack Swyteck, P.A., hadn't moved in as a subtenant. We can't possibly pay you back for all the repairs and improvements you and Andie have made around here. So we thought we could take turns working a few hours a week on your cases. Like contract attorneys, except you don't have to pay us."

Eve, the only woman Jack had known to smoke

a pipe, and Brian, who'd been wearing the same corduroy jacket since Reagan was president, had started at the Institute before Jack was in law school. Both were excellent lawyers who worked long hours for little pay.

"You don't have to do that," said Jack.

"We know. We want to. So whatcha workin' on? Bornelli?"

They'd talked about the case the way all lawyers do, mostly chitchat over lunch in the "conference room." Jack valued her opinion—Hannah didn't have her father's experience, but she definitely had his IQ.

"I'm about halfway through the grand jury transcript," said Jack. "As we suspected, the chief witness against Isa is her old boyfriend, David Kaval. He's serving time in FSP for armed robbery."

"How'd they connect him to the murder? No, let me guess: he shot his mouth off to a jailhouse snitch."

"Good guess, but no. DNA. Sosa was blindfolded when the police recovered his body. The best forensic lead was a drop of blood on the blindfold that didn't belong to Sosa. Fast forward a few years, Kaval is convicted of armed robbery. They ran his DNA through the CODIS database. Bang. They had a match."

Hannah was more than familiar with the FBI's Combined DNA Index System, which linked DNA from crime scenes to that of convicted felons and others in the database. CODIS was alphabet soup to most clients of the Freedom Institute, and usually—but not always—it spelled death by lethal injection.

"So Kaval cut a deal in exchange for testimony against Isa?"

"Yup," said Jack. "He gets ten years for his role in the kidnapping and murder of Gabriel Sosa, to be served concurrently—in effect retroactively—with his current sentence."

"In other words, he gets a free pass on the Sosa murder."

"That he does."

"Is he a credible witness?"

"Can't tell from the grand jury transcript. But we're in luck," he said as he reached for the DVD on his desk. "The state attorney's initial plan wasn't to take this case to a grand jury, so the prosecutor went to FSP and questioned him under oath before Isa's arrest warrant was issued. You want to watch with me?"

"Wow, what a coincidence!" she said, throwing up her hands. "It was next in my Netflix queue."

Bonnie knocked on the door frame and poked her head into the office. "Isa Bornelli is here early."

"Good thing I didn't pop the popcorn," said Hannah, rising.

"No, stay," said Jack. "I'd like your impression, if Isa has no objection."

"No objection to what?" asked Isa, as she entered the office.

Jack made the introductions, and Isa was fine with Hannah staying to view Kaval's video. Bonnie backed herself out of the office and quietly closed the door. Jack explained what was on his desk and then led her and Hannah to the sitting area. Hannah arranged the chairs to face the wall-mounted LCD. Jack cued up the DVD and took the chair between Hannah and his client as the first image appeared. It was just the name of the witness and the date of the examination—black letters and numbers on a white screen—but Jack suspected that it was enough to get his client's pulse racing.

"You okay?" he asked.

Isa nodded.

The name and date vanished, and David Kaval was suddenly staring straight at them.

Isa recoiled and looked away. "Oh, my God," she said, breathless.

"You sure you're okay with this?" asked Jack.

She didn't answer. Slowly, her gaze returned to the video.

Kaval was seated at a wooden table, filmed straight-on, his head and upper body centered on the screen. Orange is for death row at FSP, so he wore the standard-issue blue V-neck T-shirt. He was clearly no stranger to the prison weight room: he had the chest and biceps of a boxer, and his bulging forearms were covered in purple tattoos. Jack had interviewed many inmates at those same FSP tables, and the way Kaval dominated it, Jack estimated that he was over six feet tall. Beautiful women fall for bad boys all the time, but Isa Bornelli with David Kaval struck Jack as an extreme case.

"He looks so different," said Isa. "So hard."

"Prison can do that," said Jack.

"No," said Isa. "I romanticized him in college. I had it in my head that he was ruggedly handsome. He was just a thug."

Sylvia Hunt's voice interrupted—"*Please state your name*"—but the camera never left Kaval. Over the next few minutes, the prosecutor led the witness through his personal background, his criminal history, and his deal with the state attorney's office. Then she turned to his "relationship" with Isa Bornelli.

"*We dated off and on in college.*"

"*For how long?*"

"*A year or so. We met when she was a freshman at the University of Miami. I was in my fourth year at Miami Dade College.*"

"*You were a senior?*"

"*No. Like I said, it was my fourth year, but—no, I wasn't a senior.*"

"*You said your relationship was off and on. What was your status in March of Ms. Bornelli's sophomore year?*"

"*Off.*"

"*How 'off' was it?*"

"*We had a big argument on Valentine's Day. She said it was over.*"

"*Was it?*"

"*In her mind, maybe.*" He flashed a confident grin. "*I always knew she'd be back.*"

"What a creep," said Isa.

Jack paused the video. "If there's anything you

want to correct along the way, tell me, and I'll stop."

"I just don't want the two of you to think that I was in love with this man. Love had nothing do with us."

"Understood," said Jack. He hit PLAY, and the video resumed.

"Did you in fact see Ms. Bornelli again after that breakup?"

"Yeah. She called a few weeks later and asked me to stop by."

Isa grabbed the remote and hit PAUSE. "That's a lie. He must have tried me on my cell a hundred times. I never answered. Then one morning he just showed up outside my dorm. He stood there and waited 'til I came back from class."

Jack made a note of it on his legal pad. "Got it," he said, and the video continued.

"What did you do on that day?"

"Nothing special. We went for a walk. Got lunch. We just hung out together. But I could tell something was wrong with her. I asked if it was me—if she wanted me to leave. She said no, I definitely should stay. She said she just wanted me to be there for her. She needed someone she could count on."

"Did you have any idea what she meant by that?"

"Not at the time. But later on I did."

"What happened?"

"We went to dinner. Around eight o'clock I drove her back to her dorm and parked. We were sitting there in the dark, and for no reason she started crying. I asked her what was wrong, and that's when she told me."

"Ms. Bornelli told you what?"

"She said she went on a date. And I said, baby, no big deal. What's one date? Then she looked over at me and said, 'He raped me.'"

"What was your reaction?"

"I couldn't believe it. I'm like, how? Who did this to you?"

"Did she tell you?"

"Not at first. She said she didn't report it, so it didn't matter who did it. I said 'bullshit'—sorry. 'Isa, you gotta tell me who did this to you. You gotta tell me.'"

"Did she give his name?"

"'Give' probably isn't the right word. I kind of had to pull it out of her. She was bawling her eyes out. It was like, you know, she'd never talked to anyone about this. All kind of tears running down her face."

"What did you do?"

"I told her it was okay to cry. But she had to tell me his name. I switched on the locks so she couldn't open the door and said, 'Isa, we're not going anywhere 'til I get the name of that fucking coward who did this.'"

"What was Ms. Bornelli's response?"

"She was still crying. I took a minute to calm myself down and not sound so pissed off. Finally she seemed to get it under control. I asked if she was ready to tell me. She said, 'His name is Gabriel Sosa.'"

"What did you say?"

"I said, 'Good girl. You did the right thing. Thank you for telling me.'"

"Was there any further discussion?"

"You mean while we were in the car that night?"

"Yes, Mr. Kaval. While you were in the car."

"I asked her to tell me more about this guy Sosa."

"What did she say?"

"She was sniffling, not really looking at me. More like looking out the window. So I asked her again. 'Isa, is there anything else you want me to know?'"

"What was her response?"

"She shook her head. Then she said, 'I just wish he was dead.'"

"Those were Ms. Bornelli's exact words to you? 'I just wish he was dead'?"

"Yes. Those were her exact words."

Jack paused the video. Silence enveloped the room. He gave Isa a moment; they all needed one. Then he asked, "Did you tell him that?"

Isa lowered her eyes and brought a hand to her forehead. "I . . . I don't remember."

"Isa, please. Think hard. Is he lying? Or is he telling the truth? This is important."

"I don't—" she started to say, then stopped. "I could have."

"You could have said it?"

She nodded, tormented. She still wouldn't look at Jack, but he could see the agony on her face.

"I probably did."

"Probably?"

"I did, okay? *Yes.* I said it. That doesn't mean I *meant* it," she said, probably louder than intended. An awkward silence hung in the room. Isa gathered her purse and rose. "Excuse me. I'm not in a frame of mind to do this."

Jack rose. "Of course. We can pick this up when you're ready. I'll have Bonnie call you a taxi."

"No, I have an app. Thank you." She hurried from the room, too fast for Jack to see her out, her heels clicking on the old wooden floor.

Jack and Hannah looked at one another.

"We've all wished people dead," said Hannah.

"Maybe," said Jack, his gaze drifting back to the frozen thug on the screen. "But we don't say it to a guy like David Kaval."

25

Sylvia met her boss for breakfast at a coffee shop across the street from the University of Miami campus. The dining area was nearly empty; for the average college student, a weekend on South Beach had a way of pushing the Monday-morning breakfast rush until about lunchtime. They took a booth by the window where they could talk privately over their Nova lox and toasted bagels.

Numbers and statistics were not Sylvia's thing, but she'd seen data that pegged the total pending sex-trafficking cases in their office at about three hundred, which made the state attorney a perfect host for the annual forum on human trafficking sponsored by the university. Benitez was scheduled to be onstage at ten o'clock to welcome guests and present the first speaker, a twenty-year-old survivor who was nearly beaten to death by her pimp at the age of sixteen. Sylvia had led the prosecutorial team and convinced a judge to put him away for fifteen years.

"Got your speech all polished and ready to go?" asked Sylvia.

The state attorney put a draft of her prepared remarks aside. "Have you ever known me to stick to a script?"

That question needed no answer. Sylvia checked her foil pack of cream cheese for the calorie count and decided it wasn't worth it. Her boss had no such dilemma, spreading her pack and then Sylvia's on her bagel halves.

"Tell me what's going on with the Foneesha Johnson investigation," said Benitez.

"I just got an e-mail from the Miami field office this morning," said Sylvia. "The FBI report and recommendation is coming by the end of the week."

"Sounds like full speed ahead."

"More like hot potato. Someone at the Justice Department wants to stay as far away as possible from the Bornelli prosecution."

Benitez scraped the foil wrapper with her knife for the last bit of cream cheese. "Both the special agent in charge of the Miami field office and his ASAC will be at the trafficking forum today. I'll touch base. What's up with our friend Michael Posten at the *Tribune*?"

"I'm sure you saw Sunday's paper. Fortunately, he dropped the story that he was planning to write about Isa's statement to MDPD that she 'just went along with it.' He turned the piece into a more generic feature on the growing epidemic of sexual assault on college campuses."

"Yes, I saw. That's putting ink to good use."

"I'm afraid the improvement is temporary. I

checked back with him this morning. The story that he said was under consideration on Saturday night—that Isa was not sexually assaulted—is apparently still in the works."

The waitress came to the table and refilled their cups. Benitez waited for her to leave and then continued. "Anything more on who Posten's source could be for that story?"

"Nothing to add to what he told me on Saturday night. He not only has *a* source. He claims to have *the* source."

Benitez stirred a teaspoon of sugar into her coffee. "Let's cogitate on that. If a journalist claims to have *the* source, he has to be talking about someone with firsthand knowledge, right?"

"You would think. But Posten is always blowing smoke. That's the way he operates."

"Understood. But let's give him the benefit of the doubt for present purposes. Doesn't *the* source have to be someone who was there?"

"Well, that would be either Bornelli or Sosa. And Sosa is dead."

The state attorney gestured—a simple turn of her hand that invited Sylvia to continue with her line of reasoning.

Sylvia offered a skeptical half-chuckle. "Seriously? You think Bornelli is his source?"

"Why not?" asked Benitez. "No rape means there was no attacker. No attacker makes it much harder for us to prove Bornelli's motive to orchestrate the murder of Gabriel Sosa. I'm sure that those implications have occurred to you."

Indeed they had, ruining her date on Saturday night and keeping her wide awake well into Sunday morning. "Yes," she said. "That would be a problem."

"I have no doubt that this 'problem' has occurred to at least one of Ms. Bornelli's lawyers as well," said Benitez.

"Are you backtracking now? Swyteck or Espinosa is his source?"

She shrugged. "I suppose Posten could say that he has *the* source if the information is coming from Bornelli's lawyer. Or maybe her lawyer put her up to it and he's actually talking to Bornelli."

"I guess that's possible. But why wouldn't they save that tack for trial? Why tip their hand now by going to a newspaper?"

"Because the defense doesn't want this case to go to trial. Isa Bornelli moved to the other side of the world to avoid just that. Throwing us a curve about the sexual assault would make us wonder about the strength of our case. The more doubts we have, the more likely we are to offer a nice plea."

"Should we offer a deal?"

"Not yet," said Benitez. "Let's wait."

"'Til when?"

"I want to see what that FBI report says. I'll talk to the special agent in charge today and see if we can get a draft of the report before they release it."

"What are you hoping it shows?"

"I'm not hoping for anything," said the state attorney. "But if the conclusion is that Bornelli lied about a threatened sexual assault by a corrections officer, and if it turns out that she also lied to MDPD about being raped by Gabriel Sosa, then we have a whole different case on our hands."

"Yeah," said Sylvia, thinking it through. "That would be one . . . one very different case."

26

Jack arrived at Manny's office late Friday afternoon. Isa was already there, and she appeared much more composed than she had on Monday, when she'd rushed from the Institute. Manny had his own set of grand jury materials, but he was unpacking a different box—one that was marked "Handle with Care," and that bore a shipping label from Christie's Art Transport.

"Can you give me a hand here, Jack?"

Jack helped him sift through the packing straw, and then together they lifted out a two-foot-tall bronze sculpture and gently set it on Manny's desk.

It was an antique, which didn't work at all with the chrome-glass-and-leather décor of Manny's ultramodern office suite.

"*Bronco Buster*," said Manny. "The first of Frederic Remington's twenty-two cowboy-themed bronzes, and the most sought after. And this one is no reproduction. See the foundry mark?" he asked, indicating the Henry-Bonnard Bronze Company in New York City. "This is nineteenth century—one of the early ones done in the sand-casting method. When the price of oil goes down, buy Remingtons. Every CEO in Houston is unloading. It's like, like—"

"Like the way Venezuelan voters unloaded the Chavistas?" suggested Isa.

Most historians linked the falling price of oil to the decline of Chavez's party after his death, but Jack interpreted Isa's remark less as a political statement and more as a personal shot at her father.

"I suppose," said Manny. "Anyway, I did the same thing the last time the bottom fell out of the petroleum market. Buy low and hold it 'til the price of oil rebounds and the rednecks want their art back—then, *bam!* Manuel 'Bubba' Espinosa makes a killing."

"Sounds like a plan," said Jack. "What do you say we talk about ours?"

"Ready when you are," said Manny, as he gathered the stray pieces of packing straw from his silk rug.

"I've already watched the rest of Kaval's testimony, but it can't hurt to see it again," said Jack. "We can pick up where I left off with Isa."

"No need," said Manny. "We watched the whole thing before you got here."

Jack was taken aback. "You should have called me."

"Sorry. You covered the first part without me, so Isa and I watched the second part. We're a team, right? Teams divide labor."

For some reason the idea of Manny alone with Isa made Jack feel like something less than "co"-counsel. "Right," said Jack. "So let's talk about it."

Part two of Kaval's testimony tracked the allegations of the indictment, some of which Isa had already confirmed were true: she and Kaval went to a club on South Beach where Gabriel frequently hung out; Isa pointed out Gabriel to Kaval and his friend; the three of them, including Isa, followed Gabriel in Kaval's van; and Kaval bumped the back of Gabriel's car to make him stop and check for damage, while Kaval and his friend got out to confront him.

At that point, the stories diverged.

"You told us that you ran back to your dorm," said Jack.

"Right," said Isa.

"Kaval says you were still there when he and his buddy overpowered Gabriel and threw him in the back of the van. That you rode with them to the automotive shop."

"Yes, that's what he says."

"He's lying?" asked Jack.

She glanced at Manny. "This was something we discussed before you got here."

"And?"

Manny interjected. "She definitely did not go back to the automotive shop."

"I see," said Jack, grasping the issue. "The question is: When did you turn and run back to the dorm—before or after Kaval and his buddy grabbed Sosa and threw him in the back of the van?"

"Precisely," said Manny.

Jack was watching his client. "What's the answer, Isa?"

"I honestly didn't remember seeing them put

him in the van," she said quietly. "But the way David described things, it felt familiar. Listening to him, it seemed like I could have been there."

"You saw them shove Sosa into the van. Is that what you're saying now?"

"Well, you don't have to say '*now*.' I'm not changing my story. Just remembering things more clearly. Coming to terms with what happened to me is a process."

"And she isn't a hundred percent certain that she did see it," said Manny. "She's flagging this for us as one of those fuzzy gray areas in her memory. You've seen this as often as I have, Jack. When a witness for the prosecution insists that you were there, or that you said such and such, it's natural to question your own memory. You start to say to yourself, Wow, maybe I was there. Maybe I did say that."

Jack had seen that happen, and it was natural. It just wasn't easy for a lawyer to know when a client was experiencing that phenomenon and when they were simply making things up.

Isa spoke up. "It's also important to stress the fact that I never, ever thought they were going to hurt Gabriel. Like I said before, I thought David might scare him. Rough him up, maybe. Not—definitely not—do the things they did to him."

"I have a couple of reactions," said Jack. "One, it's easy to see how Kaval's testimony was enough to convince the grand jury to indict you. We have to assume, however, that the prosecutor held back. No prosecutor presents *all* her evidence to the grand jury. Sylvia Hunt is saving something for trial. So, Isa, if certain things trigger more memories for you, it's important that those trigger events happen before trial. We can't be surprised by a sudden recollection in front of a jury. Do you understand?"

She nodded.

"Second point," said Jack. "Whether you ran before or after they put Sosa in the van is a game changer. You're edging dangerously close to being part of a kidnapping. At the very least, you'll lose sympathy from the jury if they hear an admission that you saw them throw Sosa in the van and didn't call the police. These are all things we will have to consider if and when we have to decide if you testify on your own behalf."

"Isa and I were talking about that right before you got here," said Manny.

"At the risk of sounding prickly, that's a matter that 'the team' needs to discuss jointly."

"Easy, Jack. No decisions were made without you. But we are being more open-minded now."

"What does that mean?" asked Jack.

Manny glanced at Isa, as if cueing her to speak. "If I can't testify—or if I choose not to testify—then maybe the point Manny has been making is right," she said, avoiding eye contact with Jack. "Maybe we shouldn't be too quick to concede that, you know, I was assaulted."

"I'm afraid that ship has sailed," said Jack. "Kaval will testify that you told him you were raped. That's not hearsay—it's your own admission. It will come into evidence."

"Kaval is not credible," said Manny. "He's a scumbag thug and a convicted felon. We can destroy him on the witness stand."

"There's also the MDPD homicide detective who wrote Isa's own words into the report: 'I just went along with it.'"

"I have some ideas on how to deal with that," said Manny.

"Whoa," said Jack. "This is a sea change. Isa, are you really on board with this?"

"I don't know. Manny thinks I should consider it."

"My concern is that while you're considering it, circumstances are going to turn it into a done deal."

"I don't understand," said Isa.

Jack looked at Manny. "Could this have anything to do with the phone call I got at lunch today from Michael Posten at the *Tribune*? He's considering a story that Isa wasn't sexually assaulted, and he claims to have a solid source."

"Well, the source isn't me," said Manny. "I'm still honoring the agreement I made with the state attorney when she agreed to let Isa out on bail, which is not to talk to the media until the investigation at the detention center is over. And you should be doing the same, Jack."

Jack's internal reaction was, *Fuck you, Manny.* But he held his tongue in front of the client.

"Then who is it?"

"You're asking the question as if I know the answer," said Manny, "and I don't appreciate that."

"Could it be my father?" asked Isa.

"I don't know, Isa. Could it be?" Jack's tone wasn't threatening, but it was firm.

"It could be anyone," said Manny. "Or Posten could be up to his usual tricks, and it could be *no one*."

"No, it's someone," said Jack. "I'd bet my bar license that it's *someone*."

27

The wind chimes stirred outside Jack's office window. Miami relished a late spring breeze, as the march toward summer meant not just heat and humidity but heavy air and flat seas. Jack had noticed the chop in the bay on his morning drive from Key Biscayne, and the windsurfers and kiteboarders were eating it up. As teenagers he and Keith had missed more than few days of school on windy days. By lunchtime, he could no longer suppress the impulse. He dialed Keith's cell.

"Hey, dude. I know you can see the bay from your office. This is no teaser breeze. It's honking out there."

Keith chuckled. "'Honking.' Now there's some lingo I haven't heard since the Miami Dolphins didn't suck."

"Let's go."

"You serious?"

"It's after midnight in Hong Kong. Don't pretend you're busy. We can rent wet suits and boards right on the beach."

"Do you know how long it's been since I've windsurfed?"

"It's like riding a bicycle. You think you never forget, but at least you fall in the water instead of on the fucking pavement."

"All right, Swyteck. You're on."

"I'll pick you up outside your building in fifteen minutes."

By one o'clock they were on the water. They weren't the studs they once were, but by one thirty they were cutting each other off and stealing the other guy's wind—"gassing" was what surfers called it. Jack still considered himself a runner, and those long jogs with Max on a leash were paying off. Keith's legs gave out first. A whitecap took him out, and he was straddling his board, resting. Jack paddled alongside him.

"Happy we came out?"

"Yeah," said Keith. Then his smile flattened. Jack noticed that his gaze had drifted toward the shoreline—toward the Four Seasons high-rise, in particular.

"You thinking about Isa?"

"Melany, actually. It just feels so amazing to be out here again. It made me think, wow, I want to teach Melany to do this. And I will. I definitely will. But, typical me, I started overanalyzing the practicalities and realized, oh, of course we'll have to take off her audio processors. And then I started to notice—really notice—all the things she won't hear when she's out here. Puffs of wind. Waves splashing. The hiss of the board when you're dialed in and carving through butter. That plunge into the bay when the chop wins. Melany will never hear any of that."

"Sorry, man."

"Don't be. Just be thankful. Be thankful for what you've got."

That probably wasn't the mantra back at the IBS headquarters in Zurich or its Hong Kong office, and Jack was glad he'd taken Keith out for a glimpse of their old friendship. They drifted for a while longer, the Florida sun baking their wet suits dry. They were soon in flatter, shallow water, practically in the shadows of the office towers and condominiums that ran the length of the coastline from downtown Miami to the southern tip of the Brickell area.

"We drift any farther and we'll be looking at the walk of shame," said Keith.

The "walk of shame" is when a boarder is unable to surf back to his launch spot and must beach himself, walk back while carrying his gear—and that's the guy who buys the beer that night.

"I won't tell anyone if you don't," said Jack.

Keith smiled and then turned serious. "Can I talk shop for one minute?"

"No," said Jack. He was lying back on his board, enjoying the sun on his face.

"Come on. Seriously. This is important."

Jack sat up. "One minute."

"Isa tells me that Manny is getting on your nerves."

"Really? We're out here floating in paradise, and you want to talk about Manny?"

"This isn't about Manny. It's about my wife."

"Let me ask you a question," said Jack. "Does Isa go home and tell you everything she and her lawyers talk about?"

"No. At best I get the high-altitude overview from thirty-six thousand feet. But we do talk generally about how everybody is getting along."

"Look, Keith. You can't put two lawyers in a room without somebody getting annoyed. Manny has his own style."

"You're sure it's just a matter of style?"

"Yes. I told you before that I could work with him."

Keith watched a pair of windsurfers pass, two college guys carving the way the younger and less burdened Jack and Keith used to. Then he looked back at Jack. "I just want to make sure you're in this 'til the end."

"What would make you think I'm not?"

"Isa came home from the meeting in Manny's office and was on edge all night. I asked her what was wrong. It took a while to drill down on it, but basically she's afraid you might not stick around."

"I don't understand why she would say that."

"She's pretty intuitive, Jack. And she is a pretty advanced student of psychology. I just want you to know that Isa sees you as lead counsel in this arrangement. Manny is second chair."

"I have no problem being cocounsel."

"No, I want you to understand. It would be absolutely devastating to Isa if you were to decide that you couldn't be on this team anymore."

"Why would I decide that?"

"I'm talking hypothetically. For whatever reason

there is. Whatever might come up in the future. Before you walk away from Isa—from Isa, Melany, and me—think about what I'm saying."

"Keith, you're being way too dramatic. I'm not walking away from anybody. I won't leave unless Isa tells me to leave."

"You promise?"

It seemed like an odd request—more unnecessary drama—but it was clearly important to Keith, so Jack went along. "Yeah. I make that promise."

"So I don't need to call in the favor?"

Keith was smiling, but Jack sensed that he wasn't entirely kidding, and he knew exactly what "favor" Keith was talking about. "Whoa. You said you would never do that."

Keith looked off to the shoreline, as if following the ocean breeze through a stand of spindly coconut palms on the beach. "I never thought I'd be married to a woman indicted for murder," he said.

28

Sylvia walked quickly from the courthouse to the Graham Building. Her morning hearing had run into mid-afternoon, and she was eager to return the call she'd missed from the warden's office at Florida State Prison. It was about their star witness in the Bornelli case. Of course she feared the worst.

Please don't tell me Kaval is dead.

The elevator let her off on the seventh floor. She went straight to her office and got through to the warden himself. It was a short conversation. Kaval was still very much alive, but the news was important enough for Sylvia to head straight to the state attorney's office and share it immediately.

"Our boy David Kaval tried to call Bornelli on her cell phone. Collect, of course."

Sylvia was standing in the doorway, and the state attorney invited her in with a wave of her hand.

"When?" asked Benitez.

"Saturday night," said Sylvia, as she settled into

the armchair. "I'm told Bornelli did not accept the charges, so they didn't speak."

The state attorney leaned back in her desk chair, puzzling. "How is it that Kaval was even allowed to place the call in the first place? FSP has very strict rules on collect calls to cell phones. I should know. I was part of the panel that reviewed them. Inmates can't just place collect calls to the pope or their drug dealer or whoever else they feel like calling. They have to submit a list of cell numbers to the warden, and they can only make collect calls to preapproved numbers."

"I raised that with the warden. But guess what? Isa Bornelli's cell number is on Kaval's preapproved collect-call list."

"That is very interesting. What do her lawyers have to say about that?"

"I haven't heard from them. I just heard this myself ten minutes ago."

"So, wait a minute. Kaval placed the call two days ago, and her lawyers have said nothing to you?"

"Nope. My cynical side tells me that they put her number on the approved list and wanted him to reach out to her. He might say something they can use. They're probably coaching her right now on how to take the sting out of his testimony—maybe even turn him into a witness for the defense."

The state attorney considered it. "I don't think that's what the silence is about. If her lawyers were behind this, she would have accepted Kaval's call. She didn't."

“That’s true,” said Sylvia.

The state attorney rose, thinking as she walked slowly across her office to the window. She was looking out toward the river, her back to Sylvia as she spoke. “I’m more inclined to think that the reason we haven’t heard from Swyteck or Espinosa is because Ms. Bornelli hasn’t told them about Kaval’s collect call.”

“Why would she keep that information from her lawyers?”

“For the same reason she wouldn’t tell her lawyers that her cell phone was on Kaval’s preapproved call list.”

“Okay. But, again, why not tell them?”

She turned and faced Sylvia. “Now there’s a question I would love to have answered.”

“Do you want me to confront Kaval about this?”

“No. We need to be much more clever than that.”

“Clever in what way?”

“The fact that Bornelli is on the preapproved list tells me that our star witness was lying through his teeth when he told you that he’s had no contact with Ms. Bornelli since she left the U.”

“That would appear to be the case,” said Sylvia.

“So here’s what we’re going to do. I want you to call the warden back and tell him to do nothing.”

“Nothing?”

“Nada. He is to leave Bornelli’s number on the preapproved list. If Kaval wants to try her number again collect, FSP should allow it. Next time Bornelli might accept the charges. She might say something we can use against her. All calls are monitored, so we don't even need a warrant."

"Isn't that kind of risky? Kaval might also say something stupid and kill our case."

"He might. But let me ask you this: Based on what we have right now, how sure are you that you can prove Bornelli's guilt beyond a reasonable doubt?"

"I feel confident."

"Sylvia, all it will take to lose this case is one juror—probably one woman juror—to decide that the victim of sexual assault should never be charged with the murder of her attacker. You understand that, right?"

"I understand."

"There will be groups of protesters outside the courthouse for the duration of this trial. Those jurors will walk past their signs and slogans every day on their way to and from the courthouse. You realize that?"

"Yes."

"And here we have a shot at getting an admission straight from Bornelli's mouth that she planned, directed, and participated in this murder. Agreed?"

"That could happen."

"I say we take that shot. I say we let FSP monitor those calls the way they monitor every call from an inmate, and we get to the bottom of this. What do you say, Sylvia?"

It had been years since the state attorney had tried a case in a courtroom, but any one of her lawyers would attest that her cross-examination skills were as sharp as ever.

"Okay," said Sylvia. "Let's do it."

29

Jack waited until well after dark. Then he took a ride with Theo into the paint-and-body-shop district south of the University of Miami.

More than a decade had passed since the murder of Gabriel Sosa, but the garage where Kaval and his friend had taken him was still in business, two commercial blocks west of the elevated Metrorail station, in the crowded warehouse and auto-repair zone. This wasn't an official visit to the crime scene. Jack just wanted a rough impression of what it might have been like on that night. Might there have been a security guard at another garage who'd seen something? Could someone on the nearby Metrorail platform have heard Gabriel screaming? Would a jury believe Isa's old boyfriend when he looked them in the eye and said Isa had indeed come to this place?

"There it is," said Theo. He stopped the car and killed the engine.

They were at the end of a blind alley, this neighborhood's version of a cul-de-sac. All of the businesses in the area had closed for the night, their windows and doors protected by iron bars or roll-down shutters. Not another vehicle was on the street, but about a dozen cars were parked on the other side of a twelve-foot chain-link fence. For any would-be thieves looking for easy pickins, a coil of razor wire stretched across the top like a man-eating Slinky.

"Let's check it out," said Jack, as he opened the passenger door.

"You're getting out here, white boy?"

"No, *we're* getting out," said Jack.

They weren't far from Theo's old neighborhood, where the Knight brothers and Grove Lords had once ruled. On the other side of busy U.S. 1 was the intersection of Grand Avenue and Douglas Road, the heart of the old Grove ghetto. Theo had shared the history with Jack. It was there, outside the run-down bars and package stores, that a fifteen-year-old Theo had come across a crowd that had gathered in the street around the body of a woman that someone had discarded like so much worthless trash. His Uncle Cy had struggled to keep him back, but Theo was drawn in, as if he needed to see with his own eyes what drug addiction and a string of violent men had finally done to his mother.

Jack shut the door, and one step toward the garage was all it took to send a vicious Doberman charging toward him. Jack's heart leapt to his throat, but thankfully the guard dog was on the other side of the chain-link fence, growling and baring its teeth between barks.

"If they brought Sosa here to scare him, they chose the right place," said Jack.

They stopped and stood on the cracked asphalt, and Jack allowed himself a few quiet minutes to get a feel for the place and take an imaginary journey back to that night.

"So where was your friend Keith when all this happened?" asked Theo.

"Zurich. He'd left New York and was just getting started with IBS."

"Funny," said Theo. "People say they don't get how you and me is friends. I don't get you and Mr. Swedish banker."

"Swiss. Meatballs are Swedish."

"No, meatballs are Italian. Porn is Swedish."

Jack looked at his friend and blinked twice. "I feel like we've had this conversation before."

"Côte d'Ivoire. Two thousand eight. When you found that doctor without borders to fix your love life and thought you could follow her anywhere."

"You make it sound so pathetic."

"It was pathetic."

Jack blinked again. "Exactly what are we talking about?"

"Sorry. You and your rich friend."

"Be glad he's rich."

"Why should I give a shit?"

Jack had never told Theo the story, but it was probably about time he did, particularly in light of Keith's mention of "the favor" while out on the bay. "Do you have any idea how much it cost to conduct a DNA test when I worked at the Freedom Institute?" asked Jack.

"Never really thought about it," said Theo.

"Think six figures," said Jack. "Ever wonder who paid for the test that got you off death row?"

"Uh-uh," said Theo.

Jack had believed in Theo's innocence, but the Freedom Institute barely generated enough revenue to keep the lights on. The Innocence Project and others who fought for funding of DNA tests were just getting traction. In what Jack had thought was a long shot, he'd turned to his one friend who was making big bucks before his thirtieth birthday.

"Let me just say this," said Jack. "You owe Keith as much as I do. Probably more."

He seemed to take Jack's point. "Huh. That's cool."

"Yeah. Keith's a pretty cool guy."

Theo glanced at the barricaded entrance to the garage. "What does he think of all this?"

"That's a complicated question," said Jack.

"That's such a lawyer's answer. You know what I think?"

"No, but I'm pretty sure you're going to tell me."

"I think no matter how this turns out, Keith is gonna be left wonderin' what the hell kinda people his wife hung out with in college."

"Maybe."

"And he's gonna be wonderin' if she ever tells the truth."

"People work through these things."

"Do they?"

"Yeah. Not always. But sometimes."

The Doberman growled. He was looking at

Jack as if he were a steak dinner. Or a Swedish meatball.

"Are you making any progress on tracking down Isa's old man?" asked Jack.

"No. I've gone through almost the whole list of hotels you gave me. I've smooth-talked enough reservationists to get myself half a dozen free hotel nights. No Felipe Bornelli at any of them. He could have gone back to Venezuela."

"I don't think so," said Jack.

"Why not?"

Jack told him about the story Mike Posten had on hold at the *Tribune*. "I've heard two people say they have proof that Isa wasn't raped. Posten is one. The other is Felipe Bornelli."

"You think Felipe is his source?"

"He's the first person Isa talked to after it happened. I don't see who else Posten would consider credible, apart from someone who was there, and Sosa is dead."

"Well, what if there was more than two people there?"

"It happened in Isa's dorm room. There were no witnesses."

"I didn't say *a witness.*"

"You mean two attackers?"

"I mean three adults. One's dead. One's alive and says Sosa raped her. The third's alive, too, but is telling the *Tribune* a totally different story."

Jack paused. "I actually hadn't thought of that."

"That's because you were a married old fart before you were a married old fart."

"But why would this unnamed third person

suddenly talk to a reporter after being silent all these years?"

"I dunno. Stranger things have happened in Miami."

"Yeah," said Jack, his gaze drifting back toward the garage. "Much stranger."

30

It was after midnight in downtown Miami, and the gentle breeze from the bay was still warm enough for Isa to sit comfortably on the terrace. She was dressed for bed and covered in her bathrobe, her face aglow in the light of her tablet's LCD. The opening of the sliding glass door startled her. Keith was just getting home from the office.

"Why are you still up?" he asked as he leaned over and gave her a kiss.

"Not sleepy," said Isa.

He took a seat in the patio chair beside her. "Wish I could say the same. I have another conference call with the Hong Kong office in fifteen minutes. They think it's lunchtime."

"I'm sorry. This time difference must be brutal."

"It is what it is," he said, and then he reached over and took her hand. "But I am going to have to fly back this weekend."

"Oh," she said. "For how long?"

"At least a week. Maybe ten days if I stop in Zurich on the way back."

"I thought IBS told you to take all the time you need."

"And they meant it, too—as long as my needs don't interfere with my work."

He was smiling, but Isa knew it wasn't a joke. Travel had always been part of Keith's job, and he didn't have to tell her that living in Miami would only make it worse. Isa understood. She just didn't like knowing that he would be on the other side of the world, and that, no matter what happened, she couldn't leave this place. "Melany and I will be fine," she said.

"I know you will."

Isa glanced at her tablet. "I was on the Internet looking at schools. Jack says it's almost certain that we'll still be here when Melany starts kindergarten in the fall."

"He told me the same thing."

"I want to be sure she goes someplace where they will make every effort to mainstream her."

"Did you find anything?"

"A couple of them look promising. I thought I'd make some calls tomorrow and set up interviews."

"Sounds like a plan."

Isa waited for him to say something more, but he didn't. "Don't you want to know which schools?" she asked.

No response. He was checking an e-mail.

"Keith?"

"Huh?"

He was in serious work mode, and she didn't fault him for that. "It's okay. Never mind."

Keith rose and gave her another kiss. "Sorry, I have to dial in for my conference call."

"You go ahead."

He left, and the sliding door closed behind her. Isa laid her tablet aside, walked to the rail, and looked up at the sky. Somewhere between the Four Seasons and a billion stars a jet passed in silence. She wondered where it was coming from. It was hard to believe that just one week earlier they'd landed in Miami. Harder still to believe how everything had changed since then.

Isa's gaze dropped from the sky to the horizon, and she held it there. *Look up or out* was her rule, never straight down. It wasn't tied to a phobia. She'd read case studies of people who avoided balconies or climbing on roofs because they felt an inexplicable urge to jump. "High-place phenomenon" was the not very inventive label that psychiatrists put on it. For those people, the urge to jump had nothing to do with a death wish. It was simply their flight instinct kicking in to tell them why they felt scared. Isa's rule--never look down—was born of something else entirely. Once in her life, she'd climbed up on a railing ten stories up. She'd looked down and even selected a landing spot. It wasn't a psychological disorder or compulsion; she'd felt that jumping was her only choice. It was before Melany. Before Keith. When she was single. After she'd decided never to go back to Venezuela and that she'd never return to the States.

It was right after David Kaval found out that

she was leaving the University of Miami and moving to Zurich.

"Are you scared, Isa?"

She was, and David knew it, but that wasn't the point. He wanted to hear her say it.

"Yes," she said, but it was barely audible. She was flat on her stomach, and the weight of David's body on top of her made it difficult to breathe, let alone talk.

He grabbed her by the ponytail, jerking her head up from the floor. Tears clouded her vision, but it was too dark to see anyway.

"Do you know the most dangerous place, Isa?"

She was afraid to give the wrong answer, but she didn't really understand the question. "What?"

He pulled her hair harder, until her chin was almost pointing to the night sky. "The most dangerous place," he said, hissing. "Do you know where it is?"

"No," she said, her voice shaking.

"Then I'll tell you," he said. "And I'm not making this up. This is FBI statistics. The most dangerous place for a woman to be. Guess where it is."

"I can't."

She felt his hand slide around from the back of her neck to her throat. "*Guess*, damn it!"

"I don't know. A parking garage?"

He squeezed her throat, then released. "No. Guess again."

"A subway station?"

"*No!* You are so fucking stupid, Isa."

She didn't answer. She felt his breath on the

back of her neck as he leaned closer. "The most dangerous place a woman can be," he said in a low, threatening voice, "is in a relationship. With a man."

Isa felt chills, but she said nothing.

Kaval's grip on her throat tightened. "Do you believe that?"

He released the tension on her ponytail for an instant—just long enough for her to nod once.

"Yeah, you better," he said in that same even, threatening voice. "Because wherever you go, no matter how far away. No matter where I end up, or how much time passes. You and me will always be in a relationship. Don't you ever forget that."

Isa froze, unable to speak.

"Did you hear me?"

She nodded again.

"Then say it, you fucking bitch."

Isa swallowed her fear and answered in a voice that cracked. "I will never forget."

Summer

31

Jack parked his rental car and stepped into a meteorological wet blanket of relentless heat. It was a typical July afternoon in central Florida: 97 degrees and 97 percent humidity.

Random sprinkles brought no relief, the raindrops vaporizing instantly on the sun-baked asphalt. Jack had a short walk to the prison entrance, but even with his suit jacket draped over his arm, a "V" of sweat soaked the back of his dress shirt. A guard opened the door, and Jack thanked him for the cool wave of air-conditioning.

Never had a man been so happy to enter Florida State Prison.

Jack checked in at visitor reception. He was alone, having made this trip without Manny or his client. A corrections officer was seated on the other side of the three-quarter-inch glass. "I'm here for the deposition of David Kaval," Jack said.

Kaval was one of over a thousand inmates at FSP who weren't on death row. Still, eight years in the general prison population was no picnic. More

Florida inmates died by their own hand than by lethal injection.

The guard led Jack through a set of secure doors to the attorney visitation room. Visits with attorneys and clerics were among the limited exceptions to the no-contact visitation rule, but the prisoner had not yet arrived. There was a rectangular table in the center of the windowless room. A stenographer was set up with her machine, seated beside the empty chair for the witness. Sylvia Hunt rose from the government's side of the table, and the lawyers shook hands.

"Kaval is meeting with his attorney," said the prosecutor.

A witness has a right to be represented by counsel, and the sweetheart deal that Kaval had cut in exchange for his testimony against Isa was solid evidence that Kaval's lawyer was no slouch. Maddie Vargas was a pit bull who had parlayed years of experience at the public defender's office into a successful private practice. Kaval was typical of her clientele: men facing or serving long prison sentences for violent crimes who nevertheless managed to tap into mysterious sources of funds to pay private attorneys their handsome fees.

The metal door on the opposite side of the room opened. A corrections officer entered first, followed by the shackled prisoner in the company of another guard. Kaval was an imposing figure, even in his prison jumpsuit—Jack's height, but built like Theo. Maddy Vargas entered last, a middle-aged woman who wore too much makeup and not just one but two heavy gold bracelets on each wrist. Her auburn-colored hair was cropped a little too severely, not much longer than her client's prison cut.

"Nice to meet you," Jack said.

The chains rattled as Kaval took his seat at the end of the table, nearest to the stenographer. Vargas sat to his right. The guards assumed their posts on opposite sides of the room, one at the door to the cellblock, two at the door to freedom. The stenographer swore the witness. Jack was ready to begin. A deposition, however, was not a musical, and while the "very beginning" might be "a very good place to start" for Julie Andrews and the Trapp Family Singers, Jack liked to mix things up and catch his witness off guard. He started at anywhere but the beginning.

"Mr. Kaval, when was the last time you had any communication with Isabelle Bornelli?"

"Uh, what do you mean by communication?"

"Talk. Write. Text. E-mail. Sign language. Smoke signals. Any form of communication ever known to the human race. I think that about covers it."

"I object," said Vargas. "Your question assumes that Mr. Kaval knows Ms. Bornelli."

Jack rolled his eyes. There was no judge to rule on objections, which was normal in any deposition. Vargas was merely making a record. But some records were not worth making.

"Mr. Kaval is the chief witness for the prosecution against my client," said Jack. "I'm perfectly willing to accept that he has never met Ms. Bornelli, has no idea who she is, and has no firsthand knowledge of anything he testified about before the grand jury. Is that your point, counselor?"

The prosecutor intervened. "I think Ms. Vargas would like to withdraw her objection."

"Withdrawn," she said.

Jack continued. "You can answer, sir."

Kaval drew a breath, thinking. "Last time we communicated . . ."

"That is the question," said Jack.

"Does that include blow jobs?"

His lawyer leaned forward. "Just answer the question, David. The transcript does not reflect jokes."

"Especially tasteless ones," said Jack.

Kaval folded his arms across his chest. "Honestly, I don't remember."

"Let's break it down. Have you had any kind of communication with Isa Bornelli since you were incarcerated?"

"Yeah, sure."

Jack tried not to show his surprise, even if it was the first time he'd heard it. "How many times?"

"I don't know. Twice maybe. I wrote her a couple of letters. One was when I first got here. Another one maybe six months later."

"Why did you write her?"

"I asked her for money. She got herself a rich old man. She could afford it."

"Did she owe you money?" asked Jack.

"Why don't you ask her?"

"I'm asking you, Mr. Kaval."

"I'd say she owed it, yeah."

"Why did she owe you?"

He leaned closer, his eyes narrowing, as if he resented the question. "I was good to her, that's why. Better than she deserved. Least she could do is help me out when I'm in trouble."

"How much did you ask for?"

"I don't think I put a dollar figure on it, or a euro figure—whatever the fuck money she had in the bank."

"Try not to curse," said his lawyer.

"Sorry," said Kaval. "I asked her to send what she could afford."

Jack made a note to himself—*extortion*—and continued. "Did Ms. Bornelli answer your letters?"

"No."

"Did she send you any money?"

"No."

"So these two letters were one-way communications," said Jack. "You reached out to her, but you got no response."

"I guess that's right."

"Did you have any other communications like those? Let's call them attempted communications."

"No."

"Well, let me speak up here," said the prosecutor, "because I have no interest in getting into arguments at trial about the completeness of the answers that Mr. Swyteck received in this deposition. The collect telephone call that Mr. Kaval placed to Ms. Bornelli clearly was an 'attempted communication.'"

Jack froze. He knew nothing about a collect phone call, but it was hardly a tactical advantage to let the prosecutor know that his client had neglected to tell him about it. "Let's make the full record anyway," said Jack, bluffing through it. "Tell me about that collect call, Mr. Kaval."

He did. Jack listened, jotted down a couple notes, and then continued as if he'd heard nothing new. "Why did you try to call Ms. Bornelli?"

"I wanted her to talk dirty to me."

His lawyer groaned. "I told you, David—no jokes."

"I'm not joking. Isa can talk like a fucking street whore. And she would have, if I told her to. That's why she didn't accept the charges."

"I'm sure that's the reason," said Jack.

He smirked at Jack. "You don't know her very well, do you?"

"Mr. Kaval, I ask the questions here," said Jack. "That's the way this works."

"Ask away."

"I've represented many clients in FSP. Most of them on death row."

"Guess they should have hired a better lawyer."

Kaval's lawyer snorted, then apologized. "Sorry. That one was kind of funny."

"My point is this," said Jack. "Inmates can't just haul off and place collect calls to anyone. There's an approved list of people they can call. Was Isa Bornelli on your approved list?"

"Yeah."

Jack was getting deep into unknown territory, but a deposition was the place to ask the open-ended "why," "how," and "what" questions that a lawyer would never ask on cross-examination at trial. "How did she get on your list?"

"I put her there."

"I understand. But the list needs the warden's approval, and he wouldn't grant it simply because Isa was your old girlfriend. What exactly did you do to get her approved?"

He glanced uneasily at his attorney, and Vargas spoke for him. "Mr. Kaval will decline to answer any questions about how Ms. Bornelli got on his approved call list."

"On what basis?" asked Jack.

Vargas leaned closer to her client and whispered into his ear. Kaval looked at Jack and said, "On counsel's advice, I invoke my right under the Fifth Amendment not to answer, on the grounds I may incriminate myself."

"What?"

"You heard him," said Vargas.

"Allow me to explain," said the prosecutor. "Our investigation has revealed that Mr. Kaval provided false information to the warden in order to get Ms. Bornelli on his approved call list."

"What was that information?"

She reached into a file at her feet. "As required by law, we will be making a full production to the defense of all exculpatory evidence later this week. But in the interest of fairness, let the record reflect that I am now providing Mr. Swyteck a copy of a Certificate of Marriage for David Kaval and the defendant, Isabelle Bornelli."

Jack examined the certificate, which certainly

looked authentic, and then his gaze returned to the witness. "Is this real?"

Kaval looked to his attorney for guidance. "You can answer that question," she told him.

"It's real," he said.

It still didn't quite compute for Jack. "So, were you married to Isabelle Bornelli?"

"Yes," said Kaval.

"Just to be clear," said the prosecutor, "the state of Florida does not dispute the authenticity of the marriage certificate. Mr. Kaval's misrepresentation to the warden was his failure to disclose their divorce when he put her name on his call list."

It seemed like a simple thing to check, but with over 100,000 inmates statewide, the Florida Department of Corrections had higher priorities.

"When were you married?" Jack asked, barely able to hide his incredulity.

"It's on the paper."

"I see it," he said, checking the date again. "So this was right before Isa left for Zurich. Roughly two months after the death of Gabriel Sosa."

"About right."

Jack was still staring at the certificate. It didn't happen often, but he was speechless—and it lasted more than just a moment.

"We're all waiting," said Vargas. "Do you have any more questions, counselor?"

Jack took a breath. "Yeah," he said. "I have a whole lotta questions."

32

The deposition of David Kaval ran late, and Jack missed the last flight back to Miami. Motels near the Jacksonville airport were booked, so he took a room downtown near the St. Johns River. Jack went downstairs for a late dinner at the terrace café. By eight p.m. it was comfortable enough to sit outside, but not cool enough to explain his sudden craving for a hot cup of coffee.

"Don't you love that fresh-ground smell?" asked the waitress.

"You smell it too?"

She pointed out a tall building on the other side of the river, the Maxwell House manufacturing plant. "They're roasting beans as we speak. Been here over a hundred years now—almost as long as me, heh-heh. Folks up in Hoboken lost their plant, but we kept the Max in Jax."

She smiled—it was an obvious source of community pride—and then took his order. Jack thanked her for the unintended reminder—"Max"—and as she stepped away, he connected on FaceTime with

Andie, Riley, and the lone male in residence at the Swyteck household.

"Kiss Max good night, Daddy." The image of a wet, slurping tongue suddenly filled his iPhone screen.

"Good night, Max," said Jack. "Riley, how's my big girl?"

Her little face returned to the screen, her lower lip protruding. "Sad."

"Why are you sad?"

"Cuz Uncle Theo came over and told me a sad story."

"What was the story?"

"Fatty and Skinny went to bed. Fatty rolled over, and Skinny was dead."

"Honey, that's just a joke. No reason to be sad."

"Skinny's not dead?"

"No. Skinny is fine. I promise."

She giggled. "Silly Daddy. I knew that. I was just messing with you."

"Messing with me, huh? Did Uncle Theo teach you that too?"

"Uh-huh. He says you're easy. Mommy says so too."

"Ooh-kay," said Andie, as she appeared on the screen behind Riley. "Bedtime for blabbermouth."

They said good night, and Andie promised to call after Riley was asleep. Jack disconnected, and as he laid his cell aside, he couldn't help but think how strange life could be. A man he'd saved from the electric chair was now his best friend and was teaching Riley to "mess with him." His closest friend from high school was working on the other side of the world, wondering if his wife might spend the rest of her life in a Florida prison. He felt sad for Keith—on many levels. Just one night away from home, and Jack was already lonely. Keith had spent nearly an entire month in Hong Kong without his family. FaceTime was his lifeline.

Working behind Neil Goderich's old desk had had its advantages, Jack supposed.

The busboy filled his water glass, and Jack reviewed his notes from the deposition while waiting for his meal. His plan was to think about Kaval's testimony overnight, digest things, and speak with his client in the morning—until his phone rang. Isa was not so patient. He took her call.

"How did it go, Jack?"

He drew a fragrant breath of air—*good to the last drop*—and started with the marriage certificate. He recounted what Kaval had told him, which was met by silence on the line. Finally, she spoke.

"It's a fake."

"It's not a fake," said Jack. "I covered that in the deposition. The certificate is a valid public record. Even the prosecutor vouched for it. You were married almost five years, and there's an order of dissolution of marriage to prove it."

"Yeah, five years of marital bliss," she said with sarcasm. "And the first I found out about it was about four years and eleven months into it."

"How can that be?"

"I told you before, this man is crazy. David wanted me to marry him. Actually, that makes it sound too romantic. He said, 'You and me are getting married, bitch, whether you fucking like it or not.' I said no. I told him I was leaving Miami. That was when things got really bad."

"How bad?"

She told him about the last time she'd seen Kaval—the night he'd knocked her to the ground and pressed his hand around her throat. "David said that no matter where I went, we'd always be in a relationship. I guess I didn't fully understand what he meant until about five years later, when he sent me a letter from prison."

"That's the next thing I was going to ask you about," said Jack. "He told me he sent you two letters from FSP. So you got them?"

"I only got one. I don't know anything about a second letter."

"Okay, you never know with prison mail. But you did get a letter from him, right?"

"Yes. That's when I found out about this completely bogus marriage certificate that he got from—I don't know where he got it. Somewhere. Probably off the Internet."

"So there was no ceremony, no exchange of vows?"

"No! There was *nothing* except this piece of paper he created. He said if I gave him money, he would make it go away."

"That wasn't exactly how he characterized his letter."

"Of course it's not. He's a liar. Do you believe *him* or me?"

"He said he simply asked you for money."

"Technically speaking, yes, he did. But did he tell you there was a copy of the marriage certificate with the letter?"

"He left that part out."

"He's not stupid, Jack. David wouldn't have written a letter from prison that is blatant extortion: 'Pay me a hundred thousand dollars to make this problem go away.' He knew there was a chance that some prison screener might read it and say he's committing a crime."

"A small chance," said Jack. "Prisons would like you to think that every letter coming and going is read, but that's not the case. The only thing you can be sure of is that incoming mail is opened to make sure nothing illegal is inside."

"Okay, but he still had to be careful, because I could have taken the letter to the police and charged him with extortion. You have to look at the whole picture. I was engaged to Keith when I got this letter. David asked for money and included a copy of the marriage certificate. It didn't necessarily scream 'extortion' to an outsider, but the message to me was clear enough."

"Did you send him money?"

"No!"

"You just ignored the letter?"

"I went to see a lawyer in Zurich. He said I had a choice. I could go to a lot of aggravation and expense to clear this up and spoil the happiest time of my life; or I could enjoy my wedding, look forward to a future with the most wonderful man I had ever met, and go on with my life. I went on with my life."

"If you ignored him, how did the dissolution of marriage come about?"

"I don't know. Ask David."

Jack had asked him, but he wanted Isa's answer. She apparently had nothing to add—or nothing she wanted to share. Jack moved on. "What did you do with Kaval's letter?"

"I threw it away."

"Did you show it to Keith?"

"No."

"You and Keith were about to be married. How could you not tell him about the marriage certificate?"

"I did *tell* him. You asked me if I showed it to him. Look, this was totally bogus. It all boiled down to the fact that an old boyfriend was trying to shake me down for money."

Jack watched a yacht cruising upriver—downriver, actually. The St. Johns was the only major river in America that flowed south to north, which at the moment seemed about as odd as the flow of information from his client.

"You keep a lot of secrets, Isa."

"I told Keith."

"I don't just mean the letter. There's a little matter of a collect phone call from FSP that came up in the deposition, too."

She paused. "I'm surprised David admitted to that."

"I'm even more surprised that you didn't tell me."

"You're my lawyer, not my life manager, Jack. These are my problems. I can deal with them."

"If they come up in the courtroom, they're my problem."

"Well, now you know about it. Problem solved."

"Do you plan to tell Keith?"

"Are you talking to me now as my lawyer or Keith's friend?"

"It's a question I would ask any client."

She scoffed, and her voice grew louder in Jack's ear. "What could Keith do about any of this? For that matter, what can *you* do about it?"

"I could get a court order to make Kaval stop calling you."

"And what would that accomplish?"

"Give you and your family peace of mind. Send Kaval a message to back off."

"No, no, *no*," she said, her exasperation clear. "You'd be playing David's game. He told me that we would always have a relationship. Don't you get it? If I go to the police or a judge. If I get my husband involved. If I hire a lawyer. If I respond to his letters or his collect calls in any way—if I credit his actions with any kind of *reaction* from me—to David, *that* is a relationship. That's the 'relationship' we will always be in."

The waitress brought Jack's dinner. He gave her a silent thank-you, and when she was gone, he wrapped things up with Isa.

"When is Keith coming back to Miami?"

"This weekend."

"We should all sit down and have a meeting—you, Keith, and me."

"Why Keith? Aren't you the one who always says he's not your client?"

"True," said Jack. "But this isn't strictly about the case."

"What's it about?"

Jack's gaze drifted toward the northerly flowing river again. "Relationships."

33

On Tuesday morning Isa took her daughter to Jackson Memorial Hospital for her eight-week checkup.

Melany had been doing incredibly well post-op. Antibiotics were SOP for implant surgery, but Melany had shown no sign of infection, and there had been no need to continue the regimen beyond week one. By week three the incision had healed cleanly, and they were able to activate the implant. The one in her healthy ear had been working all along, so it wasn't the dramatic moment they had experienced the first time—the realization that Melany could "hear." But it still brought tears to Isa's eyes. She wished Keith had been able to be there.

The nurse led them to the examination room. Dr. Balkany was in Paris to deliver a lecture on the surgery he'd pioneered, and Isa was confident that Melany's operation was yet another success under his belt. Dr. Miles Vinas, a young resident in the otolaryngology department, told Melany to hop up onto the table and started the examination.

"Okay, Melany, let's make sure your heart's okay." He placed his stethoscope on her knee, which made her giggle.

"Yup, everything seems to be ticking along just fine."

Isa had never met Dr. Vinas, but she liked him so far. Melany had seen scores of doctors in her short lifetime, and the bedside manner ran the gamut, from "born to treat children" to Cruella de Vil.

"Could we leave Melany here with the nurse for a minute?" he asked. "I'd like to speak with you. In private."

Isa's heart skipped a beat. She didn't ask aloud, but the question was on the tip of her tongue: *Is there something wrong?*

"It will just take a minute," said the doctor.

"Sure," said Isa, unable to hide the anxiety in her voice. She kissed her daughter on the forehead and said, "Mommy will be right back."

The doctor led her out into the hallway and closed the office door.

"Is there a problem?" asked Isa.

"No, Melany is doing beautifully."

Isa could breathe again. "That's a relief."

"I just wanted to ask: Do we have *all* the medical records for Melany in our file?"

"Yes, of course."

"Are you sure?"

"Yes. I'm totally on top of Melany's medical history. You have all of it, from the day she was born."

"I'm not just talking about doctor visits. I mean everything. Clinics. Emergency room visits. Trauma centers."

Trauma centers? "Is there something specific you think is missing?"

He paused, as if measuring his words. "Here's the situation. I don't know if the doctor in Hong Kong botched the first surgery or not."

"Honestly, I don't care one way or the other," said Isa. "All that matters is that Melany is fine now. That's why I brought her all the way here to see Dr. Balkany. I wanted it done right. I'm not looking for a medical malpractice lawsuit against the first surgeon."

"No, that's not where I'm going with this," he said.

"Then I'm not following you."

"I've looked at Melany's file. I studied it carefully. Dr. Balkany would know better, since he performed the corrective surgery. But based on my review, I have some questions."

"About what?"

"As I indicated, I wouldn't jump to the conclusion that the first surgery was botched. In fact, I would tend to believe that it was a success."

Isa shook her head, incredulous. "How can you say that? Melany couldn't hear a thing, and if we had let this go any longer, the ossification would have progressed to the point that she would no longer be a candidate for an implant."

"But the surgery wasn't a failure from the very beginning. The audiology reports seem to indicate that there were signs of reception."

"Not for very long. Personally, I believe those early reports were false positives."

"That's possible. My point is this: it is also possible that something happened after the surgery. Something unrelated to the surgery itself. An external event."

"Meaning what, in lay terms?"

"A well-documented reason for failure of cochlear implant surgery is the displacement of the magnet of the CI receiver stimulator package. The case studies I've seen suggest that this displacement is usually due to trauma."

That word again. "Trauma?"

"In particular, head trauma."

Her eyes narrowed, and she didn't like the implication. "Are you asking me if someone hit Melany in the head?"

He just looked at her, saying nothing, which made his question even clearer. "You're asking if *I* hit her, aren't you?"

"I'm a health care professional. It's my legal duty."

Isa's mouth fell open. "Do you think I would *hurt my own child*?"

"I'm just asking the appropriate questions."

"Melany is raised in a loving home. She's everything to me. We flew all the way from Hong Kong to take care of this problem. I did that for *her*, and I end up getting—" She stopped herself, feeling the anger rising up inside her. "You've been watching way too much local news, Doctor."

She gathered herself, trying to stop the tears. It was a cumulative effect that she'd felt since the indictment, what she felt every time she spoke to her own lawyers, and what she knew she would face for the rest of her life, even if she were acquitted of all charges: suspicion. Jack had the audacity to accuse her of keeping secrets. Why did he think she hadn't told him, or her husband, or anyone else the things that everyone in hindsight thought she should have spoken about freely, as if there were no consequences? Isa knew the drill. Sexual assault was in a category by itself. The victim was associated with the crime; and all too often, the victim became the criminal. The more you say, the more you pay. She could only imagine what Dr. Vinas was writing in Melany's permanent medical record. *Possible head trauma. Mother potentially violent.* For more than a decade, Isa had managed to keep Gabriel Sosa from following her everywhere. Now there was no escape. Not for her. Not for her daughter.

She opened the door, went quickly to the examination table, and wrapped Melany in her arms.

"Are you okay, Mommy?"

She fought back tears, not showing her face to Melany until she was certain that her emotions were under control. Then she lifted Melany from the table and put her on her feet.

"Yes, sweetie. Mommy's fine. Let's go home."

She took Melany by the hand and hurried out of the office, saying nothing to Dr. Vinas as they passed him in the hallway on the way out.

34

Jack picked up Theo at Cy's Place around nine p.m. It was time he and his investigator hopped back on the trail of evidence.

The deposition of David Kaval had produced much more than a certificate of marriage. Jack had promising leads. At the top of his to-do list: nail down "John Doe" in the indictment. According to Kaval, the name of his accomplice really was "John." Beyond that, Kaval had been less than helpful: "Never knew his last name" and "got no idea where he is now."

"That's such bullshit," said Theo. He was working behind the bar, checking the cash levels in the register.

"Maybe not," said Jack. "John Doe probably never knew Kaval's last name, either. That's just the way these guys operate."

He closed the register. "The state attorney knows. She's just not telling you. I'll bet your car on that."

"My *car*?"

"Yeah, your car. You're getting a new one, anyway. Riley says she wants you in a minivan. Preferably pink, with denim upholstery."

"Gee, I wonder who gave her that idea."

Theo just laughed. Jack waited for him to give the assistant manager the "quick and dirty" on how not to burn the place down while he was away. Then they left through the kitchen, got in Jack's car, and started across town.

"So, we're going back to the body shop where this guy worked?" asked Theo.

"No and no," said Jack.

"That was one question. What's up with the double no?"

"No, we are not going back to the body shop. And no, John Doe didn't work there. That's why we've had such a hard time finding him."

"Then how did Kaval and his buddy get into the body shop?"

"They broke in. They took Sosa to a place that the police couldn't trace back to them or to anyone they knew."

"Smart. So where are we going now?"

"Club Inversion on South Beach. Kaval gave me something to go on. That's where John Doe used to earn an honest living."

"Honest? Are you high?"

"No, I'm being facetious."

"If feces-ish has anything to do with talking shit, then you're right on the money. Club Inversion is like a spigot for Miami's drug pipeline from China. I'm talking the synthetic shit. Molly.

Spice. Flakka. All the shit that chemists cook up in their labs in Shanghai and that college kids can't get enough of. The deals are cut at Club Inversion. It's common knowledge."

"Yup. And that's why you're going with me."

"Then I need to change clothes. Gotta look the part. And we need a plan."

"We can stop by your place on the way there."

"Nuh-uh," said Theo. "I don't work that cheap. We're stopping by the mall."

"Lookin' hot," Theo said to a couple of young women. They were dressed to kill and pleading their case to a rock-solid bouncer who was the keeper of the gate to the hottest dance club on South Beach.

The taller one checked him out. "Lookin' pretty hot yourself."

Theo did. They'd stopped by the Armani shop at Brickell City Centre, which was on the way to South Beach. The shirt alone had set Jack back three hundred bucks, and if Theo moved the wrong way his pecs might pop the buttons, but Theo was right: they needed to look the part.

The waiting line extended down the sidewalk, around the corner, and halfway up the block again. Most of the hopefuls would never see beyond the bouncers. Fat chance for the khaki-clad conventioneer from Pittsburgh who was dressed to sell insurance. The Latin babe in the Staccato heels was a shoo-in. Most of the rejects would shrug it off and launch plan B. Others would plead and beg, to no avail, only embarrassing themselves.

A few would curse at the bouncers, maybe even come at them, driven by a dangerous combination of drugs and testosterone, only to find out that these guys didn't just *look* mean.

Jack put on an air of confidence and walked straight to the front of the line. "Hey, good to see you, my friend," he said as he slid a fifty into the bouncer's hand.

The guy was a tattooed pillar of Brazilian marble, but money always talked.

"Next time don't pretend to fucking know me," he said as he tucked away the cash.

Theo stepped between them—and the stone-faced bouncer actually smiled.

"Hey, Mr. Theo Knight. How you doin', my man?"

Jack watched as he and Theo shook hands eleven different ways, finishing with a smile and an exchange of pulled punches to their rock-hard biceps, the standard prison-yard ritual.

"Richie, this here's my best buddy," said Theo.

"Looks more like your accountant."

Jack had expected him to say "lawyer," but he was somehow even more offended. Theo laughed and said, "Nah, he's cool."

"Then we all cool," he said as he reached into his pocket for Jack's cash. "Here, lemme give back—"

"No, no," said Theo, pushing the money back into his pocket. "It's the price of admission for an amateur. But, hey, maybe you can help me with some business." *Bi'niss.*

"What kinda business?"

"*The* business."

He clearly knew what Theo meant, and he took them aside, out of earshot from the people in line. "What about it, Theo?"

"I need to talk to someone who goes way back. Knows the old-time players."

"Like how far back?"

"Ten years or more."

Richie thought about it. "You got the wrong club, bro. Anyone who goes back that far is in Club Fed now."

"Gotta be someone still here," said Theo.

Richie gave it more thought, and then he suddenly seemed to have something. "Sammy."

"How do I meet this Sammy?"

"He's upstairs, in his private space."

"Can you take us?"

Richie laughed. "No way. I can let him know he's got visitors. If he's interested, he'll send for you. Just hang out by the bar for a while. I'll see what I can do."

Theo gave him a friendly slap on the arm, his way of saying thank you. The red velvet ropes parted, the bouncer stepped aside, and Jack and Theo entered, much to the envy of the block-long line of beautiful people waiting to get inside.

Club Inversion was once known as Club Vertigo, until a major undercover bust for trafficking in synthetic drugs sent the original owners to prison and their company into bankruptcy. The DEA connected Vertigo to a network of drop points across Miami-Dade County that received three hundred different varieties shipped from chemical factories clustered in the Hebei region outside Beijing—including tons of methylone, the main ingredient in a drug that Madonna made even more popular by walking onstage at South Beach's annual "Ultra" concert and shouting, "Has anyone seen Molly?" The club had a new name and a new owner, but the look and feel of the place was the same, the gaping interior of a four-story warehouse having been gutted and completely reconfigured with a tall and narrow atrium. The main bar and dancing were on the ground floor, and several large mirrors suspended at varying heights and at different angles made it difficult at times to discern whether you were looking up or down. With even a slight buzz on, the pounding music, swirling lights, and throngs of sweaty bodies were enough to give anyone a case of vertigo. The sensation worked both ways, with hordes of people watchers looking down on the dance crowd from tiered balconies.

"Over there," said Jack. He led Theo to a couple of stools at the far end of the bar, away from the action, where they could at least hear themselves talk.

"That chick is checking me out," said Theo.

He meant the woman at the other end of the bar, a dark-haired beauty wearing a clingy white dress and a gold necklace that played beautifully off her brown skin. She was peering over the sugar-coated rim of her cocktail glass—straight at Theo.

"Stay focused," Jack told him.

Jack knew Theo's type, and if this one kept

cutting eyes at him, it wouldn't be long before Theo was caught up in her, the music, the energy, the intoxicating mix of perfumes wafting up from the crowd—the whole package. As if there weren't enough distractions, "Albino Girl" was now onstage at the other end of the club, a Vegas-style act in which a dancer managed to keep time to the music while a thirteen-foot, lemon-yellow albino python coiled itself around her sculptured body.

The woman at the bar tossed her hair, but when she glanced back in Theo's general direction, her gaze came to rest on Jack.

Theo smiled. "Whaddya know? She's into white dudes."

"Sorry. My prenup with Andie allows me to have extramarital sex only with Eva Longoria, and then only if she initiates it."

"Hmm. Who'd Andie get in that deal?"

"Brad Pitt. But only if he can jump back into that movie where he aged in reverse—*Benjamin Button*—and make himself look the way he did in *Thelma and Louise*."

Theo arched an eyebrow, shooting Jack an exaggerated look of disapproval. "This is not something you're making up on the fly. You and your woman actually had this stupid fucking conversation, didn't you? Don't lie to me."

"I plead the Fifth."

"Ought to plead guilty by reason of marital insanity."

Jack's gaze drifted back toward the woman in

the white dress, who was talking on her cell. The call ended quickly. She tucked her phone away, climbed down from the barstool, and walked over, stopping a few feet away. She tossed her long, dark hair again, this time with attitude, and spoke in Spanish. "Sammy will see you."

Dominican, Jack guessed. His ear for Spanish was better than his tongue, so he answered in English.

"You must be one of his messengers."

"You must be Einstein," she said. *Joo muss . . .* "Come."

She led them up a curved stairwell to the second floor, which was essentially a mezzanine overlooking the dance floor. There was another velvet rope at the top of the stairs, but Sammy's messenger gained them hassle-free entry. A host of privileged partiers were standing at the balcony rail, peering down at the dancers. Designer clothes and flashy jewelry were everywhere, people outfitted to show off their money, a buff body, collagen lips, Botoxed brows, and, in many cases, an utter lack of taste. One trend was especially obvious. Some women seemed to think it stylish to rip the designer label from their jeans, and the seat of their pants right along with it, so that their bare skin somehow managed to brush up against any guy they passed. Jack figured that by the time he left this place, he'd know how to say "nice ass" in at least five different languages.

The real action, however, was in the private rooms. Jack counted at least a dozen, each set well back from the rail, one after the other, like cabanas at a beach club. Most had open access to the mezzanine area, with invited guests having a good time in plain view. Their Dominican escort took them to one that was making use of the privacy curtain. She peeled back the white linen drapery and entered first, presumably to tell Sammy that his guests had arrived.

"Let me do the talking up here," Theo said under his breath.

Jack agreed.

A moment later the Dominican summoned Jack and Theo and introduced them to Sammy. Beside him but stone silent was his bodyguard, a Jamaican who was bigger than Theo.

Jack had visited so-called clubs within a club before, and his reaction to Sammy's space was no different: *What's the big deal?* It had the usual sectional couches that visitors sat in at their own risk, preferably wearing a body condom. There was a pair of flat-screen TVs on the wall, one for sports, the other for porn. Sammy was wearing a shiny silk suit, and the matching diamond ring and earrings would have made a Kardashian jealous. At his signal the Dominican and two other women in tight skirts left the room. Jack and Theo sat with their backs to the privacy curtain, opposite Sammy and his bodyguard. On a table beside Sammy was a large glass-encased colony of ants.

"You like the bugs?" asked Sammy.

"Interesting," said Jack.

"That case is left over from the days when this was Club L'fant—short for leafcutter ant. They're from South America. The signature drink here used to be the Leafcutter vodka martini. Has kind of a walnutty taste. And they're an aphrodisiac."

"So you go *way* back?" asked Theo. "All the way to Club L'fant. That's even before Vertigo."

"Yep," said Sammy. "I'm like the historian here. Make sure we don't repeat our mistakes, if you know what I mean."

Jack did, but he honored his agreement with Theo to let him do all the talking.

"Richie says you have some business to discuss. Tell me about it."

"It's a niche business," said Theo. "I been looking for a go-to guy. Doing lots of homework. I keep hearing one name. A guy named John who used to work here. Long time ago. Thought you might know him."

"John, huh?"

"Yeah. John."

"You got a last name?"

"No. Do you?"

Sammy glanced at his bodyguard, who got up from the couch and walked around the cocktail table. Theo knew better than to remain in the disadvantaged seated position. He rose, and the two biggest guys in the room were suddenly eyeball-to-eyeball. Sammy kept talking, and they kept staring each other down, a couple of bulls ready to bang heads.

"Funny thing," said Sammy. "MDPD detectives came here not too long ago. They were looking for John, too. No last name."

Theo answered, but his eyes remained locked with the bodyguard's. "We're not cops. We got a business proposition for John."

"Business, huh? Tell me about this business."

Jack swallowed hard. He hoped to God that Theo had something.

"Lister-agra," said Theo.

Jack's heart sank. Sammy made a face. "What the fuck are you talking about?"

"It's a pill," said Theo. "A double-whammy knockoff that combines the chemical formulas for Listerine and Viagra. I got the inside track on the only ED medication in the world that comes in the form of a breath mint. Perfect for guys with bad breath and a limp dick. Like musclehead here."

The bodyguard growled. "You motha—"

Theo backed him right down.

"Easy," said Sammy.

The bodyguard stepped away, giving Theo space. Sammy had an inquisitive look on his face. "I really hope you're not shittin' me about this. Cuz I like the concept."

"I got a test shipment coming in next month from a factory in Bangkok. We're talking millions on the club market. I was looking for John to bring the Miami Beach action through here."

Sammy seemed even more intrigued. "If you're for real, I'll take John's cut."

"No. I want to talk to John."

"Not gonna happen, dude."

"Why not?"

"John smashed his motorcycle into a big-ass truck. Left a nice pile of brain salad on the highway."

Theo glanced quickly at Jack, as if wondering if that was a good thing or bad for Isa. Jack showed no reaction.

"When did that happen?" asked Theo.

"Two years ago."

"Are we talking about the same John?" asked Theo.

"Google it," said Sammy. "Motorcycle. Dead at the scene. John Simpson."

Jackpot, thought Jack.

Sammy sighed, as if ready to wrap it up. "It seems I've given you something for nothing. Which means that if I find one pill—just one Lister-agra on South Beach—and I'm not part of it, I'll find you chumps. And let me say this: John Simpson didn't fuck around. Neither do I. You understand what I'm saying?"

"We do," said Jack, rising. "Let us talk with our Asian contacts."

"We'll get back to you," said Theo.

"Fine," said Sammy. "I got a couple of fine 'Asian contacts' upstairs, if you and your accountant are interested."

Accountant? The second time in one night. *What the fuck?*

"Maybe next time," said Jack. There were no handshakes, just parting glares between Theo and the insulted "musclehead." Jack parted the linen curtain and stepped out. Theo followed and they headed to the stairway.

"*Lister-agra?*" Jack said under his breath. "Really? We're lucky to be walking out of this place alive."

Theo smiled. "Night ain't over yet, chief."

35

Isa rode the Metrorail to Coral Gables and walked Melany another block to Pee-Wee Art Camp. Melany loved to paint, and three days a week she got to share her passion with nineteen other preschoolers and two very brave art instructors.

Rather than turn right around and ride the train back to Brickell Avenue, Isa stopped at the coffee shop across the highway from University Station. It was a pleasant morning, and she found a shaded table outside to enjoy some alone time. She was halfway through her latte, and reading an article in the *Journal* about the stock market crisis in China—Keith's turf—when a young woman approached.

"I'm sorry to interrupt. You're Isabelle Bornelli, aren't you?"

Isa looked up from her tablet. The woman was dressed like a typical college student, right down to the Uggs on her feet. "Yes, I am," said Isa.

"Emma Barrett," she said as she extended her hand, and Isa shook it. "I'm a senior at the U. I've been following your case ever since the charges were brought and—well, I just want to say that I'm on your side."

"Thank you," Isa said with a polite smile.

Emma seemed to have more on her mind, but she started away. Then she stopped. "Uhm, do you mind if I sit down for just a minute?"

Isa wasn't looking for company, but she didn't see the harm. "Please."

Emma eagerly took a seat and laid her backpack at her feet. "I didn't come over to your table intending to tell you this, and I hope it doesn't make you uncomfortable. But I'm also the victim of campus date rape."

Isa had no immediate response. She hadn't seen that coming, and then it occurred to her: Emma was the first person ever to address her as a fellow victim of date rape. "I'm very sorry," said Isa.

"I was a freshman. Just like you were."

"It's a horrible crime at any age, but especially for a teenager."

"I almost flunked out. I thought about transferring to another school, but I decided no, I'm not going to let my attacker win. I stayed right here."

Isa blinked. "I went to Europe."

"I know," said Emma, and then she suddenly seemed mortified. "I wasn't judging you. Everybody deals with it in their own way. I was very vocal, but not everyone is. It's a personal decision. I'm president of SASA now. Students Against Sexual Assault."

"I guess I just didn't have that in me. But good for you."

"Have you heard of SASA?"

"No. I don't think it was here when I was a student."

"It wasn't. I started it."

"Really?"

"I had to do *something*. What I went through was horrendous. The administration put together this college inquiry panel that supposedly investigated my allegations. Of course they completely absolved my attacker. These bozos weren't even qualified. One of the old men on the panel asked me, 'So, Ms. Barrett, how is anal rape even possible?' What does he think—that a woman gets wet at the thought of vaginal rape, so that's possible, but anal rape isn't possible? How was I supposed to respond to an idiotic question like that?"

"Unbelievable."

"Anyway, at least we have SASA now. We're not completely idiotproof, but it's a start."

"You're quite an amazing woman."

"Thanks," she said with a little smile. "So are you."

Isa looked away. "Not really."

The noisy Metrorail screeched to a stop at the elevated station across the street, then went quiet.

"Hey, can I ask you a favor?" asked Emma.

"What?"

"I'm trying to start up a SASA chapter at Miami-Dade College. There's a 'campus rape awareness' event scheduled for a week from tomorrow at MDC South. Would you be willing to attend?"

Isa fumbled for a response, flustered. "I—I don't think so."

"I know it's a lot to ask. But it would be so meaningful if you—"

"I can't."

"You don't have to speak if you don't want to. I could just point you out and mention that you came to show your support and—"

"No, I just can't."

"Please don't say no."

"*No,*" she said, more firmly than she'd intended. "You'll have to excuse me, but I really have to go." Isa pushed away from the table and gathered her things.

"Okay," said Emma.

Isa accidentally knocked over the rest of her coffee as she rose. She dabbed the tabletop clean, and she was so beside herself that she stuffed the soggy napkins into her purse before slinging the strap over her shoulder. "I'm sorry I can't help your organization," she said.

"Sorry I asked," Emma said quietly.

It felt like a punch in the chest. Isa absorbed the blow, then turned and headed for the Metro station.

36

The mid-morning sun shone brightly through the conference-room window on the ninth floor of the Graham Building. The state attorney had called a ten o'clock meeting at her office. Jack and Manny were seated on the sunny side of the rectangular table. Sylvia Hunt and a junior prosecutor sat across from them with their backs to the window. It was a bush-league litigation ploy that Jack had witnessed in countless other meetings and depositions: arrange the seating so that the enemy was staring straight into the blinding sun.

Jack shielded his eyes and reached for his sunglasses. "Sylvia, please. Either adjust the mini-blinds or Manny and I will have to sit here looking like a couple of secret agents."

"Oh, is that bothering you?" she asked with phony concern. Her assistant promptly remedied the situation. Jack thanked him, and then Sylvia started the meeting with her promised announcement.

"The Justice Department has completed its

investigation into the allegations against the correctional officer at the detention center. The official report will be released tomorrow, but as a courtesy I'm giving you a preview. Here's the formal conclusion: there is no evidence that a correctional officer was planning a sexual assault of Ms. Bornelli, or that he solicited the assistance of Ms. Bornelli's cellmate in order to carry out such a plan."

"Then the investigation is a sham," said Jack. "You can't say there is *no* evidence. There's the statement of her cellmate, Foneesha Johnson."

"Ms. Johnson has recanted her prior statement."

Manny scoffed. "What a surprise."

"I can understand your cynicism," said Sylvia. "But Ms. Johnson didn't simply recant. She set the record straight. A Justice Department attorney questioned her under oath, and her testimony is that she was paid ten thousand dollars to make a false accusation."

The junior prosecutor reached across the table and handed Jack a copy of the transcript. He thumbed through it, but there wasn't time to read it in detail.

"The suspense is killing me," Jack said dryly. "Did Ms. Johnson allege that it was my client who paid her ten thousand dollars?"

"No. In fact, that's the principal reason I called this meeting. I wanted you to know that Ms. Johnson does not link your client to this scheme in any way. She testified that she and Ms. Bornelli never discussed the accusation or the bribe."

"Then how did this happen?" asked Jack. "Allegedly."

"Ms. Johnson's boyfriend was the go-between. Someone approached him on the outside and paid him ten thousand dollars. The quid pro quo was Ms. Johnson's accusation that the corrections officer was planning to sexually assault Ms. Bornelli."

"What does the boyfriend say?" asked Jack.

"He denies it, of course."

"Do you have any proof that the boyfriend was actually paid ten thousand dollars?"

"No, but we have good reason to believe that he and his new girlfriend are ten thousand dollars richer."

"New girlfriend?"

"Yes. Ms. Johnson got used, which is why she came clean. It is fully documented that the so-called boyfriend made three separate visits to Ms. Johnson after Ms. Bornelli became her cellmate. He hadn't visited a single time in the six months prior."

"Are there recordings of the conversations between Ms. Johnson and her boyfriend?"

"No."

"Then what proof do you have that he directed Foneesha Johnson to make false accusations?"

"As I indicated, we have the sworn testimony of Ms. Johnson."

"Who is now a proven liar."

"I don't think that's been proven," she said.

"She made the accusations, which were credible enough for the state attorney to agree to release my client on bail before trial. She now recants and says she was bribed. She has to be lying about something."

"This isn't a debate about the quality of the evidence. The bottom line is that the corrections officer has been absolved."

"Are you planning to bring charges against anyone?" asked Jack.

"Not at this time."

"But you're not ruling it out?"

The prosecutor paused to frame her response. "The FBI's investigation is over. MDPD's isn't. We will reevaluate if additional evidence surfaces."

"Let me get right to my immediate concern," said Jack. "Will this have any impact on my client's release on bail?"

"No."

"Isa will remain free?"

"Yes—until she's convicted, of course."

"We'll see about that," said Jack, and the meeting ended on that note. The junior prosecutor walked Jack and Manny to the elevator, and the defense lawyers rode down alone.

"Just to clear the air," said Manny, "you don't think that *I* jeopardized my law license and paid that boyfriend ten thousand dollars, do you?"

Jack was watching the blinking numbers over the door. "No. I don't."

"Who do you think did? If it happened."

"I don't know. But I can tell you this: I plan to have a very serious conversation with my old friend Keith when he gets back from Hong Kong on Saturday."

"I was thinking the same thing," said Manny.

The elevator doors opened, and they walked across the lobby.

"Are you surprised that the state attorney is leaving Isa out on bail?" asked Manny.

"No," said Jack. "You?"

"Not at all. In fact, it's a smart strategy."

"Agreed," said Jack. "Leave her out on bail, watch her on the outside, and see who she talks to."

Manny exited through the revolving door first, and Jack followed. "Let her hang herself," said Manny, "figuratively speaking."

"Exactly," said Jack.

"So what's our next move?" asked Manny, still walking.

They were beyond the shadow of the state attorney's office. Jack stopped to put on his sunglasses.

"We make sure no one hands our client a rope," he said, and then he started toward his car.

37

Isa picked up Melany from art camp at noon. After lunch they stopped at Alice C. Wainwright Park, south of the Brickell area. The park's green space was relatively small, but it was right on the bay. A five-star view of the city skyline from a limestone bluff beneath the palm trees was alone worth the visit—though Isa was already finding herself somewhat numb to that experience, waking day after day in the Four Seasons with Miami's natural and manmade beauty at her feet. Every few minutes a biker or jogger passed on the asphalt trail that stretched along the mainland coastline and over to Key Biscayne, but mother and daughter essentially had the park to themselves. Melany headed straight to the swing set. Isa watched from a park bench in the shade of a giant oak.

"Be careful," Isa called out.

Melany was pumping hard and flying high. They were beyond the four-week post-op ban on all strenuous activity, but it was hard for Isa to shift out of mother-bear mode.

"Look at me, Mommy!"

She was dipping her head back and pointing her toes to the sky, her beautiful hair blowing in the wind, the links of chain creaking in back-and-forth rhythm. Isa resisted the impulse to tell her again to take it down a notch. Once was enough. There were plenty of other people in the world to tell her what she couldn't do.

Suddenly, she jumped from the swing, launching herself into the air.

"Melany!"

Isa leapt from the bench, but there was no chance of catching her. Melany landed on the grass with a thud, and Isa was a second too late to break the fall. She was on her knees at Melany's side.

"Are you okay?" she asked with urgency. "Are you hurt?"

Melany wasn't crying, at least not at first. She seemed stunned for a moment, but as soon as she sat up and fully realized what had happened, the tears came in abundance.

"Tell me where it hurts," said Isa.

She didn't answer. Isa quickly checked the audio processors, first the left and then the right. Everything looked fine—at least on the outside.

"Can you hear what I'm saying?"

Melany was still crying, but she nodded in the affirmative. Then she burrowed her face into her mother's shoulder.

"Honey, you scared me to death."

The sobbing continued, but it seemed to be coming under control. Melany seemed more frightened than injured.

"Why did you do that, honey?"

Melany sniffled and said, "That man again."

"What?"

"That man. I saw him over there."

She was pointing toward the cinder-block building that housed the restrooms. Isa looked but saw nothing.

"What man?"

"Scary."

Isa held her daughter's head steady, forcing her to look her mother in the eye. "Melany, tell me what the man looked like."

She'd stopped crying, but her eyes were still cloudy. "Scary."

"Melany, listen to me. Was he taller or shorter than Daddy?"

"Shorter."

That ruled out David Kaval, which had been Isa's first thought, however irrational. "Older or younger?"

"Older."

"White or black?"

"Medium. A little darker than you."

Isa felt chills. It wasn't a lot to go on, but the way Melany had put it—"a little darker than you"—sent Isa's mind whirling in a familial direction.

"You said again."

Melany blinked, confused. "What?"

"You said you saw 'that man *again*.' Have you seen him before?"

She nodded.

"Where?"

"The park."

"Which park?"

"The one by Harbour City Mall."

It took a moment for Isa to process what she was hearing. "Do you mean Kowloon Park? Back in Hong Kong?"

She nodded. "When Soo Hong took me."

Soo Hong was their babysitter. The aviaries at Kowloon were Melany's favorite. "Are you sure it was the same man?"

"Yes. He was watching me."

"Did he—did he get close to you?"

"Kind of."

Isa was breathing faster. "How close?"

She didn't answer. Isa suddenly recalled a visit to Kowloon about a month after the first implant surgery, when Melany returned with a bruise on her leg. In broken English Soo Hong had told her that Melany had taken a fall.

"Melany, how close? How close did he get to you?"

Her eyes welled. "Stop yelling at me!"

Isa wasn't yelling, but Melany's aural processing was more dependent on visual cues than most children's, and Isa's demeanor must have created that impression. "I'm sorry, honey," Isa said, struggling to display a more relaxed and pleasant expression. "I just want you to tell me as much as you possibly can remember, okay? Now—how close did the man get?"

"Kind of close."

Isa swallowed the lump in her throat. "Close enough to talk to you?"

She nodded once.

Isa could barely get out the next question. "Did he? Did he speak to you?"

A tear trickled down her daughter's cheek, and it was all the response that Isa needed. Isa reached for her phone to call the police. She needed to report this and—*and say what*? That Isabelle Bornelli, who failed to report her own rape, would now like to report that her daughter saw a scary man in the park?

Melany suddenly sprang to her feet, moving much more quickly than Isa could react.

"Melany!"

Isa jumped up and started after her, but Melany had a sizable head start and was running faster than Isa had ever seen her move. She raced past the picnic tables and was headed down the slope toward the limestone bluff at the waterfront. Isa followed, calling out her name, commanding her to stop. Melany made it to a low stretch of leafy sea grapes and ducked inside the bushes. Isa caught up a few seconds later and found her sitting cross-legged in the undergrowth, hiding in the tangle of thin branches and exposed roots that supported the canopy above. Mother and daughter were breathing heavily from the fifty-yard dash. Isa got on one knee and looked her daughter in the eye.

"Don't ever run from me like that!"

Melany didn't answer. Isa was in no frame of mind to scold her any further. Her tone softened. "You don't have to run, sweetheart. You did nothing wrong."

Melany shook her head firmly. Perhaps it was

an expression of disagreement. Or maybe it was her way of saying that even though her mother's lips were moving, she couldn't hear a word of it. Isa noticed that she'd removed her audio processers and was clutching one in each fist.

Isa was still holding her cell phone, but she tucked it into her pocket. She wouldn't be calling anyone. She stood up slowly, her head and shoulders rising above the low-slung canopy of sea-grape leaves as she gazed out toward the bay.

I will kill you, she heard herself thinking. *Kill you, if you ruined what I have with my daughter.*

38

Jack and Theo drove to the Billfish 24-Hour Diner in the upper Keys for an early breakfast. Very early. They had to arrive before six a.m., when the graveyard shift ended for John Simpson's widow.

The report from Sammy at Club Inversion had proved reliable. The Kawasaki Ninja ZX-14R was a precision machine that, in the eyes of most drivers, was little more than a blur shooting by on the Expressway. According to the police report referenced in the two-year-old *Miami Tribune* article, Simpson was doing more than 100 m.p.h. when, at approximately three a.m., his motorcycle slammed into the back end of a U-Haul truck that had run out of gas and come to a complete stop in the fast lane on I-95. At that speed, a helmet barely reduced the splatter. He was survived by his then thirty-three-year-old wife, Ilene.

A few minutes of social-media research was all it had taken to learn that Ilene Simpson lived in Key Largo and worked the graveyard shift at the Billfish Diner.

The Billfish was popular year round, and with the summer "mini-season" for Florida lobster under way, it was packed with night divers who'd already caught their limit, and with recreationalists who wanted to be on the water before sunrise. No open stools at the counter, and every table in the small dining room was taken, with barely enough room for waitresses to pass. A booth in front opened just as Jack and Theo entered. They grabbed it, and their two-hour drive in the middle of the night suddenly felt worthwhile. Duct tape on Naugahyde was the authentic Billfish experience, and they were in the glow of the legendary neon sign in the window that rechristened the old eatery—appropriately, perhaps—as the "illfish Diner."

"That's Ilene," said Theo, indicating. "The waitress standing by the pie display."

"You sure?"

Theo double-checked her Facebook profile photo on his phone. "Yeah. That's her."

Jack tried not to be too obvious about his quick glances in her direction. Ilene was a thin woman with shoulder-length, dirty-blond hair and a mosaic of colorful tattoos that coiled around her left arm from her wrist to her shoulder. She didn't seem to smile much, and had Jack not read in the *Tribune* that she was in her mid-thirties, he would have guessed older.

Another waitress came to their table and placed two mugs and a pot of coffee on the table. "You boys ready to order?"

Theo put down his menu. "I'll have Ilene's special."

"We ain't got an Ilene's special."

"Yeah, you do," he said, glancing toward her coworker behind the counter. "Ask Ilene to pop over here. Tell her Sammy from South Beach sent us."

"Fine. But you're in my booth, so you gotta order something."

Theo went for the steak and eggs with a side of blood-orange doughnuts in a creamy coconut glaze. Jack was fine with coffee and a bagel. The waitress collected the menus and headed to the kitchen.

Jack checked the clock on the wall: 5:58 a.m. "She's off in two minutes. What if she slips out the back door?"

"You worry too much. She'll sit down with us."

Two minutes later, Theo was proven right. Ilene left her apron at the counter, crossed the dining area, and stopped at their table. There was no squeezing in next to Theo, so Jack made room on his side and invited her to sit.

"How do you boys know Sammy?" she asked, as she slid into the booth.

"He gave us your late husband's name," said Jack, and then he handed her a business card. "I'm the lawyer for Isabelle Bornelli—the former UM student charged with murdering the man who raped her. You've probably seen something about her case on the news."

"I don't watch the news."

"That's okay. We're here to talk about old news. We have it on good authority that John Simpson and David Kaval kidnapped the man who raped

Isa and tortured him to death. Gabriel Sosa was his name."

"Never heard of him."

"Think hard," said Jack. "Mr. Kaval is the chief witness against my client. I don't know if it matters to you or not, but from everything I've learned so far, he's going to paint your late husband as the badass who literally took a hatchet to Gabriel Sosa."

She paused, seeming to consider what Jack was saying. "Look, Mr. Swyteck, I'm tired, and all I want to do right now is go home and climb in bed."

"I just have a few questions."

"I don't know nothin' about your case, but it sounds to me like this rapist got what he deserved. If John was involved, I don't want to hear about it."

"My client saw David Kaval and another man hassling Sosa on the night of the murder. Kaval testified that the man's name was John and that he worked at Club Vertigo—Club Inversion is what it's called now. Sammy says that would be John Simpson."

"Sammy would know," she said in a tired voice.

"Know about the murder?"

"No. He would know John."

"Would he know David Kaval?"

"I have no idea. John and Sammy knew everybody. That's what I liked about John. Other things I could have lived without."

"Like what?"

"It doesn't matter. John's gone. I'm hooked up with someone pretty special now and want to move forward. So I'll tell you the same thing I told the last guy who came in here asking questions: let John rest in peace."

"Last guy? Who was that? Someone from law enforcement, like an MDPD detective?"

"No, I'm talking more recent. A detective came by a while ago."

"Shit, man," said Theo, groaning. "I told you they knew John Doe's last name. Bastards."

Jack noted it as something the prosecution should have shared with him, but that was for another time. "Can you tell me who this guy was—the one who was asking about John?"

"I don't remember his name. Not sure I ever got it."

"How recent was it?" asked Jack.

"Last month some time."

"What did he look like?"

She gave him some basics—short, Hispanic, maybe in his sixties—which was enough. Jack scrolled through his iPhone library and retrieved a photo of Isa's father that he'd downloaded from the Web. It was taken when Felipe Bornelli worked in the Venezuelan consul's office in Miami.

"This is more than ten years old," he said, showing it to Ilene. "But could it be this guy?"

She took a closer look. "Yeah. His hair's gone grayer, but that looks like him."

Jack didn't volunteer his identity. "What did he want to know?"

"I don't remember. It wasn't a long conversation. He seemed pretty satisfied to hear that I didn't know anything about this case."

Jack shook his head, confused. “I had to take David Kaval’s deposition in prison and track down Sammy at Club Inversion to figure out that ‘John Doe’ in the indictment was your husband. How did this man even know to talk to you?”

“Got me,” she said. “I think you’ll have to ask him that.”

Jack looked at Theo across the table. “Yeah. I think we will.”

39

By ten o'clock Jack was back in Miami and sitting behind his desk. Thirty minutes later he got an e-mail that changed his plans for the day. It was from an address and a server that he didn't recognize, but the subject line said "From Felipe Bornelli," which made Jack curious enough to open it. The message read:

I want a meeting with my daughter. Just the two of us. Can you arrange it?

Jack didn't reply. He forwarded it to his tech guru to see if there was a way to verify the source. His techie would have to investigate, which would take a few hours—which in turn gave Jack time to meet with his client and cocounsel. They gathered in the sitting area of Jack's office, Isa in the Windsor chair with her back to the window and Manny on the other side of the coffee table. Jack paced before the empty fireplace as he spoke.

"I have a theory on what prompted this e-mail," said Jack, and he told them how the "Felipe connection" had been the main takeaway from his conversation with Ilene Simpson at the Billfish Diner.

"I share your suspicion," said Manny. "It wasn't public information that John Simpson was John Doe. So you have to wonder what led Felipe to Ilene before you got to her."

"And now that I've talked to Ilene, is it really a coincidence that he suddenly wants to meet with his daughter, whom he hasn't spoken to in almost a decade?"

Isa was silent, which wasn't what Jack had expected. "Isa, what are you thinking?"

"There's more to the picture," she said.

Jack stopped pacing, rested his elbow on the mantel, and listened. Isa took her time, careful not to leave out anything important as she told them about Melany's "Felipe sighting" in Alice C. Wainwright Park the previous afternoon—and possibly in Hong Kong. "I was almost expecting some kind of follow-up from him," said Isa. "Maybe this proposed meeting with me is it."

"Are you sure that the man Melany saw was your father?" asked Jack.

"Yes. I showed her a photograph when we got home from the park. She was certain that it was him—both in Miami and in Hong Kong."

"That could be a little suggestive," said Jack. "It would have been preferable if you'd shown her three or four pictures and she'd picked your father."

"Fine. Maybe this wouldn't stand up in a court of law. But I'm confident it was him."

Jack took a seat. "Let's start with this question: Are *you* interested in a meeting with your father?"

Isa looked away, then back. "I'm interested to know what he was trying to say to my daughter."

"My assumption is that he isn't going to sit down with your lawyers and tell us anything. So would you be willing to meet with him alone?"

"Alone?"

"That's his request."

"I don't know how to answer that question," she said. "I could say yes to you right now, and five minutes before the meeting I could change my mind. There's a lot of history here."

Manny leaned forward in his chair, as if to announce that it was his turn to talk. "When you say there's a lot of history, do you mean only between you and your father? Or is there something between your daughter and her grandfather that is so upsetting?"

"There is no history between Melany and my father."

Manny stayed with it. "Exactly. Who's to say that this isn't just a grandfather trying to reach out—literally—to the granddaughter he hasn't been allowed to meet?"

"That's what he would say," she said, scoffing.

"What are you saying?" asked Manny. "That he traveled ten thousand miles from Caracas to Hong Kong to—do what? Molest your daughter?"

"No! Who said anything about molesting?"

"Does he have a history of child molestation?" asked Manny.

"No. I told you he was an abusive husband. I saw him hit my mother."

"Did he physically or sexually abuse you?"

"No. Why are you asking this?"

"Did you ever accuse him of it?"

Isa glared at Manny—a glare that might have knocked him from his chair had it been any more intense. "I see where you're going with this," she said. "I'm the one with a history. I'm a false accuser. I wasn't raped."

"Don't get angry."

"Then don't insult me."

"I am simply preparing you," said Manny. "Every woman who has ever been raped and gone public has had to fight the label of false accuser. You have a luxury most victims don't have. Your attacker is dead. You don't have to take the witness stand and point him out in a courtroom. You don't have to testify and endure the cross-examination."

"I'd hardly call that a luxury."

"Then you've never sat through a rape trial."

Isa looked away, and there was only silence. Manny's style wasn't Jack's, but he had a way of making his points. And at least he knew when to back off.

"Should we take a little break?" asked Jack.

"No," she said in a clipped voice, her gaze shifting from Jack to Manny and then to Jack again. "What you don't understand is how evil my father can be—how he can manipulate a little girl's mind. When I was Melany's age, he used to tell me things."

"Sexual things?" asked Manny.

"Will you quit already, Dr. Freud?"

"Manny, just listen," said Jack.

Isa drew a breath. "When he really wanted to hurt my mother, he didn't hit her. He didn't even raise his voice. He would take me aside and tell me stories about her."

"Stories?"

"Oh, my father was a wonderful storyteller. Very convincing. None of it was true, but he filled his stories with such elaborate details that I believed every word. He told me that she had another family. That she had another daughter—a perfect little girl exactly my age who was prettier and smarter than I was. He said my mother loved that family more than us. That's why he had to hit her. If he didn't, she would leave, and I would never see her again."

Isa's gaze drifted off to the middle distance, and Jack filled in the moral of Felipe's story.

"It was all her fault," said Jack.

Isa nodded, and then the sadness in her eyes gave way to resolve. "I've made my decision. Tell my father I'll meet with him."

"Are you sure?" asked Jack.

"Yes," she said. "And I'll do it on his terms. Just the two of us. Alone."

40

•

Isa wished Keith were home. Except that Miami wasn't "home." She wished her whole family could be somewhere else. Not Hong Kong, necessarily. Just anywhere but Miami.

Regrets. She had a long list of them, starting with her decision to stay in Miami for college. It wasn't for lack of options. She was an A student in high school and, having spent grades six through twelve in Miami's International Studies Magnet Program, she spoke English and German as well as her native Spanish. She wanted a top-tier university in a big city. She'd earned acceptance letters from NYU, Northwestern, and Boston College, but opted for warm winters. If only she'd preferred sweaters and boots over a bathing suit and flip-flops. Gabriel Sosa would never have found her. She would never have met David Kaval. She wouldn't be in this mess.

Then again, she wouldn't have fled to Zurich. She would never have met Keith. She wouldn't have Melany.

"Where to?" asked the taxi driver.

"Cy's Place," she told him. "Coconut Grove."

"You got it."

That was the agreed-upon venue for Isa's eight p.m. meeting with her father. Jack had arranged it. Cy's Place had been Jack's idea, but it was an accommodation in response to a specific demand. "He insists that you meet in a public place," Jack had told her after his exchange of e-mails with her father.

What did the old fool think—that Isa might pack a pistol in her purse and blow him away? That unless there were at least a dozen witnesses around them she would empty an entire ammunition clip into his chest, squeezing off round after round at point-blank range, shredding his ribs and sternum with a dozen copper-jacketed projectiles, and then dropping her gun in the dead center of the glistening crimson rose on his crisp white shirt as she turned and said, "Die, you worthless piece of shit"?

Not that she hadn't fantasized about it.

"That's a fun place," said the driver as they pulled away from the motor court at the Four Seasons.

"Excuse me?" said Isa.

"Cy's Place. I been there myself. It's cool. You'll enjoy it."

She crossed her legs and laid her purse in her lap. "I'm sure I will."

Jack and Manny waited inside Theo's business office. It was without windows, only slightly larger than a prison cell, and it doubled as a storage room for nonperishables, so the floor-to-ceiling shelves on three walls were stuffed with boxes of napkins, toilet paper, and other dry goods. Jack sat in a squeaky office chair behind the clunky metal desk, and Manny pulled up a stool on the other side. It was cramped, but the lawyers had promised to remain out of sight and within immediate reach for the meeting between Isa and her father.

"Do you think Isa told us the truth?" asked Manny.

"About what?"

"Her history with her father—whether he sexually abused her."

"I do. I think she's genuinely afraid he'll turn Melany against her, the same way he poisoned Isa's mind with lies about her mother."

"Maybe," said Manny. "But I've been thinking more and more about this since that night at the bar in the Four Seasons, when Keith asked me about the 'abuse excuse.'"

"I remember," said Jack.

"It's hard to come up with a better explanation for why Felipe doesn't want his daughter saying she was raped. It would be rational for him to fear that at some point Isa will have to explain why she didn't report it. Past abuse would be one compelling explanation."

Jack reached for a paper clip and started unbending it into a metal pointer. "There has to be a better one."

"Now you're going back to where I started. She wasn't raped."

"I'm sure that's what this meeting is about. His 'proof.'"

"Proof?"

"That's what he told Keith and me in my office—that he had 'proof' she wasn't raped."

"You think he has it?"

Jack laid the somewhat straightened paper clip on the desk. "Hard to know," he said, reaching for another clip. "A nagging part of me says it's not a total bluff."

41

For the first time since her mother's funeral, Isa sat across from her father and looked him in the eye.

He'd changed in ten years, though probably not as much as Isa perceived. The image in her mind was the old photograph that hung in the consul's office when she was in middle school, when he was handsome in his own way, much more fit and—at least as she remembered—even taller. He was dressed casually, in chinos and a short-sleeve blue guayabera.

No crisp white shirt.

"Where do we start?" she asked.

They were alone at a table for two. The small stage was empty; in the tradition of Uncle Cy and the old Overtown Village, live jazz at Cy's Place didn't start until much later. Tables were starting to fill nonetheless, a mixed crowd of well-dressed couples on their way to dinner or the theater, and the more casual drinkers who had no better place to hang out.

Her father leaned into the table just a bit, his

hands resting earnestly on the tabletop, as if he had nothing to hide. "The first thing I want you to know, Isa, is that this is all about helping you."

"*You*, helping me? This is going to be a very short meeting if that's what this is about."

"Show some respect, young lady. How do you think you got out of jail?"

"You had nothing to do with that."

"I paid ten thousand dollars to your cellmate's boyfriend. He took it from there. I thought he came up with a pretty ingenious plan—the way he and Foneesha Johnson put that guard in the hot seat and put you in the driver's seat."

Isa stared back in disbelief. "Are you saying that guard never planned to rape me?"

"I'm told he definitely had a thing for you."

Foneesha's crude warning came back to her: "*Everybody know he like Latina pussy.*"

"But whether he was going to act on it or not doesn't matter," said Felipe. "This wouldn't be the first time you made false accusations."

Her anger spiked, and it was probably a good thing that the gun in her purse and the crimson rose on the clean white shirt were just a fantasy. "Is this why you wanted me out of jail? You think you can control me?"

He forced a little smile. "No, *gorda*."

Fat girl was the ironic term of endearment he'd used when telling stories to his skinny little daughter—those vicious lies about Isa's mother. "Don't you dare call me that."

"I just want to help."

"I don't want it."

"You *need* my help."

"How does it help me when you meet with my husband and lawyer and tell them that I was never raped—that you have proof that I wasn't raped. How does it help me to plant a story with the *Tribune* that I was not raped. I assume that was you. Am I right?"

He didn't deny it. "That story never ran."

"Because it's not true. I was raped."

"You keep forgetting, I have proof that you lie."

"What is your 'proof'?"

"Alicia Morales."

Mere mention of her name cut like a knife. Alicia had been her best friend in high school and the oldest daughter of Felipe Bornelli's administrative assistant at the consulate. One night when the girls were alone, Alicia confided that Isa's father had come on to her. Isa was certain that "*el jefe*" had done much more than come on to her—Isa could see the real story in Alicia's eyes and hear it in her voice. Isa stood up for her friend and took the matter straight to the consul. It put her father's job in jeopardy—until he crushed Alicia and her allegations. Within a matter of days, Alicia's mother was dismissed from her position at the consul's office, and the entire Morales family was sent packing. Alicia never graduated from high school and ended up working a shit job in a garment factory in Caracas with her mother.

They never forgave Isa.

"I can't listen to this," said Isa as she pushed away from the table.

"Sit *down*," he said through his teeth. "Let me help you, Isa. Or I will destroy you."

She stopped and considered it. Jack had coached her to control her emotions, not to get up and walk away in anger—just listen to what he had to say. *Information is power, Isa. Get all you can.*

She settled back into the chair.

"Smart girl," he said. "Now, I want you to understand why it is better for all concerned that you never testify in this case, and that you never tell anyone that Gabriel Sosa sexually assaulted you."

"You can never make me understand that."

He laid a sealed envelope on the table between them. "This will."

"What is it?"

"This is for you, Isa. It's what I tried to give to Melany when she and her nanny were in Kowloon Park."

Confirmation that Melany had indeed spotted him in Hong Kong was one of the key objectives of the meeting, but it still seemed crazy. "If you wanted me to have this, why would you travel all the way to Hong Kong and hand it to my daughter?"

"If I had sent it to your apartment by FedEx, would you have accepted the package?"

"Only if I didn't know it was from you."

"And if you had unknowingly accepted it and seen it was from me, would you have read what I wrote?"

She gave the honest answer. "No. I would have thrown it in the trash."

"But if Melany had come home from the park

with this envelope and told you that her grandfather had given it to her, wouldn't you have opened it to see what was inside?"

"I suppose—out of concern for Melany's safety."

"And wouldn't you have read it?"

"Only to find out what kind of poison you were trying to put in my daughter's mind."

"Yes, of course. This is your precious daughter. It's your duty to protect her. You would have read it, right?"

She didn't respond right away, but when she did, she again answered honestly. "Probably."

"There you go," he said, gesturing like the man who is always right. "That alone would have made my trip worthwhile. Unfortunately, Melany got scared and ran away before I could tell her who I was and give her the envelope."

It still struck Isa as bizarre, but Felipe Bornelli was a bizarre human being. "What's inside?" she asked.

"The truth," he said.

"About what?"

"About Gabriel Sosa."

Isa felt a chill. She glanced at the envelope on the table, then back at her father.

"Share it with no one," he said in a low, almost threatening tone. "But read it. Read it as many times as you have to. Read it carefully, and then you will see things my way."

42

At 5:45 p.m. Saturday the Swissair nonstop from Zurich touched down at Miami International Airport. Keith traveled business class, not first. The difference in fare was astounding, and Keith somehow felt compelled to save the money, having spent his entire Friday at IBS headquarters trying to defend the Hong Kong office's worst second-quarter performance since the 1997 Asian financial crisis.

Landed, he texted Isa.

On Thursday evening Keith had landed in Zurich loaded with facts for his meetings. The Asian market was still feeling the effects of Black Monday, when the Shanghai main share index lost 8.49 percent of its value in a single trading day. Manufacturing in China had contracted for ten consecutive months. For the first time in history, trading on the Shanghai and Shenzhen stock exchanges was halted under new "circuit breaker" rules to avoid all-out free fall. All of that was true. It was also true that Keith had spent forty-seven of the previous sixty days half a world away from his family. His review committee, however, seemed interested in only one thing: Keith had a "major personal distraction" in his life.

Yay! Love you! Isa texted back.

Keith cleared customs, which took another forty minutes, then walked with the steady flow of passengers into the main terminal. It was the same corridor through which he'd entered upon arrival from Hong Kong in April—and that had ended with Isa in handcuffs. Going to work and spending nights alone in their Hong Kong apartment had, in some ways, made the arrest and aftermath feel as distant as another lifetime. Returning to the airport, however, and putting one foot in front of the other on the same black terrazzo floor brought it back in painful detail. It was as if he could see Jack with his wife and daughter waving from the other side of security. He could almost see Riley's face beaming as she met her new friend from Hong Kong. He could see a pair of uniformed officers from the Miami-Dade Police Department waiting at the end of the corridor. *Really* could. They were actually there.

What the heck do they want?

The more muscular officer approached. "Keith Ingraham?"

Keith stopped. "Yeah. Is something wrong?"

"You're under arrest."

The other officer cuffed Keith's hands behind his back.

"You gotta be kiddin' me," said Keith.

* * *

Jack and Andie were dining at Hillstone's Restaurant on Miracle Mile when his cell vibrated. KEITH flashed as an incoming call. It was an implicit nuptial vow that he didn't take calls from clients while on a date with Andie on a Saturday night, but technically Keith wasn't a client.

"Welcome back," Jack said.

"I've been arrested."

Jack almost dropped the phone onto his seared bluefin tuna. Keith was at the Miami-Dade police station and gave Jack as much information as he could.

"I'm on my way," said Jack, and then he quickly told him all the things *not* to say or do before his lawyer arrived. They hung up, and Jack gave Andie the bad news.

"Should I come with you?" she asked.

"I think someone needs to be with Isa."

Andie agreed. She would get their meals boxed up and cab it to the Four Seasons. Jack kissed her good-bye, but she grabbed his hand before he could dash away from the table.

"What is Keith charged with?" asked Andie.

"A second-degree felony," said Jack. "Accessory after the fact to murder."

43

Jack called Sylvia Hunt on his drive to the police station. On another Saturday night he wouldn't have expected her to answer, but Keith's arrest couldn't have happened without her involvement.

"Hello, Jack. I was just about to call and make sure you were aware of the latest developments."

Two fire trucks and an ambulance passed on U.S. 1 with sirens blaring. Jack adjusted the volume on his Bluetooth connection and returned his hands to the wheel. "This is unacceptable," he said. "There was no need for you to arrest Keith this way. You could have called me with a heads-up, and he would have surrendered himself."

"I understand what you're saying, but I assure you that this wasn't a stunt. Mr. Ingraham travels abroad more frequently than most commercial pilots. Our concern was that if we gave any advance notice, he wouldn't return to Florida."

"Seriously? You think he would flee from his wife and daughter?"

"This is a pointless debate, Jack. Let's move

forward. I'm a reasonable person. The good news for you is that bail is not an issue. We'll agree to the release of Mr. Ingraham on his own recognizance. Just surrender his passport."

"He needs to travel to make a living."

"I can't agree to let him leave Miami-Dade County. My suggestion is that you surrender his passport tonight, so he doesn't spend the night in jail, and you can go before the judge on Monday to try and get it back."

Jack didn't see much choice. "Fine. We'll do that."

"And I will send you a copy of the indictment."

"Can you e-mail it now, please?"

"Absolutely," she said. "It's on its way."

Still driving, Jack hung up and immediately dialed Manny. Manny was perfectly happy to let Jack handle the Saturday-night duty without him. It was a blurry situation anyway. Jack would help his friend get out of jail tonight, but going forward, it wasn't clear if Keith would need counsel separate from his wife's defense team. It was an issue Jack flagged in his next call—to Isa—when he told her that he'd reached the police station and was waiting for MDPD to bring Keith to him. He was still thinking about it when the door opened and Keith entered the room.

"Can you fucking believe this?" asked Keith as he seated himself in the chair at the table.

Jack signaled him to stop talking until the MDPD officers left. When the door closed and they were alone, Jack answered the pending question. "Actually, I can."

Jack told him the good news about bail, but he could make no promises that the judge would allow him to leave the country.

"If they keep my passport, you realize I will be looking for a new job," said Keith.

"Sylivia Hunt is well aware of that. Frankly, that's why she indicted you, in my opinion."

"To ruin me? What is she, a psychopath?"

"It's a strategic move. Isa is of course the primary target here. Indicting a family member is a tried-and-true method of extracting a guilty plea from the principal defendant. I've seen it a hundred times before. The usual scenario is to go after the mother who hid her son—the 'good boy'—while he was on the lam."

"You're saying that the prosecutor indicted *me* so that Isa will plead guilty?"

"She didn't tell me that. It's just my first instinct. We'll probably see some kind of plea offer in the next few days."

"But wait a second. The prosecutor can't just make up charges against me."

"She went back to the grand jury to get your indictment, so that gives her some protection from any claim that she made this up."

"How am I an accessory after the fact to the murder of Gabriel Sosa? I didn't know Isa when that happened. I wasn't even living in Miami."

"Accessory after the fact doesn't mean you were driving the getaway vehicle. The government has to prove three things. One, Isa is guilty as charged. Two, you knew she was guilty. Three, you committed some act to conceal her involvement or to make it harder for police to apprehend her."

"They can't prove any of those things," said Keith.

"You're going to have to search your memory—go way back in your relationship."

"Let's stop talking in the abstract. First, she's not guilty. But what does the prosecutor say I did to protect her? Move to Hong Kong? That's bullshit."

"No. A husband can't be charged as an accessory to a crime committed by his wife—or vice versa. That's the law in Florida. So it has to be something you did before you married Isa."

"There's nothing."

"Actually, the indictment says there is."

"What?"

Jack narrowed his eyes, making it clear that he wanted the truth. "The indictment alleges that you paid David Kaval twenty thousand dollars to keep quiet about Isa's involvement."

Keith froze for a moment, then sat back in his chair, thinking. "Before we were married," he said in a hollow voice.

"Yes. Right before. You want to tell me about that?"

"It's not what it seems," said Keith.

"I'm all ears," said Jack.

Keith's head rolled back as he breathed out heavily toward the ceiling. Then he looked at Jack.

And he told him.

44

Jack drove Keith to the Four Seasons and went up with him to the apartment. Melany was asleep. Keith was jet-lagged. Isa was wide awake. She hugged him the way a wife might hug a husband back from the battlefield. "I'm so, so sorry, honey. This is all my fault."

Jack let them have a few minutes alone, which turned into a few minutes more as Keith headed down the hall to check on Melany, Isa's "Please don't wake her" notwithstanding. Andie was in the living room, but she needed to leave and let Riley's babysitter go home. Jack walked her down to the motor court, and she got a taxi to Key Biscayne. By the time Jack returned to the apartment, Manny was sitting on the L-shaped leather couch in the living room with Isa and Keith. Isa had called him an hour earlier.

"I wanted him to be part of this," said Isa.

"Good. We're all here," said Jack.

"Not to be a party pooper," said Keith, "but I'm on Zurich time. It's going on four a.m. to me."

"I'll make coffee," said Isa.

"No more caffeine," said Keith. "I say we all get a good night's sleep and reconvene in the morning."

"How do you expect me to sleep?" asked Isa. "I don't even know what's going on."

"Frankly, neither do I," said Jack. "Keith and I talked at the station. I now have three different versions of the letters that David Kaval mailed from FSP to Zurich before you two were married. One story from him, one from Isa, and now one from Keith."

"Letters?" asked Isa. "There was only *one* letter."

Keith blinked. "No, Isa. There were two."

"No, I'm sure of it. Jack, I *told you* there was only one letter. I got *one* letter from him. That's the truth."

"Yeah," said Keith. "That is the truth. Because I was the one who checked the postbox on the day the second letter came. You never saw it."

"Keith, what are you saying?" she asked with trepidation.

"There was a bank account number in the second letter. I wired twenty thousand dollars to get Kaval to leave us alone."

Jack had already heard Keith's story, but Manny and Isa's reaction was no different from what his had been—stunned silence.

"I don't understand," said Isa.

Jack said, "Keith has been indicted for allegedly paying twenty thousand dollars in hush money to David Kaval. In essence, the charge is that Keith bribed a witness to keep him from implicating you in the murder of Gabriel Sosa."

"Did the second letter say anything about Sosa?" asked Manny.

"No," Keith said firmly. "It's like I explained to Jack already. This was about two months before our wedding. Isa told me that a crazy old boyfriend forged a marriage certificate and was going to make trouble for her. She said that she'd gone to see a lawyer, and he told her to ignore it. That seemed like bad advice to me. Then this second letter came. We don't get a lot of mail from maximum-security facilities, so I knew it was from the same guy. I opened it and read it. At this point I totally disagreed with the advice Isa got from her lawyer to just ignore this."

"Did you talk to Isa about it?" asked Manny.

"No" and "no," they answered, Keith and Isa speaking almost in unison.

"Isa was planning a wedding," said Keith. "I *did* agree with her lawyer in one respect: don't let this ruin your happy occasion. I decided to take care of it myself. I got my own lawyer to draft a dissolution of marriage and sent it to Kaval for his signature. I paid him twenty thousand dollars to sign it. I signed for Isa, and got it filed with the court. Problem solved."

"You wired twenty grand to David Kaval and never said a word to Isa?" asked Jack, incredulous. "Come on, Keith. Cut the shit."

"It's true," said Isa. "He never told me."

"All right," said Keith. "It wasn't just a matter of Isa planning a wedding. It wasn't easy for Isa to tell me—her fiancé—about that first letter from Kaval. Let me be clear about this: there was never any mention of Gabriel Sosa. I never heard the guy's name until Isa was arrested at the airport. But long before that, going back to the night Isa told me about the letter, Isa seemed terrified of this guy Kaval."

"I was," she said quietly.

Keith reached over and took her hand. "I didn't want her to know that I was having any dealings with him. I just wanted to solve the problem and keep her out of it. I did what a lot of husbands, or husbands-to-be, would do. I took care of it for her."

Jack considered the enhancement—Keith's new and improved version of the letter and the twenty thousand dollars. Jack's cocounsel spoke up before he did.

"Wow, that was awesome," said Manny.

"What do you mean?" asked Keith.

"Either all of that is absolutely true, or you two missed your calling. This is Academy Award material—Best Actress and Best Actor, right here in your living room."

"That's not funny," said Keith.

"There's something else that's not funny," said Jack. "You say the money you sent to Kaval had nothing to do with Gabriel Sosa or the charges against Isa."

"It *didn't.* Even Kaval kept quiet about it when you deposed him."

"Probably because he didn't want to be charged with extortion on top of everything else," Manny interjected.

"Let's keep the focus on you, Keith," said Jack. "Almost from the beginning of this case you *knew* that Kaval was the chief witness against Isa. But you didn't say anything about your own dealings with him. Not to me. Apparently not even to Isa. That's inexcusable."

"How is that inexcusable? Shit, Jack, we're friends, but you're kind of an odd duck when it comes to criminal-defense lawyers. I thought you guys never wanted to know *anything* unless you asked for it."

Manny piped up. "That's a whole nother debate."

"A debate we're not going to have tonight," said Jack.

"Damn right we're not," Keith said, and then he rubbed his eyes with the base of his palms, as if trying to bring himself back to life. "You made your point, Jack. I should have told you. I'm sorry. I fucked up and kept this to myself, okay? But this wasn't about Gabriel Sosa, and if I hear his name one more time tonight my head is going to explode. Since Thursday night I've flown from Hong Kong to Zurich, had my ass chewed out by one Swiss banker after another, got on another plane today and flew to Miami, and then ended up in a police station under arrest. I honestly can't say that any other day since Isa's arrest has been any less chaotic or any more fun than the last forty-eight hours. Can we pick this up again tomorrow? I need to go to bed."

Keith rose, but Jack didn't.

"I'm serious," said Keith. "I need to sleep."

Jack rose, and the others followed suit. "Sure thing."

Isa and Keith walked the lawyers to the door.

Keith shook their hands. Isa gave Jack a hug. It was the first time she'd done so.

She seemed to intuit where Jack's thoughts were leading him.

They said good night, and the lawyers went to the elevator. Jack hit the call button, and the elevator was already there. They were alone on the ride down.

"I may be out," said Jack.

"Out of what?"

"The case," said Jack. "Keith and I are old friends, which makes this hard enough. The fact that he's been less than straight with me about David Kaval may be the straw that breaks the camel's back."

"Oh, please. Like you've never represented a client who held back from you."

"It's different when friendship's involved."

The elevator doors opened. Jack and Manny stepped into the lobby.

"Fine," said Manny. "You can represent Isa. I'll represent Keith."

"Are you serious?" asked Jack.

"Why not?" said Manny as they walked out to the motor court. "No question, Isa's the marquee defendant in this case. But this could be fun, you and me. I got no problem with that."

"That could work, if the clients agree. Very gracious of you, Manny. Surprisingly gracious."

Jack would have to wait for his car, but Manny's Aston Martin was parked up front with the Bentley Continental GT, the red Ferrari 458, the yellow Lamborghini Gallardo, and a half dozen other vehicles priced north of a quarter mil. The valet attendant opened the door and handed Manny the keys, but Manny stopped and looked back at Jack before getting in.

"Funny thing, Jack. People say I'm all about serving my own ego. But that's not true at all." He flashed a little power grin and climbed behind the wheel. "I'm basically about the money."

The attendant closed the door for him. The engine roared, and Manny pulled away as if in pursuit of the checkered flag.

Jack was still standing at the curb.

"Is Mr. Espinosa a friend of yours?" asked the attendant.

Jack handed him his valet ticket. "You know, I'm not really sure."

45

Isa wanted to keep talking. She followed Keith into the master bathroom and checked the dry patches beneath her eyes in the vanity mirror. Keith was brushing his teeth at the "his" basin.

"I met with my father."

Keith stopped brushing. "When?"

"Thursday night. Jack and Manny agreed that I should. I was going to tell you, but you've been harder to reach than usual the last couple of days."

He rinsed his toothbrush and put it in the rack. "What came out of it?"

She told him about the envelope—and how her father had told her that it was about Gabriel Sosa. "He said that if I read what was inside, I would see things his way."

"What was in it?"

"I don't know. I still haven't opened it."

"Doesn't Jack think you should?"

"I haven't told him about it."

"Why not?"

She turned away from the bathroom mirror,

her eyes meeting his. "I wanted us to talk about it first."

"You want us to read it together?"

She took a step closer and touched his hand. "Yes. Together."

Keith nodded. She opened the envelope and removed a handwritten letter. It was in Spanish. Keith watched as Isa read it to herself. Then she looked at him.

"Do you want me to translate?" she asked, swallowing hard.

She was giving her husband one last chance not to know all, and Keith seemed to appreciate the gravity of the situation.

"Yeah," he said finally. "Translate."

And she did.

Keith lay awake in the darkness. Isa was sound asleep on her side of the bed. Keith had slept little in the previous two days, but apparently Isa had slept even less. She'd agonized over the letter from her father—whether to tell her lawyer about it, whether to read it before Keith got home, whether to read it at all. She'd admitted to having retrieved it from the garbage twice. There was no doubt in her mind that it would be filled with lies. Reading it together, with her husband, would be cathartic for her. A burden lifted. Or shifted—to him.

I gotta get to sleep.

He was exhausted, but rest wouldn't come.

Keith slid out of bed and walked quietly across the room. The door was open, so he made it into the hallway without disturbing Isa. He continued to Melany's room. Another open door. Her Winnie-the-Pooh night-light cast an orange-yellow glow across the carpet. He tiptoed as he entered. Even with her audio processors removed for the night Melany could sense movement across the floor. Keith stopped at her bedside and watched her sleep. Such peacefulness. He leaned over and kissed her forehead.

"My angel," he whispered.

He stepped back slowly and left the room. Seeing Melany had been exactly what he needed. The perfect reminder that all of this would be worth it—that the past didn't matter.

Or did it?

Keith went to the kitchen, got a glass of milk, and walked to the window. The cityscape was still aglow, though it was nowhere near as bright as it had been just a couple of hours earlier, when he and Isa had taken seats at the kitchen counter, sliced open the envelope from her father, and read the letter the way she'd wanted to read it—together.

Until the letter, Gabriel Sosa had been an abstraction to Keith. Isa's father—he still didn't think of him as a "father-in-law"—had changed everything. Maybe the letter was nothing but lies, as Isa had said. Lies or not, the effect on Keith was the same. Gabriel Sosa had never felt like part of *them* before. The letter, even more than the indictment, brought him into their marriage. Partly because of what the letter said. But mostly because it made Keith realize that he may have lied to Jack. He'd sworn to Jack that he had never heard the name Gabriel Sosa until Isa's arrest.

But he had—possibly.

It was early in his relationship with Isa, years back, probably the fourth or fifth time they'd slept together. They'd been out late and both had had too much to drink. They undressed each other and fell into the bed. It was sloppy and awkward sex. They were so drunk, in fact, that they even laughed off a guffaw that might have destroyed another relationship. All these years later, it didn't seem funny at all.

Keith couldn't be certain. His memory wasn't clear, and so many years had passed. But one thing he was sure of. As he rolled on top and found his way inside her, Isa had called him by the wrong name.

The name had long ago escaped him. But the letter—written by the man who had traveled all the way from Venezuela to tell Jack and Keith that he could prove Isa wasn't raped—had brought it back to him. Or was the past playing tricks on him? Keith didn't think so. In the back of his mind, deep in his memory, he could hear Isa's voice on that night. He was almost certain that in that breathless heat of passion, she'd brought her lips to his ear and whispered a name that, at the time, had meant nothing to him.

"Gabriel."

46

On Monday morning the court bailiff called two cases for a single hearing.

"The *State of Florida v. Keith Ingraham* and the *State of Florida v. Isabelle Bornelli*," he intoned, and the case numbers followed.

From high on the bench Judge Gonzalez greeted the lawyers. They rose at their respective tables to announce their appearance—first the prosecution and then the defense. Which made it official: Manny's proposed arrangement had carried the day.

"Jack Swyteck, for defendant Isabelle Bornelli."

"Manuel Espinosa, for defendant Keith Ingraham."

As planned, the defense team had reconvened on Sunday morning, and the lawyers had laid out the many good reasons for husband and wife to have separate counsel. Isa didn't want to choose and was relieved that Jack and Manny had essentially chosen for her. Keith was pleased to know that he wouldn't be shelling out another hundred-thousand-dollar retainer to a third lawyer.

Monday's hearing marked the first time that all four were seated at the table for the defense.

"Give me one sec," the judge said, and a frantic self-search commenced beneath his robe for a missing pair of reading glasses. The courtroom was silent, but it was far from empty. Media coverage of the case had subsided over the summer, but Keith's indictment had sparked interest anew. Virtually every significant news agency in south Florida was represented in the press gallery, and about half of the seats for the general public were filled. Jack noticed none of the "Rape Victims Matter" demonstrators from Isa's arraignment, but that didn't mean they weren't coming.

The judge affixed his spectacles, checked the notepad before him, and cleared his throat. "I understand that the parties have stipulated to Mr. Ingraham's release on his own recognizance."

Sylvia Hunt rose but remained at the prosecution's table, near the empty jury box. "Provided that the court retains possession of his passport," she said.

The judge's expression soured. "That seems extreme, don't you think, Ms. Hunt?"

"The defendant is charged with a felony punishable by up to fifteen years in prison. I don't think it's too much to ask that he stay in Miami-Dade County and not travel to a Communist country where extradition would be virtually impossible."

The communism argument. *Here we go again*, thought Jack, but it was Manny's turn to speak.

"Your Honor, my client is an international banker who runs the Hong Kong office for IBS.

He doesn't travel there to pledge allegiance to the Communist Party. I would also add that his wife surrendered her passport in April, awaiting trial, and she has never attempted to flee. If the court is truly concerned that Mr. Ingraham might not return for trial, we would agree to post a bond."

"Done," said the judge. "Bail is set at fifty thousand dollars. Mr. Ingraham's passport shall be returned immediately. He is free to travel to his workplace in Hong Kong, but he is prohibited from entering the Chinese mainland."

Keith leaned toward Jack and whispered, "I can live with that."

Manny thanked the judge and took his seat at the table beside his client. Jack rose for the main event.

"Next issue," the judge said. "I have a motion from the prosecution to consolidate these two cases for *all* purposes, including a single trial in which husband and wife will be codefendants."

"That's correct," said the prosecutor. "We believe that is both efficient and fair to both defendants."

"We disagree," said Jack. "Judge, the prosecution wants to prejudice the jury against Isa Bornelli by injecting into her trial the question of whether her husband made an illegal payment to David Kaval, the state's chief witness against my client. That's improper."

"Why would a joint trial be improper?" asked the judge. "This all seems intertwined."

"It's a simple matter of law and logic," said Manny, rising.

It was a bit of hijacking, as the defense team had agreed before the hearing that Jack would cover the issue of a joint trial.

"Who's arguing this motion for the defense?" asked the judge.

"I will, if cocounsel will yield," said Manny. "If anyone is prejudiced by a joint trial, it's my client, who is facing relatively minor charges and will be forced to stand trial with an accused murderer."

Jack didn't want to yield, but he also didn't want to send a message to the prosecutor that her obvious plan was working—that division was already brewing in the defense camp.

The judge took Manny's bait. "Proceed, Mr. Espinosa."

Jack returned to his seat. Manny buttoned his coat, and he paraded forward in a manner that belied his words to Jack in the motor court on Saturday night—that he was about the money, not ego.

"Here's the thing, Judge. Mr. Ingraham cannot be an accessory after the fact to the murder of Gabriel Sosa unless his wife is guilty of murder. It only makes sense to let her trial play out first. If she is acquitted, the 'accessory after the fact' charges against my client must be dismissed. If she is convicted, the court can proceed with a trial on the accessory charge."

The judge made a face. "Two trials instead of one? That makes no sense. This is a lot like a conspiracy case. Coconspirators stand trial together every day in the court systems."

"It's not really a conspiracy charge," said Manny.

"David Kaval and Ms. Bornelli are the alleged conspiracy."

"The same logic applies," said the judge. "The motion to consolidate is granted. Mr. Ingraham and Ms. Bornelli will stand trial together. Anything else?"

Jack rose. "Your Honor, I'd like to be heard on this."

"I'm not going to give the defense two bites at the apple on every issue that comes up. The cases are consolidated. Coordinate your strategies accordingly. We're adjourned," he announced with a bang of the gavel.

All rose on the bailiff's command. Judge Gonzalez stepped down from the bench and exited through the side door to his chambers. Jack stepped closer to Manny, speaking under his breath so as not to be heard by his client. "Don't you ever pull a fucking stunt like that again."

"I had the judge eating out of my hand on bail. It wasn't time to change horses. I went for it. You would have done the same."

A bustling courtroom wasn't the place to debate it. Both Isa and Keith had questions, but the media were standing behind them, just on the other side of the rail. Jack told Isa to "save it" until they were back at his office. Jack gathered his papers, but the prosecutor stopped him before he could step away.

"My office, Jack?"

"Excuse me?"

Sylvia wasn't smiling, but she was clearly pleased with the judge's decision to consolidate. "No prosecutor would want to put a victim of sexual assault through the added ordeal of a murder trial if justice can be served without one. I have an offer for your client," she said. "And it's the best offer she's going to get."

47

Twenty minutes after Manny and the newly anointed "joint" defendants arrived at the Freedom Institute, Jack joined them. His meeting with Sylvia Hunt had been brief, with no need to retreat to the state attorney's office. Jack had all the details by the time they left the courthouse.

"It's not a bad offer," said Jack.

They were in Jack's office, though the seating arrangement was a little different for this meeting than previous ones. No one had choreographed it, at least not overtly, but husband and wife had ended up on opposite sides of the table. Isa was beside Jack, Keith beside Manny.

"If Isa pleads guilty to voluntary manslaughter and accepts a prison sentence of forty-two months, the prosecution will drop all charges against Keith."

"I won't do it," she said. "No way."

"I agree," said Keith. "This prosecutor has built a case of first-degree murder on the back of David

Kaval—a lying scumbag. Even with his lies, they can't put Isa at the scene of the crime."

"They don't have to prove she was there," said Jack. "They have to prove she planned and directed it."

"Which they can't," said Keith. "This has been the prosecutor's strategy from the beginning. Overcharge Isa and then hope that she caves and cops a plea to a lesser charge."

"I agree that's the strategy," said Jack. "Charging you puts more pressure on Isa to cut a deal. The possibility that both Melany's mother *and* father may end up in jail has to weigh heavily on a mother's mind. We may not like that game, but we still need to evaluate the deal."

"If I'm sentenced to forty-two months, how much time would I actually serve?"

"Florida law requires you to serve at least eighty-five percent of your sentence. A few days short of three years."

"That's too long," said Isa.

"If you're convicted at trial, it's a mandatory life sentence. And life in Florida means life. There is no parole."

There was silence in the room. At this stage, Jack had expected another knee-jerk response of "No deals," but Isa actually seemed to be considering it—at least for a moment. Keith seemed to be putting his emotions aside as well. Practicality was setting in.

"I could see where someone in Isa's shoes wouldn't want to roll the dice," Keith said, addressing the group. Then he looked at Isa. "Honey, I'm not pushing you one way or the other. But I want you to know that I'll be here for you. Three years is—"

"Three of the most formative years of Melany's life," she said in a sharp tone. "Kindergarten is when we mainstream her, Keith. These next three years—the next *year*, really—will define who she is for the rest of her life. I can't spend that time in jail."

"I know, but—"

"No buts," said Isa. "And it's not just about doing time. Entering a guilty plea would be a lie. How would I ever explain that to our daughter?"

Keith fell silent, then nodded. "I think it's unanimous," he told the lawyers. "No deals. At least none that involves jail time."

Jack felt compelled to point out the elephant in the room. "We all know where this is headed if Isa turns down this deal."

"We do?" asked Isa.

Manny did. "Sylvia Hunt will offer Keith a deal."

"What kind of deal?" asked Keith.

Manny moved to the other side of the room, closer to Keith, his client. "My guess? She'll offer to drop the charges in exchange for your testimony against Isa."

"That's not gonna happen," said Keith.

"That won't stop the prosecutor from trying."

"What could I possibly say to hurt Isa?"

"The prosecutor would be most interested in

anything Isa might have said to you that could be construed as her admission of guilt."

"There's nothing like that," said Keith.

"Or some piece of evidence that she may have shared with you," said Jack.

Keith hesitated just long enough for Jack to notice. "Nothing," said Keith.

"This doesn't make sense to me," said Isa. "I thought we all agreed that I can't testify against Keith and Keith can't testify against me. Our conversations as husband and wife are protected by the marital privilege."

"That's true for conversations after you were married," said Manny. "But it doesn't apply to anything you shared before you were married, even if you shared your deepest, darkest secrets in complete confidence."

"The policy behind this privilege is to protect the institution of marriage," said Jack. "If it wasn't said in the context of a valid marriage, no privilege attaches."

Keith put a finer point on it. "So if I wanted to, I could testify about things Isa and I talked about before we were married?"

"Yes," said Manny.

"That goes both ways," said Jack. "Isa could testify against you if she wanted to. You couldn't stop her."

Husband and wife exchanged glances. "That would never happen," said Keith.

"No," said Isa. "Never."

"Just to be clear," said Keith. "I will never agree

to any deal that sends my wife to jail. Any more than she would cut a deal that sends me to jail."

Jack nodded, but he'd seen it all—spouses turning against spouses, mothers turning against their own sons. It was impossible to predict what deals a client might consider or even accept as trial approaches and the prospect of serious prison time looms.

And Jack just didn't trust Manny.

"I'll tell Sylvia Hunt no deal," said Jack. "Is that the decision?"

"Yes," said Isa.

"Final decision," said Keith.

48

David Kaval could taste freedom. It was on the other side of the prison door—the final step in a journey that had begun 3,104 days earlier.

Eight and a half fucking years.

Kaval's last day at FSP had started at two a.m., when a corrections officer entered his cell and told him, "Pack your shit." Kaval had known for some time that this day was coming, but he hadn't prepacked. He'd told no one on the block about his release, not even his cellmate, since getting the news. He'd followed his daily routine to the letter: the same vocational class, same workout schedule, same walk in the prison yard. He'd done absolutely nothing out of the ordinary—nothing that might signal to other inmates that his release was imminent. Kaval wasn't stupid. No sense putting the prison world on notice that time was running out for anyone planning to even an old score with Inmate Y-37980.

Like everything in prison life, the release process was painfully slow. By three a.m. he'd finally reached a holding tank with other inmates. For all but Kaval and one other lucky guy who felt like he'd won the lottery, however, this wasn't a happy day. Most were simply being transferred to another facility as part of routine population control. At five a.m. the guards escorted the entire group to the cafeteria, where Kaval ate his last prison meal. Then it was off to another holding tank. More waiting, but he was too pumped with adrenaline to be bored. Some of the corrections officers he'd come to know over the years walked over and shared parting words, things along the lines of "Keep your head up, Kaval," and "Don't come back." One guard, however, kept his distance. Kaval kept looking in his direction, determined to lock eyes with him at least once before leaving.

It was the asshole who'd nearly derailed Kaval's early release.

Inmates at FSP can earn "gain time" to shave off as much as 15 percent of their court-imposed sentence. It's a tool the Florida Department of Corrections uses to encourage satisfactory inmate behavior and participation in prison programs. Gain time is based on a point system: sixty days for earning a GED, another sixty days for performing an outstanding deed, and so on. Kaval had earned enough gain time to reduce his ten-year sentence by eighteen months. A single disciplinary report for fighting or other bad behavior, however, could cost an inmate all of his gain time. Who could spend eight years in a box and not lose his cool? Kaval had unloaded his anger on a Puerto Rican pedophile who kept singing "I kissed a girl and got arrested" to the tune of Katy Perry's "I Kissed a

Girl"—for two hours, nonstop. Kaval smashed his fucking head into a urinal, and it cost him. No one had ever heard of an inmate getting his gain time reinstated. There was a first time for everything, however, and Kaval had pulled it off.

But not without help.

At six a.m. the door opened, and the transferring inmates filed out—a line of losers linked one to the next by metal handcuffs. Kaval felt no spirit of camaraderie. It was every man for himself inside these walls, and he'd lived by that creed for more than eight years. There was no doubt in his mind that most of those guys—especially the lifers—would have slit his throat in a minute, if that was what it took to trade places with him.

"Let's go," said the guard.

Kaval grabbed his personal property bag and followed the corrections officer into the next room to meet a clerk seated at a desk. She asked a series of basic questions—name, age, DOB, FSP number—which she entered into the log. The guard took him to an adjoining room for fingerprinting and a photograph. Then it was time for the final strip search. About once a month some idiot failed to ditch his contraband before release. Not Kaval.

"You're clean," he said.

Kaval left his prison uniform on the floor. The guard handed him street clothes, which he pulled on quickly. Not stylish, but adequate. When he was dressed, the guard led him back to the clerk's office. She pushed the desk phone toward him. The hold button was blinking.

"Sylvia Hunt wants to speak to you," said the desk clerk. She handed Kaval the phone and opened the line with a punch of the button.

"Kaval here," he said.

"You understand the terms of your release, right?" she said, no small talk.

"Yes, ma'am."

"If you leave the state of Florida before Isa Bornelli's trial, it's back to prison."

"No problem. Gonna just lie on the beach."

"If your testimony at trial deviates by one word from what you told the grand jury, you are going straight back to prison."

"Got it."

"And let me reiterate. The only time you are to get near Isabelle Bornelli is when you see her in the courtroom. If you get within five hundred yards of her outside the courthouse, we will lock you up. You understand?"

He smiled thinly. "I hear you."

"Do you *understand*?"

"Sure. No problem."

"Good. Stay out of trouble."

The call ended, and Kaval hung up. The guard walked him out of the office and wished him well. Another guard at the exit made one last check to make sure they had the right inmate. Then the door opened. Kaval walked into the morning sun and heard the door close behind him. He stopped and turned around, threw his hands into the air, and shouted at the top of his lungs:

"Good-bye, you motherfuckers!"

A blue Chevy was at the curb with the motor

running. Kaval walked quickly down the sidewalk, opened the car door, and climbed into the passenger seat.

"Hey, baby. Time to have sex."

Ilene Simpson smiled. "There's a motel two miles down the road."

He smiled back. "This is going to be so fucking good."

She reached across the console and slid her hand between his legs. Kaval was more than ready.

"You are such a bad boy."

The smile left his face. "You love it, bitch."

Fall

49

Autumn brought butterflies. Isa felt them in her stomach, as summer's end meant the start of the long-awaited trial.

Nineteen weeks—April to October—had passed since Isa's indictment, which probably should have been time enough to prepare mentally and emotionally. But it almost didn't seem real, not even as she and Keith took their seats at the mahogany table beside their lawyers.

Jury selection had consumed all of Monday and half of Tuesday, with lawyers for the prosecution and defense employing some combination of voodoo and pop psychology to pick the perfect group of strangers to decide if this husband and wife should live out their lives together, as parents, or separately, as inmates. Judge Gonzalez—the same judge who had denied bail to Isa—presided at trial.

"We have a jury," Judge Gonzalez announced.

Isa sized them up. Six adults who had never been convicted of a felony, which was all that Florida law required in a noncapital case. Four women and two men: an elementary school teacher, a janitor, a nurse, a bus driver, a grad student from FIU, and a self-proclaimed musician. The prosecution had wanted men. The defense preferred women. Beyond that, who were these people? What baggage would they carry into the jury box? The rest of Isa's life and Keith's future were in their hands. Isa wasn't terribly comfortable with that arrangement, but Jack and Manny had seemed satisfied. Then again, so had Sylvia Hunt.

The trial broke for lunch, and they returned to the courtroom for opening statements. Keith's parents sat in the front row of public seating, directly behind their son. Isa had no family to show support. The press gallery was filled to capacity, well beyond the handful that had shown up for jury selection. Likewise, the general audience had nearly doubled in size. It was as if the scouts had phoned their friends to tell them that things were about to get interesting. Isa had the sickening sense that they were.

"Ms. Hunt," said Judge Gonzalez, "please proceed."

The prosecutor rose and stepped to the well of the courtroom, that stagelike opening before the bench where lawyers could seemingly step away from the action and speak directly to the jury, like a Shakespearean actor delivering a soliloquy. Hunt buttoned her blazer, bid the jurors a good afternoon, and dove straight into her thesis.

"Gabriel Sosa did not deserve to die."

She paused for what seemed a painfully long

stretch of silence, as if to ensure that the message sank in. Then she stepped closer to the jury and continued.

"Mr. Sosa was twenty years old when his bloodied and shirtless body was found in a ditch on the side of a road. He had been tortured to death.

"The defendant, Isabelle Bornelli, was a nineteen-year-old college freshman. A month before Mr. Sosa was murdered, they went on a date. She invited him up to her dorm room, where one of two things happened. Mr. Sosa and Ms. Bornelli had consensual sex, or Mr. Sosa sexually assaulted her.

"In this trial, you will see no police report of a sexual assault. Ms. Bornelli never filed one. However, you will hear the testimony of another man who dated Ms. Bornelli in college, David Kaval. Now, Mr. Kaval is no saint. In fact, he has spent almost his entire adult life in a maximum-security prison. Ms. Bornelli chose to tell *him* that she was raped by Mr. Sosa. Mr. Kaval will explain what happened next. He will admit the role he played in the murder of Gabriel Sosa. And he will tell you how Ms. Bornelli planned, participated in, and orchestrated this brutal revenge killing.

"I urge you to listen to Mr. Kaval's testimony carefully. Listen to *all* the testimony in this case. But no matter what you may hear in this courtroom in the coming days, remember the very first thing I told you. Gabriel Sosa did not deserve a death sentence. Isabelle Bornelli has no right to decide who lives and who dies."

Isa shrank on the inside as the prosecutor thanked the jurors and returned to her seat.

"Mr. Swyteck, your opening statement?" said the judge.

As Jack rose, Isa was fully aware of the joint defense team's advance strategy on opening statements. But having felt the weight of the prosecutor's words, and having witnessed the impact on the jury, she was having second thoughts.

"Defendant Bornelli will defer her opening statement to the start of her case," Jack announced, sticking to the plan.

"Very well. Ladies and gentlemen of the jury, defendant Bornelli has elected to save her opening statement until after the state of Florida has presented its evidence. It's her right to do so, and if any defensc is necessary, you will be hearing from her lawyer at that time. Mr. Espinosa, you may proceed on behalf of defendant Ingraham."

Manny rose and stepped to the lectern. Behind Isa was a quick shuffle of reporters jockeying for position, then silence. Manny began, serious yet cordial in his delivery.

"A revenge killing? Really? If things were that clear cut, this jury would have the easiest job on the planet."

He stepped out from behind the lectern and continued. "But your job isn't as simple as slapping the label 'revenge killer' on Isa Bornelli and sending her and her husband to prison. Your job is to make the prosecution prove its case against Keith Ingraham and Isa Bornelli beyond a reasonable doubt. That standard applies to each of them. They are husband and wife, but the charges against them are very different. Ms. Bornelli is charged with murder; Mr. Ingraham is charged as an accessory after the fact. The prosecution would like you to lump this all under the heading of one big 'revenge killing' and conclude that they are both criminals. That *they* are criminals." Manny shook his head, saying, "Ms. Hunt has it all wrong, folks. There is no *they*. There is no conspiracy. There is no revenge killing."

He paused, and for a split second Isa thought he might say "no rape."

"Clearest of all, there is not a shred of evidence that my client, Keith Ingraham, has done anything wrong. He's not an accessory after the fact to a murder. He's a complete afterthought—of an overzealous prosecutor."

Manny returned to his seat. Isa tried not to be obvious in making her assessment, but she was drawing on every ounce of her training and education in psychology to gauge the jury's reaction. It was a stoic bunch—or perhaps they had already condemned her.

Judge Gonzalez broke the silence. "It's almost five o'clock, so let's reconvene tomorrow at nine. Jurors are reminded of their oaths. We're adjourned," he said with the bang of a gavel.

All rose as the judge exited the courtroom. Isa tried to catch Keith's eye, but he had turned his head to reassure his parents, which made her feel even more alone. She could have used some reassurance. All this talk about reasonable doubt was nice. Manny's mention of "no evidence" against Keith had been poignant.

But it would have helped to hear someone say that *she* was innocent.

50

Jack led the way from Judge Gonzalez's courtroom to the main courthouse exit. Isa and Keith joined hands and followed, with Manny bringing up the rear. The gaggle of media around them made for a slow-moving glob of humanity that funneled through the revolving door to the courthouse steps. Camera crews stood right outside the building. Jack was immediately met by an array of black microphones thrust in his face, as effective as punji stakes in bringing the caravan to a halt. Jack had prepared a sound bite for the evening news, and this was the time to deliver.

"The victim in this case is Isa Bornelli. She and her husband are innocent of the charges against them, and we are confident that this jury will return a verdict of not guilty."

Jack pushed forward, with *push* being the operative word. The media wanted more. One reporter after another fired questions at Isa—some of them routine, others plain obnoxious.

"Did you do it, Isa?"

"Did Gabriel Sosa sexually assault you?"

"Hey, Isa, does a rapist deserve to die?"

He'd coached Isa not to respond in any way, and she followed the plan as they made their way down the final tier of granite steps, toward the group of demonstrators on the sidewalk. Jack was certain that they meant well, and "Rape Victims Matter" was a welcome show of support, but he worried how Isa would hold up if this gauntlet became a nightly occurrence.

"You did nothing wrong, girl!"

"We love you, Isa!"

Keith had arranged for a car service, and the team piled into the stretch limo at the curb. Jack and Manny took the forward-facing bench seat; Isa and Keith sat opposite them, with their backs to the driver. Manny yanked the door shut, and the driver pulled away.

Isa exhaled loudly. "Isn't there another way out of the building?"

"I'm afraid not," said Jack.

"Not unless you're going to the stockade," said Manny.

Jack would have been content to leave out that point of clarification.

"What's that stuck to your computer bag?" asked Manny.

"Huh?" asked Jack. He looked down and saw a yellow Post-it attached to his bag. It wasn't a handwriting he recognized. He removed it and read it to himself.

"*She will not testify*," it read.

"What is it?" asked Isa. She'd apparently read his expression.

"Stop the car!"

The driver slammed on the breaks.

"Jack, what is it?" asked Isa.

Jack jumped out of the car, hopped onto the sidewalk, and ran the half city block back to the courthouse steps. Reporters and their crews were in the middle of the "live from the courthouse" wrap-up, and the crowd was dispersing. But Jack knew that, in the confusion of their exit, someone on those steps had just moments earlier reached through the crowd and slapped the Post-it onto his computer bag. He was making a mad dash in desperation, but this was his only shot at catching a glimpse of whoever had done it.

He raced up the courthouse steps, looking left and right, then stopped at the revolving doors. He looked out across the street, then up toward the Metro station. He saw nothing suspicious, but, then again, he didn't know who or what he was looking for. He pulled his iPhone from his pocket and took some quick video, scanning the entire area. It was a long shot, but a study of the video might reveal a clue. He let it record for a minute and then made a call to the prosecutor.

"Sylvia, I'm outside the courthouse," he said, and he quickly told her what had happened.

"What do you want me to do about it?" she asked.

"I read this message as a threat against my client."

"A threat? How?"

"It's saying that if she testifies there will be consequences."

"It's a statement of fact: 'she will not testify,' meaning that your client fears the truth and doesn't have the guts to testify at trial."

Jack hesitated, never having considered that reading. "I think it's a threat."

"I don't. But if it is, who made it?"

"I don't know. That's the point. I want the note checked for fingerprints."

"Fine. Wait where you are. I'll have MDPD come to you and collect it properly."

He thanked her and hung up.

Sylvia Hunt phoned MDPD, and then got in her car and took the turnpike south to Homestead, to the Eden Park mobile home community.

Eden Park was twenty-seven acres of manufactured housing, a flat and treeless tract of agricultural land that Miami-Dade had rezoned "residential" to accommodate thousands of migrant workers who worked the surrounding fields of beans and tomatoes each winter. Some mobile home parks were beautiful, having made it from one hurricane season to the next with nary a sign of damage from wind or rain. Eden Park was not one of them. When it came to tropical storms, Eden Park was like that unknowing kid in middle school who walks around all day with the "Kick Me" sign pasted to his back. It bore the scars of every major storm to make landfall in the last decade. Empty lots aplenty, the demolished houses long since hauled away. Some home owners bought storm-damaged units on the cheap and fixed them up, good as new. Some bought as-is but were unable to afford the necessary repairs. Windows remained boarded with plywood year round, the roof perpetually covered with blue plastic tarps, the "temporary" fixes turned permanent.

David Kaval's trailer was at the end of the dusty gravel road that bisected the park. Sylvia parked and got out. It was one of those balmy autumn evenings that felt more like summer, a feeling that was amplified by swarms of mosquitoes that apparently didn't care if it was October. It wasn't lost on Sylvia that she was less than a mile from the Everglades, and even closer to the lonely road where the body of Gabriel Sosa had been found ten years earlier—bloodied, shirtless, and in a ditch, as she'd told the jury.

David Kaval was shirtless when he answered her knock on the door.

"Hey, baby, what's up?" he said from the other side of the screen.

"Don't give me that 'baby' crap. I need to talk to you."

"We need to do this outside," he said coyly. "Got some business going on in here."

Sylvia could only imagine what he was up to, but his credibility with the jury was already hanging by a thread, and her star witness could ill afford an arrest for possession of narcotics added to his impressive rap sheet. Sylvia stepped away from the door, and Kaval came outside.

"Jack Swyteck got a note today after trial," she said. "Did it come from you?"

"Nope."

"Did you have someone give it to him?"

"Uh-uh. Don't know nothin' about no note."

She studied his expression. "Have you had any contact with Isa Bornelli?"

Kaval breathed an exaggerated sigh of exasperation. "We have this conversation every week. No, no, and again, no. I haven't been anywhere near her since the day I got out of FSP."

"We're in the homestretch, David. It's just a matter of days before I call you to the witness stand. Keep away from her."

"Fine by me."

Sylvia started away and then stopped. "For what it's worth—and this is just me reading tea leaves—I don't think Isa Bornelli is going to testify on her own behalf."

"Oh, I'm *sure* she won't."

Their eyes locked. Sylvia wasn't often the one to blink in a stare down, but this time she was. A thin smile creased Kaval's lips.

"Gotta get back to business."

"Stay out of trouble," she said.

"You, too, baby," he said in a cold, even tone. Then he opened the door and disappeared into his trailer.

The defense team regrouped in Jack's office. Manny ordered delivery from Tropical Chinese, insisting that it served the best dim sum in Miami. Jack had his own favorite, but he held his tongue for more important points of disagreement with his cocounsel.

Isa wasn't eating.

"You okay?" asked Jack.

"I don't know if I'm bothered more by the note or by Sylvia Hunt's reaction to it."

Jack had shared the prosecutor's view that "she will not testify" simply meant that Isa was afraid of the truth. He wished he hadn't.

Jack pulled up a chair and faced her. "Let me ask you something, and I need a completely honest answer. Has David Kaval reached out to you at any time since he got out of prison?"

"No."

"So the last time he tried was that collect call he made from prison. Is that right?"

"Right. Last I know of."

"What do you mean that you know of?"

"She doesn't mean anything," said Keith. "Isa has been a virtual prisoner since Kaval was released. How could he possibly contact her without us being aware of it? It's not healthy, Jack. She spends twenty-two hours a day on the sixty-first floor of the Four Seasons."

"How would you know, Keith? You spend twenty-five days a month in Hong Kong."

"Okay," said Manny, raising his arms like a boxing referee. "Everybody take a deep breath."

"Manny's right," said Jack. "This is exactly what Sylvia Hunt wanted to happen when she indicted Keith. She wants you to go at each other."

Keith went to his wife and took her hand. "I'm sorry, honey. It's been one hell of a day."

"It's okay."

Hannah Goldsmith knocked on the door and entered the room. Jack had taken her up on the offer to pitch in with legal assistance on spot assignments. She laid a one-page letter on the table in front of him. "Here's a first draft," she said.

"What's that?" asked Isa.

"The video I took from the courthouse steps is useless," said Jack. "But I'm hoping one of the news stations may have caught someone in the act of putting that Post-it on my laptop bag. I'm asking all the stations for their raw footage of us leaving the courthouse."

"That's a good idea," said Manny.

Jack read it and made only minor edits. Hannah left with instructions to sign for Jack and get it out ASAP.

"I don't think it was Kaval," said Keith. "If it has any meaning at all, I think her father is behind it."

"Why do you think that?" asked his lawyer.

"For all the reasons we've talked about ever since he walked through that door and told Jack and me that she wasn't raped."

"Isa, do you have any reason to believe that your father is in Miami?" asked Jack.

"No."

"He wouldn't dare come to Miami now," said Manny. "Why risk getting slapped with a trial subpoena by us or by Sylvia Hunt and being forced to testify? He's safe in Venezuela."

"Is that true?" asked Isa.

"It is," said Jack. "Unless he's stupid enough to come here and get tagged by a process server, there's no way Felipe Bornelli ends up being a witness in this trial."

"Unless he does so voluntarily," said Manny.

"But that's not going to happen. Not in a million years."

"Or, maybe," said Jack, thinking aloud, "not unless Isa promises that she won't testify."

"What are you talking about?" asked Isa.

"Maybe the note *is* from him. Maybe he's willing to say something that will help you—but only if you don't get on the witness stand and tell the world what a complete ass he was when you called home and told him that you'd been raped."

"No," Isa said firmly. "No way that's what this is."

"How can you be so certain?"

"You're just wrong, Jack. Okay? You don't know my father."

Jack sensed that she was pushing back too hard. "Or maybe I still don't know everything that you and your father talked about at your meeting at Cy's Place."

"How many times do I have to apologize for not showing you his letter right away? I wanted to go over it with Keith. We did. Then we gave it to you. What he said to me at the table, and what he wrote in the letter, it was the same message. 'This is *your* problem, Isa, I'm not one of those parents who will lie under oath to protect his child, I'm not going to lie to protect anyone.' It was his typical self-serving b.s., and as usual his words have no connection to the truth and no purpose except to hurt me."

That was a fair summary of what his letter said. But Jack still had doubts that the letter was a full recap of what Isa and her father had talked about face-to-face. It was just human nature to avoid putting the most damning statements in writing, and, despite his flaws, Felipe Bornelli was still human.

Jack's cell rang. He took the call without leaving the room. It lasted only a minute. Then he shared it with the group.

"The lab came back with nothing. The only fingerprints on the Post-it are mine."

"Okay," said Keith. "What do we do now?"

"Move on and refocus on what matters," said Jack. "First witness for the prosecution. Tomorrow. Nine a.m."

51

Jack's day began with no surprises. He'd predicted a science lesson, and Sylvia Hunt delivered: witness one for the prosecution was Herbert Macklemore, M.D., one of seven full-time physicians at the Miami-Dade Medical Examiner Department who specialized in forensic pathology.

The prosecutor was twenty minutes into a direct examination, the witness having explained his impressive credentials and his role as lead pathologist on the Sosa homicide investigation. The defense team was seated at its assigned table to the judge's right. On the wall to their left was a projection screen, which faced the jury on the other side of the courtroom. The first image on the screen was a headshot of Gabriel Sosa taken from his passport.

The victim, brought to life.

Jack gauged the jury's reaction. To them, Gabriel must have looked—normal. Nothing about those sincere brown eyes said, "I'm a rapist." It took no stretch of the imagination to see him as a nice young man whom Isa had dated and invited back to her dorm room. This was the guy you'd expect Isa to take home to meet her parents.

He was no David Kaval.

"Next slide," said the prosecutor.

The jury squirmed, and a collective catch of the breath was audible throughout the courtroom. Jack tried not to react, but his client was less impassive.

"What are we looking at now, Doctor?" asked the prosecutor.

Macklemore adjusted his eyeglasses, applying his long, thin fingers to the tortoiseshell frame with a surgeon's precision. He showed no signs of nervousness and, for that matter, barely any sign of personality. He reminded Jack of his college anthropology professor.

"We have here a gaping head wound over the left front and mid scalp," he said, using a laser pointer to help the jury follow along. "With a comminuted skull fracture and rupture of the meningeal membranes, which reveals the frontal lobe of the left brain hemisphere."

Two of the jurors averted their eyes.

"What is a comminuted fracture?" asked the prosecutor.

"A fracture in which a bone is broken, splintered, or crushed into a number of pieces."

"It would suggest severe trauma, correct?"

"In Mr. Sosa's case, definitely."

"Did you measure the wound?"

"The laceration was fifteen centimeters from the medial eyebrow ridge to the top of the head.

The fracture was nine centimeters in length, with the deepest point of penetration at three centimeters."

It was big.

"Doctor, I realize that I may be asking you to state the obvious, but based on your autopsy, were you able to determine a cause of death?"

"Yes. Incised wounds and blunt trauma to the head."

"From multiple blows?"

"No. A single blow from a heavy but sharp instrument, such as a meat cleaver or machete."

"Thank you. Let's talk about the manner of death. Next slide."

It was a pair of photographs. "These are left and right images of Mr. Sosa's upper torso and shoulder, with particular focus on the area extending from the axila—the armpit—to the clavicle."

"What does this show?" asked the prosecutor.

"A matching pattern of wounds on the left and right sides, including serious abrasions and tears to the epidermis."

"You say a pattern. What does the pattern suggest?"

"Significantly, the wounds are not horizontal. On both sides, the bruising and abrasions run vertically—upward—from the armpit, toward the shoulder."

"What does that tell you, Doctor?"

"This is an issue we confront in strangulation cases. Are the wounds on the neck horizontal, which would suggest ligature strangulation? Or are they in a more vertical or inverted V pattern, which would suggest hanging? Here we have a vertical pattern."

"In terms of forensics, what does that tell you about the manner of death?"

"Well, we have five choices for manner of death: natural, accidental, homicide, suicide, or undetermined. These wounds indicate that at some point in time before his death, Mr. Sosa was suspended in the air by either a rope or a chain."

"Perhaps by a steel-chain engine hoist that you might find in an automotive repair shop?"

Jack could have objected, but what was the point? There was no disputing that the murder of Gabriel Sosa had been merciless. It all came down to whether Isa played a role in it.

"Possibly," said Macklemore. "I can say that the wounds are consistent with some form of torture, which in turn indicates that the manner of death was homicide."

More photographs followed. Cuts and bruises on his back indicated that Sosa had been whipped and beaten with either a hose or an electrical cord. The red dots on his abdomen were burns from lit cigarettes. Swollen and bruised testicles suggested that Sosa had been a human punching bag for the amusement of his assailant.

The courtroom was silent, and the jurors struggled with the courtroom version of battle fatigue, clearly in need of a break.

"Just two more slides," said the prosecutor, and she brought up the image of the victim's knees.

"Multiple abrasions and contusions on the epidermis," said Macklemore.

"Skinned knees, in layman's terms?"

"Yes."

Finally, the ghastly image of Sosa's right hand: he was missing three fingers.

"These are what are commonly referred to as defensive wounds," said Macklemore. "The kind of injuries one would sustain when fending off a knife attack, for example."

"To sum up, Doctor: All of this says *what* about the manner of death?"

Gruesome. Horrific. Unimaginable cruelty. Those were just a few of the words that came to Jack's mind.

"Mr. Sosa was hoisted into the air and tortured. At some point he was on his knees," he added, pausing to let the jury fill in the blank with the obvious implication: *begging for his life.* "The severed fingers are wounds that Mr. Sosa likely sustained while fending off an attack, which ended with a catastrophic blow to the head and traumatic brain injury. In short, the manner of death—"

He stopped in response to a loud gasp from the public seating area, which was immediately followed by the echo of footfalls on tile flooring. Jack turned to see a woman running up the center aisle and then pushing through the double doors in the rear of the courtroom. The heavy doors swung closed, but even that could not completely muffle the sound of her wailing in the hallway.

The judge had his gavel in hand, but he had yet

to strike it. He knew what had happened, as did everyone else.

"Gabriel's mother," Manny whispered, in case Jack had not yet deduced it.

"The manner of death is homicide," said Macklemore, finishing his answer.

Jack's gaze drifted toward the jurors. All six were reading Isa's reaction. Watching her. *Judging* her.

The judge checked the clock on the wall. "I think we could all use a break. Let's all be back in fifteen minutes," he said with a bang of his gavel.

Sylvia Hunt seemed content to leave the photograph burning onto the projection screen. Jack waited for the judge to exit and then did the only thing he could.

He went to the projector and turned it off.

52

The defense found an empty conference room down the hallway. Jack closed the door, and the lawyers took seats at the round table. Keith and Isa remained standing, embracing one another. Jack gave them a minute, and then they joined the lawyers at the table.

"I can't take this anymore," said Isa. "I just feel so . . . guilty."

The word seemed to hang in the air.

"Guilty?" asked Jack.

"Yes. For months I've been focusing only on the fact that I had nothing to do with the murder of Gabriel Sosa. Now I see these pictures, and I see his mother running out of the courtroom, and I can barely stomach the thought of what happened to him. Yes, he did a terrible, terrible thing to me. But this is an absolute horror that I could wish on no one."

"So you don't mean guilty, as in—"

"No, *no*," she said. "Guilty is not the right word. Selfish, maybe?"

"I understand what you're saying," said Manny.

"This is a horrific crime, and this jury will want to hold someone accountable for it, whether you were raped or not."

"Are we back to that?" asked Isa. "Whether I was raped or not?"

"No," said Jack. "I think Manny's point is that even though Sosa raped you, Sylvia Hunt mapped out an effective strategy in her opening statement. He didn't deserve to die. He certainly didn't deserve to die like *this*."

"What do we do about that?" asked Keith.

"I have a thought," said Manny. "Though I hesitate to raise it now, on the heels of this discussion of feeling selfish."

"Just say it," said Jack. "This is a joint defense."

"Actually, that's the point. My client is stuck in a joint trial, which in my opinion is not the safest place for a guy charged as an accessory after the fact. The gruesomeness of this murder is irrelevant to anything Keith is alleged to have done. If Isa is found guilty, this jury will find Keith guilty. I'm not so sure that would be the case in a separate trial."

"That argument has been made and lost. Judge Gonzalez has made it clear that there's not going to be a separate trial," said Jack.

"I understand," said Manny. "But I'm putting this out for consideration. Isa turned down the deal that Sylvia Hunt offered. But it may be time for Keith to think about cutting his own plea bargain. With or without Isa."

"No," said Keith.

Jack and Isa were conspicuously silent.

"It's a bad idea," said Keith, looking at Jack. "Don't you agree?"

It was a delicate matter in any joint trial—offering guidance to another lawyer's client. It was especially complicated where the question was coming from one of Jack's oldest friends. In Keith's mind the most important thing was his marriage. But if Jack were Keith's lawyer, Jack would be telling him that he had a child who needed him and that the most important thing was his liberty.

"When Sylvia Hunt presented the deal, she said it was the best offer that *Isa* would receive," Jack said. "I interpret that to mean the door is still open for Keith."

Keith was about to say something, but his lawyer stopped him. "We don't have to decide this right now," said Manny.

Jack's cell rang. Hannah Goldsmith was calling from the Freedom Institute. She'd been reviewing the raw footage from the television news stations all morning, searching for any clues as to who had reached out from the crowd and stuck the Post-it on Jack's computer bag—the "She will not testify" message.

Jack put her on speaker. "Whatchya got, Hannah?"

"The *Action News* footage is the winner. I've been over it a dozen times now, breaking it down frame by frame."

"What do you see?"

"No face. No body. Just a hand reaching out with the Post-it."

"That's something," said Jack.

"Yeah, it is something," said Hannah. "Something you may not have expected: the hand is a woman's."

"Are you sure?" asked Jack.

"I'd bet money on it. I can get a video-analysis expert to weigh in, if you like."

"Yeah," said Jack. "Let's definitely do that."

53

Relaxed. That was the word that came to Jack's mind as the second witness for the prosecution swore the familiar oath. Testifying at trial and facing the sometimes brutal cross-examination of a criminal-defense lawyer wasn't high on the list of favorite pastimes for most law enforcement officers. Retired MDPD detective Victor Meza appeared to be the exception. For three years he'd led the department's investigation into the murder of Gabriel Sosa. The case was officially "cold" when he'd put away his shield, filed for his pension, and moved to Naples. He seemed pleased that the case, at least from MDPD's standpoint, was finally resolved.

Or maybe he was just glad as hell to be anywhere but on a shuffleboard court.

"Detective Meza, what finally led you to Defendant Bornelli?"

Meza's opening testimony had covered the recovery of Sosa's body, the leads, the follow-up investigation, and a series of dead ends. Then the prosecutor turned to the meat of her examination, a point in time roughly one month into the investigation—the detective's interview of Isa.

"We examined Mr. Sosa's cell phone records," he said. "We interviewed everyone he had spoken to or texted, going back ninety days prior to his death."

The victim's call report was marked as a trial exhibit and, at the prosecutor's request, Detective Meza pointed out two communications between Isa and Sosa.

"Where did your interview of Ms. Bornelli take place?"

"My partner and I coordinated with the university police. We waited for Ms. Bornelli outside the lecture hall for her morning class. When she came out, we approached. She identified herself as Isabelle Bornelli. I asked if she knew Gabriel Sosa."

"What did Ms. Bornelli say?"

"She immediately asked, 'Is he dead?'"

"Those were her first words: 'Is he dead?'"

"Yes."

"She didn't ask, 'Did he kill someone?'"

"No."

"She didn't ask, 'Did he rape someone?'"

"No."

"Ms. Bornelli asked you, 'Is he dead?'"

"That's correct."

The prosecutor paused, making sure that her point had registered with the jury. "Then what?"

"Ms. Bornelli agreed to talk to us, so we walked two minutes to the campus police station, where we could speak in private. My partner and I then questioned her in a conference room."

A second exhibit was marked—the detective's report of his interview. The prosecutor used it as a reference point for her subsequent questions. "On page two of your report it says: 'Subject stated that she was the victim of date rape.' Did you ask her if she had been sexually assaulted?"

"No. She volunteered that information."

"After you had told her that Mr. Sosa had been murdered, correct?"

"Yes, correct."

The prosecutor went back to the report. "The next line says: 'Subject stated that she told her on-and-off boyfriend, David Kaval, about the rape.' Was that the first time you had heard the name David Kaval?"

"Yes. Frankly, we were out of leads at this point. So this was of great interest to us."

"Why?"

"Well, I asked Ms. Bornelli if her boyfriend was angry at Mr. Sosa for what he had done to her, and she confirmed that he was 'very angry.' I then asked if her boyfriend had done anything to suggest he might retaliate."

"And her response?"

"She said no. As I wrote in the report, she said, 'David was just there for me.'"

"What did you do next?"

Meza shifted in the witness chair, sitting more erect, as if he were getting to the good part. "You have to understand, a lot of what a detective does is instinctual—you follow your gut. I had a suspicion about this guy Kaval. So, at this point, I turn things over to my partner, who was a woman. She's now the 'good cop.' I excused myself and called back to the station to run a background check on Kaval. Well, my instincts were right. Kaval had no convictions, but quite a lengthy arrest record."

"What did you do with that information?"

"I kept it to myself," said Meza. "But when I returned to the interrogation—we all know the drill—I was the 'bad cop,'" he said, making air quotes.

"What does that mean, Detective?"

"I was a more—stern, let's put it that way. I told her, 'Look, miss, if you know who killed Gabriel Sosa, this is the time for us to talk about it, because we don't want you getting into something that later on you might not be able to get out of.'"

"How did she respond?"

"She appeared scared to me. Nervous. But she just sat there, staring."

"Did you keep at it?"

"Yes, ma'am. I told her about Sosa's wounds. The blow to his head. The evidence of torture. I said that these are the kinds of things you see when the attacker is *very* angry. 'Have you ever seen your boyfriend that angry?' I asked her."

He was starting to ramble, and Jack was tempted to object, but his instincts told him that Meza was the kind of cop who, if given enough rope, would say something to hang himself. And he did.

"I said, 'Don't try and protect anybody, miss. Somebody that has a nice build like you, gets raped by this guy, gets caught between a rock and hard place.'"

Jack drew a noose on his notepad.

"'Is there anybody you're trying to protect? 'Cause don't do that,' I said. 'You were a victim, so I want to keep it that way.'"

"Did she offer any further information?" asked the prosecutor.

"None," said Meza. "She wanted to know if she was free to go."

"How did you leave things with her?"

"I told her I couldn't make her stay. But before she left, I planted a seed. I said, 'I hope you're being completely honest with us. Because murder is the kind of crime that doesn't go away. The investigation never stops.'"

"Thank you, Detective. That's all the questions I have."

The prosecutor stepped away from the lectern and returned to her seat. The judge invited cross-examination, and Jack rose, promising that he would be quick. He planted himself in front of the witness, close enough to exercise a level of control, but not so close as to draw an objection for badgering the witness. He had his notes with him, but only for effect, as he pretended to read the detective's testimony back to him.

"'Someone with a nice build like you,'" said Jack, his voice loud enough to rattle the witness. "That's what you said to her?"

"Yes."

"You were a fifty-year-old man?"

"Fifty-two."

"You're what? Six-three, two hundred forty pounds?"

"About that."

"You're a law enforcement officer?"

"I was."

"You were talking to a nineteen-year-old college student who told you that she was sexually assaulted?"

"That's what she told me."

"And you knew that, for whatever reason—maybe she was scared, maybe she was embarrassed, maybe she was too traumatized—she decided not to report her rape to the police. You knew that, right?"

"I knew she didn't report anything."

"And yet, you were utterly surprised that she didn't open right up and tell you everything, huh? You played 'the bad cop' and put the teenager with the 'nice build' completely at ease—but *she* was the one hiding something. It was *her* fault."

"Objection," said the prosecutor.

"Sustained."

Jack was fine with it. His read of the jury was that his point had registered.

"One final question," he said, again checking his notes. "Detective Meza, you mentioned that murder is the type of crime that doesn't go away. The investigation never stops."

"Yes. I said that. And I believe that."

"What about rape? Is that the kind of crime that doesn't go away?"

The detective shifted nervously. "I don't know how to answer that."

"I didn't think so. No further questions, Your Honor."

Jack returned to his chair. Manny rose, which Jack hadn't expected, and he stepped toward the lectern. "I have just a brief follow-up on behalf of Defendant Ingraham," Manny announced.

The judge didn't seem happy about the double-teaming, and Jack couldn't imagine what questions Manny would have for this witness.

"Keep it brief," said the judge.

"Detective Meza, you also said that, in a murder case, the investigation never stops. Is it fair to say that in this case, the investigation into the rape of Isa Bornelli never *started*?"

"Objection," said the prosecutor.

"I'll rephrase," said Manny. "Did MDPD open an investigation into the rape of Isabelle Bornelli?"

"There was no need. Her attacker was dead."

"You were a homicide investigator, right?"

"I think that's been pretty well established."

"Did MDPD ever have an investigator who specializes in sexual assault interview Ms. Bornelli?"

He paused, at least appearing to think about it. "No."

"True or false, Detective Meza: MDPD didn't bring in a sexual assault investigator because you didn't believe Ms. Bornelli had been raped."

Manny paused, as if bracing for the prosecutor's objection. Jack had expected one—hoped for one actually, wishing he could have objected on Isa's behalf, but that wasn't an option.

The prosecutor let it go.

Meza appeared to struggle for a response, then copped out. "I don't really recall."

"We'll leave it at that," said Manny. "Nothing further."

Jack said nothing as Manny returned to his chair, knowing that the jury and the press were watching. But he was angry.

To borrow Meza's words, Jack was *very angry*.

54

"What the fuck did you just do in that courtroom, Manny?"

Trial had ended for the day, but Jack had pulled the entire team into the open conference room down the hall. What he had to say to Manny couldn't wait until they returned to the office for debriefing.

"I was just picking up on the theme you started," he said.

"The hell you were," said Jack. He was up and pacing, trying to cool down. Manny was standing, too. The clients were at the table.

"After Dr. Macklemore testified," said Jack, "I didn't think it was possible for the jury to forget those images of Gabriel Sosa. But I took Detective Meza's own words and reminded them that Isa is a victim, too. In ten seconds you erased any sympathy the jury felt toward her: you turned her into the false accuser who made it all up."

"It's not the mistake you think it is," said Manny.

"It's not the strategy we agreed on! We dumped

'no rape means no motive; no motive means no conviction.' You're injecting it into the case anyway."

"The two approaches are not incompatible."

Jack stopped pacing, incredulous. "How can they *not be*? Isa can't be a victim *and* a false accuser."

"The victim angle works coming from you, Jack, as counsel for Isa. But 'no rape, no motive' also works—as long as it comes from me, as counsel for Keith."

"I don't follow this at all," said Isa.

Manny took the chair next to Isa, appealing to her directly. "It all comes down to reasonable doubt. If it exists in the mind of the jury, the defense wins. If I develop this theory as part of Keith's defense, you don't 'own it' directly. But you still benefit. At the end of this trial, there is no way this jury is going to know *beyond a reasonable doubt* whether you are a victim or not a victim. Whether Sosa was a rapist or not a rapist. Whether you had motive to hurt him, or no motive at all. It's like a puzzle. If the pieces don't fit, the jury must acquit."

Jack watched Isa's reaction closely. It was obvious that her heart was not on board with this strategy, which was a good thing. Jack couldn't have disagreed more with Manny, and at the risk of starting nuclear war, this was the time to lay it on the table.

"Isa told David Kaval that she was raped," said Jack, "and Kaval lined up the thug who killed Gabriel Sosa. If Isa wasn't raped, it doesn't absolve her of anything. As long as David Kaval *believed* what she told him, and if Isa stuck to her lie all the way through the kidnapping and the murder, Isa goes to jail for the rest of her life. In fact, if Sylvia Hunt is smart, she'll turn your 'no rape' argument against us and convince this jury that it was Isa's *lies*—not her sexual assault—that got Gabriel Sosa murdered. What better way is there for the prosecutor to make the jury hate Isa, feel no sympathy for her as a victim, and convict her? If that happens, neither Isa nor Keith stands any chance of acquittal."

There was silence. Jack could see that Manny wanted to disagree with him, but he couldn't. Jack was dead right.

"I was raped," said Isa, her voice shaking with anger. "Manny, if you utter one more word in the courtroom to cast doubt on that, Keith will fire you. Jack can defend both of us. Right, Keith?"

He didn't answer.

"Keith, right?"

Jack caught Keith's eye and did a double take. A feeling came over him, albeit just for a split second, that Manny had cleared this with his client—the resurrection of the "no rape" strategy—before springing it on Jack and Isa. Jack knew his old friend, and he had seen an unmistakable flash of regret.

"That's absolutely right," said Keith in a hollow voice.

55

Sylvia Hunt walked out of the courthouse with her head up. It had been a good day at trial. She had nothing to say to the media on the courthouse steps. She kept walking, and they didn't follow her—probably waiting for the money shot of Isabelle Bornelli. She passed the group of demonstrators on the sidewalk. They were fewer in number tonight, she noticed, but it was the core, vocal group.

"*Rape victims matter!*"

Did they honestly think she disagreed? She suspected that their numbers would continue to dwindle as the trial progressed. Yes, things were going well for the prosecution. But the best was yet to come.

Sylvia walked to the Graham Building and went up to her office. The support staff had already gone home, so she was on her own to make any last-minute changes in exhibits or slides for the next day of trial. She worked at her desk until seven p.m. and grabbed takeout on the way home. The grand jury testimony of David Kaval was her dinner companion. She reviewed it one more time while eating her cold Thai chicken salad.

A friend called. Did she want a quick break from trial prep, grab a quick coffee?

"No, I have a meeting."

"You're a big-shot prosecutor. Bump it back half an hour. You need to get out, Sylvia. It'll be good for your sanity."

At 8:30 p.m. sharp there was a knock on her door. The meeting was with Manny Espinosa. Apparently not all Latinos operated on Cuban time.

"I gotta run," she told her friend, and then hung up.

Sylvia invited Manny inside, and they sat in the living room. It was a discussion she would have preferred to have in her office, but she'd forgotten to request afterhours A/C at the Graham Building, which meant that the temperature there was somewhere between baked brisket and slow-cooked ribs. It didn't matter. Once she'd told Manny that she had an offer for his client, it was Sylvia's impression that he would have traveled to Mars or Venus, had she selected either venue.

"So you have an offer?" asked Manny.

Sylvia laid her notes on the coffee table. "The felony charge of accessory after the fact is reduced to criminal facilitation, a first-degree misdemeanor. His sentence is a fine in the amount of one thousand dollars. No jail time."

Misdemeanor was the magic word. No jail was the icing. Manny's interest was obvious.

"What do you want from my client?" he asked.

"Truthful testimony."

Manny shook his head. "His conversations with his wife are protected by the marital privilege. Even if he wanted to testify, Isa could stop him."

"Their conversations before marriage are not privileged."

"I've made him aware of that. There's nothing."

Sylvia leaned forward, her expression very serious. "Convey my offer to him. Maybe something will come up."

Keith took Manny's call on the terrace. Isa was in Melany's bedroom, reading aloud with her. Keith was alone, leaning on the rail and looking out over the city lights as his lawyer explained the deal.

"That's a nonstarter, Manny. I'll never testify against Isa."

Manny reemphasized how meaningless a misdemeanor conviction was—and how devastating a felony conviction could be to Keith's career, even if he didn't get prison time.

"This felony has nothing to do with banking or securities," said Keith. "I've already checked with the IBS in-house attorneys. There's no automatic ban from the SEC or any other agency to stop me from doing business as usual."

"Keith, you are not Citibank. You are not too big to fail. Maybe the Securities and Exchange Commission won't care. But do you think IBS wants a convicted felon running its Hong Kong office? They will dump you."

"Not if I don't get prison time."

"I can't guarantee that you won't if you're convicted."

"I thought you said I'd get probation."

"I told you there's no minimum *mandatory* prison time for a second-degree felony. You have no priors, so yeah, you'll probably get probation. But you won't be traveling to Hong Kong while on probation."

The glass door opened behind him and Isa stepped onto the terrace. "Who you talking to?"

"I gotta go, Manny," he said into the phone. His lawyer said they'd talk more, and they hung up.

"What did Manny want?"

Isa still looked distressed, even after the calming effect of time alone with Melany. Keith didn't want to upset her further by telling her that he'd been asked to testify against her—something that would never happen.

"Manny's trying to get my charge down to a misdemeanor," he said, leaving it at that.

"That's great," she said.

"Yeah. It would be."

"Then you would be out of the case, right?"

"Right."

She walked the rail and stood beside him, and together they gazed out toward the Everglades, the darkness that lay beyond the blanket of city lights.

"We should do everything possible to make that happen," Isa said.

"I'm not sure we can."

She turned her head to look at him. "You have

to, Keith. We can't afford to risk both of us going to prison. That's not fair to Melany."

"That's the argument Manny is making, but I don't think it's a serious risk that I would actually get prison time. I want to talk to Jack about it and see what he thinks."

She looked out again toward the city. "Okay. But that aside, I'm starting to think that I'd be better off with Manny out of the case."

"Jack will bring him in line."

She breathed deeply, and Keith could hear the stress. "I'm afraid the damage has already been done by Manny's strategy. What if Jack is right? What if the jury thinks I lied to David when I told him I was raped?"

"They won't think that, Isa. It doesn't make sense."

"Yes, it does. Here's how it could have happened. Kaval comes to see me. He wants us to get back together again, like we've done a dozen times before. Break up/make up/break up/make up. I tell him it's really over between us this time. He doesn't accept it. I tell him he better accept it: I had sex with Gabriel. He flips out. He can't believe I would sleep with a guy I hardly know. He—he's gonna hit me. I freak. I don't know what to do. I tell him it was rape. Gabriel raped me, I say. And then . . . well, then the rest happens."

She'd laid it out so quickly that Keith, too, felt breathless. It was a bit unnerving the way Isa had stitched together such a plausible false-accuser scenario. If the prosecution was able to present that theory of the case in convincing fashion, Isa was cooked.

"That's not what happened, though. Right?" he asked.

"No! Good God, Keith, how could you even ask that question? I told you what happened. You know the truth."

"I do," he said as she laid her hand atop his on the rail.

But he didn't.

56

The first witness on Thursday morning made Jack a little sick to his stomach, figuratively speaking. Ironically, it was a doctor who was making him feel that way. Cassandra Campos was the physician on duty when Isa had visited the student health center on Saturday morning.

"Did Ms. Bornelli state that she had been sexually assaulted?" the prosecutor asked.

"No. She reported only that she'd engaged in unprotected sex the night before."

"What was the purpose of her visit?"

"I don't recall any purpose other than to report that she'd had unprotected sex."

"Those were Ms. Bornelli's words—'unprotected sex'?"

"That's what I wrote in my notes. 'Unprotected sex.'"

If the words *unprotected sex* found their way into the Q-and-A one more time, Jack would nominate the prosecutor for "Witness Coach of the Year."

"Did you prescribe any course of treatment for Ms. Bornelli's unprotected sex?" asked Hunt.

"I see here in the patient record that she was written a prescription for a 'morning-after' pill."

"Anything else?"

"I'm sure I would have told her that the morning-after pill does not prevent sexually transmitted diseases. Other than that, no."

"Nothing further."

Ten minutes, and the prosecutor was finished. And Jack knew exactly where Sylvia Hunt was headed. No rape. Isa's false accusation had cost Gabriel Sosa his life. There was only one victim in this case.

Manny's "no rape" strategy had backfired.

Jack approached the witness and did the best he could. "Dr. Campos, you testified earlier that you wrote Ms. Bornelli a prescription for the morning-after pill, correct?"

"That's right."

"Did you see Ms. Bornelli before or after August 24, 2006?"

The doctor seemed to recognize that the date had some significance—or she was at least vaguely aware that Jack was setting a trap. "After, of course."

Jack approached the bench and handed up the applicable FDA regulation. "Judge, I'd ask the court to take judicial notice that, effective August 24, 2006, the morning-after pill was available over the counter, without a prescription, to any woman eighteen years of age or older."

The judge granted the request and so stated for the record. Jack continued with the witness.

"Doctor, would you like to reconsider your testimony?"

"Uh, yes," she said, stammering. "I apparently was mistaken when I said I wrote a prescription for Plan B. I probably told her to go to the pharmacy and buy it."

"She didn't need a prescription, did she?"

"Not at that time, no."

"Ms. Bornelli could have walked into any pharmacy and purchased the morning-after pill for about twenty-five bucks."

"In theory."

"No, *in reality*, she didn't need to see a doctor to get the morning-after pill, did she, Dr. Campos?"

"No. She did not."

"So let me ask you a few more questions about this, because I really want you to help me and the jury to understand why Ms. Bornelli went to see a physician. Ms. Bornelli made an appointment to see a doctor, correct?"

"Yes. If you have no appointment, you see the nurse practitioner."

"She kept her appointment," said Jack.

"Obviously."

"She told you that she had engaged in unprotected sex."

"That I remember very clearly."

"And your only response was to tell her what every college freshman in America already knows: she could get the morning-after pill over the counter from the pharmacy."

"Objection," said Hunt. "Argumentative."

"Overruled. Please answer the question, Dr. Campos."

"Well, like I said. I also told her about sexually transmitted diseases."

"Great. Nice work."

"Objection."

"Sustained. Easy, Mr. Swyteck."

"Doctor, did it ever occur to you that this young woman had gone to see a doctor—a medical *doctor*—for some reason other than to be told that she could buy a morning-after pill at the drugstore?"

The silence was, as they say, deafening. It was as if at that very moment—in a crowded courtroom, under cross-examination by defense counsel—the thought finally *had* occurred to Dr. Campos.

"I don't really recall," she said in a weak voice.

Jack didn't relent. "You didn't ask if she'd been sexually assaulted, did you?"

"No."

"You didn't check Ms. Bornelli's body for cuts or scratches?"

"No."

"You didn't examine her for any signs of forced entry?"

"No. She said she had unprotected sex."

"Yes, we heard you the first fifteen times," said Jack.

"Objection."

"Sustained. Really, that'll do, Mr. Swyteck," said the judge.

"Just a couple more questions," said Jack—and these were from Isa. "Dr. Campos, how much time did you spend with this patient? Five minutes?"

"I don't recall."

"Could it have been less than five minutes?" he asked, his tone more assertive.

"We're very busy on Saturday mornings. Short-staffed, too. It very well could have been a quick in and out."

"Less than two minutes?"

"I don't remember."

"Possibly less than two minutes?"

It wasn't a concession that Jack would have gotten at the top of his examination, but the witness seemed beaten. "Possibly."

"Thank you, Doctor." Jack returned to the table and took his chair beside Isa.

"Great job," she whispered.

Jack gave his client a little nod of appreciation. It wasn't the killer cross-examination that blew a case wide open, but it was a helpful first crack in the government's new theory that the rape was a fabrication. Cracks could win trials for the defense. Or they could draw reinforcements from the prosecution.

Either way, Jack knew the battle was far from over.

57

"The state of Florida calls David Kaval," Sylvia Hunt announced.

Jack showed no reaction, but he saw Isa reach beneath the table and squeeze her husband's hand. They'd all known this day was coming, and Jack had told Isa on their way to the courthouse that Kaval would likely make an appearance before the lunch break.

Kaval came down the center aisle, like any other witness, no longer a prisoner who had to enter through a side door in the company of law enforcement. He stepped through the swinging gate on his way to the witness stand. He was wearing a long-sleeve dress shirt and a tie—at the insistence of the prosecution, Jack presumed, in order to hide the tattoos. His black shoes were polished and his gray slacks were pressed. He was clean-shaven, with his hair neatly styled and combed. Jack wasn't close enough to see, but he wouldn't have been surprised to find that Sylvia Hunt had manicured his fingernails as well. The transformation was remarkable. The contrast between

Gabriel Sosa and David Kaval—between the boy next door and the man who'd wanted him dead—had evaporated. If Jack had asked a stranger to pick out the bad boy Isa had dated in college, he probably would have guessed Keith.

Appearances could be so deceiving.

Kaval swore the oath, took a seat, and looked pleasantly at the jurors—more good coaching.

"Good morning, Mr. Kaval. Would you please introduce yourself to the jury."

The next few minutes unfolded like a job interview. Kaval told the jury where he lived, where he'd grown up, where he'd attended high school.

"You've made some mistakes in your life, haven't you, Mr. Kaval?"

He had, he told the jury, but his good behavior at FSP had shaved eighteen months off his sentence, and he was determined to turn his life around. He was planning to re-enroll at Miami-Dade College and was looking for a job. No drugs and no trouble with the law since his release from FSP, not even a traffic citation. His deal with the prosecution in this case—no jail time for his role in the murder of Gabriel Sosa—was just one more step toward putting the mistakes of the past behind him.

"Tell us about your relationship with the defendant, Isabelle Bornelli," said the prosecutor.

"It was special," he said, and for the first time since entering the courtroom, his gaze drifted toward the defense table, straight at Jack's client. "Me and Isa had a very special relationship."

The reaction from Isa was so visceral that Jack

sensed it. Kaval's mere use of the word *relationship*, it seemed, had nearly knocked her off the chair.

Kaval told an attentive jury how he'd met Isa during her first week on campus, how inseparable they were throughout the fall, and how his heart had broken when she'd told him that they should "see other people."

"When did you find out that she'd gone on a date with Gabriel Sosa?"

The questions kept coming, and his answers flowed like a polished script. Jack had read the transcript of Kaval's grand jury testimony many times, so nothing came as a surprise. Still, reading it on a printed page had been one thing. Words that seemed dead on the printed page took on new effect in a packed courtroom. His recounting of the conversation in which Isa had told him about the assault had been particularly convincing—and helpful, Jack thought. As Kaval told it, Isa sounded like anything but a false accuser. Nor did she sound like a woman particularly set on revenge. Until the final question before the lunch break—regarding the last thing Isa had said to him on the day she'd told him she was raped.

"'I just wish he was dead,'" he said, quoting Isa.

"Those were Ms. Bornelli's exact words to you?" the prosecutor asked, a verbatim replay of the grand jury examination. 'I just wish he was dead'?"

"Yes. Those were her exact words."

Sylvia Hunt paused. More than paused. She stopped long enough for all six jurors to shift their gaze from the witness to the accused.

"It's almost noon," the judge said, his words

coming like an eleventh-hour stay of execution, a welcome break to the uncomfortable courtroom silence. "Let's reconvene at one o'clock."

He cracked the gavel, all rose on the bailiff's command, and the judge exited to his chambers. The clerk's office had accommodated Jack's request to use the conference room down the hall for lunch so that the defense team didn't have to fight the media getting out to a restaurant and back. They took the side exit to the corridor. A young woman approached Isa as they rounded the corner in the hallway. She looked familiar to Jack, and he thought he might have seen her once or twice outside the courthouse with the other "Rape Victims Matter" demonstrators.

"There's another rally," he heard the woman tell Isa. She handed Isa a flyer, said she hoped Isa could come, and stepped away. Jack and Isa continued down the hall.

"Who was that?" asked Jack.

"Her name is Emma. She organizes student rallies to increase awareness of sexual assault on college campuses."

Jack took the flyer from Isa's hand and read it. "The rally is *this Saturday*. That's smack-dab in the middle of your trial. You know you won't be going, right?"

"I have no intention of going."

Jack stopped and looked her in the eye, making sure she understood. "You're not going."

"I said I had no intention."

Coming from most clients, that answer would have sufficed. Not from Isa. "The prosecution will probably rest its case tomorrow—maybe by the end of today, depending on how Kaval behaves. Then the ball is in our court. This is *the* weekend, Isa. This is when we decide if you take the stand in your own defense. I'm not asking if you have any intention to go to that rally. I want this to be clear: you're not going. Got it?"

She nodded, though Jack's words seemed to trigger a sobering, if not numbing, realization that it was getting late in the game.

"Yeah," she said. "I got it."

58

Jack returned to Judge Gonzalez's courtroom expecting a rough afternoon.

I just wish he was dead. The judge had given the jury an entire lunch hour to chew, swallow, and digest those words. Jack had been mulling them over for weeks. He knew Isa's side of the story—that she hadn't meant it literally. Jack had expected something very different from Kaval. He'd worried about it. He wondered how Keith would react. He'd even dreamed about it.

Do you really mean that, Isa? You wish this guy was dead?

Yes.

Really, really mean it?

Yes! I want him dead!

Okay.

You'll do it, David?

No, baby. We'll do it.

The time for speculation and bad dreams was over. The jury was seated. The judge reminded the witness of his oath. Sylvia Hunt picked up exactly where she'd left off, with Isa's own words.

"Mr. Kaval—what did you take Ms. Bornelli to mean by that?"

Jack braced himself. Isa was looking down, her vague reflection staring back at her from the polished mahogany tabletop.

Kaval leaned closer to the microphone and said, "I didn't take it literally that she wanted me to kill him."

Jack wondered if he was still dreaming.

"What did you understand her to mean?"

"That she wanted me to scare him."

Manny scribbled out a note and passed it to Jack: *WTF?*

"What did you do?" the prosecutor asked.

"I called my buddy John Simpson and we made a plan."

"What was your plan?"

A series of questions followed. Kaval described the scene at the club, where Isa pointed out Sosa as her attacker and they followed him to his car. They tailed Sosa in their van and bumped his car on purpose. When he got out of his car to inspect the damage, they hassled him, trapping him between the two vehicles.

"What did you do then?"

"Simpson and me threw him in the back of the van and drove to the automotive shop."

"Was Ms. Bornelli with you?"

This was it, thought Jack—the point at which Kaval's story would no longer match Isa's, where Kaval would reveal himself as the star witness for the prosecution.

"No," said Kaval. "As I recall, Simpson and

me were hassling Sosa. Isa got out of the van and started freaking out. So I told her to get lost. She ran. Then we put Sosa in the van."

Jack did all he could to keep his jaw from dropping in front of the jury. *What the hell is going on?*

"Where did you take Mr. Sosa?" asked the prosecutor.

"Simpson had a buddy who worked at a body shop in south Miami. He stole a set of keys and gave Simpson the alarm code. That's where we took Sosa."

"Then what happened?"

"We pulled Sosa out of the van."

"Did he fight back?"

"A little. But at this point his hands were tied behind his back. Duct tape on his mouth. One of us put a blindfold on him."

"Where did you take him?"

"We went in through the office door. Then went right into the main garage area and took off the blindfold."

"Why did you remove his blindfold?"

"It's a scary place after hours. These heavy chains hang from the ceiling to lift engines out of cars. We wanted him to see all that. You know, like I said, the idea was to make this scary."

"Did you use the engine chains?"

"First John ripped off his shirt."

"Then what?"

"We wrapped the engine chains around him. One on each side, under the arms and up over the shoulders."

Jack made a note. That was consistent with the wound pattern described by the medical examiner.

"Was Mr. Sosa resisting at this point?" asked the prosecutor.

"Not really. More begging—or whimpering. He still had duct tape on his mouth."

"Did you hoist him up?"

"Not yet. Simpson—John could be a really scary guy—he starts laying out all these tools on the garage floor in front of Sosa."

"What kind of tools?"

"Pliers. Screw drivers. Wire cutters."

"Things that someone might use as instruments of torture?" asked the prosecutor.

"Yeah. Things that would really scare him."

"What did you do?"

"I walked up to Sosa. He wasn't quite as tall as me, but I squatted a little and got right in his face. And I started yelling."

"What did you yell?"

"You want me to yell it like I did? Word for word?"

"Yes. As best you can remember."

"I yelled—and it was loud. Really loud. '*Did you fucking rape my girlfriend? You piece of shit! Did you rape Isa Bornelli?*'"

It sent a collective chill through the courtroom, and it drew another visceral reaction from Isa—one that told Jack more plainly than words that his client had heard the man yell like that before.

"Did Mr. Sosa respond?"

"He shook his head back and forth. And I could

hear him trying to say, like, 'No, no, no,' through the tape."

"What did you do?"

"John hoisted him up. Not too high. Just enough to get his feet off the ground."

"So he was hanging by the chains?"

"Right."

"What did you do next?"

Kaval shrugged and said, "We left."

"You left Sosa hanging by the chains?"

"Yeah. We knew someone would find him in the morning."

"You didn't torture him?"

"No."

"He was alive when you left?"

"Yeah. His legs were kicking."

"Why did you leave?"

"The plan was to scare him so he wouldn't do to some other girl what he done to Isa. That's what we did."

The prosecutor walked to her table and conferred quietly with the junior prosecutor. They seemed satisfied. "I have no further questions, Your Honor."

The judge leaned back in his leather chair and addressed the defense. "Any cross-examination?"

Jack requested a moment, and the judge gave it to him. The defense lawyers conferred quickly at their table, exchanging whispers. Manny shared Jack's assessment—no damage. At least none that could be repaired through cross-examination of this witness. Jack knew that the worst mistake a criminal-defense lawyer could make was to cross-examine when none was needed. He played it safe, emphasizing the only point that deserved emphasis.

Jack approached the witness, using a far less aggressive tone than he'd planned to use with this witness. "Mr. Kaval, you're no longer in prison, are you?"

"No."

"You're not going back to prison for shoving Mr. Sosa into the back of a van, are you?"

"No."

"You're not going back to prison for taking Mr. Sosa to the garage and hoisting him up on those chains."

"No."

"You're not going back to prison for leaving him hanging in midair."

"No."

"In fact, the state attorney promised that you're not going back to prison. That was your deal, right?"

"Yeah. As long as I told the truth."

"And everything you said here today is the truth?"

"Yes, sir."

Jack thanked him and stepped away. The prosecution had no redirect.

"Mr. Kaval, you are excused," said the judge.

He stepped down from the witness stand and walked toward the rail. He glanced once in Isa's direction as he passed between the tables for the prosecution and defense, but Isa wasn't looking at him. The gate squeaked as the witness passed into the public seating area, and his footfalls echoed in the quiet courtroom as he walked up the center aisle.

And just one thought burned in Jack's mind.

I gotta be missing something.

59

It was time for a beer. "But only one," said Jack.

Isa had gone straight to the apartment after trial. Jack, Keith, and Manny stopped at Cy's Place on the way home from the courthouse and took a seat at the bar. Theo put a couple of ice-cold bottles of IPA in front of them. Manny was in a celebratory mood. Jack was cautious. Keith seemed somewhere in between.

"I still say we're missing something," said Jack.

Kaval could have done so much more damage. He could have testified that Isa planned the murder. He could have testified that he told Isa in no uncertain terms that they intended to torture and murder Sosa. Instead, he testified that, as far as Isa knew, the only plan was to "put a scare into Sosa."

"They can't convict Isa on this evidence, can they?" asked Keith. "Who can blame the victim of sexual assault for wanting a couple of thugs to put a scare into her rapist? To make sure he didn't rape someone else."

"Well, here's what the prosecutor will tell the jury about that," said Jack. "If all she really wanted was to make sure he didn't do it again, she should have called the police and put him in jail."

"Okay, she should have. But lots of rapes go unreported. That doesn't mean she wanted him murdered—that she *planned* his murder."

"Jack, you are always such a doggy downer," said Manny. "Sure, Sylvia Hunt will twist everything to fit her theory of the case. She will hammer hard to the jury that Sosa shook his head and even through duct tape tried to deny that he ever raped Isa. But even if Isa lied to her boyfriend about being raped, that doesn't make her a murderer. I've said it all along—no rape, no motive. No motive, no conviction. Right now, we have reasonable doubt. That's all we need."

Manny excused himself and walked to the restroom. Jack and Keith remained at the bar, thinking about what Manny had just said. Keith was unusually quiet, tugging at the label on his IPA.

"You okay?" asked Jack.

Keith shook his head. "Not really."

"Maybe Manny's right," said Jack. "I do tend to worry."

"It's not that," said Keith.

Jack took a pull from his bottled beer. "Something you want to get off your chest?"

Keith looked at his beer, then at Jack. "Six months ago, people would have said I had it all, right? Yeah, sure, life threw us a curve with Melany's ears. But I earn enough 'fuck you' money to say 'Fuck you, world, I can fix it.'"

Jack stayed quiet, sensing that Keith had more to say.

"The truth is, we're living on a bubble. All of us. Most of my life I managed to steer clear of the really bad choices that derail guys like me. I listened to my mom and didn't do drugs. I listened to my dad and never made a bet I couldn't afford to lose. I ignored Nike and didn't 'just do it.' I was careful and worked hard and married this incredibly smart, beautiful woman. Then in a nanosecond—in less than the time it takes for a bubble to burst—everything changed."

"Hey, come on," said Jack. "You can beat this, too. Manny is right in this respect. All we need is reasonable doubt."

"Yeah, I get that. In the courtroom that's all we need. But I guess what I'm saying is this, Jack. At some point, I'll have to decide for myself if my wife was responsible for the death of another human being. At some point, I'll want more than reasonable doubt. Do you understand what I'm saying?"

Jack studied his friend's expression. He saw the pain. The angst. "Yeah," said Jack. "I get what you're saying."

Theo came by. "Another round?" he asked from the business side of the bar.

"We're good," said Jack.

Keith laid a ten on the bar to cover the beer. "Can you drop me at the Four Seasons on your way to Key Biscayne?"

"Sorry, buddy. We're headed in the opposite direction."

Theo caught the "we" part. "You mean you and me?"

"Yeah. I need you to take a ride with me."

"Where to?"

"South," said Jack, swallowing the last of his beer. "Back to the 'illfish Diner. I think I know what we're missing."

60

Friday. Jack thanked God it was—even if Sylvia Hunt was determined to spoil it.

"The state of Florida calls Ilene Simpson," said the prosecutor.

Jack's hunch had proved correct. His return trip with Theo to the Billfish Diner, however, had been a waste of time. Ilene still waitressed there, but the manager was ready to fire her. Her attendance record since August had been abysmal—either late for her shift or didn't show up at all. The problem was that she'd moved too far away. "Living up in Homestead now, with her new boyfriend." Jack took a stab and asked if the new boyfriend's name was David. "Yeah. David. A real asshole. Told him not to come around here anymore. That guy's trouble."

The manager had it dead wrong. *Ilene* was trouble.

The witness was sworn and took a seat. Ilene was wearing flat shoes, navy-blue slacks, and a peach-colored blouse, with simple jewelry and minimal makeup. "Nothing sexy" had been the fashion edict from the prosecutor, Jack surmised. She sat with her hands in her lap, and the way she clenched them into tight fists suggested that she was far less at ease than Kaval had been in the role of star witness. Her apparent nervousness, however, only seemed to make the jury more attentive to her every word.

"Ms. Simpson, you are the widow of John Simpson, correct?"

The jury immediately made the connection, and some took notes as Ilene described her life with John Simpson. "He was a strange man," she said, summing up.

"Strange in what way?"

She struggled for a moment, as if embarrassed. "Sexually."

"Is it fair to say that he was into things that you were not into?"

"I'm not a prude, okay? But yes, John pushed things."

The prosecutor glanced at the jury, as if gauging their appetite for this type of testimony.

"Ms. Simpson, this trial isn't about what went on in your bedroom. We're not interested in yet another installment of *Fifty Shades of Grey*."

"Amen to that," said the judge.

"But in all seriousness," said the prosecutor, "it is important for the jury to understand John Simpson as a person. Did he ever inflict pain on you?"

"Yes."

"Did he ever burn your body with a cigarette?"

The prosecutor glanced at Jack, as if expecting

an objection, but the question harkened back to the testimony of the medical examiner—the wounds found on Sosa's body. It was relevant. More important, Jack didn't want to convey the impression to the jury that Isa's lawyer was in any sense of the word "defending" John Simpson. He let it go.

"Yes."

"Did he ever whip you with an electrical cord?"

Ilene swallowed hard, as if answering these probing questions in public was proving more difficult than expected. "Yes."

"Did he ever suspend you from the ceiling?"

"Yes."

"With chains?"

"Yes."

The prosecutor did another quick check of the jury, taking the collective pulse. "Would you say that it gave John Simpson pleasure to inflict pain on others?"

"Without a doubt."

The prosecutor returned to the lectern and flipped to the next page of her notes. Several jurors seemed relieved to see that she was moving on.

"Ms. Simpson, I want to take you back to the specific night that is in question in this case. Where were you that night around midnight?"

"I was at work. I was a cocktail waitress at Club Vertigo. It's called Club Inversion now. John was a regular. That's where we met."

"Just to be clear, as of the night of Gabriel Sosa's death, you already knew John Simpson, correct?"

"Yes. We weren't exactly living together. But I slept at his place four or five nights a week."

"Did you sleep at his place on this night?"

"I was supposed to."

"What happened?"

"I got off work around one o'clock. Got to John's condo about one thirty."

"Was he in bed?"

"No. John was in the shower."

"In your experience, was it his regular practice to shower at one thirty in the morning?"

"I would say no."

"What happened next?"

"I wasn't really sleepy. I watched TV until he finished his shower. He came out with a towel around his waist and was going to sit down on the couch next to me. But his cell rang on the kitchen counter. That's where he kept his charger. He went over and answered it."

"Do you know who the call was from?"

"No."

"Did you hear what John was saying?"

"Not really. I wasn't paying attention. It sounded like he was arguing with someone. Even shouting into the phone at one point."

"What happened after the call ended?"

"John got dressed really quick. I asked him where he was going."

"Did he tell you?"

"He said to meet him in one hour at some auto repair shop. He gave me the address."

"Did you question him about this?"

"No. I could tell he was still fuming about this phone call. When John got like this, nobody asked questions. You just did what he said."

"Did he tell you anything else?"

"Yes," she said, and her gaze shifted to the other side of the courtroom—toward the defense. "He said to bring Isa Bornelli with me."

The jurors, too, shifted their gaze in Isa's direction. Jack ignored the impulse to turn his head, playing it cool, keeping his focus on the witness.

"Did you know Ms. Bornelli?" asked the prosecutor.

"We weren't friends or anything. But I'd seen her at the club before. With David Kaval."

"Help me understand something here," said the prosecutor. "We're talking somewhere between two and three in the morning. How were you supposed to pick up Ms. Bornelli at this hour and bring her to a garage?"

"I asked the same question. John said, 'Just tell her it's about Gabriel Sosa and it's important. She'll come.'"

"Did you pick up Ms. Bornelli?"

"Yeah. I called her, and she came down from her dorm room."

"Did she ask any questions?"

"Yeah, but I did what John told me: I told her it was about Gabriel Sosa. She wanted to know what, specifically, and I told her I didn't know. But it was important."

"Then what?"

"Like I said, Isa came down and got in my car. I drove to the garage—to the address John gave me."

"What did you do when you got to the garage?"

"I parked outside and called John on his cell. He came out."

"How would you describe his appearance?"

She lowered her eyes. Her voice quivered. "He had blood on his shirt."

"What did he do?"

"He went to the passenger side and opened the door. Isa tried to scream, but he put his hand over her mouth and told her to shut it."

"Did she go quiet?"

"Yes. Then he grabbed her by the arm and took her into the building."

"What did you do?"

"I was scared. I didn't know what to do. This wasn't the first time I'd seen John in this—in this zone, I guess you'd call it. But all that blood on his shirt, that wasn't like anything I saw before. Honestly, I was afraid for Isa. So I went inside after them."

"Did you catch up?"

"Yeah. John had her by the arm and took her through the office real quick. I followed them into the garage area."

"What did you see?"

Ilene drew a breath. "There was a man on the floor."

The prosecutor showed the witness a photograph that had previously been marked as a trial exhibit. "This man?"

Ilene nodded. "Yes."

"Let the record reflect that the witness identified the man on the floor as Gabriel Sosa," said the prosecutor.

"It shall," said the judge.

Hunt set the photograph aside. "Are you sure Mr. Sosa was on the floor?"

"Yes. On his knees. He had no shirt on. Lots of cuts and bruises."

"Was he bleeding?"

"Yeah. He was beat up and bloody."

"What happened next?"

"Isa started screaming at John. He grabbed her by the jaw and made her shut up. He took her over to the man—to Mr. Sosa. John said, *'Look at him! Look at him!'* "

"What happened next?"

"Mr. Sosa said something to her."

"What did he say to Ms. Bornelli?"

"I don't know. It was something in Spanish."

"Then what happened?"

"Isa was crying. She screamed at John. 'It wasn't him! Let him go! He didn't do anything!' John just grabbed her by the jaw again and said, 'It's too late for that.' "

"What did you do next?"

"I did what John told me. I took Isa away and drove her back to the dorm."

"How long was the ride?"

"I don't know. Five minutes maybe."

"Did Ms. Bornelli call the police on the way to her dorm?"

"No. She didn't call anybody."

The prosecutor gathered her notes and stepped back from the lectern. "Thank you, Ms. Simpson," she said in a matter-of-fact tone. "I have no further questions."

The judge looked at Jack. Judge Gonzalez was stoic as ever, except for that one little hitch in his left eyebrow that Jack read as, *Good luck with this one, counselor.*

"Cross-examination?"

"I'd like a sidebar, Your Honor."

The judge waved the lawyers forward and they gathered on the side of the bench that was farthest away from the jury box and the witness.

"I want permission to voir-dire the witness," said Jack. It was lawyer-speak for questioning a witness outside the presence of the jury.

"Voir-dire her about what?" asked the judge.

"The prosecution's failure to disclose a possible third-party deal with this witness."

The prosecutor was beyond indignant. "What?"

"That's a very serious accusation," said the judge. "If Ms. Hunt failed to tell you that she promised something to Ms. Simpson in exchange for her testimony, I would have to declare a mistrial."

"There's absolutely no basis for this accusation," said Hunt.

"There is," said Jack. "Ms. Simpson is currently living with David Kaval, which is interesting, since she puts everyone *but Kaval* at the garage when Mr. Sosa was actually being tortured."

"Judge, the state attorney has made absolutely no promises to Ilene Simpson that she will not face charges."

"That's why I called it a third-party deal," said Jack. "I want to find out if David Kaval got out of prison because Ilene Simpson—his new 'girlfriend'—agreed to be the star witness against my client."

"That's absolutely preposterous," said Hunt.

"You know, Judge, that's the third time I've heard Ms. Hunt use the word *absolutely*, which is usually a pretty good sign that a lawyer is 'absolutely' blowing smoke."

"All right," said the judge, "that's enough. I'm denying the request to voir-dire the witness at this time. But, Mr. Swyteck, file a motion, and if you can set forth a reasonable basis for the possible existence of a secret deal between this witness and the state, I will reconsider. Ms. Hunt, let me ask you this. How many more witnesses do you have?"

"None. Ms. Simpson is the last one."

"So the state will rest after cross-examination?"

"Yes, Your Honor."

"Perfect," said the judge. "It was my goal to finish with the prosecution's case before this jury retires for the weekend. Mr. Swyteck, proceed with your cross-examination."

"Judge, to be quite honest, much of this witness's testimony has taken me totally by surprise. I would love the opportunity to regroup over the weekend."

"Mr. Swyteck, you've tried many cases. You know what will happen if Ms. Hunt does not rest her case before we leave here today. She'll show up Monday morning and have five more witnesses to present. This trial will never end."

Jack couldn't disagree, and he actually liked the

idea of forcing the government to rest its case. But he had a better way to get there.

"Your Honor, I'm happy to proceed today with limited cross. But I would request permission to recall Mrs. Simpson to the witness stand as a hostile witness, should the defense choose to put on its case next week."

The judge paused to consider what Jack was requesting, and he seemed to appreciate the genius of it: Jack was forcing the state to end its case today, and he was preserving his ability to prepare to his fullest and take his best shot at Ilene Simpson next week.

"Come on, Judge," said the prosecutor, "Mr. Swyteck wants to have his cake and eat it, too."

"That's probably true," said the judge. "But I like cake. Mr. Swyteck's request to recall Ilene Simpson next week as a hostile witness is granted. Proceed with your cross-examination."

The prosecutor and Manny returned to their respective tables. Jack took his place before the witness. Since he had the ability to recall her next week, Jack would keep his examination brief. His only goal was to soften some of the sting of her testimony before the jury retired for the weekend. If Jack could score just one point, it would be a victory.

He zeroed in for the kill quickly.

"Mrs. Simpson, you testified that when you pulled up to the garage in your car, John Simpson physically took Isa Bornelli by the arm and pulled her from the passenger seat. Correct?"

She paused, obviously distrustful of anything

Jack said, and reluctant to agree. But there was only one answer. "Yes, that's what I said."

"And when you were in the garage, again John Simpson took Ms. Bornelli physically by the arm, and he led her to where Gabriel Sosa was kneeling."

Another pause, and Jack could almost see the wheels churning in her head as she tried to figure out where this was headed. "Yes," she answered.

Jack went to his table and checked his notes. "And when he had Ms. Bornelli right in front of Mr. Sosa, he shouted something at her."

"Yes."

"'*Look at him!*'" Jack shouted, and then he repeated it, pounding out each word with a tap on his notepad: '*Look . . . at . . . him!*'"

"Yes," she said, her voice shaking a bit. "That's what he said."

Jack laid his notepad on the table. "Mrs. Simpson: You know why he told you to bring Ms. Bornelli to the garage at three o'clock in the morning, don't you?"

"I—I'm not sure."

"You *know*," he said, his voice rising, "that John Simpson wanted Isa Bornelli to *look at* the bloody and beaten body of Gabriel Sosa. That's what he said, right? '*Look at him!*'"

"Yes."

"You *know* that John Simpson was sending Ms. Bornelli a message, don't you?"

"I—"

"Objection!"

Jack didn't wait for a ruling, his cadence even

faster: "You *know* he was telling Ms. Bornelli that if she *ever* told *anyone* what happened on that night, that *this* is what would happen *to her*!"

"Objection, Your Honor!"

"*Isn't that true*, Mrs. Simpson?"

"Mr. Swyteck, that's enough. The objection is sustained."

Jack turned away and did a quick check of the courtroom pulse. The judge was glaring at him. Sylvia Hunt was fuming. The jury appeared to be in shock. The media were eating it up.

And back at his table, seated beside Jack's empty chair, Isabelle Bornelli was sobbing into her own hands, her husband's arm draped around her heaving shoulders.

"Your Honor, I have nothing more for this witness. At this time," Jack added, portending more to come. Then he returned to his chair.

61

"The state of Florida rests."

Jack thought that those would be the final words before trial broke for the weekend. Manny had another idea. He waited for the judge to dismiss the jury, and then he played his hand.

"Your Honor, we haven't heard a thing in this courtroom to support the charge against Keith Ingraham. Even if the court assumes that there is sufficient evidence to show that Isa Bornelli was involved in the murder of Gabriel Sosa, not a shred of evidence has been offered to show that Mr. Ingraham knew anything about it. As the court knows, under Florida law a husband or wife cannot be an accessory after the fact to a crime committed by his or her spouse, so the only relevant conduct is *before* they were married. There's nothing, Judge. Nothing before and, for that matter, nothing after. Keith Ingraham is not an accessory after the fact to murder. I request that the court enter a judgment of acquittal as to my client."

"Ms. Hunt, any response?"

The prosecutor rose. "Your Honor, at this time the state of Florida withdraws the charge against Keith Ingraham."

Judge Gonzalez shook his head in tremor-like fashion—it reminded Jack of his crazy dog Max shaking off the rain—as if to say, *Haven't we had enough surprises for one day?*

"Done," the judge said. "Mr. Ingraham, you are free to go. Ms. Bornelli and Mr. Swyteck, I will see you Monday morning at nine a.m. sharp. We are adjourned."

"All rise!"

A murmur coursed through the courtroom as the crowd rose and the judge stepped down from the bench. His chambers door closed with a thud, which sent the media racing to the rail like sprinters after a starting gun. Manny went to them. Isa and her husband remained in their chairs, locked in an embrace. Jack walked straight to Sylvia Hunt.

"It sucks what you did to Keith Ingraham," he said.

"It sucks what you did to Ilene Simpson."

"No. Ilene is fair game. You charged Keith as a pawn. He was purely leverage to get Isa to cut a deal and agree to plead guilty to your offer of manslaughter."

She packed her briefcase and locked it. "And as it turns out, the trial is going quite well. I don't need leverage, and all deals are off the table. Keith Ingraham is superfluous. So I let him walk."

"Are you for real?" asked Jack.

"You don't have to thank me. In fact, you won't

want to thank me, after the jury convicts your client and she's sentenced to life. See you Monday, Jack," she said as she turned and headed toward the gate.

Jack watched as the swarm of reporters that had gathered around Manny suddenly rushed to the other side of the courtroom, eager for a quote from the prosecutor. One of them called out to Jack by name—*"Hey, Swyteck!"*—but Jack continued toward the defense table. Keith and Isa were still in their seats, still sharing a private moment in a public place. They occupied two of the four chairs. The defense table was half full. Or half empty. They would find out soon enough.

Yes, Sylvia. We will see you Monday.

62

Jack saw the first signs of discord in the limo ride from the courthouse.

As usual, Jack and Manny were in the forward-facing bench seat, and their clients rode with their backs to the driver. But there were a few extra inches of daylight between Keith and Isa on this trip. They seemed more interested in the view outside their respective windows than in the person beside them. At first, Jack thought it could have been simple fatigue. Or perhaps Keith was feeling a bit of "survivor's guilt"—he was free, but Isa was still on trial. By the time they reached the Freedom Institute, however, it was clear: not all was simpatico between them.

It was around three o'clock when they gathered in Jack's office to debrief. Manny had been on his cell since leaving the courthouse. Whether he would remain on the team to help Isa was one item on the afternoon agenda. Keith had something else he wanted to discuss.

"Was Jack right?" Keith asked.

"Right about what?" asked Isa.

"His cross-examination of Ilene. Is that the reason you didn't go to the police—because John Simpson threatened to do to you what he did to Sosa?"

It was a question he could have asked in private, strictly between husband and wife. But it was as if Keith had decided that he wasn't the only person in the room who deserved an honest answer from Isa.

"Yes," she said with a slight edge to her tone. "I told you three times in the courtroom. *Yes.* I was nineteen years old. I was scared to death. I probably should have gone to the police. But I swear, I thought they were done punishing Gabriel for what he had done. I begged them not to kill him. I stood in front of the man who had raped me and told John Simpson that Gabriel was innocent—anything to convince Simpson to let him go."

Keith was silent. Isa prevailed on him. "Keith, I swear on my life. I swear on *our daughter's life.* Simpson told me it was over. When I left that garage, Gabriel was alive."

"Not for long."

"That's not my fault!"

"That's debatable."

"Oh, my God, Keith. Why are you being like this to me? You didn't know Gabriel Sosa. Do you have any idea what kind of person he was?"

"I don't know anything about him."

"He's the man who raped your wife! *That's* who he is. He pulled a knife on me and raped me for two hours in every part of my body, in any way he wanted. Do you want more details, Keith? Is this what a woman has to say in order for people to believe her?

"And it didn't end there. Gabriel didn't go away. He started showing up at the Wellness Center when I would work out. He would show up at Starbucks when I was having coffee. He knew my routine, and he would be there, just so I'd have to see him—so I'd have to feel him looking at me. And *then*—after I *defended* him in that garage and told John Simpson 'You got the wrong guy, please don't hurt him!'—do you know what Gabriel did?"

No one asked. They simply gave Isa time to steady her voice and continue.

"You heard Ilene's testimony," she said, "how Gabriel said something in Spanish that she didn't understand. That was true. Gabriel looked up at me and said, '*Valió la pena.*'"

She didn't translate. The words hung in the air.

"What does that mean?" asked Keith.

Isa swallowed hard, unable to answer.

Jack's Spanish was serviceable enough. "It was worth it."

Isa sprang from her chair and hurriedly left the room. The men were stone silent. No one made eye contact. Finally, Keith spoke.

"I had no idea about the knife."

"There was no knife," said Jack.

"You think she was lying?"

"No. I believe everything she said except the part about the knife. I think she was making a point there."

"A point?"

"Ten years ago, there had to be a knife. Or a gun. Something. Something more than a nineteen-year-old woman's word that she invited a man into her dorm room and didn't consent to sex. With no weapon, the doctor at the campus clinic wouldn't believe her. The police wouldn't believe her. Not even her own father believed she was raped."

"Point well taken," said Manny.

"Except—" Keith started to say.

"Except what?" asked Jack.

"It's not just attitude or chauvinism that kept Felipe Bornelli from believing Isa when she called home and said she was raped."

"Do you know something I don't?" asked Jack.

"Isa told me what she and her father talked about when they met in Cy's Place. Not everything was in the letter he gave her—the one she showed you."

"What was left out?"

"According to her father, Isa has made at least one false accusation in the past. It had to do with her father and one of her friends in high school."

"Do you have the girl's name?" asked Jack.

"Alicia Morales."

Jack pulled his chair closer and looked his friend in the eye. "Tell me about that, Keith. For once, please. I need *someone* to tell me everything there is to know."

63

The phone call at 4:59 p.m. that Friday from Sylvia Hunt surprised Jack. Her message surprised him even more. "It's your lucky day," she said.

"Excuse me?"

"I told you in the courtroom that I would see you in court—no deals for Ms. Bornelli. I still feel that's the wisest course. But there is at least one person here at the Office of the State Attorney who feels differently."

Jack understood clearly: he'd always known State Attorney Carmen Benitez to be reasonable.

"What are you putting on the table?"

"I'm not doing this on the phone. Talk to your client. Get prior authorization from her as to what is acceptable. Meet me in my office at six o'clock and I'll present my offer. You either accept it or reject it on the spot. Those are the rules. Take it or leave it."

Jack took it. He arrived at the Graham Building before six. A rookie prosecutor met him outside the building, got him through weekend security, and took him up the elevator to Sylvia Hunt's office. Sylvia closed the door. The meeting was just her and Jack.

"Well?" said Jack. "What's your offer?"

She leaned forward in her chair and folded her hands atop her desk. "Before I get to that, there are a few things I want to clear up. First, there is no third-party deal, as you described it to Judge Gonzalez. I didn't promise to go easy on David Kaval in exchange for testimony from Ilene Simpson."

"Then you have nothing to worry about," said Jack. "But I'm still going to ask her about it."

"Do what you have to do," she said. "Second, I was angry, I admit, after trial today. I said things about your friend Keith I shouldn't have. I want to assure you that this office didn't charge him as a pawn, as you characterized it. We presented evidence to a grand jury, and there was probable cause to believe that he paid twenty thousand dollars to David Kaval to keep quiet about his wife's involvement in the murder of Gabriel Sosa. In the course of this trial, I sorted out that Kaval wasn't even at the garage when Gabriel was murdered. It became clear to me that Mr. Ingraham's payment wasn't hush money. It really was just to clear up the marital records. That's why I took a dismissal."

"All's well that ends well, I guess," said Jack. "Hopefully we have a good ending for Isa."

"Yes," said the prosecutor. "I've been authorized to put my previous offer back on the table. Voluntary manslaughter, four years in prison."

"You have to do better than that," said Jack.

"I don't have to do anything."

"You could be fair."

"This is more than fair."

"You don't see Isabelle Bornelli as a victim at all here, do you?"

She glared at Jack, and her eyes began to cloud with the same anger that he'd seen in the courtroom. She yanked open her desk drawer, gathered up a shoe box, and emptied the contents onto her desktop.

It was a stack of letters. Some were still in postmarked envelopes. Some were opened.

"What's this?"

"Take a look. Look who signed them."

Jack took one of the letters. It was handwritten and two pages in length. Jack turned to the back of the second page. It was signed "Fatima Sosa."

"Gabriel's mother," said Sylvia. "Take your time. Read it."

"I don't need to," said Jack.

"And you don't need to tell me who the victim is in this case," she said, taking the letter back from him. She gathered up the papers and put them back in the box. "Now, do you accept my offer? Or do you reject it?"

Jack already had his decision from Isa. Four years in prison was not acceptable. He rose and said, "We'll see you Monday."

Jack left the Graham Building and went to his car. Isa was waiting to hear from him, but she was not the first person he needed to call. Something else was on his mind—a question that had been burning since seeing those letters from Fatima Sosa.

Jack needed a quick answer. He dialed Michael Posten at the *Miami Tribune.* Over the years, Jack's relationship with Mike had ebbed and flowed between trust and distrust, friend and foe. Their dealings in Isa's case had been no different. But Posten might be willing to help Jack sort out this latest quandary, especially if he didn't know he was helping.

"Mike, hey, it's Jack Swyteck."

"Jack, buddy. Just the man I wanted to talk to. I'm doing a story for Sunday's paper. I could use a quote."

"Sure. But maybe you can do me a little favor."

"How little?"

"You did a story right before the start of trial. I seem to recall a couple of quotes from Fatima Sosa, Gabriel's mother."

"Yeah, I interviewed her."

"In Miami?"

"Yeah. She lives here."

"Fatima Sosa lives in Miami?"

"Yeah. Bird Road and Ninety-seventh Avenue."

"And how's her English?"

"Nonexistent. We spoke Spanish. Why do you ask?"

Jack wasn't about to tell Posten. "Ah, it's not important."

But that was a lie. Jack knew it was important. It *had* to be important. Fatima Sosa lived in Miami and spoke only Spanish.

The letters that Sylvia Hunt had spilled out

onto her desk were written in English and postmarked Caracas.

"Now, about my quote," said Posten.

"Sorry, Mike. I'm going to have to get back to you on that."

64

Isa wanted to be alone. The news from Jack wasn't good, but it wasn't unexpected. She just needed a few minutes to recover.

She put a pan of Tater Tots in the oven for Melany—the deal was that she got them only if she ate the spinach salad that was on its way up from the hotel's kitchen—and went to the master bedroom. Keith was outside, on his cell, pacing from one end of the terrace to the other, waking up everyone he knew from Zurich to Hong Kong and sharing the good news about his acquittal.

Isa tried not to lie down. If she did, she would surely pass out from exhaustion, and the Tater Tots would go up in flames. She sat on the edge of the mattress. The framed photograph on the nightstand caught her eye. Keith and her on their wedding day in Zurich. Happy times. No worries. Not like today.

Isa was worried about many things, and not just the jury that she would face alone on Monday morning. She worried about Melany losing her mother if she was convicted. She worried about her future with Keith—even if she was acquitted.

Isa had withheld information from her husband, no question. Her actions had left doubts in his mind about her, she knew. Keith had managed to convince himself that their life together would have been so much better, that they would be in such a better place now, if only Isa had told him everything from the very beginning.

You are so wrong, Keith.

There was a night early in their relationship that Keith and Isa never talked about. They were both drunk. They got naked and jumped into bed. It wasn't the best sex two people had ever had. It wasn't even the best sex she'd ever had with Keith. In fact, it was awful. It was the worst by far—and not just because of a moment that, afterward, Keith had tried to laugh off with her as "awkward." Keith was under the impression that Isa had whispered another man's name in the heat of passion, which of course would have been "awkward."

Awkward didn't begin to describe what Isa had felt, or what had actually happened.

She loved Keith, and Isa never wanted him to think that sex was anything but a strong point in their relationship. The very last thing she wanted was for him to fear that he was forcing himself on her in the bedroom. But the truth was that, on that particular night, she didn't want sex. Keith was smashed, and in his drunken confidence he *had* pushed it. The situation was so confusing, so murky, and so negative that it triggered a memory that Isa had managed to suppress for years. She was hardly aware that she'd verbalized it, that in a moment of psychological transference she'd seen her lover in that light. For one horrific instant—in anything but "a moment of passion"—she'd felt so helpless and repulsed by the man she loved that she couldn't stop the words from coming, even if they hadn't come as audibly or as clearly as she remembered.

"*Get off me, Gabriel!*"

"Hey, honey," said Keith, and his voice startled her as he entered the bedroom. He sat beside her on the edge of the mattress.

"Hey," she said, breathless.

"You okay?"

"Yeah. I guess I was zoning out for a second there."

"I just wanted to say I'm sorry. I'm sorry for what happened to you. Sorry for what you've gone through. But I want you to know that I'm going to be here for you. I'll be there for the rest of the trial. And when it's over, I'll help you through this."

He hugged her, but it didn't make Isa want to hug back. He couldn't possibly have understood, but this was the very reason she hadn't told him in the first place. Keith was a fixer. A problem solver. Isa didn't want his help. She didn't want a savior. She wanted her husband back. Her man.

Keith just kept hugging her, and he wouldn't let go.

That was awkward.

65

Jack picked up his grandmother and drove west on Bird Road. They were headed to Fatima Sosa's house.

"Is she a Communist?" Abuela asked in Spanish.

"No. I'm told she is anti-Chavista."

"*Bueno.* Then we will be great friends."

In Abuela's book, the only thing better than an enemy of Castro was an enemy of Castro's protégés—even the dead ones. Jack told her the mission: find out who really wrote those letters to the state attorney in English and mailed them from Venezuela.

Jack knew from Michael Posten the general area in which Fatima lived. He'd searched online unsuccessfully for the exact address, so he'd enlisted the faithful and reliable assistance of Bonnie the Roadrunner. She got it in thirty seconds, reminding him that there was this thing called a phonebook that was actually still in print and that provided the name, address, and phone number for every landline in Miami-Dade County.

The sun was setting as Jack and his *abuela*

pulled up and parked across the street from the ranch-style house on Southwest Fortieth Terrace. Jack ran through the mission one more time. Abuela said she understood. They agreed that the mere sight of Jack would cause Fatima to slam the door in his face. Jack waited in the car and watched from across the street as Abuela walked alone to the front door and rang the bell.

No one answered. She turned around, looked at Jack, and shrugged.

Then the door opened.

Jack wasn't sure what Abuela would say. Frankly, he never knew what might come out of her mouth. But he'd made it clear that this was important, and he knew that she would do her best. The two women appeared to be talking, which Jack took as a positive sign. A minute later they were still talking—a very positive sign. Still talking. Jack checked his watch. It was going on five minutes.

Jack couldn't imagine what could hold these two old women in conversation for so long. Maybe the fact that they'd both lost a twenty-something-year-old child gave them a point of connection. Finally, the front door closed. Abuela turned, walked back to Jack's car, and climbed into the passenger seat.

"I should work for the CIA," she said.

"You got it?"

"*Sí*," she said as she pulled the door shut.

"Who wrote the letters?"

"La novia de Gabriel."

"Gabriel Sosa's fiancée?"

"*Sí*. Alicia Morales."

Jack took a breath, thanked Abuela, and then dialed Theo on his cell. "Pack an overnight bag, dude. And your passport."

"Where are we going?"

The postmark on the envelopes was their destination. "Caracas," said Jack.

66

At 1:40 a.m. Saturday, Santa Barbara Airlines flight number 1526 began its descent into Simón Bolívar International Airport. It was the last nonstop of the day from Miami to Caracas, and Jack and Theo were on it.

Jack had a window seat and slept all but the final thirty minutes of the three-and-a-half-hour flight. He woke in time to glimpse the countless twinkling lights that stretched across the hills near the airport. *Los ranchitos*—the mud huts and tin-roofed shacks of crime-ridden barrios—seemed peaceful and pretty enough at night from an airplane, but no sane visitor dared to enter, day or night, not even with a bodyguard.

The flight attendant cleared away the empty mini-bottles from Theo's tray in preparation for landing. A steady supply of rum and Cokes had made quick friends of the ladies across the aisle, Mercedes and her even more attractive sister, who swore that her name was Benz.

"I'm sure," said Jack, speaking more to himself

than to Theo. "And who are their parents? German engineering?"

The flight landed just after two a.m. They cleared customs and took a cab to the VIP Caracas, a modestly priced boutique hotel in the relatively safe business district. Their rooms had no air-conditioning, but since they were on the second floor, the desk clerk assured them that it was safe to leave the window open. Jack's mattress was reasonably comfortable, and he slept for another couple of hours. He and Theo met for breakfast in the dining room at eight a.m.

"Catch any z's?"

"Yeah, thank God," said Jack. He'd been getting about four hours per night throughout the trial.

"You didn't hear the gunshots around five?"

Theo had obviously taken the clerk's word for it and kept the window open. Jack had played it safe. Caracas consistently ranked second or third in any worldwide ranking of violent crime in major cities that weren't considered war zones. On any given weekend, murder tallies as high as forty were not uncommon. Gun ownership was legal only for the army, police, and Venezuela's booming private security industry, which meant that illegal ownership tallied somewhere in the millions.

"Didn't hear a thing," said Jack.

Theo made his first run at the breakfast buffet. Jack checked his e-mails on his phone and was happy to see that a friend of Andie's had come through for him. Jack would never ask his wife to tap directly into FBI resources, but she knew plenty of retired agents-turned-private-investigator who could nail down a current address for the right Alicia Morales—and there were hundreds, by Jack's estimate, in Caracas.

"Alicia lives in the Catia borough," said Jack.

Theo took a monster-sized bite of fresh pineapple. "Where's that?"

"West of here. Actually not far from the presidential palace."

"Is it safe?"

"No."

"Are we going?"

"That's why you're here, pal."

After breakfast they walked to the motor court in front of the hotel. The fifth cabbie they approached was either brave enough, stupid enough, or hungry enough to take them to their destination. Ten minutes into the ride, however, Jack was starting to question the route they were taking. His Spanish was a continual work in progress, but he was determined to raise Riley bilingual, and since her birth Jack had improved his own skills sufficiently to challenge the driver. The man's impassioned explanation seemed to be on the up-and-up.

"What did he say?" asked Theo.

"He says he doesn't take the highway past the slums anymore. The gangs throw rocks from the overpasses. When the driver stops to check the damage, the other gang members run out from the bushes and rob him. One of his friends was shot in the head two weeks ago."

"Nice," said Theo.

Caracas sits in a valley by Mount Avila, a nine-thousand-foot peak that separates the city from the Caribbean Sea and dominates most of the city's landscape. The rich lived to the east of the central business district. In the western hills were the barrios, home to roughly half the city's population of some five million. Jack and Theo's driver took them along the Avenida Sucre in western Caracas and past the Mikro supermarket, where a few hundred people of all ages had queued up in the morning sun. "Hoping to reach the door before the sugar and flour runs out," the driver told Jack. The roads worsened and the ride got bumpier as the taxi climbed higher into the hills. Like many Venezuelans, the driver loved conversation. He talked about everything from the dry toilet project in La Vega barrio, a district with no access to the municipal water grid, to the lyrics of the late political activist Alí Primera, who once sang passionately about the truth of Venezuela, which was in the hills—the people, and their unrest. If that was so, "the truth" was right outside Jack's window.

The cab stopped. The driver pointed to a house across the street. He gave them some final advice, speaking Spanish slowly enough for Jack to understand. *Be careful. Don't flash money. And remember, in the barrios, like many places with terrible reputations, most people are friendly. Just keep your eyes open for the bad ones.*

"*Gracias,*" said Jack. He paid the fare and gave the driver an extra fifty bucks to wait for them so that they would be sure to have a ride back to the hotel. The driver gladly agreed and took the money. Jack and Theo climbed out of the cab and closed the door.

The tires squealed as the driver got the hell out of there.

"I guess fifty bucks wasn't enough," said Jack as he watched the taxi speed away from them.

"Hope you have a plan B, dude."

Jack was still working on it. Theo followed him across the street. This wasn't the tin-roof and mud-house neighborhood that stupid American tourists ventured into in hopes of spicing up their vacation postings on Instagram, only to end up lying in a ditch somewhere, naked, penniless, and wondering how they were going to get home with no phone and no passport. But it was poor by any standard, and Jack was glad to have Theo's muscle in his company.

"Does Felipe Bornelli live around here, too?" asked Theo.

"Not anymore. Isa said her parents grew up in this area, but Felipe did well for himself under Chavez. He lives on the east side now. I doubt Isa ever set foot here."

"But Alicia Morales was her friend, right?"

"Her friend from Miami, when Alicia's mother worked for Felipe."

"So this is where you end up after you work in the Venezuelan consul's office?"

It did seem strange, and Theo's question went to the heart of the enigma.

The Morales residence was a one-story house

of unpainted blocks and sloppy masonry. The low-slung roof sagged in the middle, and the foundation listed badly to the left, matching the slope of the hill. Laundry flapped in the breeze on a line that hung like a sad smile between Alicia's house and their next-door neighbor's.

Jack went to the front door and knocked. No one answered. Jack noticed the home security system: broken bottles and other jagged spikes of glass cemented onto the window sills to deter a break-in, or punish anyone who tried.

"Hey, Jack—say cheese," said Theo, as he snapped Jack's picture from the street.

"Are you crazy?"

"It's on its way," said Theo, and Jack's phone chimed in his pocket with the message.

"Damn it, Theo! Put that phone away before you get us mugged."

The next-door neighbor came to the fence, looking at them suspiciously. "Who are you?"

Jack answered, and they continued the conversation in Spanish. The man didn't know who Isabelle Bornelli was, but he knew the name Felipe Bornelli.

"Alicia is not here," said the neighbor.

"Where can we find her?"

"I wouldn't tell you if I knew. She has no interest in helping anyone in the Bornelli family."

"Why is that?" asked Jack.

"*Why?*" he asked, incredulous. "Felipe Bornelli sent her fiancé to Vista Hermosa."

"Vista Hermosa?"

"In Ciudad Bolívar. It's a prison."

"Hell on earth," said Theo, speaking only to Jack. "I seen grown men cry at the thought of being deported and sent there. FSP is a fucking five-star hotel compared to that place."

Jack continued with the neighbor in Spanish. "What was his crime?"

"Political prisoner. Which is false. He was a Chavista. Like all the people of the hills."

Jack didn't argue with him, but he knew for a fact that Gabriel's mother wasn't. Abuela wouldn't have lasted fifteen seconds on the front porch of a Chavista.

"Jack," said Theo, "incoming at three o'clock."

Jack glanced toward the side street. A group of eight young men were approaching. They could have been looking for a ninth to field a *béisbol* team, but Jack trusted Theo's instincts. He'd also read enough travel advisories to know about the neighborhood enforcers who replaced police presence—thugs who enforced their own rule of law.

"Not safe here for you," the man said. "You should go."

A horn tooted, and a taxi pulled up. The *same* taxi. Their cabdriver had returned.

Thank God.

Jack thanked the neighbor, and then he and Theo hurried to the taxi and jumped in the backseat.

"I thought you left us," Jack told him in Spanish as they pulled away.

"No, no. I have to keep moving. Those boys would slit my throat for the cash you gave me."

Jack settled into the backseat.

"What did he say?" asked Theo.

Jack glanced out the rear window. A dog ran across the street. A barefoot young girl chased after it. The gang of eight was watching her.

"He says I shouldn't be doing this shit anymore," said Jack. "I have a two-year-old."

67

Isa felt drawn to the U.

Keith and another dad from Melany's kindergarten class took their daughters bowling on Saturday. Isa rode the Metrorail to University station. Her purse was in her lap, along with the flyer from Emma about the campus rally at the University of Miami.

Isa had told no one that she was going. She hadn't made up her mind until that morning. She was staring at her reflection in the bathroom mirror, contemplating who she was.

Victim? Murderer?

Victim? False accuser?

Victim? Liar?

The meeting with her father at Cy's Place had been the low point—until Ilene Simpson's testimony, which became the new low point. Then came the lowest point of all: the meeting in Jack's office, where it became painfully obvious to Isa that there was an inborn processing defect in all men—even good men—that made the concept of "date rape" almost impossible to compute.

A small crowd was gathered on the quad. Some were standing, and maybe a couple dozen were seated in folding chairs on the lawn, facing a small stage. Isa stood toward the back. It was no accident that an event to promote awareness of sexual assault on college campuses was held near the residence halls, and Isa was all too aware of the fact that she was just two buildings away from her old dorm room. The "Students Against Sexual Assault" banner stretched between the trunks of two palm trees. Campus television was covering the event. Isa moved to an open seat in the last row of chairs as the president of the student body yielded the podium to SASA president Emma Barrett.

There was brief applause, and then the crowd settled in to listen.

"Have you ever noticed there are no sorority houses on this campus?" Emma asked from the podium. "We have sororities, and there are fraternity houses aplenty, but not a single sorority *house*. Ever wondered why? One salacious rumor has it that it was illegal for more than five women to live together in the same housing unit. It was considered a brothel. That fits nicely with the legend of Al Capone hanging out at the Biltmore Hotel. But it's rumor, not fact. The truth, however, is even more bizarre.

"The philosophy in the early 1960s, when Greek houses were popping up on this campus, was that UM was a 'finishing school' for young ladies. Women were required to live in residence halls on campus. We had to sign in and out, and there was a 'house mother' assigned to every floor to make sure the 'ladies' adhered to the rules outlined in 'The Little Green Book,' which was published by the dean of women.

"The 'Little Green Book' no longer exists. Rules have changed. Attitudes have changed more slowly. What we're here to talk about today is this: that the way to make college campuses safe for women—and respectful of women—is not to impose dress codes, curfews, and Little Green Books. It's to change a culture in which sixty percent of rape and sexual-assault victims continue to keep silent."

Isa joined in the applause, startled by her own enthusiasm. It was the first time since coming to Miami that she'd been out in public and made to feel like something other than a criminal. Isa glanced left, then right. She saw other women. She knew she wasn't the only one in the crowd who'd felt drawn to this event, who hadn't reported, and who made up that silent 60 percent.

"Isa?"

She turned at the sound of her name and caught her breath. She was suddenly speechless. Even after all these years, Isa recognized the face immediately, but the woman reintroduced herself anyway.

"It's me. Alicia."

68

Jack's return flight put him in Miami early Saturday evening. Isa had called him in Caracas after the SASA rally at the university. Before Jack could tell her what a bad idea it had been for her to attend, she filled him in about Alicia Morales—which made him forgive all. It was time for Jack to meet her. He took a cab straight from the airport to Brickell Avenue.

At sixty-four stories, the Four Seasons is Florida's tallest building and a pillar of luxury even by Miami standards. Jack couldn't honestly say he'd want to live there, but the endless stream of repairs at the Freedom Institute sometimes left him thinking that five-star service and twenty-four-hour pampering didn't sound so bad. Having spent his morning in the western hills of Caracas, Jack could only wonder how it made Alicia feel about the hand fate had dealt her and the life her best friend from high school was living.

"I hated her," said Alicia. "Every day I woke up hating Isa with every bone in my body."

They were in Isa's kitchen, seated around the

polished granite counter. It was just the three of them. Manny was out of the picture. Keith had taken Melany to Coconut Grove for pizza.

Isa looked out the window. The resentment was undoubtedly something Isa had known about for years, and perhaps Alicia had told her to her face before. Nonetheless, the words coming from Alicia's lips seemed to sting.

"I don't blame you," said Isa.

"No," said Alicia. "My hatred was directed at the wrong person."

Jack listened as Alicia continued to speak from the heart, confirming all that Jack had learned from her next-door neighbor in Catia—and more. Jack interrupted only when necessary. Alicia paused every few minutes to collect herself. She and Isa exchanged an occasional glance or a sad smile, but Jack didn't take that as a sign that they had in any way scripted or rehearsed Alicia's words. Isa had withheld information from him before, spoken in half-truths, and even lied to him. But in her kitchen on that Saturday night—when it was just Jack, his client, and her best friend from high school—nothing was fabricated. That was Jack's firm take.

"Isa, did you and Alicia talk about the Post-it note?"

"No," said Isa.

Jack told her about their dash from the courthouse after a full day of trial and the message Jack had found stuck to his computer bag when they piled into the limo: *She will not testify.*

"We did a frame-by-frame examination of

video from the news stations. It shows someone in the crowd reaching out and putting it there as we left the courthouse. The hand appears to be a woman's."

Alicia looked away, then back. "An older woman, you mean. Someone who isn't computer literate and doesn't trust cyberspace enough to believe that an e-mail would actually get to you, so she had to do it in writing."

Those weren't questions. Alicia was guiding Jack to an answer.

"Gabriel's mother?" he asked.

"Yes. I wrote the note for her. In English. Just like I wrote her letters to the state attorney."

"Fatima obviously doesn't want you to testify," said Jack.

"No. She doesn't."

Jack glanced at Isa, and her expression made it clear that if anyone was going to ask Alicia for a favor, it needed to be Jack.

"It's Isa's turn to present evidence to the jury on Monday," said Jack. "Is the note your final word on the subject?"

Alicia paused. Clearly a bond remained between Alicia and the woman who would have been her mother-in-law, and Alicia wouldn't lightly disregard whatever pact they'd reached on Alicia's involvement in the trial.

"It's not final," she said in a firm voice. "I *will* testify."

69

Monday came quickly. The trial of Isabelle Bornelli resumed at nine a.m.

Jack was standing behind his chair at the table. Isa was seated to his left. It was just the two of them.

"The defense calls Alicia Morales."

Alicia had been staying with Isa since Saturday night, but even as Jack was driving to the courthouse that morning, he'd feared a frantic phone call from Isa telling him that Alicia had changed her mind and was on her way back to Venezuela. Hitting her with a court-issued subpoena might have compelled her appearance, but it might also have turned her into a hostile witness. It was no small relief to see the double doors in the back of the courtroom open as Alicia began her walk in silence down the center aisle.

Jack had little doubt that these two old friends had been the prettiest girls in their high school class, and that like sisters they were able to share clothes. The navy suit and burgundy blouse borrowed from Isa was a good look for Alicia. Faux pearls were an appropriately understated accessory, and she walked comfortably in modest heels. Appearance wasn't everything, but there was no such thing as a second first impression. And Alicia *was* being watched. The press section was so packed that media representatives had spilled over into the public seating area, which was also filled to capacity. Anticipation was high, fueled mainly by rumors that Isa would take the stand in her own defense. Alicia, Jack hoped, would make that unnecessary.

"Do you swear to tell the truth, the whole truth . . ."

The administration of the oath was no mere formality, but Jack found his gaze sweeping slowly from the witness to the jurors, and then out toward the crowded gallery. Keith was in the first row behind the defense table, the polished rail separating him from his wife. For the first week of trial, Gabriel's mother had seated herself on the prosecutor's side of the courtroom. She was back for week two.

Jack approached the witness. "Good morning, Ms. Morales."

Her smile was a little tentative. "Good morning."

Jack walked her through her nervousness with simple background questions. Born, Caracas. Current home address, Catia. No, never finished high school. Last worked in a factory making T-shirts.

"Where have you lived for the past two months, Ms. Morales?"

"I've been staying with Fatima Sosa. Gabriel's mother. She is a legal resident and lives here in Miami. I'm here on a three-month nonimmigrant visa."

Jack paused, giving the jury time to appreciate the significance of the fact that the first witness for the defense was living with the victim's mother. Jack could have pressed the point. He could have revealed how Fatima had told Jack's *abuela* that Alicia wrote the letters to the state attorney but failed to mention that Alicia had been living in her house since summer's end. Indeed, Fatima had even led Abuela to believe that Jack needed to travel to Venezuela to track her down. But all eyes were already upon Alicia, including those of Fatima Sosa, and Jack didn't need to up the pressure by attacking the mother of a dead son.

"Let's back up a little," said Jack. "Your English is quite good, Ms. Morales. Where did you learn to speak it?"

"Here in Miami. My mother worked for the Consul General of the Bolivarian Republic of Venezuela on Brickell Avenue."

"How long did she work there?"

"Five years, when I was in middle school and high school. I was an ESL student—English as a second language."

"Who did your mother work for at the consulate?"

"She was an administrative assistant to Señor Felipe Bornelli."

Jack guided the jurors' attention to his client;

he hoped Isa was ready for it. "Is Felipe Bornelli the father of the defendant, Isabelle Bornelli?"

"Yes."

"Did you know Ms. Bornelli?"

"Yes. We were close friends," she said, glancing again in Isa's direction. "Best friends. Until the very end."

"How old were you when you and Isa stopped being best friends?"

"Seventeen. We were high school juniors."

"What happened?"

Alicia hesitated. Jack's list of easy questions had come to an end. The silence continued. The judge spoke up. "Perhaps you can be more specific in your question, Mr. Swyteck."

"Of course, Judge. Ms. Morales, did you say anything that caused the rift between you and Isabelle Bornelli?"

Jack sensed that the prosecutor would have liked to object, but it wasn't hearsay for a witness to repeat her own words. "Isa and I told each other everything. One night, when we were alone, I guess I wasn't acting like myself. I told her what was wrong."

"What did you say to her?"

"This—this was very hard for me. But I said that her father came on to me."

"You told Ms. Bornelli that her father made an unwanted sexual advance, correct?"

"Yes," she said quietly.

"Did you tell anyone other than Ms. Bornelli about this?"

"I didn't want to. I was afraid my mother might lose her job."

"But did you tell anyone?" asked Jack.

"Yes. We made a written complaint to the consul general."

"You said 'we.' Did anyone help you with that complaint?"

"Yes. Isabelle Bornelli."

"How did she help?"

"She—Isa really *made* me write it. And Isa was the one who got us in to see the consul general. My mother was a secretary. Her father was a diplomat. She had status. We went to the consul general's office together and handed it to him personally."

"What was the final resolution by the consul?"

"None that I'm aware of."

"What happened after you presented your complaint?"

"About a week later, my mother was fired. We were sent back to Venezuela."

Jack stepped away from the lectern briefly, for no purpose other than to give the witness a break. Then he resumed.

"Did you tell anyone else that Felipe Bornelli had 'come on to you'?"

"Not in Miami. I didn't tell anyone until my mother and I moved back to Caracas."

"Whom did you tell?"

She glanced toward the jury. "I told Gabriel Sosa."

Even the judge perked up, Jack noticed. "How did you know Mr. Sosa?" asked Jack.

"We met about three months after my return to Caracas. We started dating. Pretty soon after that we got engaged."

"How did you come to tell him about what happened in Miami with Felipe Bornelli?"

She paused to choose her words. "It was after we were engaged. I was getting distant with Gabriel. It wasn't because I didn't love him. I did. I told him it wasn't his fault—that something had happened to me in Miami."

Jack didn't like having to ask the next question, but this trial left no room for ambiguity.

"It's important to know exactly what you told him, Ms. Morales. Do you remember your exact words?"

She drew a breath, then answered. "I told him that Mr. Bornelli raped me."

Jack could have left it there. The logical follow-up—*Did* he sexually assault you?—was extremely risky. An answer of "no" would turn his star witness into a false accuser. But if Jack didn't ask the question, Sylvia Hunt would.

"Ms. Morales, I know this may be a difficult question for you to answer, but were you sexually assaulted by Felipe Bornelli?"

Silence. She didn't answer.

The judge prodded. "Ms. Morales, you must answer the question."

"I'm sorry. Could you ask again?"

Jack did. He waited. The courtroom waited.

"No," she said. "That was a lie."

It was as if the floor had collapsed beneath Jack's feet. It wasn't the answer he'd expected. It wasn't the story she'd told him on Saturday night in Isa's apartment.

Judge Gonzalez interjected. "Mr. Swyteck, do you have another question?"

Jack's pause had been longer than intended. He would have to move on and figure out a way to work around Alicia's change of heart—and change of story.

"What did Gabriel Sosa do after you told him you were sexually assaulted?"

"He went to speak to Mr. Bornelli. I begged him not to. But he did."

"In Miami?"

"No. By then the Venezuelan government had closed the consul's office in Miami. Mr. Bornelli was back in Caracas working for the Chavez government."

"What happened after Gabriel met with Mr. Bornelli?"

"About two days later, Gabriel was arrested and sent to prison at Vista Hermosa."

"What was he charged with?"

"Inciting violence, which is a charge the Chavez government brought against political opponents."

"*Was* Gabriel Sosa an opponent of the government?"

"No."

"How long did he stay in Vista Hermosa?" asked Jack.

"Six months."

"Did you visit him?"

"No. I tried one time."

"What happened?"

"Too dangerous. The place was built to hold four hundred inmates and has more than fifteen hundred. The only part of Vista Hermosa that the guards control is the front gate. Inside is run by the inmates. Rival gangs are led by a *pran*—like a crime boss. They have guns. They have knives. If you break the gang's rules, they—"

"Objection," said the prosecutor, rising. "Your Honor, this is way beyond the witness's personal knowledge."

"Sustained."

Jack was confident that the jury had the gist. Even a good day at Vista Hermosa was cruel and unusual punishment. "When did you next see Gabriel?"

"When he was released."

"What was he like when he came out?"

She lowered her eyes, her voice laden with sadness. "He was a different person. Angry. Violent. Extremely violent."

"Did he ever hit you?"

She paused, then nodded. "Yes."

Jack was tempted to ask if he had ever sexually assaulted her—she'd hinted at it on Saturday night—but Fatima Sosa was in the courtroom, which might color Alicia's testimony, and Jack couldn't afford another setback from this witness.

"Did you and Gabriel Sosa remain engaged?" asked Jack.

"No. I ended it."

"Did he stay in Caracas?"

"No. He went to Miami."

"What did he plan to do when he got to Miami?"

The prosecutor rose. "Objection. Calls for speculation."

"Sustained."

It was the correct ruling, but even with the objection, the answer was obvious. Jack didn't like ending on a weak note, but he probably had enough to argue to the jury that Gabriel Sosa went to Miami to even the score. "One moment, please, Your Honor. I may be finished."

Jack checked his notes. The more he thought about it, the less comfortable he was with the way things stood. Alicia's credibility with the jury was critical. She painted herself as a liar—a woman who had lied to her own fiancé and told him that Felipe Bornelli was a rapist. She would be skewered on cross-examination. Jack had to rehabilitate her. Like it or not, he had to revisit the most difficult part of her testimony.

"Ms. Morales, you testified earlier that you feared retaliation by Felipe Bornelli. In your view, Mr. Bornelli was a very powerful man, correct?"

"Yes."

"He's still a powerful man, isn't he?"

"Objection, Your Honor."

"Judge, all I'm asking for is this witness's present perception," said Jack.

The judge mulled it over for a moment. "The witness may answer."

"Yes," said Alicia. "As I understand, Mr. Bornelli is still held in high regard by the party and the current administration."

"After you made your complaint about Mr. Bornelli to the consul general, your mother was fired from her job and sent back to Caracas. Correct?"

"Yes."

Jack had seen the house they lived in. He thought it important for the jury to see it. The only photograph he had was the one that Theo had texted to him—the one Jack had nearly strangled him for taking. Jack pulled it up on his iPhone, showed it to the judge and the prosecutor, and then shared it with the witness.

"Is this the house in Caracas that you and your mother moved to?" asked Jack.

She seemed surprised that Jack had a photo—perhaps even more surprised to see Jack in it. "Yes."

With the court's permission, Jack showed it to the jury. Then he returned to the podium. "Ms. Morales, there are worse houses than this one in Caracas, are there not?"

"Yes. Definitely."

"There are parts of the Catia borough where crime is out of control. True?"

"Some places I would never want to live."

"This house is not the most dangerous place that you and your mother could end up. Is it?"

Alicia seemed to understand Jack's point, but the prosecutor interrupted. "Objection, Judge. I don't see the relevance of any of this."

"Nor do I. Sustained."

Jack wanted to explain that it was relevant—that this witness had stopped short of telling the jury the horrid truth about Felipe Bornelli, and that she'd done so out of the same fear of retribution that had tormented her as a teenager.

"Judge, I—"

"I've already sustained the objection, Mr. Swyteck. Please move on."

"Can I change my answer, please?" asked Alicia.

Jack's spirits soared. Alicia was looking straight at Isa, and Jack sensed that both his client and the witness had understood where he was headed with his line of questioning—and that the two old friends had come to a silent understanding that it was time for the truth to be told.

The prosecutor didn't know what to say, but she spoke anyway. "Judge, there is no question pending."

"I'll fix that," said Jack. He was still operating on a hunch, but one glance back at Isa confirmed that his instincts were spot on. He framed his question with confidence.

"Ms. Morales, I understand how difficult this may be for you, but can you please tell us: Were you sexually assaulted by Felipe Bornelli?"

Silence. She didn't answer.

You can do it, Jack told her, but only in his thoughts.

The judge prodded. "Ms. Morales, you must answer the question."

"I'm sorry. Could you ask it again?"

Jack did. He waited. The courtroom waited.

Be strong, thought Jack.

"Yes, that's true," she said, swallowing hard. "Felipe Bornelli raped me."

She'd said it. Aloud. In a packed courtroom. And Jack saw no signs of regret.

"Ms. Morales, you testified earlier that you told Isabelle Bornelli that her father made sexual advances. Was that what you told her?"

"Yes. I was afraid to say more."

"You testified earlier that you told Gabriel Sosa that you were raped by Felipe Bornelli. Is that what you told him?"

"Yes. I told him that because it was the truth."

"So when Gabriel Sosa came to Miami, he knew that Isabelle Bornelli's father had raped you."

Again Jack sensed that the prosecutor wanted to object, but she didn't pull the trigger.

"Yes," said Alicia. "He knew. Because that's what I told him."

Jack smiled with his eyes at Alicia—nothing obvious, just enough to let her know that she'd done the right thing. Then he stepped back from the podium.

"I have no further questions, Your Honor."

70

Monday ended with a whimper. Jack could not have been more pleased.

Sylvia Hunt's cross-examination of Alicia had done no damage. The prosecutor spent the rest of the afternoon trying to convince the judge that her testimony should be excluded as prejudicial.

"Of course it's *prejudicial*," Judge Gonzalez told her. "I don't think Mr. Swyteck called her to the witness stand to *help* the state's case. The testimony shall stand as admissible."

Trial adjourned at five p.m. Jack made the decision to say nothing to the media. His direct examination of Alicia had given them plenty to talk about on the evening news. It was also important that Isa and Alicia leave the courthouse separately. The defense could ill afford an accusation of exerting undue influence on a witness and manufacturing evidence.

Isa and Keith went to their apartment. Jack returned to the Freedom Institute. He had serious work to do.

Jack's toughest decision was whether to leave

things as they stood or present additional evidence in Isa's defense. It was clear enough from Alicia's testimony that Gabriel raped Isa to even the score with the Bornelli family; the rape of Felipe Bornelli's daughter was Gabriel's notion of "justice" for Alicia. The second part of Jack's argument was purely deduction: Felipe ordered the torture and execution of Gabriel Sosa to avenge the rape of his daughter. Jack didn't have that evidence. Nor did he know how to get it—short of calling Isa's father to the witness stand.

"Any leads on where we might find Felipe Bornelli?" Jack asked.

Hannah, Brian, and Eve were in the room with Jack. The whole team from the Freedom Institute was helping him at this stage, and the energy level was high. Victory seemed within grasp.

"I have three investigators on it," said Hannah. "Not even Andie's friend—the retired FBI agent—has turned up anything."

"If he's not in Miami, and we can't subpoena him, I may have to make *the* decision tomorrow," said Jack.

Everyone knew what "*the* decision" was: Would Isa testify in her own defense?

"Are you ready, if you have to call her?" asked Hannah.

"I spent most of the weekend focusing on Alicia. It would be nice to have another day and put off Isa's testimony 'til Wednesday if we can."

"You could recall Ilene Simpson," said Brian. "The judge said the defense could put her back on the stand as part of its case."

"That's a great idea, Brian. Can you get me a draft outline?"

"Sure thing."

They divvied up a few more tasks—exhibits that they planned to offer, evidentiary objections they might face, and more. The others retreated to their offices. Jack was alone when he got the phone call from Alicia.

"How are you doing?" asked Jack.

"Oh, I'm okay," she said.

Jack could hear the stress in her voice. "Are you sure?"

"Uhm—I'm with Fatima Sosa. At her house."

Jack could certainly see how that would be stressful. "Is everything all right?"

"Fatima would like to talk to you."

"Now?"

"Yes."

"What about?"

"What do you think?"

That was a fair response. Jack hoped it was the breakthrough that would end the case. But it might have been something else. "I could be there in twenty minutes."

"I think you should come," she said, the stress still evident in her tone. "I'm *asking* you to come."

The way she'd put it was a little curious, but she'd definitely conveyed that it was important.

"Okay," said Jack. "I'm on my way."

71

Jack drove to Fatima Sosa's house—the address was still in his GPS from the trip with Abuela—and this time he parked in the driveway. Alicia answered the front door and invited him into the living room. Fatima wasn't home.

"But you said Fatima wanted to talk to me," Jack said.

"Alicia lied," said Felipe Bornelli as he emerged from the dark hallway, joining them in the living room. "But it was at my direction."

Felipe was a holding a pistol. It was pointed at Jack. "Put the chain on the door, Alicia."

She obeyed, the chain rattling in her shaking hand. They stood in a triangle—Alicia near the door, Felipe closest to the hallway, and Jack at the window, in front of the drawn curtains.

"Felipe, you're making a huge mistake," said Jack.

"You made the mistake, Mr. Swyteck, when you underestimated me."

"There's nothing you can accomplish by shooting me."

"This is true," he said. "That's why Alicia is going to do it."

"No! I won't," she said.

Keeping his pistol trained on Jack, Felipe pulled a small revolver from his jacket. "Take it, Alicia."

"No."

He laid the gun on the end table. "Pick it up. Point it at his chest. And pull the trigger. That's how this is going to play out."

Jack had no weapon, only his words. He tried to engage Felipe. "Who did you hire, Felipe? David Kaval or John Simpson?"

"This isn't a courtroom. You don't get to ask questions."

"Gabriel raped Isa, so you paid her badass boyfriend to kill him? Do I have that right? You're the revenge killer?"

He smiled sardonically. "Revenge had nothing to do with it. Gabriel landed in prison because he tried to extort me. I put him where he belonged. Unfortunately, prison only seemed to make him bolder. I knew he wouldn't stop with the rape of my daughter. He would blackmail me the rest of my life. He had to go."

"That's not true," said Alicia.

"Sad, but true," he said with a heavy dose of insincerity. "Aw, does that spoil it for you, Alicia? Did you think that after you told Gabriel you were raped he confronted me to protect the honor of his fiancée? Your knight in shining armor? Hardly. He wanted fifty thousand dollars."

"That's a lie!"

"Pick up the gun, Alicia."

"No."

"You're making a very bad choice. It will not end well for you. I'll shoot you and Swyteck, and I'll have your mother living in a mud hut at the end of the fucking runway at Simón Bolívar. I'm offering you the only way out. Swyteck forced you to lie about me and Gabriel on the witness stand. You resented it. You shot him. You will be halfway to Venezuela before I call the police. That's my guarantee."

There was silence. Then, slowly, Alicia reached for the gun on the table.

"Don't do it," said Jack.

She took the revolver and held it loosely in her hand.

"You've shot a gun before, haven't you?" asked Felipe. "Living in Catia?"

"Yes. Don't make me do this."

"I can destroy you and your whole family, Alicia. Is that what you want?"

"I'll shoot *you*," she said, but she wasn't aiming at him. The gun lay flat in her palm.

"No, you won't. I'm a powerful man, Alicia. That was the one thing you said in court today that was true."

"Everything I said in that courtroom was true."

"I raped you?" he said, scoffing. "Really? As I recall, I gave the little teenage whore exactly what she wanted. Now hold the gun like you mean it, take aim, and pull the trigger."

Alicia clasped the revolver in both hands. It

was visibly shaking as she raised and extended her arms to assume the marksman's pose. The barrel was pointed straight at Jack's chest.

"That's it," said Felipe. "Now pull the trigger."

"Don't do this," said Jack.

The agony was all over her face. Her eyes welled, her hands shook, and Jack saw the quiver in her lower lip.

"Don't let him take any more from you, Alicia," said Jack.

"Ignore him," said Felipe.

"He took what didn't belong to him. He took your life in Miami. Your fiancé. Your future. Your body."

"Pull the trigger!"

"Now he wants your soul," said Jack.

"Do it!" shouted Felipe.

Her grip tightened, and Jack knew that his window of opportunity was about to close. He searched his mind for a hook, some convincing angle to turn this moment against Felipe in an instant. He suddenly remembered the conversation on Saturday night in Isa's apartment, how Isa and Alicia had reconnected at that rally at UM. Something had drawn Alicia to that event, just as Isa had been drawn there.

"What would Emma Barrett do?" asked Jack.

To Felipe, it was a strange name that threw him off guard for a split second; to Alicia, it was the tipping point.

"Who?" asked Felipe, but before he could react, Alicia's aim shifted from Jack to Felipe, and she squeezed the trigger. Then she squeezed it again. And again, and again.

She stopped only when all six chambers were spent. Then she dropped the gun and fell to her knees. Tears flowed, seemingly without end, and her shoulders bounced in cathartic heaves.

Jack checked Felipe for a pulse, but he was dead. He went to Alicia, knelt beside her, and put his arm around her. Then he put into words what he had told her only with his eyes in the courtroom.

"It's okay, Alicia. You did the right thing."

72

Jack was in court Tuesday morning for Sylvia Hunt's formal dismissal of the case against Isa. Judge Gonzalez announced a judgment of acquittal from the bench.

"Good luck to you, Ms. Bornelli. You're free to go."

She went without delay.

Isa, Keith, and Melany were booked on the late flight to Hong Kong via Toronto. An intern at the IBS Miami office would pack whatever they couldn't fit in a suitcase and ship it to them. Key Biscayne wasn't on the way to the airport, but they stopped by the house to say good-bye to Jack, Andie, and Riley. Isa wanted a minute alone with Jack. They stepped onto the back patio. Jack closed the sliding door, and they sat at the glass-top table, just the two of them.

The cool breeze from the bay was starting to feel more like autumn in Miami. Jack could hear the chop in the bay in the darkness.

"I know I wasn't the model client," said Isa. "I probably drove you crazy at times."

"Nah, you—well, actually. Yes."

They shared a little smile, and then Isa turned serious. "I don't want anything bad to happen to Alicia."

"She'll be fine. Felipe was armed and threatening to kill both of us. Clearest case of justifiable homicide I've ever seen."

"Does the state attorney feel the same way?"

"Yes. I called Sylvia Hunt after the judge tossed out your case. It turned into more than the standard 'no hard feelings' conversation. Alicia will never be charged. Can't say the same for David Kaval and Ilene Simpson."

"She's going to prosecute them?"

"Ilene Simpson never hired a lawyer. She really did fail to protect herself with a formal immunity deal. She was all about protecting her new boyfriend Kaval, so she left herself wide open to prosecution. Sylvia says she's going after her."

"And Kaval?"

"He screwed himself. His whole deal was contingent on staying away from Ilene until after the trial. The dumb shit practically had Ilene move in with him. He's going back to prison."

"Well," said Isa. "Who would have guessed it? A happy ending."

"Except that it's not the ending, is it? You didn't pull me out onto the patio to hear what I had to say. You wanted to tell me something."

Isa glanced toward the bay. It took a minute for her to begin, and finally she sat up straight and spoke with the demeanor of someone who had prepared her words but wasn't necessarily sticking to them.

"This won't excuse all the aggravation I caused you. But it may help you understand some of my actions. I wanted you to know about this."

Isa reached into her purse and laid a single-page handwritten letter on the table. It was in Spanish.

"What is it?" asked Jack.

"This is a letter that my mother wrote to me before she died. She was sick—too sick to mail it. Or maybe she just didn't want me to have it until after she was gone. My father was supposed to give it to me nine years ago at her funeral. He didn't. He gave it to me when we met at Cy's Place."

"Did you show this to Keith?"

"No. I've never told anyone about it."

Jack took the letter. He could read Spanish fairly well, but cursive in the darkness was beyond his ability. It was bad cursive, too—the distorted handwriting of a woman on her deathbed.

"It's an apology," said Isa, seeing his difficulties. "My mother wanted me to know she was sorry."

"Sorry for what?"

Isa glanced out toward the bay, then back. "Just so you understand, this is how my father tried to convince me that I should never tell anyone I was raped. Manny was pretty intuitive when he latched on to 'no rape equals no motive.' My father was of the same mind. Except that this letter isn't about *my* motive for revenge against Gabriel."

"It's about your father's?"

"No," said Isa. "My mother's."

Jack blinked hard, trying to comprehend what he'd just heard.

"Your mother's?"

"My father never visited me in college. My mother did. She met David Kaval. She knew he was a thug. She hated that I was seeing him. After I told David I was raped, I called my mother. I was scared. I told her how angry David was, and I was afraid that he might take things into his own hands. I never knew it, but she followed up with David." She paused, then added, "It wasn't to stop him."

Jack suddenly felt things falling into place. "Your mother asked David Kaval to—"

"To teach Gabriel a lesson. Not to kill him."

"But your father admitted to me that *he* was behind Gabriel's torture and murder."

"Somewhere along the line my father got involved. My mother must have told him about her conversation with David. My father took control, like he always did, and it went to the next level—he twisted it to fit whatever agenda he had."

Jack caught his breath. "Wow."

"Yeah," she said flatly. "Wow. So if this trial had ever played out to the end—if my father had lived to tell his story of rape and revenge—my mother would have been the villain. And she had no way to defend herself. Except through me."

Jack was silent.

"My father abused her even in death," said Isa. Then she looked Jack in the eye and said, "I'm glad he's dead. I suppose that's a terrible thing for a daughter to say about her own father, but it's true."

Jack nodded but said nothing.

Isa rose and extended her hand. There was no hug, just a handshake. "Thank you, Mr. Swyteck. Thank you for everything."

As they turned and headed back into the house, Isa's words—*I'm glad he's dead*—replayed in Jack's mind, and suddenly it occurred to him:

For the first time since spring, he was absolutely certain that his client was telling the truth.

Acknowledgments

Readers first met Jack Swyteck in my 1994 debut, *The Pardon*, as an idealistic and somewhat naive young lawyer whose love life could have filled an entire volume of "Cupid's Rules of Love and War—Idiot's Edition." He's grown a lot since then. So have I. *Most Dangerous Place* is my—*gulp*—twenty-fifth novel.

No. 25 is a milestone, and I'm grateful to the team behind this run. To my good fortune I've had the same publisher (HarperCollins) and literary agent (Richard Pine, and his father, Artie, before him) since *The Pardon.* More than twenty years ago Carolyn Marino stepped in as my editor to make sure I didn't become a "one-hit wonder," and since then, nothing has happened to Jack without passing the "Carolyn test."

My beta readers are the unsung heroes. Janis Koch—once known as "Conan the Grammarian" to her students—has been an irreplaceable member of the team since *Got the Look.* Janis and my long-time friend Gloria Villa have corrected hundreds of errors that would have otherwise gone to print.

Readers can thank them for the polish and blame me for any remaining errors.

Finally, thanks to my wife, Tiffany, who was there for the pre-*Pardon* crash and burn, who knows why *Most Dangerous Place* is not No. 26, and who has shown only love and support through good and bad, success and setback.

JMG, May 2016